Junius Podrug writes, travels and practises law.
This is his second novel.

Also by Junius Podrug

Frost of Heaven

Winterkill

Junius Podrug

First published in 1995
by HEADLINE BOOK PUBLISHING

First published in paperback in 1995
by HEADLINE BOOK PUBLISHING

A HEADLINE FEATURE paperback

10 9 8 7 6 5 4 3 2 1

ISBN 0 7472 4446 4

Typeset by Keyboard Services, Luton, Beds

Printed and bound in Great Britain by
Cox & Wyman Ltd, Reading, Berks

HEADLINE BOOK PUBLISHING
A division of Hodder Headline PLC
338 Euston Road
London NW1 3BH

For those who made it happen:
Hilda, Carol McCleary, Steve Jones,
Pamela Hopkins and Cate Paterson.

Chapter 1

ST BASIL'S CATHEDRAL, MOSCOW

A cathedral built with blood, a city founded on murder.

'Isn't it interesting? Moscow's history is full of murder and intrigue,' the old woman yelled over the roar of a mob invading Red Square. 'The guide said the city was built because of a murder, some prince or another avenging the death of his brother at the hands of an unfaithful wife. I love cities with dark histories, don't you? Like London and the Ripper stories. I went to Milwaukee to look at the house where Jeffrey Dawmer ate those people...'

The woman was a step ahead of Lara as the tour group rushed for the cathedral entrance with a riot threatening in the square.

Dark histories. Lara almost blurted out that she had a dark history, that she had left Moscow as a terrified little girl over twenty years ago, that on a bitter winter day after her mother packed her lunch and sent her off to school, unthinkable things had happened.

'Ivan the Terrible had the eyes of the architects gouged so they would never create anything as beautiful again,' the guide shouted as the group of women hurried toward the great cathedral.

'They say you can just feel the haunting,' the old woman

1

said between clouds of breath. 'He killed millions, you know, Ivan the Terrible. I heard someone say he used the blood of his enemies in the mortar holding the cathedral together. Isn't that interesting?' The woman's plump cheeks were inflamed from the cold; her nose, turning cobalt, appeared ready to break off. She carried a shopping bag in each hand, swinging the bags as if they were paddles. When Lara had attached herself to the group earlier, she had discovered the woman and the other members of the tour were retired telephone company employees from Chicago.

Lara was not a tourist; she had come back to the cathedral to face the violent stranger that had haunted her dreams since she was a child. The summons had come to her office in San Francisco, murder in black and white – a grainy police photo of a naked woman slashed and mutilated on the floor next to a bed. The picture had arrived in an envelope without a return address, but the postmark was Moscow. Staring at the photo, her stomach juices poisoning, her throat constricting, she knew she would have to return to Moscow to unravel the mystery behind the violence that had left her mother dead and herself a battered and violated seven-year-old orphan.

The photograph had been bait sent by someone who wanted her back in Moscow. And St Basil's was where the nightmares of her childhood had been conceived. Now as she approached the great cathedral, icy wind slashed at her exposed cheeks and stung her eyes while fear burned within her. The night wind was brutal in a city where the first breath of fresh air on a winterkill morning set lungs afire.

Behind her the mob was growing in size and threat, thousands of diehard communists shouting slogans and carrying flaming torches. Just as suddenly, troops loyal to Boris Yeltsin converged on the square. Lara felt the frenzied commotion in the hollow of her stomach as her ears rang with communist battle cries: 'Kill Yeltsin! Return Russia to communism!'

'Do you think there'll be fighting?' the woman shouted above the din.

'I don't know,' Lara said.

'Isn't it exciting?' The woman giggled with pleasure at the thought of being able to tell the folks back home about witnessing a riot in Moscow. It had been three months since the August coup had failed and in a tornado of political shocks the Communist Party had fallen from power as the Soviet Union disintegrated.

'It's history,' Lara said. Not wanting to become a historical statistic, she moved quickly to enter the cathedral while the mob roared by, the flickering light of their torches igniting the already riotous colors of the church. Ignorant armies on darkling plains, she thought, not remembering where she had read the phrase.

Inside the vestibule the group paused as the guide explained the tour. The women had earlier seen the frescoes of the chapels that made up the cathedral and they were back for a tour of the inner sanctum, the stairways that wormed through the chapels and domes. The cathedral, actually nine chapels clustered under the exotic domes of a 110-foot tower and eight onion-shaped cupolas, was like no other church; in fact it was not really a church at all, the small chapels were not designed for worship but as monuments to battle and bloodshed.

'The singing you hear is that of the Don Cossack Choir,' the guide said. 'The choir is making a Christmas broadcast from the cathedral.'

A Christmas broadcast from Moscow! Three-quarters of

a century had passed since the last national Christmas celebration; now communism had been swept away, leaving Moscow and the rest of the country cold and hungry and scared, bread shelves empty, as Russians faced their first Christmas since the Tsar, his wife, his four daughters, and his young son had been murdered.

Anxiety and paranoia blew through the city like bad breath. Lara sucked in the fear-infested atmosphere as an emotional leech, dread gripping her, as it had from the moment she had arrived at the airport two weeks ago.

Each day she had come to Red Square to stare at the cathedral, the crowning glory of a mad ruler, exotic and barbaric in its startling colors and shapes which captured the clash of Oriental and Western cultures that symbolized Russia. But she had never entered the church, had never mustered the courage until she latched onto the tour group this afternoon.

Someone had lured her back to Moscow.

The church was part of the nightmare.

Her constricting throat threatened to smother her and blood pounded in her temples as she followed the tour group up a gloomy stairwell. Images, pieces of memory as unspeakable as the cruelties of mad Russian rulers, broke off from a dark place buried deep in her subconscious and floated to the surface.

She was seven years old, being led up the steps. A voice in the darkness, a muffled whisper from a woman whose face was hidden behind her mother's red scarf. Beckoning her. Come closer, Lara . . .

'You don't have to stay with me,' a voice beside her said.

'What?'

'I'm old and fat, but I'll make it.'

The woman with the shopping bags thought Lara had stayed to the rear of the tour group to keep her company.

Lara decided it would be a struggle for the poor woman to carry her own weight up the stairs never mind the shopping bags as well. 'Let me help you with your bags.'

'I'm fine, there's nothing in the bags anyway. You could have fired cannon balls down GUM's aisles and not hit any merchandise. You look pale as a ghost, my dear,' the old woman huffed. 'Am I going to have to carry *you* up the stairs?'

'I'm all right,' Lara said. She touched her neck and self-consciously pulled her scarf higher. The sensation of choking, of strangling, which had brought her out of childhood nightmares fighting for breath, had returned when she received the photograph. She worked to calm herself, to keep her breathing normal as she followed the woman and the rest of the tour group up the stairs.

The chill in the stairwell was heavy and still, cold as a headstone.

From the rear, swelling the stairway, came the powerful voices of the Don Cossack Choir. The somber music filling the stairwell played on her emotions. The song was of Christmas among Volga boatmen but, as with so much Russian music, the tone was of hardship and toil, voices rising from the black soil of Mother Russia, stirring images of peasants stooped over from back-breaking labor and frozen tundras, of retreating Russian armies burning their own cities to foil foreign invaders, of famine and grief and cannibalism caused by war and the mad dreams of tsars and commissars.

A memory rushed at her, fueled by the dark tones of the Cossacks and the grave chill of the stone.

She was in the second grade at the little school just off Red Square.

'Your mother's come for you,' her teacher said, standing at the window and pointing down at the woman waiting

outside, bundled in the long gray coat, hat and red scarf her mother always wore, the scarf pulled up over her mouth and nose to protect against the treacherous wind-chill.

They left the school together and walked down Red Square to the cathedral.

She skipped alongside her mother, holding her gloved hand, her cheeks nipped by the biting winter wind.

They entered the cathedral and went up the dark and deserted stairway, higher and higher toward the 110-foot summit of the main tower.

She asked her mother why she had been taken out of school, why they had come to the cathedral, what was at the top of the high tower.

The woman didn't answer her and they were near the top before Lara saw the woman's eyes . . .

Experiencing the terror again, goose bumps rose on her thighs and crawled up her back. Lara rubbed her throat, trying to relax the muscles. They said it was my mother but wasn't true, she told herself. Her mother loved her, would never have harmed her. Her senses told her she was right. The sickening repulsion she was feeling now in the stairwell wasn't consistent with the loving memories of her mother – cookies and milk, being hugged to her mother's warm bosom, a kiss on the cheek before being bundled off to school.

She wanted desperately to turn and run down the steps, to get back to the sanctuary of her hotel, but each time she felt herself weakening she thought about the photo, the woman on the floor next to a bed, covers pulled partly over her face and breasts as if she had attempted to hide her nakedness even as she was dying from savage wounds. Dark stains, blood, splattered her bare flesh and the bedding in which she was tangled.

Thinking about the horrible photograph and the warm,

wonderful person her mother had been fueled her anger
and kept her feet moving up, step after step.

'St Basil's was built to commemorate the victory of Ivan
the Terrible over the Tartars at Kazan and Astrakhan,' the
guide told them as the group paused on a landing to remove
coats and scarfs. Lara kept her coat on. She was trembling
despite the beads of sweat rolling down the sides of her
face.

'Russians had been under the brutal heel of the barbaric
Tartars and paid tribute in the form of gold and golden-
haired Russian maidens. Tsar Ivan drove the hordes from
our cities and in turn raped their women.'

'Isn't that interesting?' the older woman said to Lara.
'Ivan was mad, you know. Killed more Russians than
foreigners. He and Stalin. Stalin's wife killed herself. Or
was it his son? Maybe he killed both of them. Crazy too,
you know. Aren't you going to take off your coat, dear?
You're sweating.'

'I'm cold,' she lied, embarrassed to tell the woman that
she was shaking from fright. Fear and memories dried her
throat, turned her skin cold and clammy.

*She stopped trying to be playful after they entered the
stairwell, stopped humming a school tune as they climbed
higher up the great tower.*

*She became frightened and tried to hang back as the
woman wearing her mother's coat and red scarf gripped her
hand tighter and pulled her along.*

She asked where they were going, but no answer came.

She stared at the cold, unfamiliar eyes.

'You've got to come, my dear.'

'What?'

'We're moving on, up, up, up,' the older woman told
her.

Lara shook away the memories and kept her wobbly legs

moving on the stairs. 'That music, the Russians are so damn soulful, aren't they?' she said, using the sound of her own voice to beat back the nightmare waking in her head.

'You're an American, aren't you?' the older woman asked. 'We were wondering because we heard you talking to the guide in Russian when you asked to join the tour of the cathedral. Are your parents Russian?'

Lara shook her head. 'American and British. I . . . I was born in Moscow, went to school here before I returned to the States.'

'Oh, parents in diplomatic service. I so envy people in the diplomatic corps, though it must be hard for the children.'

Lara didn't correct the woman's assumption that her parents had been diplomats. They were, in a sense, but not in a way that the woman would have understood. She might have recognized her mother's name if Lara had mentioned it. Angela Patrick had been a household name in the turbulent 1960s. A young Berkeley professor, she had been an early leader of anti-war activists, firebrands who took the cry against war out of the classroom and into the streets. She had fled America after a demonstration turned ugly and the streets bloody.

The woman would not have recognized Lara's father's name. Welsh, born in a poor coal mining town, he was a poet and social revolutionary; a lover, a drinker and a fighter, he threw away his life on some idealistic and misbegotten mission to save Africa for the Africans. He was, like Angela Patrick, a child of the sixties. Lara's father had been killed not long after she was born, but Lara had felt his love through her mother. They were wonderfully passionate people, Lara thought, filled with a zest for life and love for all living things.

Her mother had filled her with that same passion,

instilling in her a love of life and people, but the passion had been smothered in her when she was still a child. She had to find that passion again, just as she had to find a murderer.

'Coming back for a visit now that communism has fallen?' the woman huffed beside her.

'For a visit,' Lara repeated mechanically. A return to a private hell that had nothing to do with politics. If stories of murder and perversion titillated the woman, Lara could tell her things that would turn her stomach. She was a prosecutor with the San Francisco District Attorney's office, supervising deputy of the Special Crimes Unit which specialized in crimes of violence against women and children, prosecuting criminals whose sick minds would have embarrassed even Ivan the Terrible.

'Too bad about that scaffolding outside on the main tower, isn't it?' the woman said. 'They would decide to paint it just when I come to Moscow to take pictures.'

Lara looked up the stairway, beyond the woman. The main tower, the 110-foot center sphere of the cathedral. That was where the woman in the gray coat and red scarf had taken her.

At 5:30, closing time, the guards left their positions at the cathedral entrance and went down the corridor where they stood and watched the famed Russian choir. They left the door unlocked because the tour group in the stairwell, the last of the day, would be leaving in a few minutes.

One of the guards felt a cold draft at the back of his neck and he turned to see the figure of a woman disappearing into the antechamber to the rear where access to the stairwell was located.

'What's the matter?' the other guard asked.

The first one shrugged. 'A woman in a gray coat came in. Tourist catching up with the rest of the group.'

Chapter 2

A cathedral built with blood, a city founded on murder.

The words chased her as she went up the dark winding stairwell.

This was the way, Lara thought, this is where I was led.

Memories of that last morning in Moscow began at the apartment she had shared with her mother. She remembered impatiently pulling away from her mother's last-minute adjustment of her coat and scarf so she could run and join her friends en route to school. They had stood on the landing outside the door to their apartment—

The landing. What was it about the landing that nudged a memory? She shook her head and rubbed her temples, ignoring the look of the older woman from the tour group.

'Got a headache, honey?'

'No,' Lara said. She wished it was that simple. I have to keep my thoughts straight, she told herself. Forget the landing outside the apartment. Only the stairway in the cathedral was important. But the memory hung there.

When her mother had finished fussing with her coat and scarf, she gave Lara a kiss on the cheek and slipped an extra cookie into her side pocket. Lara grabbed her book bag and turned to race down the stairs when something caught her eye. A woman in a nurse's white uniform on the landing above them . . .

A spike of pain shot between her temples. She stopped in

11

the church stairwell and leaned against the wall. Tension round her neck created the sensation that her windpipe was closing. She knew it was only a panic reaction, that her throat was open, but she couldn't control the choking it triggered.

She pushed herself away from the wall and told herself to keep moving, to keep putting one foot in front of the other. And to keep remembering.

Everything had been buried for so long, locked inside her since the day she had left Moscow traumatized and orphaned, put on a plane bound for America to a grandmother she had never met. She remembered leaving the school, being taken to St Basil's, the stairwell, but then there was a gap, and her next memory was of the airplane, of a sympathetic stewardess who had given her a teddy bear another child had left behind.

Somewhere in the upper recesses of the great Russian cathedral was the answer to that lost time; to the nightmares that had made her wake up screaming every night during her first days in America until a doctor 'cured' the nightmares with a drug that put her into a deep, dreamless sleep at night.

The tour guide's voice floated down as they paused at another landing. 'Not even Stalin, in all his might and power, Stalin who they say killed thirty million people out of madness and ambition and defeated the Nazi beasts in the Great Patriotic War, not even he could soil this cathedral that symbolized the power and glory of all Russia . . .'

A tempest pounded in Lara's head, fed by the mournful music that came up the stairwell like a powerful wind, a crazy jumble of thoughts and fragments of images. Thirty million killed by madness . . . Nazi beasts . . .

A small room, hardly more than a cubbyhole. She was so

12

small, so scared. The red scarf and hat covered most of the woman's face but she saw the eyes staring at her . . .

Burning eyes. The eyes of her mother. *No!* They were not her mother's eyes. Her mother was not a monster crazed by drugs. What had happened to her that day was not something a loving mother would have done to her own child.

In the dark room a hand reached out for her, a muffled whisper from a shadowy figure beckoning. Come closer . . .

The guide's voice jarred Lara back from the memories.

'This is the end of the tour. We will return to ground level by a stairway on the other side.'

As the group moved down the corridor toward the descending stairs, Lara hung back, her heart beating in her throat.

The older woman had caught up with the main group and was talking to another tourist as the group disappeared round a turn in the corridor.

Lara stared at the stairs leading to the top of the tower. The room was up there. She had to climb the stairs, find the room. She had to complete the chain of memory that she had avoided for twenty years.

As she took her first step she heard a noise to the rear and stopped. It had sounded like footsteps on the stairway where she and the tour group had just been. She stood still and listened but no other sound came. She took deep breaths to calm her nerves. There are good reasons for people to be on the steps, she thought. This is a church, and Russian Orthodox priests, dressed in flowing black robes and tall headdresses, would be about.

She went slowly up the steps, fighting her fears, the powerful music a hand at her back. These were the same steps she had been forced to go up. Her body heat rose and she loosened the scarf round her neck.

13

At a landing two flights up she paused; the stairwell split, one set went to the right, the other to the left. She hesitated, unsure of the path she had followed as a little girl, and finally chose the one to the left.

It led to a dead end and she went back, but stopped in her tracks as she heard a creaking noise, the sound of a heavy foot on a wooden step, though whether it came from above or below, she could not tell. She paused again where the stairwell split into two paths. Determined not to fall victim to her own imagination, she forced herself to take one step, then another, and slowly went up the stairway on the right.

Moments later she stopped in an open doorway to a small room. The room was cast in shadows; only shallow light from the dim light bulb in the corridor pushed into the room, leaving deep holes of darkness in the corners. The ceiling was low, the head of a tall man would brush the beams. This was the place the woman had brought her.

She made out wooden crosses of various sizes on the walls and it gave birth to another memory. The room was used to store crosses which hung from braces on the walls. The crosses might have been stored here untouched for over seventy years, she thought; church crosses had not been in high demand during the communist era.

She remembered she had worked her hand loose from the woman's and had stood in the doorway as the woman stepped further into the room. The woman had taken something out of a coat pocket, a piece of rope, and she did something with the rope with her back to Lara. Then the woman turned.

Come closer, the woman said, holding out her gloved hand for Lara. The woman pulled her closer and started to . . .

Her mind rebelled at the memory. *The woman had*

14

undressed her. She had removed Lara's hat and scarf and coat and . . . the memory repulsed her.

Oh God, I was naked. It was cold and I was naked. I cried, I know I cried when she undressed me. She took off all my clothes and I stood here naked and crying and pleading. I begged her to leave me alone.

Terrified by her memories, a nerve next to her left breast twitched as if her heart were shaking in her chest. Tears that wouldn't flow burned her eyes. She wanted to run, race back down the stairs and back to her hotel room and hide her head but she knew if she did she would never be able to face the past – or the future. Nothing to fear but fear, she told herself. She wasn't a helpless little girl but a grown woman. And the bogey man wasn't here.

As she forced herself to step into the room, she heard footsteps on the stairway and spun round to face the door, her nerves on fire. Someone was out there, following her . . .

She stepped back, deeper into the dark recesses of the room as the steps grew closer.

There was no way out of the room.

The thought nearly paralyzed her. Window shutters rattled on her right, pushed by the wind outside. The window was a glassless opening, the shutters were unhooked and appeared easy to part with a shove, but it was a hundred feet down to Red Square.

Trapped. *I'm trapped.* Her breathing came in shallow gasps. The footsteps grew nearer and emotions overwhelmed her as she relived the birth of her nightmares.

The woman pulled her closer, not toward the window but to the wall behind her. Something was dangling from one of the low beams . . . a rope. The woman had hung a rope from the beam. The end of the rope was knotted into a noose.

Lara swayed dizzily, the memory swelling in her mind

like a dark cloud. A black form moved past the doorway and continued down the corridor, the thought barely registering in her mind that the person was a priest in flowing robes.

As her vision cleared, she continued to stare across the small room. Something was hanging from the ceiling and her eyes slowly brought it into focus.

A rope.

A rope with a noose.

A scream caught in her windpipe as someone behind her grabbed her throat in a vise grip. She clutched at the hand, trying to remove the powerful fingers strangling her.

Squeezing her throat with one hand, the attacker's other hand worked up her skirt and pushed into her panties. Something smooth and phallic-shaped in the hand was being forced into the private area between her legs. Darkness was flooding her mind from lack of oxygen but the intrusion of what felt like a plastic penis between her legs triggered an explosion of rage in her.

She twisted free of the hand on her throat and beat at her attacker with a wild fury of arms and fists. Staggering back, she caught a flash of long, dark brown hair and a red scarf covering a woman's face. She stumbled backwards as the person lunged at her. The wooden shutters at her back broke open as she slammed against them. Her attacker shoved her and she screamed as she fell backwards through the window . . .

Chapter 3

'Cross your legs,' the doctor told her. 'Uncross.'

The metal examining table was cold. She was limp and tired and sore after being scraped off the side of one of the world's most famous cathedrals.

'Lift your arms above your head,' the doctor said. 'That's fine. Be thankful for the slowness of Russian workers. The police officer said work on the cathedral ended a week ago but no one had got round to taking down the scaffolding.'

A fall of a dozen feet onto the scaffolding had given her no more than bruises. Guards alerted by people in Red Square had pulled her back inside. She had spent less than five minutes on the scaffolding – or a thousand years, depending on who was counting.

A young woman whimpering in pain in the examining room next to her was driving her crazy.

'What's wrong with that girl?' she asked.

'Her boy friend broke her arms because she wouldn't fuck someone who offered him drugs in exchange.'

'Can't you give her some painkillers? She sounds like she's in terrible pain.'

'Painkillers? We have a small ration to ease the last hours of the terminally ill. Antibiotics are even more scarce. Painkillers for women giving birth have to be bought on the black market by husbands. X-rays, those we ate for lunch yesterday.'

She studied him as he cleaned scrapes on the side of her leg. He was young and harried and worried – no, she thought, not worried, grim. He was losing hope, had stopped worrying, and had simply turned grim and determined. Several years younger than her twenty-eight, tension marks had formed at the corners of his mouth and worry lines creased his forehead from a perpetual frown.

Compared to high-tech American emergency rooms where the profit margin was more outrageous than that in jewelry or cosmetics, the Moscow emergency room struck her as dated, with a 1930s ambience.

'You keep touching your neck,' he said to her. 'I don't see anything significant. Just a little redness.'

'I don't bruise easily.' Her neck hurt from the attempt to strangle her but that was not why her hand went to it. The strangling sensation had stayed and she knew she had to work with herself to get rid of it. He didn't see a scar round her neck because childhood surgery had eliminated it to the casual eye. But it was still there in her mind's eye.

'Everything is rationed in Moscow. Even life and death,' she murmured, not really talking to him, just thinking aloud.

'Life and death are becoming a black-market commodity,' the doctor said. Anger showed on his face. 'A child died last week in our hospital because staff members were watering down medication to sell some on the side. Mothers and newborns become infected because there are three or four women at a time in delivery rooms and bedding doesn't get changed after delivery.'

'It's better than living under tyranny,' she said. 'The problems will iron themselves out.'

'Tell yourself that the next time you go into a store to buy tampons. If you didn't bring a supply from America, you'll have to carry a big wad of cotton in your bag as Russian women do.'

The young woman in the next room screamed again and Lara felt her pain in the pit of her own stomach.

'If you're finished I'll get out of your hair,' she said.

'You're paying with hard currency. That makes you a priority patient.' He looked up and gave her a tight smile to take the edge off his words. 'Just joking.'

She knew he wasn't kidding. Her US dollars had an exchange rate of nearly a thousand roubles to one dollar, with the rouble deteriorating further every day. She felt instantly guilty; she was getting special attention because she could pay with hard currency while the poor girl next door was suffering.

'It's not good to practice medicine when you don't have the right tools,' he said. 'We have more thermonuclear warheads than incubators for sick babies.'

She started to say something when a nurse poked her head through the curtains that functioned as a door for the examining room. 'The police officer's back. He wants to see you, doctor.'

The doctor slipped out to speak to the officer, leaving the curtain open a few inches. Lara put her clothes back on as she watched the doctor and police officer talk. She wondered if there was any news about the woman who had attacked her.

She was pulling on her second boot when the doctor came back in. His grim demeanor had changed. Now he avoided her eye. 'I hadn't finished cleaning your wounds.'

'Is the officer still out there?' she asked. 'I'd like to know if he found out anything.'

'He's gone. He said you can drop by the police station tomorrow and file a report.'

'I was almost murdered and I'm supposed to stop by and file a report? When he left a while ago he said he was going to try and find out if anyone saw the woman who pushed me out of the window.'

'Are you sure it was a woman who attacked you?'

'I'm not sure of anything. The person was strong, stronger than the average woman, but hell, I don't know, lots of women work out in gyms today. But that wasn't a penis trying to penetrate, it was too ... too smooth, like plastic, what we call a dildo in my country. I told all this to the police officer.'

'A woman with a gray coat and red scarf.' His voice was neutral and it sent a shot of anger through her.

'Yes, gray coat, red scarf.' She knew her voice betrayed her panic. She could sense the words coming, mimicking what the doctor was about to say.

'Just like the last time,' he said.

'Yes, yes, just like the last time. Only that time a priest found me hanging and cut me down.' Her voice lost its control. 'He told you I was crazy, didn't he?'

'No. This is what he told me.' His words were carefully chosen. 'That you came back to Moscow after leaving here as a child. That you have visited the police and questioned the cause of your mother's death which occurred twenty years ago. That you were ... brutalized as a child. Sexually—'

'And while reliving the past, I just happened to fall out of the window.' She slung on her coat angrily. 'Great theory, saves police work. I suppose he told you my mother hurt me when I was little, but that's a lie. She was a caring, loving—'

'Your mother was a foreigner, an American campus radical. There was a question of psychedelic drugs—'

'That's a lie too.' She dug money from her purse. 'Thanks for the help. The rest is to buy painkillers for the girl next door.'

His angry voice followed her out of the room. 'We have enough problems in Russia. Why don't you go home and be crazy.'

Chapter 4

The third-floor corridor at the Gorky Hotel had the stark ambience and cold, fleshy smell of a meat locker. The rooms were kept just chilly enough so she was never quite comfortable.

What a dump, she thought, walking past wallpaper that had peeled from the wall. Even though the Gorky looked like a hotel – lobby, elevators, hallways, rooms, beds, dressers, toilets – the place had the feel of a government office facility. It lacked human comforts and amenities; everything was utilitarian and nothing worked. The fixtures and furnishings were sturdy and graceless, as if a society that boasted of being classless was also faceless.

It was going to take weeks, maybe even months to get the information she needed and the Gorky was the best she could afford without running up an enormous tab on credit cards that she wasn't sure she would be able to repay.

Her hand shook as she inserted the key in the lock to her room door. She opened the door and went in. There was no dead bolt on the door and once inside she placed a chair under the handle.

Sitting on the edge of the bed, she held her face in her hands. Her head was pounding and her stomach seemed to be lined with acid. She needed to cry, her mind and soul needed the cleansing, the release, but tears failed her now as they always did. She took deep breaths to get her body under control. And tried to force herself to remember.

In her heart she knew it was all a lie, everything they claimed about her mother – the acid trip, the battering and molestation of her own daughter, the wild driving that took her into a head-on collision with a gasoline tanker.

The car crash had left nothing to bury. Angela Patrick remained in a state of oblivion, with no grave in which to lay her head, no grave stone to mark her stay on earth. Lara was her mother's only earthly memorial. And at long last she had come back to Moscow where her mother's name had been blackened, where her mother's last day on earth was one of infamy.

And someone was trying to kill her. The same person who had tried it when she was a little girl.

Breathe deep, breathe deep.

It started coming, that surge up her throat, and she ran for the bathroom. It was rushing out by the time she made it to the sink, the spoiled contents of her stomach boiling up her throat and out of her mouth.

Afterwards she flushed her mouth out with water and brushed her teeth three times. The image in the bathroom mirror was not a pretty one. Chestnut hair, hazel eyes, smooth, fair complexion; a guy at work had sent her a passionate letter telling her she was beautiful but she had decided it was a joke and trashed it. She never thought of herself as beautiful, never thought anyone else would consider her beautiful, although in the last few years as her life seemed to be going the way of a dried prune she had wondered if her brain didn't need an overhaul.

The young man who had thought she was beautiful had probably just been shy; he had not approached her because her body language told the world to stay away. The 'ice

queen' is what one frustrated attorney called her after she
rejected several lunch dates.

'I hate you, damn it,' she told her reflection. 'You have
nobody because you're scared. Admit it, you're afraid to
get involved. You're afraid to show any emotion.'

Like the doctor, the features were too grim, too serious.
She tried a smile but her lips were so tight she decided they
would shatter if she pushed it.

She left the confrontation with herself at the mirror and
went back into the bedroom. Too tired to take off her
clothes, she crawled under the covers with her ski jacket,
sweater and skirt still on and buried her head under the
blankets.

She closed her eyes and felt her sore throat. *Somebody
was trying to kill her.*

Erupting from the blankets, she grabbed the phone to
call the hotel operator, letting the phone ring and ring as
she lay in bed staring up at the cracked ceiling.

Calling to be connected to the airlines.

She was going home.

Not worth it, she told herself. Someone had tried to kill
her. Someone had brought alive her nightmares. She would
go back home, stay in her condo for a while, go back to
work for a few months, maybe a year, save up money and
then come back again when she had the strength and
courage. Maybe then the city wouldn't be rampant with
rumors of cannibalism.

She dropped the phone back in the cradle. One good
thing about the Moscow phone system, it didn't let you
make rash decisions. There weren't even phone books in
the city. No phone books, no way to make quick connec-
tions – that had been one way the communist regime had
kept control.

If she ran she would never come back. She had to face

her fears and conquer them. She had to face the past and her enemy from the past.

Life in San Francisco as a deputy prosecutor, living in a new condo two blocks from the water, had been . . . okay, just okay. She had a cat instead of a man. A career instead of a family. It wouldn't have been so bad if that part of her life had just been on hold while she launched an exciting new career, but it had been her life history. A teacher had told her that she was one of the prettiest girls in her high school but she didn't believe it – and she didn't have a date for the prom. Pretty is as pretty does, her grandmother used to say.

She was nearly thirty and had not had anything more than casual relations with men, and no close women friends. No close friends, period. And no relatives she knew of now that her grandmother was in her grave.

All alone in the world and she was tired of the loneliness, tired of a sterile life. There had been passion in her life, passion for living, love for other people, but she had had an emotional lobotomy at the age of seven and all her emotions were bottled up. She was ready to explode with lust and love and friendship and zest for life, but like a volcano with a cork in it, all of those wonderful emotions were stuck in her throat.

Her mother had been full of life and love and laughter, emotions she shared with her daughter. That's why Lara knew her mother would never have harmed anyone, why the talk of psychedelic drugs was nonsense.

Sure, her mother had been a campus radical, but she had fought for life, to get the US out of Vietnam and save lives on both sides of the war. When a demonstration went to hell on a Berkeley street and someone got killed, her mother had found herself on the police list even though she had not caused the tragedy. She fled to Canada and later accepted an invitation to teach in the Soviet Union. If the Soviets had been looking for a propaganda piece in her, they were disappointed. She was not a communist and refused to get involved in anti-American dialogue.

'Why haven't I ever experienced a love like my parents'?' Lara asked herself.

In Moscow her mother fell in love with Keir Thomas, a wild and impulsive Welsh poet-political activist, a political fugitive accused of talking about blowing up parliament on Guy Fawkes Day. As fiery and idealistic as his poetry, he joined a group of other young foreigners living in Russia who went off to Africa as unpaid mercenaries to remove some last vestige of European colonialism, only to be caught on the wrong side of a tribal war and killed by the people he had come to liberate.

True to their nature and those heady, idealistic days of the sixties, Lara's parents had not bothered formalizing Angela's pregnancy with a wedding ceremony. Things like marriage and planning for your children's education meant nothing to a generation that tried to conquer the world with the power of love, pot, and an occasional confrontation with authority.

Lara had never met her father, he was in Africa when she was born, but she knew him through the stories her mother had told her. When it thundered and stormed at night and she snuggled into bed next to her mother, each with a mug of hot chocolate, Angela told her of her love for Keir and of his love for life.

Her death made Lara a seven-year-old orphan whose only known relative was a grandmother halfway round the world in San Francisco. The subject of her mother's death, of what had happened to Lara on her last day in Moscow, had been taboo in her grandmother's house. The only comment she had heard her grandmother make was that the Soviets had killed Angela, but Lara had never accepted it. She could never explain to her grandmother why; it wasn't something she could put into words, especially not to the older woman who had been ready for retirement, and maybe even ready for an unhappy early grave, when a seven-year-old child had suddenly been dropped in her lap.

Her grandmother considered herself a failure. Her husband had died years before she was ready for widowhood, and her only child had gone overnight from a bright-eyed flower-loving peacenik to a front-page fugitive. She had found refuge accepting Jesus and hiding behind biblical quotes until an ill wind had carried her daughter's child to her. Raising Lara had been a burden.

Lara had left Moscow with terrible secrets sewn inside her like a cancerous tumor. Her grandmother had never tried to heal the hurt. The pain had lain dormant for over twenty years while Lara grew from frightened child to cautious woman, never probing that corner of her mind where mad dogs played. For most of her life she had simply accepted her fate, that this was her, a determined workaholic respected by police officers and her fellow prosecutors for her bright mind and assertive actions; respect at work, a cat who loved her, a condo two blocks from the ocean, what else did a woman need?

The bubble had burst when the cryptic summons to Moscow had arrived and she started reliving the past. And thinking about all the lost years in between.

Lara closed her eyes and had started to doze when pounding came at her door. She grabbed the telephone by her bed, fumbled and dropped the receiver. Getting it back in hand, she called the front desk, her heart thumping.

No operator was on duty at this time of night. Would the front desk clerk answer? The pounding came again and her blood pressure surged. Leaving the telephone off the hook so it would keep ringing, she went to the door, hoping it was just the floor warden come to complain that Lara had not checked in with her.

'Who is it?'

'Gropski.'

Relief flowed through her. Gropski was hotel security, a short stump with fat lips, wide nose, huge head, and ugly brown blotches on his flesh that gave him the appearance of a frog left out in the sun too long, a not too likely scenario in Moscow where sunshine was not a threatening commodity.

'What do you want?'

'You asked me questions.'

A slur to his voice suggested he had had too much vodka, a common condition in a country where the leading cause of almost everything was too much vodka. She wasn't going to open the door for him; he was a creepy jerk with a broad, flat nose red from being stuck in too many glasses of booze and too much dirty laundry. 'It's the middle of the night,' she said. That wasn't quite true. In a couple of hours it would be morning.

'You've been gone.'

'What do you want?' she repeated.

'I have information for you,' came through the door in a drunken slur. Thinking of his round face, watery jaundiced eyes and fat nose, she imagined a frog in heat.

'Put it under the door.'

'The door? Lady, don't be stupid. The information is from my mouth.'

Definitely wouldn't fit, she thought. 'Look, I'm not opening this door. And I have the front desk on the line and I'm going to ask them to send someone up if you don't tell me what you want or go away.' From where she stood she could hear the continuing ring of the phone. Still no answer from the front desk.

'Send someone up? This is Gropski, I'm the security officer. You call, I get sent up.'

'Gropski, listen to me. Tell me what you want or I'm going to make a complaint with the ministry in the morning.' She didn't have the faintest idea which ministry was responsible for hotel security officers now that the KGB no longer existed.

'Information has a price,' he purred, with all the sexual innuendo a squat little frog could muster.

'Tell me what you're offering. If I think it's worth anything I'll slip some money under the door.'

'No money, we can make other arrangements.'

'*I'm calling the ministry!*'

'All right, all right, on Lenin's grave, I'm just trying to help. You asked me to inquire as to how you can arrange access to, uh, certain matters.'

'Yes?'

'I have made contact with the man who can make the arrangements. He is a master of blat.'

Blat. The fine art of peddling influence to get things out of the government, anything from a refrigerator to a dacha. With the fall of communism, the billions of documents detailing seventy years of Soviet atrocities were being bid for. She wanted access to records about her mother's death, records that would show the hypocrisy of the official version.

'There's a price,' the frog whispered through the door.

There was always a price.

'Who is this person?'

'I have the information written down for you. Open the door and I'll give it to you.'

'Slip it under the door and I'll put a hundred dollars under.'

'Money first.'

'We'll do it at the same time.'

No honor among thieves or anyone else in Moscow, she thought. These were hard times. A few months ago people like Gropski had a small amount of prestige, even as a security officer at a fleabag like the Gorky. Now he was relegated to selling information about the government to the same type of people he had been spying on.

Lara grabbed a hundred dollar bill from her purse and bent down by the door.

'I'm ready,' she said.

Gropski slipped just enough of the paper under for it to poke out on her side. She slid the bill slowly under, pulling in the paper as he reeled in the money.

She got to her feet to read the message, her aching bones reminding her of her injuries.

'Mr Belkin. 8:00 tonight. Patriotic Park. South entrance.'

She leaned closer to the door. 'Why do we have to meet in a park at night when there's a lounge downstairs. Gropski? Gropski?' The frog had left.

She sighed wearily. All alone, no one to hold her, comfort her, share with her. Even her damn cat was halfway round the world.

She staggered to the bed, pausing to put the phone back on the hook, and crawled under the blankets, shaking, aching and miserable.

Chapter 5

By eight o'clock Moscow had been dark for hours and the street outside the Gorky was a shade past midnight.

'They're rationing the street lights,' the porter told her. 'Turning off the lights at every other sector to conserve energy. Tomorrow night we'll have lights. Very democratic,' he said.

She didn't know if he was trying to be funny with the last comment. He was small and wrinkled, with white hair, rotten yellow teeth and unhealthy gray skin. In his heavy uniform of tattered purple wool and tarnished gold epaulets, he looked like a dwarf king from Alice's Wonderland.

'No taxis again?'

'No, they're all at the better hotels. They're rationing the petrol for buses, too,' he said. 'Buses run out of gas on their route.' He shook his head. 'Just like the war, the Great Patriotic War. Everything was rationed. People are hungry again. Just like the war.' His mind lurched back to her transportation problem. 'Do you want a taxi called?'

'They never come.'

'That's true. They stay around the better hotels. They're low on gas, too. It was like that during the war, but there were no lights anywhere. The bombers...'

She left his remembrances of the Second World War and stepped out onto the street, gasping a little as the below zero air burnt her throat and lungs. She quickly covered her mouth and nose with her scarf and pulled her hat down until only her eyes were visible. The cold even attacked her eyes, making her blink as they smarted.

The streets were dark in every direction and she wondered how big the 'sector' was that had been blacked out. Was the intersection where she was meeting the man named Belkin also suffering a black-out? Damn, damn, damn. That idiot Gropski should have set up the meeting at the hotel lounge, at *any* hotel lounge. Hell, she would risk his friend in her room rather than walk along dark and frigid Moscow streets. Not only had someone tried to kill her, the world's safest city had taken on a big dose of crime during the past few years as communism waned and the tight controls disappeared. She had slept most of the day and had crawled out of bed only a couple of hours earlier. She had tried to find Gropski to get him to change the meeting place, but he was out, no doubt living it up with a bottle and a prostitute on her hundred dollars.

No taxis, no buses, dark deserted streets, it was insane to go out alone. But it's only eight o'clock, she told herself, and it was just a few blocks.

She turned round and went back to the hotel. She gave the porter a 500 rouble note. 'Stand outside and watch me as I go up the street,' she told him.

'Watch you?'

'Muggers and rapists.'

He nodded as he followed her outside. 'The streets aren't safe. Nothing works, not even the police. They say now we're free, but when the communists ran the country our jobs were safe, the streets were clean, and the buses ran on time. What's the use of being free if you have to be scared? Back during the war, if a mugger was caught . . .'

On the street she hurried in the direction of the

rendezvous, the porter's words drizzling behind her in the frigid night. Only an occasional car drove by, headlights setting the darkened street aglow, tires hissing on the wet road. The Gorky was located in an area of government offices, which became deserted when the buses stopped running at seven in the evening after hauling away the last of the workers. The buildings were all Soviet generic: big, solid structures of dull concrete, with no character, grace or even architectural interest.

Her feet crunched on packed snow. The municipal street cleaners still managed to keep most of the traffic lanes clear of snow, but they piled the snow up along the gutters in a long dirty mound that spilled over onto the sidewalks.

She looked back over her shoulder, making sure the porter was still keeping watch in front of the hotel.

Cold, cold, cold.

She hated being cold. Wearing a California ski jacket, woolen pants, long underwear, boots, heavy socks, sweater, hat, and scarf, she was bundled up for a Himalayan trek and was still cold, still shivering. One of her few pleasant memories of the Moscow she had left as a child was the clean white snow at Christmas time. But Moscow was no longer a lily white city and she wondered if the damn place had got colder, too.

She stopped at the next corner from the hotel and silently cursed. The street was dark for blocks. At the hotel, the porter had turned to go back inside.

She gritted her teeth and hurried down the street, her eyes darting toward the dark entrances in front of each building, at the street behind her, at the spaces between buildings. Can fear make you colder? she wondered.

Her fear of someone jumping out of a dark alley or doorway got the best of her and she stumbled over dirty snow and started running down the street.

33

* * *

Half a block from the rendezvous, she spotted him, big, solid, a well-fed slab of Russian beef.

He was standing in the shadows just outside the glow of the street lamp on the corner, reassuringly conspicuous. She was grateful that the park was not part of the blackout.

He watched her progress across the street. As she stepped up on the sidewalk on his side, he suddenly turned and started walking down the park path, signaling her with a look to follow him.

She fell in wordlessly behind him, telling herself that Russian parks weren't like American ones, that they belonged to the people, not gangs and perverts, that there was nothing wrong with a stroll with a strange man in a dark park at night. Right, she thought.

Other people were around, young and old, even a couple with a baby carriage; that kept her fear within manageable levels, but she wasn't going to follow him off the main path if he decided to communicate with nature.

He suddenly paused to let her catch up, his eyes searching the path behind them. She pulled her scarf off her face as she approached. Neither Belkin nor most of the people passing them were dressed for Arctic conditions as she was. Living in Moscow must make one's blood cold.

'Expecting someone to join us?' she asked.

'No,' he snapped. 'Are you?'

Bad move, she told herself. His paranoia level was a bit high too. 'Only you.' She smiled, but it was forced. 'Could we go someplace warmer?'

'This is better,' he said. He continued to walk and she reluctantly stepped along. An immediate dislike and distrust of the man had raised the hair on her suspicions. Gropski was a loser; this man was a bastard.

Some things about him were obvious: he was a fat cat in thin, hungry Moscow; his hat was sable at a time when desperate people were thinking about ways to use sable hats in borscht. His overcoat was cashmere, and if the lapels were any indication, the inside was lined with fine fur.

Everything about him spoke of an *apparatchik* – one of the middle management bureaucratic fascists who ran the country and bled off the cream that hadn't ended up on the lips of the Inner Circle.

But there was another quality about him, one that made her uneasy and added to the shivers brought on by the Moscow freeze. His pockmarked face, fat cruel lips, black, slicked-back hair gave him that brute-brained look of old-line communists, with their wide-lapel suit jackets and pants tailored for tree trunks. It all conveyed a sort of menace – not viciousness, not craziness, but the kind of cold bastard bureaucrat who, following orders, would walk down a line of peasants kneeling before a mass grave and put a bullet in the head of each . . .

'You have murder on your mind.'

His words jarred her.

'What?'

'You have not come to Moscow to verify that your mother was killed in a car accident over twenty years ago. You have come to expose a cover-up, a conspiracy, resulting in your mother's death.'

She took a deep breath before answering. She almost told him it was her own attempted murder that she was concerned about at the moment.

'If you're implying I'm here on some sort of political witch hunt to prove my mother was killed by the com- munists, you're wrong.' She had told Gropski the same thing. Uncovering wrongs that were rights under the old regime was not welcome in the new Russia, and for good reason. Not only were most of the people in charge today in control a few months ago when the Soviet Union fell, but communism had saturated every element of society; some gave orders, and the rest followed.

'My mother was killed by a maniac.' Lara didn't add that while her mother might not have been killed for political reasons, she believed her death had certainly been covered up for political reasons.

'At the time of your mother's death I was in a position to know a little about it. What I am saying,' he added hastily, 'is that I was in a position to read reports that were not released to the public. Your mother took a psychedelic drug, LSD or some other hallucinogenic substance. She went crazy, attempted to harm you, her own daughter, and ended up driving a car at high speed into a petrol tanker. *Boom!*' He threw his hands in the air. 'That was the end of it.'

She took another deep breath. 'Not exactly. My mother was a nineteen sixties Berkeley radical and it's not hard for people to identify her with acid trips, but I know that was not true. My mother did not take drugs. She was an anti-war activist, not a hippie. She was a college professor and intellectual—'

'Like Professor Leary, the American drug guru?'

'And,' she went on, ignoring his comment, 'my mother was a pacifist and a health nut. She was not the acid-taking radical that the newspapers tried to portray after her death.' Moscow's black winter night bit at her exposed cheeks and stung her nose. She wanted so much to tell this arrogant bastard to screw off.

'You're not fooling me,' Belkin said. 'I worked for the government. You believe your mother was murdered years ago and now you have come to hunt down the killer. Am I right? Yes, I am right.' He scowled at her like a man trying to make up his mind whether to step on a bug.

Lara turned her head so he couldn't read her thoughts. The cold-blooded bastard talked about murder, taking life's breath from a living, loving person, her mother, as if it was a statistic about the grain harvest. This throwback to the old regime was no more capable of understanding her mother than a dinosaur was of understanding a computer.

The lie detector that grows between the ears of any good prosecutor after a few years on the job was ringing alarm bells in her head like a heart monitor in cardiac arrest. Her instincts were not only telling her that he was a dangerous man who could not be trusted but that he had a hidden agenda.

Apparatchiks were bureaucrats with government-issued hearts and the soul of a metal desk, but she sensed something else about him, something that scared her. He struck a cord deep within her, reminded her of someone, but she couldn't put a face on the memory.

Calm down, don't let him get to you. Don't let the city get to you.

The dark winter night was falling closer to the ground in an icy mist, and although their way along the footpath was lit, the lamps cast only a gloomy pallor; further out, she could see shadowy trees stripped to skeletons by winter's cold hand.

The gloom made her feel sad. So much death in winter. Her mother had died on a cold winter day.

People on the path hurried by in both directions as she kept pace with Belkin. A glow lit the night in the distance and she faintly heard the sound of music.

She glanced back over her shoulder and he caught her eye. 'Just paranoid about being in a park at night,' she told him.

'Parks belong to the people of Moscow, day and night,' he said. 'We have not yet given them up to criminals as you Westerners have. But now,' he lifted his hands as if there was a communist heaven that would hear his plea somewhere in the darkness above, 'with the new regime . . .'

'We should have met in a restaurant,' she said. 'I don't know how you people stand this cold. I was born in Moscow but I can't stand cold weather. My feet are frostbitten.'

'Tell me about the photograph,' he said.

She continued walking without responding. The meeting had been set up so she could gain information, not hand it out. She decided to tell him as much as Gropski knew since Gropski had probably already filled him in.

'It's a black and white police crime scene photo of a woman who had been slashed with a knife.'

'And what do you want from me?'

She had given that question a lot of thought and was ready to reach for the golden ring.

'I want access to secret KGB files. The ones stored at the Lubyanka.'

Chapter 6

'This woman in the photograph,' Belkin said, 'it was your mother?'

'Yes.' He had not reacted at all to her request. Everyone wanted access to the KGB archives that documented seventy years of secret police abuse and intrigue. The top-secret files were rumored to be stored at the Lubyanka, the notorious former prison and KGB headquarters in the heart of the city.

He glanced at her. 'You say yes, but there is something in your voice . . .'

'I'm sure it's my mother. It's just that the woman's face is partly under bedcovers. But she is the same age and size as my mother was. Besides, there would be no reason for anyone to send me the picture if it wasn't my mother.'

'The message that came with the picture. What did it say?'

'There was no written message.'

Belkin stopped and stared at her. 'No message?'

'Just the picture. Postmarked Moscow.'

'And you came halfway round the world because of a picture with no message?'

'I came halfway round the world because I'm sure the picture itself was a message. I know my mother did not get high on psychedelic drugs and run her car into a tanker.'

'You were seven years old.'

'I'm not seven now. I came back to Moscow a couple of weeks ago and one of the first things I did was go to the accident site. It's on a deserted stretch of road about fifty miles east of the city. There's a small village nearby and I checked the police records there for the day my mother was supposed to have died. The village police still have their records, nicely handwritten, going back to Tsarist times. They were proud to show them to me.' After she had greased the palm of the constable in charge, she wanted to add.

'The day of my mother's death there was a report of a farm tractor stuck in a ditch, a wife complaining about her drunken husband, a tire stolen from someone's car. The tractor stuck in the mud rated eighteen lines but a horrendous accident involving a head-on collision between a passenger car and a petroleum tanker, an accident that killed a famous American peace activist, wasn't even mentioned.

'The tanker and my mother's car were supposed to have exploded in flames, the truck driver miraculously thrown clear as the tanker blew. It had to be the biggest event that happened in that village for decades and yet there is no record of it.'

Belkin made an unintelligible noise, something akin to a grunt, as they began walking again. 'An accident involving a foreigner would not have been handled by village police.'

'No, it would have been handled by the KGB which had jurisdiction over everything concerning foreigners. But that doesn't mean that a significant event wouldn't have been noted in the police ledger. Besides, if nothing else, the local police would have contacted the KGB and made a notation of that. I saw those types of entries for other incidents, even ones in which the KGB was called because a foreign reporter had been driving drunk. And why didn't the constable, who'd been stationed there for over thirty years, remember anything about the most sensational accident that ever occurred in his jurisdiction?'

'This picture of a woman, this message without words, you will show it to me.'

It wasn't a question, it was a command. And there was something else in his voice – eagerness. He was keen to see the picture. It set off another alarm bell in her head. Nothing was registering right with this man. Information about the past, access to government archives, was one of the hottest items on the Russian black market; conversations started with how much and ended if an amount wasn't agreed upon. But Belkin had not mentioned money. The couple of hundred dollars she had expected to pay would hardly have been a down payment on his handmade Italian boots, but even so, he wasn't playing by the rules.

To her surprise he didn't press his demand to see the photograph. 'You are a prosecutor in your country, am I right?' he said. 'You had the police authorities there examine the picture.'

He got no credit for his question – Gropski knew she was a prosecutor and that she had sent the picture to the crime lab. 'The crime lab couldn't date it, but they had a psychological make-up done on the person who inflicted the wounds.'

'A psychological profile?'

'Yes, a profile of the mental state of the person who did the killing, obtained by analysis of the wounds.'

Another grunt. He was probably used to analyzing criminals with a rubber hose, Lara thought, not with a computer.

'It was a crime of passion?' he asked.

'A crime of insanity. The . . . the woman,' she couldn't

41

say her mother, 'was mutilated by a savage attack that included slashing her sex organs. She wasn't stabbed but killed in an insane attack by someone in a frenzy.'

'I remember a similar case,' he said. 'It occurred around the same time, over twenty years ago. A seventeen-year-old boy killed a woman in the building where he lived. The woman was a foreigner, Scandinavian. No doubt the woman brought the attack on herself by provoking the boy.'

Jesus. What an ass.

'Finnish girls – that's what she was, I recall – are notorious sexual deviates. This type of crime would not have been committed in the Soviet Union without foreign influence.'

Did he really believe this bullshit? His comments were typical communist hogwash. Nothing had existed officially in the Soviet Union that reflected negatively on the party line. She wanted to remind him that Beria, the old KGB chief, used to have his men grab women off the streets of Moscow at night so he could rape and abuse them. Fathers and husbands who objected ended up dead or were sent to forced labor camps.

'You have wasted your money coming to Moscow. The picture was probably sent by some pervert to stimulate you.'

'Mr Belkin, at the Special Crimes Unit where I worked, we didn't get pictures of mutilated women in the mail every day, but those were the types of cases we frequently handled. I'm certain someone was sending me a message with the picture. The message was that the official version of my mother's death was not true.'

'Nonsense! Your mother's death was investigated by the proper officials. The findings are not open to question.'

'I went to the university where my mother used to teach.

42

There is no record of her there. It's as if she never existed. I checked the militia files here in Moscow, there's no report on my mother's so-called accident. I went to the old apartment building where we used to live. The manager is away on vacation but I persuaded her daughter-in-law to show me the tenant book from that time. A page was missing, the page that would have registered our stay in the building. Do you understand?' It was almost a plea. 'It's as if someone spat on the slate and wiped my mother off it. An entire life is missing.'

'So it is your belief that the KGB was involved in your mother's death.'

She shrugged. 'Who else could make a person invisible in the Soviet Union? But no, I don't think that the KGB was responsible for my mother's death. A different form of insanity than politics caused my mother's death.' The KGB would have put a bullet in her head, not mutilated her, but she didn't express her thoughts. He still hadn't asked for money, he wanted the picture. But why? she wondered. What did this character want with a picture of a dead woman?

'If you do not suspect the KGB of eliminating your mother, why do you want to gain access to KGB files?'

More word games, she thought. He knew why she wanted access to KGB files. 'For the reason I just said – the KGB would have investigated my mother's death. Someone went to the trouble to ensure that anything and everything connected to my mother was wiped out. I want to know who did it.'

'You believe you can track the killer through a paper trail. Bah! That is the stuff of cheap detective stores. You see conspiracies. I see government inefficiency.'

Then why do you want the picture, you phoney bastard?

Her feet were frozen and she couldn't feel her toes at all.

Her whole body had become cold. A girl from California could freeze to death in winterkill Moscow.

'What's the matter with you? You're shaking. Are you ill?' Belkin asked.

'No. I'm not used to this bitter cold weather.'

'It is the weather that makes us Russians strong. Cold weather, vodka and hot women.' He tried to slip his arm round her waist and she moved away.

The sound of music was louder. 'I hear music,' she said.

'Yes, there's a carnival. We will see it.'

Lights from the carnival created a glowing dome in the freezing mist ahead and the music gained volume with each step. Only the Russians would have a carnival tucked away in a dark park on a freezing night, she thought. Everything about the city since she had arrived had struck her as *film noir* that was just a little out of focus.

Calm down, don't let him get to you, don't let this crazy city get to you.

'That's Christmas music.' She quickened her pace and followed the sound round a bend. The path straightened and led to an old-fashioned carnival with ferris wheel, carousel, and booths selling chances to win prizes.

'Amazing,' she said. 'They've put Christmas trim on the booths, but those elves hustling people look like—'

'Gypsies.' The look on his face told her Gypsies were more bugs to squash.

Off to the right, on a massive monument to the 'Heroic Workers of the Ural Mines' who had provided the steel for Soviet tanks, chubby, rosy-faced children sang Christmas carols to a larger group of beaming parents.

Three giggling young teenage girls ran by, eager to get to the carnival games. Belkin stared at their backsides as if they were pieces of meat to hump; his big paws opened and closed as if he was squeezing a succulent piece of their anatomy.

She realized who Belkin reminded her of. A man she had prosecuted a couple of years ago, a Market Street strip joint owner who had beaten one of the girls, then taken his big hands and squeezed her inflated breasts until the silicone implants burst. In court, as she had turned from the jury, Lara had met his dead eyes and saw his big hands squeezing the end of the counsel table . . .

The cold had worked its way beneath the scarf round her neck and sent an icy sensation down her spine.

She cleared her throat. 'I need to make arrangements,' meaning payment, 'to, uh, inspect my mother's KGB file. Mr Gropski said you could get me access to the KGB archives.'

It was a moment before he spoke. 'Freaks. They have a freak show. And a dwarf.'

The freak show was ahead of them on the left, the side of the tent hung with pictures of deformed people. A small person in a tall Cossack hat and heavy fur coat stood on a platform and shook his cane at the crowd passing by, urging the people to come in and see the Fat Lady, Snake Man, Tattoo Man and the Crocodile Woman.

'Freak shows are outlawed in America,' she said.

'Freaks fascinate me.'

His response surprised her. She would have guessed that nothing fascinated this man. *Apparatchiks* were not given to imagination.

'And disgust me. Human deformities. Have you ever met a freak?'

She didn't know how to answer because she never considered disabilities as unnatural.

'I know one,' he replied. 'I have made a study of a freak.

They are interesting because they are . . . abnormal. Am I right? Yes, I am right.' And then he smiled at her.

Her unease increased. Keeping her fear and dislike of him under control was getting more difficult. She wanted to pay him and run, but he seemed to enjoy having her beside him as he strutted along, glaring contemptuously at everything he saw; with a clipboard he would have looked very much like a petty *apparatchik* recording the names of people who dared to enjoy themselves.

'Look at these fools,' he said, gesturing, 'they worry about food for their children, they use the same bone for three soups, and they come here and throw their money to thieves.'

People who should have been worried about bread were lined up several deep at every booth, trying to win a stuffed animal by getting coins to stick on slippery plates, tossing plastic loops at vodka bottles, throwing knives at balloons. Knives were so much more Russian and Gypsy than darts, she thought. At a shooting gallery, a group of drunk Russian paratroopers wearing Afghanistan campaign ribbons were having a wild contest shooting pellets at metal ducks.

The freak show was getting more attention than tall, hoary old Grandfather Frost and Snow Maiden walking among the sideshows. Lara noticed that traditional Russian Christmas characters were trying to sell colorful little gift packages, not give them away. Truly in the spirit of a free-market Christmas.

'These bastard thieves should be sent off to Siberia for re-education,' Belkin said of the Gypsies. 'Along with the fools who permit the corruption by giving them money. Not so long ago we would have swept the park clean of this trash.'

'Let them have fun,' she said. 'The economy is getting

worse every day, everyone is expecting another political coup, something like this is a good diversion. Besides, look at the faces in the crowd, the adults are as excited as the children.' She glanced back over her shoulder again.

'Are you certain you were not followed?' he demanded.

'Why would I have been followed? I don't know anyone in Moscow. I just got a little spooked walking over in the dark. I'm going to take a taxi back.'

'You need a man to protect you,' he leered at her.

What she really needed was a good old-fashioned American gun, not sexual innuendo from this bastard.

'I set the meeting at night in the park for security, you understand. But next time we will meet at your hotel. In your room, away from prying eyes.'

Not if she could help it.

A little boy carrying a balloon on a stick got too close to Belkin and he swatted the balloon, popping it. He held up his hand in mock innocence to show Lara a huge diamond ring. 'An accident.'

Lara glanced back sympathetically at the little boy.

The child gave her the finger.

She shrugged. Russian kids weren't much different from the home grown.

'You know they are selling human meat in the butcher shops,' he said.

'Yes, I heard the rumors. Something about government inspectors finding a human knuckle bone in a batch of pigs' feet. But there are always crazy rumors during bad times.'

'Cannibalism,' he said smugly. 'We had it after both wars and it is coming back again. Strangers attacked on the roadside and the bodies dragged into the forest to be butchered. Mark my words, it is no coincidence that we have this invasion of Gypsies just as we find human meat on our shelves. If those of us capable of running the country do not return to power, you will see Gypsies stealing Russian children and selling their flesh. Am I right? Yes, yes, I am right.'

An old Gypsy woman, a small person, similar in size to the man hustling for the freak show, came up beside Belkin and touched his arm.

'Let me reveal the future to—'

'Get away from me, you diseased old hag.' He jerked his arm away with such force the woman stumbled back and fell.

Lara rushed over to her and helped her to her feet. She looked back at Belkin. His expression told her he had just stepped on a bug.

'I'll be with you in a moment,' she told the bastard. 'I've never had my fortune told.' She tried to force a smile but couldn't manage it.

Following the Gypsy to a small booth set up near the freak show, she took a seat on a rickety wooden chair across the table from the woman and glanced over her shoulder to make sure Belkin was sticking around. He was looking at the billboards displaying the oddities and deformities of the freak show stars.

Dark Gypsy eyes studied her. 'You are tall and fair. Much too thin for a Russian winter. My Gypsy brothers would be attracted to you. The man you are with is not worth the price of your beauty.'

Lara blushed. 'The man is not a friend. He is providing information about . . . a personal problem. I'm sorry about the way he treated you.'

Keen eyes drilled into hers. 'I know he is not your friend.'

'Can you really tell the future?'

'You are not Russian,' the Gypsy said, 'though you speak almost as one.'

'You're not Russian, either. And your accent is much worse than mine. Are you Romanian?' It was as good a guess as any, she thought. Romania was famous for Gypsies and vampires.

'I am from many places,' the woman said, 'and from none.' She didn't smile but kept her intense eyes burning into Lara. 'That man,' she nodded in Belkin's direction. He had wandered over to a booth selling magic novelties and love potions. 'He is not a good man. He does not mean well for you.'

'That's true,' Lara said. 'I've already figured that one out.' Afraid she'd lose Belkin, she took a wad of roubles out of her purse and slipped a thousand rouble bill from it – about a dollar at the current rate of exchange and not far from the official minimum daily wage. 'I'm sorry for the way he pushed you.' She put the money on the table and got up.

The woman whipped the money up her sleeve.

'You are troubled,' she said.

Lara shook her head. 'I came to Moscow for ... for personal reasons. I think this damn winter is getting to me. Everything is so cold and gray. I'll feel better when I get home and see some sunshine.'

'A shadow walks in your footsteps.'

'Sounds like an old Gypsy tale,' Lara said, leaving the tent.

The Gypsy woman's words caught up with her as she was walking away.

'This shadow brings death.'

The woman pulled shut the curtains that closed off the front of the tent. Lara stepped back to the tent but hesitated at pulling the curtain open. It was just an act, part of the game, she told herself, but the words hacked at her and she jerked back the curtain.

49

The woman was gone. She had slipped out the back.

Lara stepped round the small table in the middle of the booth and fumbled with the curtains. Finding the opening, she stepped through, coming out behind the tent. The fortune teller was nowhere in sight, but a tall man with thick black hair, no hat, and wearing a loose-fitting, inexpensive overcoat was leaning against a lamppost. His hands were in his coat pockets and he had a cigarette dangling from his mouth.

'Hello,' she smiled. 'Did you see the fortune teller?'

He took his cigarette out of his mouth; not returning her smile, he nodded toward the back entrance to the freak show. 'She went in there. Probably to put on her crocodile skin for the next show.'

'Thanks,' she said, feeling a fool for chasing after a dwarf fortune teller who doubled as a crocodile woman.

Chapter 7

Belkin was still at the booth that sold magic and love potions. His back was to her as she left the fortune teller's tent. Crystal flakes, sprinkles just big enough to be called snow, had started falling from the night sky.

The Gypsy woman's words had shaken her. She needed to get out of the park and back to her hotel, away from the weird Christmas celebration with freaks and Gypsies and a throwback to the old regime.

This is crazy, she told herself. She couldn't let an old Gypsy woman get to her.

Trying to keep her fears under check, she concentrated on Belkin as she slowly walked toward him.

Why hadn't he mentioned money? It bugged her. Everyone she had come into contact with about obtaining information, from the hotel security man and clerks at government offices to the taxi drivers in between, had all been on the take, had all made demands for that magic money called hard currency. Belkin had been coming on to her sexually but the bribe had been arranged before they met, so sex had not been the motive for him providing information. Sex was a bonus the old bastard came up with after he met her.

What did this hard-line communist want with the picture? To bury it, or sell it?

As she came up behind him, he turned to face her. He

51

gaped at her wide-eyed, his hands clutching a bloody dagger sticking in his chest.

She stared at the dagger, her eyes locked on the blood. She tried to work her jaw muscles and finally it burst out of her, a scream that stopped all the action around them. The hustlers stopped hustling, the marks stopped pulling money out of their shoes, the dwarf on the platform in front of the freak show cut his spiel in mid-sentence, his cane raised overhead. Every eye went to her and Belkin.

Her mind went numb; she wanted to draw her eyes away from the bloody mess on his coat, the handle of the protruding dagger, but her reflexes were frozen.

Belkin's expression slowly relaxed. One of his big paws went up to his chest and pulled the dagger off. It came away with a wad of plastic blood.

A chuckle began deep in his chest and exploded as an almost girlish giggle as he pointed up at the magic sign above the booth.

Tension snapped and people all around them began to laugh; a shrill cackle from the little man hustling the freak show from atop the platform pierced the night.

Lara wanted to crawl into a hole and die.

An elderly couple walked by and the old woman shook a finger at her. 'Silly girl.'

Belkin was still chuckling as they walked away from the carnival. Lara began to wish the bastard really had been stabbed.

The freezing night, the crazy carnival, the old Gypsy and the bastard had worn her nerves and patience to breaking point.

'Mr Belkin, this meeting was set up to provide me with information. Information I need to access the KGB files in the Lubyanka. Can you help with that?'

'Have you ever been in the Lubyanka?'

'No, never. But there's a first time for everything.'

He looked at her.

'If you can make the arrangements, I will be happy to, uh, pay an appropriate fee.'

His grunt told her that the money was meaningless to him. So what was he after?

'You will be disappointed even if you find the file you seek. You will discover that the KGB was the most important organ of the state in ensuring that justice was administered evenly and democratically, that the stories you have heard about excesses, are just that – stories. Certainly, if a woman was brutalized, the KGB would have been the first to seek punishment for the perpetrator without political considerations.'

Oh sure. When Beria was executed by Khrushchev, it was not for his crimes against women, many of them teenage girls, but for his political ambitions.

Lara could imagine this man using his authority to paw and molest young women. He even looked like her mental image of the notorious Beria. Her years in the Special Crimes Unit had not broadened her tolerance of people who treated those weaker than themselves as toys they could play rough with.

'Look at the litter along this street,' he said. 'Soon the city will be as dirty as American cities. Already drugs are pouring into the country. Next there will be drive-by shootings.'

She cleared her throat and reached deep into her almost dry well of patience for just a little more to tolerate this insufferable man. 'I suppose the streets were cleaner and, uh, much better maintained under the Soviet regime.'

He pointed up at the night sky, at the light snowfall

drifting down. 'Even the snow was cleaner under us Soviets.'

God give me strength . . .

'About gaining access to my mother's file in the KGB archives . . .'

'I never said your mother would have a KGB file.'

'I thought everyone had a KGB file.'

'They did.'

'About gaining access to the archives, can you help?'

The pompous ass let the question hang in the air.

'Mr Belkin—'

'I have made the arrangements. But my fee is the picture. A copy of it,' he assured her smoothly.

'Okay. A copy of it. But not until I get what I want. Can you get me into the archives?'

'I can get you into them. Now let me see the picture.'

'I don't have it. It's back in my room.'

His eyes shot to her purse and she needed every ounce of control to keep from tightening her grip on it. He seemed to be hesitating between taking her purse by force or accepting her story that the picture was in her room. It suddenly struck her why he thought it was in her purse. Gropski had probably searched her room.

'I have it well hidden in my room,' she said. 'You can't trust anyone in a Moscow hotel. Too many thieves. And I dropped off a copy to the Legal Attaché at the American Embassy to hold for me,' she lied. 'It's in a sealed envelope. If I get admission to the archives, I'll give you a copy of the picture.'

Tension in his huge shoulders relaxed a fraction.

Jesus, I made it, she thought.

'I want to see the picture—'

'No, first I get admission into the archives. Look, Mr Belkin, I don't mean to be rude, but I've had a couple of unpleasant days. Right now I'm freezing and ready to faint. If you want to make a deal to get me into the archives, fine. If not, I hate to put it this way, but there is someone on almost every street corner offering the Soviet's old secrets for a price.'

'Fine,' he growled. 'You will see your archives. And when you are finished, you will give me a copy of the picture. If you do not . . .'

There's nothing like an unspoken threat to get across a point.

'How do I get in?' she asked.

'Tonight at one o'clock in the morning you will meet a man named Minsky at the Lubyanka Square metro station. He will be in the tea shop near the entrance.'

'Tonight? In the middle of the night? Can't we—'

'Don't be a fool. This is the archive containing top secret KGB files. The public has never been admitted to these records. Would you prefer to present yourself tomorrow morning at the Ministry of Security and tell them you wish to sneak into the archives?'

'What do I pay—'

Belkin slapped away the question with the back of his hand. 'Minsky will take care of those details. He will charge you five hundred American dollars.' He stopped walking and faced her. 'You are not to show that picture to anyone, not even that fool Gropski. Do you understand?'

'Yes, fine.'

'When you return from the archives I will be waiting in the tea shop for you. We will return together to your room and get the picture.'

'You can see the picture in my room, but I'm not giving you that one. We can have a copy made in the morning.'

She didn't know if the explanation annoyed him or if the look on his face meant he was disgusted with her, the situation, and life in general because he had to negotiate with fools like her rather than crush them.

'Tonight,' he said.

He turned away and walked toward the corner where a group of people were waiting to cross the street. She deliberately started in the other direction, heading away from him to find a taxi.

She was fifty feet away before she turned to see if he was following her. The broad back of his camel-colored coat was visible in the crowd waiting for the light to change. Turning back, sighing, wondering why God put creeps like Belkin on this earth, she heard a crash and screams behind her. She swung back round. A truck had stopped at the curb a little further down the street and a crowd was starting to gather round someone lying face down in the gutter. The person was wearing a camel-colored coat.

She ran back, nearly taking a fall as she slipped on new snow.

People surrounded the prone figure in the gutter but she pushed through them. It was Belkin. Voices babbled about what had happened.

'The man fell in front of the truck.'

'He was pushed.'

'He's dead.'

'The man is injured. Has anyone called an ambulance?'

Lara pushed in further toward the gutter to get a closer view but an elderly woman elbowed her, not about to give up her gawking space. It was the same woman who had called her a silly girl earlier when Lara had screamed.

Ignoring the woman, Lara stood on her toes and stretched her neck to get a look. She felt someone uncomfortably close to her backside and a raspy voice whispering in her ear.

'*Come closer . . .*'

She was shoved as she started to turn. She fell forward against the old woman, taking the woman to the ground with her. The woman clawed at her as Lara pulled herself away and looked for the person who pushed her.

'Did you see that nurse?' somebody asked.

'Nurse?' Lara's voice quavered.

An image flashed in her mind. *The landing outside their apartment. Her mother bundling her up for school. Someone in white . . . a nurse's uniform, coming out of a room on the next landing above . . .*

'I saw a nurse standing by you. She could have helped the injured man, but she walked away. That's the trouble with . . .'

Lara had to get away. She felt her throat constricting, her head pounding. The words came at her, words that hacked and slashed at her.

Come closer . . .

Chapter 8

Her knees shook as she walked across the lobby of the Gorky.

The clerk was bent over a newspaper spread on the front desk, supporting his chin on his hands and elbows. He looked up as she approached.

'May I help you?'

'Gropski, the security man, where is he?'

'Mr Gropski is not on the premises. Do you have a problem regarding security?'

'Yes – no, I'm checking out.'

'Yes, of course. You wish your bags transferred—'

'No, wait, I'm not checking out.' A wave of nausea hit her and she leaned against the counter for support.

'Not checking out. Does Madam need a doctor?'

'I need a . . .' she almost said gun, but held her tongue. She took a deep breath and tried focusing on the clerk. 'I-I'm sorry, I'm not checking out, not tonight, I'll check out tomorrow. I have to do something tonight.'

She turned away from the clerk and headed for the elevator. She had never taken the elevator before, it looked as rundown and dilapidated as the rest of the city was becoming, but tonight she didn't have the strength to climb the stairs.

Leaning back against the elevator wall, she unintentionally snubbed the friendly, smiling woman operating the lift.

Safely in her room, she slammed the door behind her, too drained mentally and emotionally to barricade the door. She sat on the bed and stared down at the floor.

Belkin had been hit by a truck; he was hurt; how serious, she didn't know. From the conversations she had heard around her, she had the impression that he wasn't dead but she couldn't be positive about that. Right now she wasn't positive about anything.

Focus, she told herself. That's what you do when too much is coming at you. Divide up the problems and conquer them.

She was being stalked. That was a certainty. Belkin had been badly injured. It could have been an accident – no, that would be too much of a coincidence. A more likely scenario was that the person stalking her pushed Belkin into the path of the truck. Why? Because Belkin was helping her, because he wanted the picture, because ... She didn't know all the becauses, she just knew it couldn't be a coincidence.

Last night a woman wearing a red scarf and gray coat had attacked her. Tonight a nurse had pushed up against her and whispered in her ear, 'Come closer . . .' The two people had to be the same.

The image came to her again, the nurse emerging on the landing above as she was leaving for school that fatal morning. The memory started an immediate throbbing in her temples. She shook her head and put aside the image, unable to deal with it. Deal with now, she told herself. The rest will overwhelm you, just deal with the present.

It was after nine. The appointment with Minsky and the secret KGB archives was set for one in the morning. How could she go through with it? How could she go out on the dark street and make her way to a rendezvous halfway across the city? She didn't have the strength or the guts. It was too much. She should go home, recoup.

She reached for the phone to call the airlines then slammed it back down. *No!* She couldn't go home. Someone had lured her back to Moscow, someone who knew her nightmares, someone from her nightmares. Why, after over twenty years? What had happened? Who was hiding a dark secret from the past that she threatened to expose?

One thing was clear about Belkin – he was not simply a go-between brought in by the hotel security man. Belkin knew something about the picture; if not the picture, then about her mother's death. Perhaps it arose from his job in the KGB. She was sure he was ex-KGB. What had he said? That he had been in a position to know things about her mother's death that were never revealed to the public?

He wanted the picture. For what reason? To protect someone? Blackmail? Advancement? Revenge?

She shook her head. Too much speculation, too many roads for her mind to travel. Right now she had to concentrate on the most critical problem: someone had lured her back to Moscow, someone was trying to terrorize her ... and kill her. And she had to go back out onto Moscow's dark streets to the KGB archives.

What does a person do when someone wants to kill them? she asked herself. Not just someone but probably a maniac.

Keep off the streets after dark.

Stay in public places.

Hire a bodyguard.

Get the police to investigate.

The police were a problem. It wasn't a language problem, she could speak Russian almost as a native. It wasn't just a credibility problem with them thinking she was a nut from California. The problem was that since the August coup, nothing worked quite right in the city, least of all the police. The KGB, which had been largely responsible for internal security and everything involving foreigners, had been disbanded and the local police lacked the training and direction to fill the gap. They were incapable of coping with the wave of crime currently threatening the city, swollen by the birth of the Russian Mafia and the Russian drug trade. Her mother's death two decades ago, officially recorded as an accident, hadn't aroused any interest when she had made inquiries at the Criminal Investigation Unit of the Moscow police. When she had started talking cover-up, the deputy commander had escorted her firmly by the arm to his door and told her to go back to America. 'We are not resurrecting the past to punish the living and defame the dead,' he told her. And after the incident at the cathedral, the police had written her off as a nutcase.

An ugly thought struck her. What if they blame me for Belkin's accident? No, she thought, there must have been witnesses, someone must have seen him being pushed – or fall. He was pushed, she was sure of it.

A bodyguard. She needed a bodyguard. She could hire Gropski temporarily, or find someone through him. But Gropski wasn't around and Belkin had set up a meeting for one o'clock in the morning, in four hours' time. It wasn't a meeting she could rearrange with a phone call.

She lay back on the bed, pulling the covers over her, too cold and stressed even to take off her boots. She needed a plan. She had to make that appointment. And she wasn't walking out into the dark streets by herself. She needed a bodyguard.

At thirty minutes past midnight, she went down to the

lobby. The night clerk was sleeping with his head on his folded arms on the countertop.

'Excuse me, sir, excuse me.'

The man rose from his slumber and leaned back, taking a deep yawn, nearly falling off his chair. 'May I help you?'

'Has Mr Gropski returned?'

'No, he hasn't reported in.'

'Who's in charge of security when he's gone?'

'Mr Nosenko.'

'I'd like to speak to Mr Nosenko.'

'He's on vacation at the Black Sea.'

Her temper rose a notch.

'Then who is—' No, she knew the routine by now. 'Gropski's not here, Nosenko's not here, so no one is in charge of security at the hotel while they're gone. Is that it?'

The clerk tried to shake some of the sleep out of his head. 'No, Mr Nosenko's in charge of security when Mr Gropski's—'

'But Nosenko's at the Black Sea!'

'Yes, but when Mr Gropski is gone, that means—'

'Forget it.' She spun on her heel and started for the front doors, steaming. These people have had the government telling them what to do for so long, they've forgotten how to think.

She followed the sound of snoring to locate the porter. He was spread out, asleep, on a luggage bench in a tiny alcove just behind the porter's desk.

Awoken, he came out of his cave buttoning his uniform coat and apologizing.

'I want you to walk with me over to the Metrope Hotel so I can get a taxi.'

'You want me to carry your luggage?'

'No luggage. I don't want to walk alone in the dark.'

'I can call you a taxi.'

'Will it come?'

He shrugged. 'Probably not.'

'Then let's not call one. I'll give you five American dollars if you come with me.'

Sleep popped out of his eyes and he literally snapped to attention. 'I will accompany you. It is dangerous for a woman alone at night.'

She had already turned and was pushing open the front door. Moscow freeze attacked her the moment she stepped out of the hotel and she pulled her hat down over her ears and adjusted her scarf until it covered her nose. He followed her into the night, stuffing his shirt down his pants, buttoning his heavy wool jacket.

'I'm leaving this hotel,' she told him. 'There's no security, the restaurant is poisonous – on those rare occasions when it decides to open – and there are no taxis. And the damn place is freezing.'

'Yes, yes,' he huffed beside her. 'Ah, but the old days—'

'When the snow was cleaner,' she snapped.

'Yes! You remember. Yes, it was cleaner. Why, back during the Great Patriotic War—'

'There's a taxi!'

A taxi was approaching the hotel and Lara turned to hurry back to the entry to meet it.

'Perhaps you'd like another taxi?' the old porter told her as he hurried beside her.

'I'll still give you the money.'

'This taxi is a good one. Only a few dents . . .'

Two men in business suits, ties askew, a breeze of vodka following them, exited the taxi. From their accents they appeared to be Ukrainians.

One of them reached for her arm as she moved by them to take the taxi. 'Pretty lady, join us for a drink,' came out in poor Russian as she swatted away the arm and got into the taxi, slamming the door and locking it. She rolled down the window just enough to give the porter a five dollar bill as the taxi pulled away.

'Men in this country, on this side of the world even, are a century behind in women's rights,' she told the driver, a woman. She wasn't flattered by being called pretty – her scarf had covered most of her face. 'Pretty' to a drunk was anything wearing women's clothes.

'Russian men are bastards,' the woman driver told her. 'I like the foreign ones, especially the French and Italian. They know how to treat a woman right. Where am I taking you?'

'The metro station at Lubyanka Square.'

The woman shot Lara a look in the rearview mirror as she moved through the light street traffic.

'A taxi to a metro station?'

'I'm, uh, meeting a friend,' Lara said.

The woman shrugged. 'Not that you shouldn't take a taxi, the metro's not safe at night. They're talking about putting Afghanistan war veterans with assault rifles on the trains to protect honest citizens. Pretty soon the city will be like New York. Criminals will have more guns than the police.'

Lara wondered if the woman was a defense plant lay-off – she had the look of a professional. She had heard of engineers and scientists driving taxis because of lay-offs at all types of plants. A group of prostitutes dominating the bar at the best hotel in town were formerly engineers at a defense plant.

She had to admit that prostitution was a slightly better way to feed your kids than cannibalism.

Lara stared at the Lubyanka as the taxi entered the square. True to Russian logic, the 'square' was circular.

She had seen the building in the daytime when she was making her rounds trying to dig up information about her mother, but the most notorious building in Russia took on a sinister cast with the gloom of night.

'I hear they're selling pieces of Dzerzhinsky. A friend of mine claims to have his left toe.'

Lara made a listening response and glanced at the empty pedestal where the huge statue of the founder of the CHEKA, the predecessor to the KGB, had been pulled down after the August coup attempt.

Thinking about cannibalism and prostitution to feed children and what hell the woman driver put up with driving a taxi at night, Lara gave her a generous tip and hurried away from the cab, a little embarrassed by the woman's gratitude.

The stairway into the underground station was littered with newspapers and two men huddled together sharing a bottle of vodka. She hurried by them, wishing the mysterious Minsky had chosen somewhere on street level for their meeting.

The tea shop had one customer who stared apprehensively at her as she entered.

'Mr Minsky?'

He winced and looked round to see if anyone had heard the name. The only other person in the kiosk was a heavy woman washing cups.

Lara sat down across from him, thankful he didn't have Belkin's brutal mentality written on his face. He looked more like a rabbit than KGB middle management.

The woman washing cups behind the counter looked over to her and Lara shook her head, no, she didn't want anything.

'Mr Belkin sent me. He said—'

'Yes, yes, I understand, we don't have to discuss it.'

The rabbit was a nervous wreck. She wondered if he had heard about Belkin's accident. If he hadn't, it didn't seem the right thing to mention when he was shaking in his boots at just the sight of her.

He spiked his tea with a splash of vodka from a flask and downed the drink, allowing a little to dribble on his coat front where it joined the residue of previous meals and drinks.

He was older than she had expected, probably in his sixties. Definitely not a Belkin fat cat; Mr Minsky's clothes were winter heavy but threadbare, the shoulders of his coat littered with dandruff. He had the look of a shop-worn bookworm rather than a night watchman. His straggly hair was dirty white, his eyebrows driven snow and bushy; his eyes were pink and his face had mostly sunk into jowls that weren't clean-shaven but had faint white hairs pointing straight out like tiny needles of an albino cactus. He reminded her of a big-footed rabbit, old and scuffed and ... odd. One that had just crawled out of a hole and was looking around, amazed the world was still here.

He slammed his cup down on the table and coughed onto the back of his coat sleeve. Finally he looked up at her, picking up a piece of the newspaper he had been reading and rattling it at her. 'Look, look at him, imitating the old aristocracy.'

He was referring to a newspaper article about a Moscow entrepreneur, the *enfant terrible* of the new Russian rich, who had bought a museum palace on the outskirts of the city from the worker committee that had managed it before the Deluge. The whole country was talking about it because the man was fighting the government's attempt to get it back.

'Trying to make serfs out of us poor people,' Minsky

muttered. 'He's stolen a palace and calls it his dacha. KGB one day, next day a millionaire.' Minsky's hands shook as he held up the newspaper. He was so damn nervous it was making her nervous.

'The money. American,' he whispered.

She took five hundred dollars out of her purse and put it on the table. 'Mr Minsky, I—'

He slapped the paper on top of the money and stared at her wide-eyed.

'Sorry,' she said, kicking herself for exposing the money transfer. She wasn't used to being covert. People passing bribe money was the sort of thing as a prosecutor she saw in police snapshots and hidden videos.

Minsky glanced over to make sure the counter woman still had her back to them before he slid his hand under the paper to take the money. After another furtive look around, he counted the notes, keeping them and his hands beneath the table.

If there were any undercover cops in the place, Minsky would have stood out as a flashing neon of guilty behavior.

'There is only five hundred. I must have one thousand.'

Her pulse and blood temperature rose. 'The deal was five hundred dollars. I'm not paying any more.' At the hard currency exchange rate, it was over a year's minimum wage for the man. At her own rate, it was more than she could afford.

'New deal,' he said, with an attempt at looking tough that came out more cringing than hard. 'Most people pay a thousand to get into the archives. I can lose my job, my pension. I have to have more money.'

White fluffs of hair were growing out of his nostrils. As he whined, one of the fluffs became wet with a drop of something really to fall.

She looked away, at a train coming into the station. The

metro closed down at one o'clock and the train that pulled in let off only two people but didn't take anyone on. She couldn't afford to pay one thousand dollars and even if she could, she hated being ripped off. She was no good at bribing her way into government archives. Somehow, the fact that she was in Russia made the whole thing seem not criminal, but she knew that it wasn't legal. If it was legal she would have presented herself in the morning when the building opened.

Showing more resolve than she really had, she turned back to him. 'Mr Minsky, the price I was quoted and accepted was five hundred. If that is not good enough, give me the money back. And,' she leaned in closer, 'before you entertain any notions about keeping my money, let me tell you I will be at the Ministry of Security when it opens in the morning if I don't get every cent back.'

His pink eyes bulged and his face turned crimson. 'Come with me,' he croaked.

She followed him out into the station and down the high ceilinged corridor, a deputy district attorney from California alongside a Russian night watchman she had bribed to gain access to secret government files.

Overweight, arthritic and asthmatic, he wheezed as he inhaled and wheezed as he exhaled. 'The new government with its old capitalist ideas is making thieves out of honest men.'

She glanced around at the derelicts in the underground and didn't see an honest man. It occurred to her that he might be talking about himself.

'They're trying to kill off the old people. The new Russia is for the young. They don't want to pay pensions to the old. They're killing us off with cold and starvation. Why don't they just shoot us? Better to die fast . . .'

If whining was harmful, the old man had a fatal dose of it. She changed the subject.

'You're a night guard at the archives?'

'I was once a KGB historian.' A moment's pride fell before self-pity. 'Now there is nothing to record. The KGB is gone and a wet-nosed ministry has taken over. Once I made a record of *history*. Now I sit in a chair and smoke cigarettes and watch history grow dust.'

She suddenly felt sorry for him. He had spent a lifetime under one system, worked, planned, saved, and was ready for retirement when the old system fell and inflation soared not into double digits but by *thousands* of percentage points.

'Because I no longer earn enough for meat in my soup I am turned into a criminal by foreigners who want to look into our secrets.'

They bypassed escalators leading up to street level and went behind the mechanical steps to a door with a sign that warned against entry. A dim light bulb imprisoned in a wire cage caked with dead insects hung above the door.

He pressed a button concealed on the side of the door molding and a moment later a judas window opened and an eye examined them. Just like a roaring twenties speakeasy, she thought. The door swung open and a dour man with a bushy mustache and huge belly let them in. The door was thick and solid enough to secure a walk-in bank safe.

The guard station consisted of an iron chair with a pillow on it; some newspapers, lunch and a thermos bottle were on the floor next to the chair. The guard gave her a hard stare and she met his eye. Another pensioner, but this one looked mean and cranky.

'You have to pay him two hundred dollars,' Minsky said.

'What?'

Minsky shrugged and looked away.

'I already paid him,' she told the man.

'Now you pay me.'

'I'm not paying you anything. I paid him five hundred dollars.'

The man looked at Minsky. 'So little? You give away the KGB's secrets for small change?'

Minsky shrugged again. 'I'm a hungry man.'

'You're both—' She cut it off, knowing she couldn't win. She dug five twenties out of her purse. 'I'll give you a hundred dollars. If that's not enough I'm leaving.'

The man took the money without a word and she saw a look pass between them. They would be splitting the total take later.

'There had better be no more surprises,' she told Minsky as they walked side by side down the dank corridor.

He wheezed.

The concrete corridor was poorly lit. Rusty pipes, sweaty walls, dead rats and small streams of water made up the decor.

'Where exactly are you taking me?'

'To the archives.' He wheezed again.

'Are we under the Lubyanka?'

'You'll see, you'll see,' he muttered.

What the hell did that mean? The old man was worse than Belkin. Belkin would have been manageable with a little flirting and flattery. Minsky was a hole she threw money in and got wheezes in return.

She wondered about the path her life was taking. Here she was in a dank tunnel with a strange old man who wheezed and limped as he led her under the most infamous building in Russia. If places had soul, the Lubyanka's would burn in eternal hell for the crimes against humanity committed there. People were beaten and tortured and even killed in the Lubyanka. She shuddered at the thought that her mother might have been one of those tortured.

Another door that would stop a tank was waiting at the end of the corridor.

Another guard, another chair, newspapers, a jug of coffee.

Another one hundred dollars.

'That's it,' she told her wheezing guide. 'That's all. Not a dime more. I have enough money left on me for a taxi back to my hotel. That's it.'

The man shrugged. 'What's a hundred dollars to a rich American?' He started wheezing and coughing and leaned against the wall for a moment to catch his breath. She realized that somewhere in that wheezing was laughter. 'You won the war and now you pay,' he chuckled. 'Isn't that how you Americans always do it? You win the war and then you pay.'

They arrived at another door and this time she blew.

'No, no,' he wheezed, 'this is my station.'

On the other side of the massive door was a well-lit corridor. After going a dozen feet, he led her through tall metal doors and into a different world.

Storage walls soaring fifteen, maybe twenty feet high created narrow, poorly lit aisles that seemed to go on for ever in every direction. The walls were swollen with boxes – cardboard boxes, wooden boxes, plastic bins and metal containers; boxes and filing cabinets out in the open, behind mesh screens, behind steel bars.

She walked around a little, taking it all in, cobwebs and dust, the smell of old paper, yellowing and decaying – wrongs and atrocities disappearing as the paper disintegrated. She felt as if she had just stepped into the belly of a dinosaur. A rat scrambled across an aisle and down another small ribbon of water that had a dark slime underbelly.

'The KGB archives,' she said more to herself than to him.

'Yes, but some say that the most secret documents are in Mr Yeltsin's sugar bowl.'

'Ones that can be used politically?'

Minsky shrugged and wheezed.

She looked around in wonderment and understood why the world's scholars were frantic to get inside. It all had to be here, seventy-five years of skullduggery, plots and spies, murder and mass murder, blackmail, treachery and atrocities. Thirty million people were killed under Stalin. Perhaps the record of each was in this vast concrete cavern, she thought, a last testament written by their executioners: 'Ivan confessed to anti-Soviet thoughts just before he was shot attempting to escape.'

She could sense the pathos, the human drama; these were not documents about the grain harvest, but about *lives* – people of flesh and blood, people like her mother with prides and prejudices, fears and ambitions; all that was human or inhuman about them now stored in boxes like paper souls.

'Where is my mother's file?' she asked.

Minsky turned away from her and watched a fly crawling up the wall. 'Your mother's file?'

'My mother's file. The file I've spent nearly a thousand dollars between you, your friends and Gropski to see tonight.'

Wheeze. He folded up a piece of newspaper to use as a swatter, watching the fly with what appeared to be great interest.

'You wanted to get into the archives to find your

73

mother's file. My task was to get you in so you may do your search.'

'So I can—' She shot a glance around her. It would take a team of scholars months to find a barking dog in the vast paper jungle. But then she realized there had to be an index system.

'Fine. Where's your index?'

'Index?'

Chapter 9

'You bastard!'

Minsky backed up, his fat jowls trembling, the fly swatter held up in self-defense as she shouted at him.

'I'm going to have you thrown in prison. You won't have to worry about the price of meat or vodka for the rest of your life. You're a thief, a liar—'

'You bribed me, an official of the—'

'No, I'm an innocent American tourist who was lured here under false pretenses and robbed. By the time I get through telling my story to the American public, Russia can kiss foreign aid away. And you're going to prison. I'm leaving now, but I'll be back tomorrow to hold a news conference on the front steps of the Lubyanka.'

He slowly sank to the floor. He knelt before her, sweat rolling down his jowls.

'Please, my pension . . .'

A pang of pity hit her but that prosecutor's go-for-the-kill training kicked in.

'Where's my mother's file?'

'As God is my witness, I don't know.'

A communist swearing to God?

'How do I find it?'

He waved his hands in front of him. 'You can't, not tonight. If there's a file here it would take many days to find. And you would need more information than just her name.'

'There's no indexing system?'

'No indexing system, I swear it.'

It rang true. Another element of control, like no phone books.

'Then how do you find anything in this ... this ...' she waved at the cavern.

'Most of the filing is done by KGB department, further divided by section.'

'By year?'

'Sometimes, but there would be a hundred different places to look for any particular year.'

'How do you find anything?'

'Find anything? We don't find anything. We don't look. No one wants the past resurrected.' He wheezed.

'Get off your knees,' she told him.

Minsky climbed laboriously to his feet.

'Sit down.'

He sat down. So far, so good.

'Now listen to me, you sold me information and you're going to come up with information. I don't care if you have a coronary. Understand?'

He nodded and then wiped sweat off his jowls with the newspaper he still held, leaving black ink streaks.

'You and Belkin must have discussed this and come up with something. Or you both lied to me from the beginning and—'

'Please, please, we discussed it. I told him I would not be able to find your mother's file. But there might be something.'

'What?'

'Belkin said your mother was killed in an accident involving a truck. Do you have the name of the truck driver?'

'Yes, but that's all I have about him. A name from over twenty years ago. I haven't been able to locate him.'

'We might be able to locate his file.'

'Why would you be able to locate the truck driver's file and not my mother's?'

'If the accident happened anywhere near Moscow, he probably worked for the KGB's local motorized division. There are only a small number of those files here. If you know his name and the year he drove for the KGB, you can find his file and obtain information about the accident from it.'

'I never said he worked for the KGB.'

'You said it was an accident that didn't happen. Only the KGB could make things not happen.'

An hour later she found the file of KGB motor pool driver Joseph Guk.

He had worked for the mobile support division, Moscow Area, for over thirty years, and had retired five years ago. He had had the same rural address for most of the thirty years and, if he was like most people in the country, probably still had the same address today. If he was alive.

The file confirmed all her suspicions about the accident: there was no mention of it. Joseph Guk had received annual commendations for being accident free, including the year of her mother's death. He had only two fender benders during his entire career; neither was judged his fault, both were duly related in characteristic Soviet detail. But not a word about a fiery collision between his tanker and her mother's car that supposedly destroyed both vehicles.

She was tired and dirty by the time she found and read Guk's file. At nearly three in the morning Minsky got out of his chair and lumbered along to escort her out. He asked nothing about her findings and she volunteered nothing. She wondered what exactly his relationship with Belkin was. She decided to test the water.

'By the way,' she said, 'I forgot to tell you, tonight as Mr Belkin was leaving me he was hit by a truck. I think he might have been seriously injured.'

A hoarse expulsion of breath, not a wheeze but something more akin to a death rattle, gurgled from Minsky's throat.

He backed away from her, turned and ran.

Back in her hotel she wedged the door with a chair, and for good measure backed it up with another.

After washing her hands and face, she climbed into bed with two sets of long underwear still on.

Minsky's reaction to Belkin's accident had sent the temperature soaring on her own paranoia. She knew she should be on the next plane out of Moscow, back to a nice safe job of dealing with killers and perverts. She couldn't be the first person to buy their way into the archives. Minsky and his cohorts had a well-rehearsed act going. So why was he ready to croak every time she opened her mouth? And nearly did when she mentioned Belkin's accident?

The questions spun round in her head like a dog chasing its tail. It all seemed to come back to the same question.

Who had sent for her?

Just before she fell asleep, another question slipped through a crack in her mind to add to her confusion: that wasn't an ordinary storage room she had been digging into, but an archive still classified top secret because it recorded the brutal atrocities of generations of Soviet secret police.

What was the file of an unimportant truck driver who had retired years ago doing in the country's most secret KGB archives?

Chapter 10

It was early morning when a noise at her door jerked her awake and she shot upright on the bed. The door was being forced against the chair wedged under the handle.

A man cursed. 'She's jammed it with a chair.'

She jumped out of bed and ran at the door, yelling, 'I've called the police! I have a gun!'

'We are the police! Throw your gun out or we'll shoot!'

'Wait. I don't have a gun! Don't shoot!'

'Sonofabitch.' Then silence. A man's calm voice came through from the corridor. 'Remove the chair.'

She pulled both chairs away from the door and it opened with a push from the other side.

Two men were standing at the door, one over-sized, one normal. They wore the standard uniform of Russian plainclothes police: cheap suits, wrinkled white shirts with yellowing collars and top button undone, ties sloppy, shoes which had seen too much mileage.

She backed away from the door as they came into the room, the smaller man leading the way. A look from the men reminded her she was still in long underwear and she grabbed a blanket off the bed.

'What do you want?' she asked.

The bigger man had a Cossack handlebar mustache, bald head and powerful torso. He automatically looked at the other man for an answer to her question.

79

'What's your name?' the other man asked.

'What's your name? And let me see some identification before I start screaming.'

He raised his eyebrows at his husky partner. 'First she has a gun, now she's a screamer.' He flashed her an identification card. 'Detective Kirov. My partner is Detective Stenka.'

She examined the card closely. Detective Yuri Kirov was with the Special Division, Moscow Militia. The local police.

'Now let me see your identification, please,' Kirov said.

The 'please' was not polite. Her hands were shaking as she fumbled for her passport. She knew she was going to be arrested for bribing her way into the archives. She was so stupid. Hidden cameras probably recorded the whole thing.

Kirov was quick, intense, professionally curt. He wandered around her room as she fumbled with her bag, taking in everything while Stenka folded his arms and quietly leaned against the wall by the door.

Yuri Kirov ran one hand though his thick black hair while he studied the passport in the other. She noticed his eyes were unusually dark, what some Russians would call Gypsy eyes.

And then it hit her.

'Wait a minute, I've seen you before,' she said to him. 'Last night.' She pointed her forefinger at him. 'You were at the carnival, behind the fortune teller's tent.'

'Correct. You were chasing a dwarf at the time, I believe.'

She blushed. 'I . . . I . . . What were you doing there?'

'Police business. Why have you come to Moscow?'

'Visiting.'

'Visiting who?'

'Moscow. I'm a tourist.'

'You speak perfect Russian. Your family was Russian?'

'American and British. I was born in Moscow.' Her

insides were shaking. How could she have been stupid enough to break the law in a foreign country? It was all probably a set-up, a sting operation. She was surprised she hadn't been arrested coming out of the archives. She had to call the American Embassy for help.

'What is your relationship with Nikolai Belkin?'

'Belkin? Someone I met here in Moscow.'

'Met him for what reason?' Detective Kirov wandered around the room a little more and opened her closet.

'Excuse me, but do you have a warrant?'

'A warrant?' He turned to Stenka and threw up his hands. 'How rude of you, Stenka. Show her our warrant.'

Without a change in expression the Cossack opened his coat to expose a 9mm automatic in a shoulder holster.

Kirov pointed at Stenka's gun. 'In Russia, that is what gives you permission to search.'

'This is crazy. I'm calling the American Embassy.' She went for the telephone next to her bed.

Kirov spoke as he went through her clothes hanging in the closet. 'Your phone doesn't work. Stenka had the hotel operator turn it off.' He looked back at his partner and shook his head. 'Tough cop. He's from the old school.'

He moved to her dresser and started rifling through the drawers as he talked. She felt totally helpless.

'Why are you staying at this hotel?'

'Why not?'

'It's a dump.'

'I'm not rich.'

'You're an American.'

'Don't believe everything you read about Americans.'

'Are you a prostitute?'

'What? What gives you the right to ask me a question like that? Get the hell out of my room. Better yet, I'll get out. I'm going to your supervisors.' She started for the door.

Stenka raised his eyebrows at Kirov who shook his head. 'Let her go. She'll freeze to death in her underwear before she catches a taxi.'

Shit. She had forgotten how she was dressed. She came back into the room with the blanket trailing after her and stood toe to toe with Kirov, her face burning.

'I'm a prosecutor, and in my country I work with the police. I know the difference between someone being harassed and a real police investigation. I saw you last night. You have—'

'All right, all right, calm down and I'll tell you why we're here.' He backed away from her and flopped into the stuffed chair by the dresser and lit a cigarette.

'I don't like smoking in my room.'

'So don't smoke.'

She sat on the edge of her bed and stared coldly at him. She ran her fingers through her hair and they caught in tangles. She must look like hell. She pulled the blanket tighter.

Kirov blew smoke in the air. 'I apologize for the prostitution remark, but,' he counted with his fingers, 'one, you are in a cheap hotel that does not cater for foreigners; two, you have been registered here for two weeks and appear to be neither a tourist nor on business in Moscow; and three, last night you were in the company of Nikolai Belkin about the time the subject took a nose dive in front of a truck. Besides his nose-diving, Mr Belkin is well known to the Moscow police as a sausage waver. You are a prosecutor. You know what I mean.'

She knew what he meant. In her office they were called wienie wavers: guys who liked to pull their penis out and startle women – a flasher. Relief flowed through her. They were investigating Belkin's accident, not her invasion of the archives.

'And four, an elderly woman at the scene of Belkin's

accident stated that a young foreign woman who had been with Belkin had been acting strange. The good citizen is willing to testify that the young woman appeared to be under the influence of drugs. There is also the fact that you were behind the Gypsy tents when I saw you. As you are no doubt aware, Gypsies are importing drugs into Russia in great quantities.'

'Now I'm a *drug runner*?' If it sounds like drugs, it probably is drugs, a San Francisco cop would say. But Belkin didn't strike her as someone who would be involved in drug trafficking. Violence, a little perversion, yes, but not drugs. He was old guard, not a yuppie. But she couldn't defend herself by telling the police she had met Belkin to steal state secrets, not sell drugs. 'I was looking for the fortune teller because of something she had said. Look, Officer, I don't sell drugs, I don't use drugs, and I seriously doubt Mr Belkin is either a user or a seller. Is that what you're investigating, drugs?'

'I wasn't investigating him last night. We know him from the past. I was on another case last night when I spotted you with him. What's your relationship with Belkin?'

'Nothing that is any business of the police. We're just friends.' Oh God, what a thing to say about a wienie waver.

Kirov looked at Stenka and gave him a 'what can I say' shrug. She went a shade redder but kept her mouth shut.

Kirov blew more smoke and asked, 'Have you violated any laws while in Russia?'

She leaned against the bed post, crossed her legs, pulled the blanket snugger, and gave Detective Kirov her best smile.

'Why don't you give me a list of laws, Detective, so I can tell you which ones to arrest me for?'

Stenka chuckled, and Kirov gave him a dark look but then

suddenly smiled, a genuine smile, as he ran his hand through his dark wavy hair. The smile broke up the rugged intensity of his features and made him look younger. A little gray in his hair made her estimate his age in the late thirties, but his features had the cast of a man who had seen more life than that.

She knew the smile was to disarm her. If being friendly didn't work, he'd go back to tough cop.

'We are here because Belkin was injured in an accident last night. In his pocket was a slip of paper with your name and hotel on it. A woman fitting your description was observed leaving the scene of the accident last night. As I've already said, witnesses say she was acting oddly and left in a hurry. Because of Belkin's past record, we had to investigate.'

She started to blurt out that a maniac had probably pushed Belkin in front of the truck, the same person who had tried to kill her at St Basil's, but she snapped her jaws shut so quickly her teeth hit. This detective wasn't telling her everything. She had better keep her mouth shut and see what he had up his sleeve before exposing her hand.

'Mr Belkin didn't die in the accident, did he?'

'No, I can guarantee you he survived the injuries inflicted by the truck.'

'Then why don't you ask Belkin?' A safe bet, she thought. The security man had told her Belkin was a master of blat.

'An excellent idea!' He jumped to his feet. 'Get dressed. We can question you together.'

'Together? What about?'

A radio blasted on in the room next door, someone's wake-up call. The music was rap.

Kirov jerked his thumb at the wall. 'This is what our young people are learning from their exposure to Western culture – drugs, sex and bad music. Get dressed.'

He politely left the room and Stenka followed him, leaving the door open a crack.

In the corridor Kirov lit another cigarette and positioned himself so he could watch her through the crack as she dressed.

'Checking for weapons,' he whispered to Stenka.

The big man leaned against the corridor wall and folded his arms. 'We didn't have an investigation in the park last night.'

It was her first ride in a police car where she was the suspect. Stenka drove, his big frame overwhelming the driver's area of the small militia car. She sat in the back with Kirov. Neither of them spoke. He rolled down a window and blew cigarette smoke out. The smoke came back in, along with a lot of frigid air.

Uneasiness about everything crept up on her. Yuri Kirov claimed he hadn't been in the park to watch her and Belkin. But . . . she hated coincidences. Yet being there to investigate a Gypsy drug connection would be in line with what was going on in the country. Belkin could quickly straighten them out about the drug connection, but she cringed at the thought of having to keep up a pretense of being 'friendly' with the pervert.

Yuri Kirov appeared professional and that inferred honesty to her. An honest cop could be of real use to her – as soon as she convinced him that she wasn't selling sex or drugs.

As the car approached the hospital, Kirov told Stenka to park in the rear, near the basement steps. 'It's the quickest way to his room,' he said.

As she followed Kirov down a flight of cement steps into a rear entrance to the hospital's basement, Stenka's big frame behind her, she wondered how seriously Belkin had been hurt. He obviously wasn't critical if cops and suspects could waltz in and out of his room.

Kirov flashed his ID at an attendant's station near the entry door and walked quickly by, moving down the drab corridor at a pace fast enough to make Lara stretch her legs to keep up. The hospital corridor was colder than her hotel corridor; they could freeze meat in this one, she thought.

Yuri pushed through a pair of swinging doors and into a room with white walls and glaring lights, and she flew into the room behind him. He stepped to the side and with the pressure of Stenka coming on her tail she was almost on top of a gurney before she stopped.

A naked body, a man's hairy body with his penis poking up in full erection, lay on the gurney. Belkin, black and blue marks down the left side of his body, his arm broken and separated, an open wound at his hip, was very dead.

She recoiled in shock, knocking away Kirov's hand as he reached for her.

'You sonofabitch!' She shoved by Stenka and knocked the swinging doors open, bursting back into the corridor, nearly bellying over another gurney being pushed down the corridor by an attendant. A sheet slipped off as she pulled away and an old woman with eyes wide open and mouth gaping open in death's rigor stared up at her.

She ran down the corridor and out the steps leading back to the parking lot. She was going through the door at the bottom of the stairs when she saw the sign by the attendant's desk: HOSPITAL MORGUE.

Halfway across the parking lot, Yuri Kirov caught up with her. He walked beside her for a moment without speaking.

When she reached the sidewalk, she stepped off the curb to flag a taxi.

'I'm sorry,' he said. 'I needed to know your reaction.'

'My reaction? How the hell did you think I would react to something like that?' She was shaking.

A taxi spotted her waving and swerved across traffic lanes to get to her.

'You set me up by lying about his accident injuries. Then shove a dead body in my face. I hope it gives you and your pals a big laugh when you get back to your office.'

She opened the back door and started into the taxi when he said, 'I told you he didn't die from a truck hitting him. He was murdered. Later.'

Yuri Kirov's dark eyes fascinated her. The tune to the old Russian love song, '*Oh Shishonya* – Oh Dark Eyes', played in her head as they sat across the table from each other in a coffee bar. The coffee bar sold espresso, cappuccino, café mocha and desserts. A sign on the wall said it was a joint venture owned by an Italian company and Russian entrepreneurs.

Cappuccino and espresso were one thousand roubles each. She noticed that most of the patrons looked like foreigners, which wasn't surprising because the average Russian could buy food for a couple of days on that kind of money.

He insisted upon a cup of regular coffee. 'I'm not into designer drinks. That's what the world's gone to, designer clothes, designer cars, designer drugs. That's going to be the next big problem in Russia. Right now most of the drugs are expensive. But to get money to feed their families, half the unemployed chemists in the country are making synthetic drugs in their kitchens. Either that or vodka. And some of the homemade vodka is deadlier than bad drugs.'

'I guess it beats cannibalism.'

'Cannibalism?'

'Sorry. Bad joke. You told me you were going to explain how Belkin died.' She noticed Yuri wore the same cheap overcoat he had on when she saw him at the carnival. Another sign he was honest. Moscow policemen probably made less than a hundred dollars a month, she thought. A few cups of coffee in this place was a day's wages.

He took a sip of coffee. 'In a moment of great personal fear when I thought you were going to knock me down and let the taxi run over my head, I told you I would explain how Belkin died. But . . .'

'No buts.'

'But if I explain immediately, like the magician I will have revealed how the trick works and lose my audience. Can't we just sit and relax for a moment and enjoy this wonderful treat the Italians have invented for us?'

She leaned across the table toward him. 'Detective Kirov—'

'Yuri, please.'

'Detective Kirov, you strike me as a hard-working and dedicated officer. The only time you strike me wrong is when you pull dirty tricks on me, or try to be nice. Don't try to be nice. It doesn't suit your character. Just tell me what happened to Belkin.'

'He was killed.'

'Murdered?'

'The matter is still under investigation. His death may have been an accident.'

She groaned. 'You told me a few minutes ago that the man was murdered.' Getting information out of Yuri Kirov was not going to be easy. 'Is this going to be one of those cases of suicide where the dead man shot himself in the head, stabbed himself in the back, then hanged himself without a chair?'

'Suicide? What are you talking about?'

'Another stupid attempt at humor. My reaction to you being evasive. How was Belkin killed?'

'Through an injection of potassium. It may have been an accidental injection. We are still trying to find the nurse who administered it.'

Her gut wrenched. She fumbled with her cappuccino and took a sip to hide her reaction. 'A nurse? One employed at the hospital?'

'We're not sure. One of the night attendants saw a nurse enter Belkin's room last night. She didn't recognize the person but assumed it was a private nurse. Russian hospitals aren't always administered efficiently. Lethal injections are sometimes just part of the standard of care.'

'Man or woman?'

'The nurse? A woman. I noticed when I mentioned the nurse you . . . reacted.'

'Yes. Last night, after Mr Belkin was hit by a truck, a woman, one of the people in the crowd, pointed out that a nurse left the scene when her help was needed.'

'Did you see the nurse?'

'No.'

'So you think the nurse who gave him the injection may have pushed him in front of the truck.'

'He was pushed?'

Yuri shrugged. 'We have conflicting versions. We don't know if he was pushed by someone in particular or if he lost his balance from a surge of the crowd.'

'You didn't see the accident?' she said.

'No, I was back at the carnival. I found out about it later.'

She had an urge to tell him everything, about the photograph that had lured her to Moscow, her mother's 'accident', what she had found in the archives, but she held back. It would be pretty stupid to admit to a cop she barely knew that she had spent the previous night bribing her way into government archives. In America, she could count on being arrested. In Russia, who the hell knew what could happen.

And she didn't know if she could trust him. She liked him, felt very comfortable with him, sensing a caring and reasonable human being behind the tough veneer police have to maintain as a hazard of their profession, yet . . .

She desperately needed an ally but what did she really know about him? If he was the type of cop who took bribes, he certainly hid it well; besides the cheap overcoat, his suit was well worn, his shoes dog-eared, his shirt washed and ironed at home.

Hoping he wasn't married was a sudden thought that she quickly put out of her mind.

He lit another cigarette.

Next to being cold, she hated men who smoked.

'I know, you hate smoking.'

'Can you read my mind? I know a carnival where you could get a job.'

'I was reading your face. You said you were born in Moscow. Your parents were diplomats?'

'No, quite the opposite. Both my parents were fugitives from justice.'

That got his attention.

'My mother was an anti-war activist. She was a young teacher at Berkeley – that's a university in California.'

'I know about Berkeley. Burning bras, sex in the street, fights with the police.'

'She wasn't into burning bras or public sex, but a battle with the police is what made her a fugitive. She taught at the university, political science, and was a leader in the early movement for free speech and against the war in Vietnam. She was one of the organizers of a demonstration that got out of control. Someone was killed when a car that was turned over in the street caught fire and blew up. Arrest warrants were issued for the organizers of the demonstration and my mother fled to Canada to avoid a murder charge for a crime she really didn't commit.'

'A person was killed regardless of your mother's motives.'

'My mother was a pacifist, a caring person, she didn't even eat meat because she loved all forms of life. The last thing she would have wanted was for someone to get hurt. She felt, probably with good cause, that she would be prosecuted as an example to scare others, and so she ran.

'She went to Canada. After an attempt to extradite her, she accepted an invitation to teach at the Foreign Institute in Moscow. The motive for the invitation was probably to use her for propaganda, but she restricted herself solely to anti-war issues.'

'And your father?'

She smiled. 'I wish I had met him. He was a poet, a Welsh poet.'

'Welsh?'

'Wales. It's part of Great Britain.'

'I know Wales. Exploitation of coal miners by capitalist warmongers.' He grinned to let her know he was joking.

'I've never been there but it sounds picturesque,' she said. 'Wild moorlands, crashing waves, sudden storms. Anyway, my father was a poet and, well, something of an anarchist. He got involved in some sort of foolish plot. A bunch of young college students with too much idealistic passion and not enough brains talked publicly about blowing up parliament on Guy Fawkes Day.'

Yuri choked on a sip of coffee.

'You have to remember this was the sixties,' she explained.

'Of course, I forgot, in the sixties it was permissible to blow up governments and kill people in political riots.'

'Anyway, my father fled to the Netherlands. He was apparently quite well known for his socialist poetry. While in the Netherlands, he was invited to read poetry in Moscow by a young poets' association.'

'Is he still alive?'

'No. He was . . . idealistic, impulsive – wild and crazy, I guess they'd call him today. A bunch of volunteer mercenaries were organized and sent to Africa to help some fledgling communist ruler. In my father's mind, he was off to save Africa from the last vestiges of colonialism. He died there, in some battle, I think against the army of the very man they were sent to help.

'I really wish I had met him. I have some wonderful memories of my mother, more feelings than actual events, she died when I was seven, but it's something. With my father I only have my mother's stories and letters to her own mother.' She sipped her cappuccino. 'Tell me about your parents.'

'Absolutely nothing to tell. I don't have your wonderful memories. I was an orphan.'

'Oh. But you had adopted parents, didn't you?'

'No, I wasn't one of the lucky ones. When I was a teenager I ended up in a youth conservation corps. When I was old enough, I joined the army. That's where I first became a police officer, military police. What happened to your mother?'

'She was killed in an accident.' Her voice faltered. She looked away for a moment before she turned back and locked eyes with him. 'That's why I'm in Moscow. I don't believe my mother was really killed in an accident.' She told him about going out to the police sub-station and finding no record of the crash.

He listened and sipped coffee. His expression revealed nothing and it prompted her to tell him a little more.

'It's not just the lack of a police report. Her existence was wiped out at the university, even at our old apartment. I was sent something in the mail. That's why I came to Moscow.' Damning herself for revealing too much, she told him about the photograph. She knew she was being too trusting, but she was so alone and frightened, she needed an ally. And a tough Moscow cop would be a good one.

There was a long silence between them. Finally he lit another cigarette and stretched. 'In my opinion, you are making more out of the situation than it deserves. You assume that the woman in the photograph is your mother but admit the face is not visible. You also assume that there has been a cover-up of the brutal murder of your mother. The Soviet regime was efficient to the point of inefficiency. We were so intent, so driven by the system to get things right, we never got everything done. I think you are confusing governmental inefficiency with a plot against your mother.'

'You sound like Belkin.'

'You discussed this with Belkin?'

'Well, yes, a little—'

'And he was going to assist you in obtaining information about your mother before his accident intervened.'

'Accident? He was murdered.'

'That has not been established.'

Here we go again, she thought. 'Forget Belkin. What about the photograph and the attempt on my life?'

He waved his cigarette hand at her. 'You suspect a murder took place over twenty years ago. You have no evidence and have no access to evidence. You are wasting your time in Moscow.'

'Wasting my time?' She fanned the smoke away from her face. 'You haven't listened to a thing I've said. You sound like an apologist for seventy-five years of Soviet mediocrity. No wonder you people lost the Cold War.'

'We ended the Cold War, we did not lose it.'

'Oh, excuse me, is that the current rationale for a system that couldn't grow enough grain to feed its own people?'

'A system that put the first man in space.'

'Look, Officer Kirov—'

'Detective.'

'Whatever. I don't want to argue with you. In fact, I don't want anything at all to do with you.'

She stood up and fumbled in her purse.

'And I suggest you get on the next plane back to the United States,' he said. 'It appears that some of the irrationality that runs on both sides of your family has been inherited.'

'I see, I'm crazy. That's the official line, isn't it? Poor little Lara got hurt when she was small and is now imagining it all over again. That's a great line, but it's a damn lie. The only thing I've imagined is that you're a good police officer. You have the brain of a metal desk like the rest of the bureaucrats in this country.' She slapped five dollars on the table.

He leaped up, knocking over his chair. 'What's that?'

'I'm picking up the bill,' she snapped. 'You couldn't afford . . .' She closed her mouth and started to leave.

He grabbed her arm and forced the five dollar bill into her hand.

'You are in Russia,' he said hotly. 'Men do not have their balls cut off in this country like your American men. I will pay.'

She jerked her arm away and walked out of the restaurant.

Chapter 11

In the taxi back to the hotel she cursed herself. Damn, damn, damn. There went her hopes for someone to help her. She had a chance to have a cop with muscles, a gun, and authority on her side and she got into an argument with him. Did she really have to argue with him about the Cold War? And insult him over the check, too?

There was no hope for her. She was destined to spend her life an old maid, all her romantic passions unspent, buried with her like a miser taking his coins to the grave.

Yuri Kirov definitely attracted her – until he revealed his ignorance and started spouting Soviet nonsense. These people were all still brainwashed. But for a brief moment when she was in the espresso bar with him she had felt comfortable, safe.

Now she was alone again.

Story of my life, she thought. The gray gloom hovering over the city pressed down on her, increasing her depression. She understood why populations in northern climates with long dismal winters had high suicide rates.

She wondered what it would be like to have a husband, kids, a house and stay home in a cocoon? Her mother's generation had won the battle against the enslavement of women in a social prison. But every once in a while, when the things that went bump in the night got closer, she thought about cocoons . . .

It was still early. Barely ten o'clock in the morning and she felt as if she had been through a wringer. She thought for a moment and made a decision not to waste the day – especially the *daylight* – with sleep.

St Basil's had been the first challenge she had faced in coming back to Moscow. It had taken her two weeks, and nearly cost her life, to meet the challenge and enter the building.

The second piece to her nightmares was the little school.

'I've changed my mind,' she told the driver.

She felt the headache come as the taxi neared Red Square and the school.

'I'm not turning back.'

The driver glanced over his shoulder at her. 'No English.'

'It's all right,' she told him in Russian, 'I was talking to myself.'

The Little School, as it was called by everyone even though it had an official name a foot long, was tucked away in a building a block off Red Square. The monster GUM department store was nearby. As a child, her way to and from the school had not been through Red Square, but from a street behind the square.

It was indeed a 'little' school, twenty classrooms carved out of the guts of an office structure. The closest thing to a playground had been a gymnasium above the classrooms. What the school lacked in size was made up for in prestige because only the brightest children of high-ranking Kremlin officials were admitted. Her mother had not been part of the Inner Circle, but after Lara tested exceptionally high, a friend of her mother's at the Ministry of Education managed to slip Lara in on the grounds that she would provide a 'cultural challenge' to the other children.

She knew the school still existed and that I. Malinovsky, her second grade teacher, was still on the staff. That much she had learned with a telephone call. Separation by miles of telephone wire and trips to Red Square to stare at the cathedral had been as close as she had got to the school since her return.

She fought the headache as she made her way along an interior corridor to the steps that led up to the classroom level.

She stopped at the administration office and asked the receptionist for directions to I. Malinovsky's classroom. 'I. Malinovsky' was the only name Lara knew the teacher by. She didn't know what the 'I' stood for.

'Last classroom on the right at the end of the hall.' The woman checked her watch. 'If you hurry, you'll catch her still in morning break before the children come back.'

When Lara was in the second grade, I. Malinovsky would always stay in the classroom during the morning break and correct papers or read over a cup of tea. Lara couldn't remember what the woman looked like and wondered if her memory of morning tea was an actual recollection of what the woman did or a conglomerate of memories about teachers at the school in general.

Walking down the corridor she heard the pounding of hundreds of young feet in the gym above. She remembered the gym. Gymnastics was the sport of the day for young girls when she went to the school. She had been a little too large, a little too awkward to be good at it.

Bits and pieces of other memories came to her: the smell of the white pasty glue used to stick autumn leaves to classroom windows, a patriotic song the class sang each morning about heroic workers and farmers, being scolded for racing her friend Anna to the drinking fountain . . .

*Standing at a window with her teacher, the teacher pointing
down at the street where a woman stood, a woman in a gray
coat and red scarf. 'Your mother's come for you.'*

The door to the classroom was open and she paused
before stepping in, taking a moment to study the woman
seated at the desk in the front of the classroom. I.
Malinovsky seemed vaguely familiar but once again she
didn't know how much of her impression was memory and
how much was invoked just because the woman was sitting
in the teacher's chair.

The woman was probably approaching retirement age: a
few dark streaks still toned the hair she had pulled back into
a severe bun; her wrinkles, certainly not from too much
sunshine in Moscow, created the map of a hard life on her
face.

No, Lara thought, not a hard life. The stern press to her
lips that caused lines to scar her cheeks, the spinster frown
that left creases on her forehead, and the harsh gray suit,
more uniform than fashion statement, were the marks of a
life unfulfilled.

Looking at her made Lara think of a line from an old
English poem: 'For of all sad words of tongue or pen, / The
saddest are these: "It might have been!"'

Lara felt a stab to her heart. God, this would be her in
twenty years if she didn't get her life together.

'May I help you?'

'Yes, I'm looking for I. Malinovsky.'

'I am Malinovsky.'

Lara stepped into the classroom as the woman stood up.

'If this is about one of your children, school regulations
require that you make an appointment.'

'No, it's not that. I used to be one of your students.'

'One of my students?' The woman studied her face. 'It
must have been quite some time ago.'

'Twenty years. My name is Lara Patrick.' Lara self-consciously pushed hair away from her forehead.

'Patrick. The American.' The woman's demeanor went from briskly professional to disturbed.

'Yes.'

'I remember. Yes, a little foreign girl. Your mother was an American communist.' The woman appeared to fumble for words, not at all the reaction Lara had expected. Her old teacher seemed more frightened by her sudden appearance than surprised.

'My mother wasn't a communist. She was an anti-war activist.'

The woman sat down in her chair and stared up at Lara, worry shadowing her already severe features. 'The little Patrick girl, yes, a foreigner who didn't really belong here in the school, but an intelligent, bright child.'

Malinovsky spoke as if she was talking about a third person. Ill at ease, Lara shifted her feet and looked around the classroom. Something was wrong.

'Why are you here?' the teacher asked.

'Why? To say hello. It's been a long time.'

Her answer seemed to cause the woman to relax a little.

'Oh, I see, yes, that's right, it has been a long time. You must still remember the school. You were what, about eight?'

'Seven.'

I. Malinovsky folded her hands in her lap and smiled. 'Well, we are happy when our students return to say hello.'

'Do you remember that day?' Lara asked.

The woman's smile turned down. 'Which day?'

'My last day. It was near the end of the school term. You told me my mother had come for me.'

'I don't remember.'

Anger underlined the woman's words and hostility clouded her face.

'A woman dressed in my mother's clothes came to pick me up. I never returned to school. You must remember that. I was the only foreigner in the school.'

'There are so many years, so many students, all of you become a blur after a while.'

'Who took me out of school that day, pretending to be my mother?'

'I don't know what you are talking about.'

'I need to know who came here that day and took me from the classroom.'

The woman stood up. 'That was twenty years ago. I don't remember such nonsense.'

Lara stared at her. There was an edge of fear to the woman's voice. 'I never returned to the school. I was hurt in an ... an incident at St Basil's. You must know that, there must have been rumors flying around the school, questions about why I never returned. Someone in the school must have known what happened.'

'I'm not responsible for what your mother did. You were a foreigner, you didn't belong here anyway.'

'Why did you say it was my mother? Did you speak to her? Did she—'

'I remember nothing.' Malinovsky stood up, her face dark with anger, her lips trembling. 'Get out of here, go away. I don't want to hear this nonsense.'

Lara shook her head. 'Why are you acting this way? You knew who I was the moment I said my name. You didn't have to think back twenty years. *You were expecting me.*'

'I don't know what you're talking about.'

'What are you so frightened of? Someone has been to see you, haven't they? They told you I was coming and warned you not to say anything.'

'I don't have to listen to this. You have no right to come to my classroom and speak to me this way.' She was almost yelling. 'Get out, get out or I will call the authorities.'

'Please talk to me. It's important.'

'Important?' She waved away the word with her hands. 'To speak to you? Who are you to come here from America making accusations after all these years. I am a school teacher—'

'I'm not accusing—'

'A professional teacher, do you understand, for over thirty years. My students have grown up and are running the country. They run the country and go on weekends to their fancy dachas and I sit here and decay into an old woman with nothing.'

'I need your help.'

'My help!' The woman screamed the word. Spittle hit the breast of Lara's coat. 'I can help no one, I can't even help myself. Get out, get out, go back to America. You're not wanted here. Poor Russians are trying to survive. Go back to your fat country.'

Lara paused at the door. 'It was the woman who pretended to be my mother, wasn't it? She's been back to see you.'

'*GET OUT!*' Malinovsky collapsed back on her chair as if the shout had taken the last of her strength. Lara heard her sobbing as she walked back down the corridor. Her headache had become the terrible pain of a vise clamped to both temples and tightened until her skull was being crushed.

At the bottom of a stairway she forced herself to turn left toward Red Square, the route she had avoided on her way to the school. Her knees were weak and her head ready to explode but she forced herself forward.

Memories stormed at her with every step – walking with

the woman, asking why she had been taken out of school, where they were going . . .

Lara came out onto Red Square and stopped. Her body didn't want to go any further.

Before her was the Place of Skulls, the stone platform upon which executions took place in tsarist times. Further to the right was the Lenin Mausoleum and the great Kremlin Wall. Through the gated entrances to the Kremlin were the buildings that housed the might and power of all the Russias.

She turned away from the wall and slowly walked to her left, her throat muscles constricting until it felt as if dread would suffocate her. But she kept walking, putting one foot in front of the other, looking down, following where her feet were taking her as her mind balked.

She stopped and looked up at the cathedral that was the most incredible building in all Russia, at the eight magnificent domes; a church not even Stalin had dared defile.

Blood pounded in her temples and a wave of nausea swept over her, turning her stomach, blocking her throat. Dizzy, unsteady on her feet, she forced herself to look beyond the eight domes to the great tower that rose over a hundred feet.

She saw a woman in a gray coat with a little girl in hand entering the cathedral and her head exploded. She swayed and felt herself falling as black dust swarmed her mind.

Chapter 12

Street traffic parted at the sound of the speeding ambulance's piercing siren. Lara sat on the metal floor in the back of the ambulance with a blanket wrapped round her.

'The factory that repairs stretchers is in Latvia,' the ambulance attendant told her. 'Latvia has declared its independence and won't repair Russian stretchers unless payment is made in advance in hard currency.'

He seemed young to be a paramedic, no more than in his late teens, she thought, still fighting pimples and awkwardness with girls.

'New stretchers are made in a factory in the Ukraine,' he went on. 'And they won't sell us stretchers without hard currency paid in advance either. Can you blame them? Every day the rouble buys less. Soon you will need a wheelbarrow full to buy a bottle of vodka.'

'So this board,' she nudged it with her foot, 'is your stretcher.'

'Temporarily.' He smiled. She liked him.

The ambulance had been near Red Square when they got the call that a woman had fainted not far from St Basil's Cathedral. When they picked her up, he first inquired whether she was pregnant. After she told him that would have required an immaculate conception, he asked if she was starved. After a negative on that, finding out she was an American, he asked if she had AIDS.

The ambulance went round a sharp curve in the road, siren still blaring, the driver's foot heavy on the gas pedal. A wide stretch of road opened up and the driver shot them down the middle divider, sending a traffic officer scrambling out of the way and cars swerving to avoid head-on collisions.

'Is all this necessary?' Lara asked. 'You're just dropping me off at my hotel.'

He grinned, exposing a metal filling in a front tooth. 'Olga's a relief driver from the suburbs. She doesn't get many chances to race through the downtown sector at high speed.'

Lara leaned back against the interior wall and closed her eyes. She had felt horribly embarrassed, fainting in Red Square in the middle of the day, cringing at the thought she might have been filmed and she'd see herself tonight on the Moscow Evening News. But the concern and good humor of the ambulance attendants had helped ease the embarrassment.

Misha, the attendant, was still curious as to why she had fainted, but other than telling him truthfully that she was under great stress, she avoided the subject. The truth was that when she had stared up at St Basil's she had experienced a wave of such paralyzing fear that her mind had blacked out rather than come to grips with it.

Olga took another turn at full speed. Straightening up, Lara gave Misha a wan smile. 'I'm going to throw up.'

He grabbed a metal pot off a hook on the wall and shoved it at her. 'Maybe we'd better take you to a hospital,' he said.

Bad timing. A fit of laughter hit her; choking, she almost dumped the contents of the pot in his lap.

'People die,' she gasped, 'in Moscow hospitals.'

As the ambulance pulled up in front of her hotel and the

wail of its siren slowly tapered off, Misha opened the back doors and stepped down. He helped her out as a curious crowd gathered.

'Thank Olga for me.' Lara had left a wad of 500 rouble notes in the back of the ambulance - Misha had refused to take any money from her.

'Taxi shortage,' she told the gawking porter as she walked by him and went into the hotel. It suddenly occurred to her that she had left the hotel that morning in a police car and returned in an ambulance. Well, what did they expect when everything was going crazy in the city?

Two clerks stared at her from behind the front desk as she walked by and headed for the security office. The only other person in the lobby was a sleeping man sitting on a couch with his head hanging back, snoring with his mouth open.

She opened the door of the security office, expecting to find Gropski in the room. A man cut from the same cloth as the frog, cheap pin-striped suit, belly bulging, shirt two inches short of being able to close at the neck, looked up at her from behind a steel desk. The desk and the steel chair he was sitting on were the only furnishings in the office.

'Yes?'

'I'm looking for the security officer.'

'I'm Nosenko, the security officer.'

'I'm looking for Mr Gropski.'

'Gropski no longer works for the hotel.'

Lara stared at him. 'Is he dead?'

The man's eyebrows shot up. 'Dead? I hope so. He abandoned his duty and I had to return from my vacation to do his job. If he is not dead now, he will be when I find him.'

'Does anyone know where he went?'

'To hell, for all I know.' His eyes skimmed her up and down. 'You have a security problem?' He started to rise. 'We can have a drink—'

'Thank you, but I'm in a hurry.'

She went back into the lobby. She didn't want to go up to her room. It was still morning. Finding another hotel was on her list of wants, going to see Guk, the truck driver who had miraculously survived the crash with her mother, was another.

Not able to muster the courage yet to turn up cold on the truck driver's doorstep, she left the Gorky and walked, ignoring the rare phenomenon of an available taxi in front of the hotel. The taxi driver and porter watched her as she walked down the street. She didn't blame them. Besides early morning visits from the police, being taken away in a police car and arriving back in an ambulance, she supposed she could rack up the hotel security man disappearing after talking to her. Had Gropski heard about Belkin's untimely demise and taken fright? Had someone paid him a visit? The same someone who frightened the school teacher?

She had the sensation of standing in a forest clearing as maniacs stampeded around her. Her mother's death was taking on darker and darker tones. Common sense kept telling her to get on a plane, back to her condo and her cat, but her determination was stronger than common sense.

Knowing that she was in a strange city, being watched, being stalked even, was frightening, but she had options in her waking moments and could fight back. She was more frightened alone in bed with her nightmares.

Hiring a bodyguard still seemed a good idea if she was going to stay in Moscow. She wanted to call up Yuri Kirov to tell him she needed help, but she couldn't do it.

I wouldn't ask for help if I was hanging from the ledge of a cliff, she thought. I've got to learn how to change, to deal with people. I know how to give, I've got to learn how to take.

A ruthless prosecutor had been her reputation. Defense attorneys called her 'Maximum Bob' after a retired judge who commonly handed out long sentences. Yes, she had been tough – but fair, she hoped. She knew in the back of her mind there had always been the suppressed anger and fears about her own childhood debasement and now she wondered how much of that had directed her in prosecuting people who hurt children. No, she thought, the people I prosecuted were guilty and deserved what they got. The only thing they got from her was the maximum they earned for their crimes – that and nothing more. She simply didn't plea bargain with bastards.

She crossed the street to get off the busy, store-lined sidewalk and walk along a park on the other side.

It had snowed during the night, but a sky that was only partially cloudy allowed a little sunshine over the city. The sunshine helped lift her spirits, but she still felt alone and vulnerable. No one to turn to. Lara the loner, always the loner, she thought. Her grandmother had provided her with the necessities of life, but none of the warmth. Her British relatives had never answered the letter she sent to them when she was a teenager. And she had never really established any close relationships with the people around her.

A strange child, her grandmother called her. Strange because she talked so little, played alone, seemed to be cautious of everyone. Her grandmother had blamed it on cultural shock and the death of her mother. In her own mind, she was normal. She just preferred being alone. Or so she told herself. She kept herself busy, adjusting to American schools, excelling at exams, working hard at college to get accepted at law school, graduating near the top of her class in law school, and then surprising even herself by turning down a high-paying job with a corporate firm for an assistant district attorney's position in the unit prosecuting crimes against women and children.

She threw herself into her work, dealing with those around her with polite professionalism. No one really knew her. She had never been to an office party, didn't drop by the 'watering hole' where prosecutors, cops and probation people met after work for cheap 'happy hour' drinks. She ate her lunches alone at her desk and didn't even go down to the cafeteria for breaks. She'd never had a long-term personal involvement. Friends, male and female, were people she worked with and the relationship ended when it was time to leave the office. A couple of people who cared were frank enough to tell her that she shared nothing of herself, retreating into a shell every time they tried to get close.

Having gone directly from childhood to being an adult without stopping to be a teenager had a lot to do with it. Perhaps if her grandmother had healed the wounds, had shown love rather than tolerance . . .

The photograph from Moscow had come at a time when she was wondering about who she was, a time when she lay awake at night and tried to put together the pieces that added up to her. Moscow had so far been something of a catalyst for her. Being in the city, all alone without her work to throw herself into, had made her think not only about what had happened to her mother's life, but her own.

I hate being alone, hate it, hate it, hate it. I've been lying to myself because I've spent my life frightened.

Frightened. Another piece of the puzzle to herself. I've spent my whole life afraid. The nightmares went away with medication, but the fears were just buried, not resolved.

She desperately wanted someone to love and to love her. And it would have been nice to have worked out these home truths in her cozy little condo by the sea. Her return to Moscow was not a homecoming but a victim returning to the scene of a lynching.

Something hit her in the back. She spun round as a snowball exploded at her feet.

Three kids in the park, ten- or twelve-year-olds, were her assailants. One of them yelled, 'Want to fight, lady?' Another one threw a snowball at an old woman with a cane coming down the street.

Lara saw red. She grabbed snow, molded it into a ball and threw it. Her snowball missed – it wasn't even in the ballpark. The kids howled with laughter and launched an attack.

She got behind a tree as snowballs whizzed by. As soon as she counted three balls, she stepped out and threw, this one missing by only a mile or so. She jumped behind the tree again and made snowballs. The pain in her head had gone. One, two, three – she spun out from behind the tree and got a snowball in the chest. They had caught on to her little trick. She staggered back and let one go at the kids and then got behind the tree again. A snowball hit just above her head on the tree. They had outflanked her.

She bent down and came up with another snowball as two more missiles came flying at her.

She heard tires squealing and a man was suddenly at her side. He tossed one ball, re-armed, and they both sent off another. The charging kids backed up and he said, 'Let's get them.' Lara followed his charge and threw as the kids retreated.

'Not bad, considering they had us outnumbered,' the man laughed.

He was magazine-cover material; not the Marlboro Man

type, but more like the guy in a skimpy brief staring out of a window at city lights. There was something familiar about him.

'Have we met?'

'I would have remembered you. I'm Alexei Bova.'

Oh God, now she knew who he was. The *enfant terrible* of the new Russian rich. Probably the richest man in Russia. The most eligible bachelor in Russia. Muscovites spent their morning break recounting his latest exploits and arguing whether he should be shot or deified.

War cries came from the direction their opponents had fled. The kids had added two to their assault team and the five-strong army was charging with snowballs at the ready.

'Quick, get in my car!'

Alexei was fast. He was in the car and had the engine running before Lara had slammed the passenger door. Alexei hit the gas and the car's screeching tires blew exhaust smoke back at the kids. She was compressed back into the seat as if she had just taken off in a rocket. Parked cars were a blur as they flew by.

He brought the powerful car down to a normal speed and she started to breathe again. The car's engine sounded like a jet plane. It was a red sports model with a familiar emblem. She was trying to remember the brand when he told her.

'Lamborgini. A good Russian car.' He laughed.

The price of the Italian import probably could have supported a hundred Russian families for a year. His jacket was sable, very masculine, and expensive enough to feed a small village. His laughter was rich and husky. She guessed he was older than her first impression; he looked thirtyish but probably was somewhere in his forties or even early fifties. Whatever his age, he was still model material. His golden hair had just a tinge of white in it, his tanned face was smooth and handsome with a perfectly chiseled nose and chin.

'Thanks,' she said. 'If you hadn't come to the rescue, those kids would have humiliated me on the battlefield.'

'It was fun. I think it's probably the first snow fight I was ever in.' He glanced down at his watch. 'I'm afraid I have a terribly important meeting with some very boring city officials. I'm always late for these meetings, but today I am more than politely late.' He pointed at the building at the end of the busy street.

She recognized it immediately: The Black Tower, one of the first high-rise office buildings constructed with private funds and the most controversial building in Russia.

'Now that we have fought the enemies of mankind side by side and defeated them,' he said, 'or at least made a graceful retreat, we must celebrate our victory. Please have dinner with me tonight.'

Have dinner with the richest and most handsome man in Russia? What an exciting and incredible opportunity. What fantastic luck.

'No, I'm sorry, but I really can't,' she blurted out, her face turning pink.

'Then you must come to my party tomorrow night. At the tower. Many of the most important people in Moscow will be there.'

'Well, I'm not sure . . .'

'Here's my card. Give me a call if you change your mind. Now I must drop you back at your hotel.'

'No, that's all right. Let me off right here.'

'Are you sure? I don't mind—'

'No, no, this is fine. I was coming down to look at these stores anyway.'

He pulled the car over to the curb and she shook his hand as she got out. 'Thank you, Mr Bova, for saving me from a fate worse than death.'

'My pleasure, Lara. If you change your mind, give me a call.'

She walked away, a little dazed. *Stupid, stupid, stupid.* What is the matter with me? Moscow's Donald Trump invites me to dinner and a party with the rich and famous and I tell him I'm busy. Busy doing what? Counting the cracks in the ceiling at my lousy hotel?

She kicked a street lamp. Ignoring the looks of passersby, she kicked it again. Putting her head down, she started back in the direction of her hotel. She had been too embarrassed to let him drop her off at one of the cheapest hotels in Moscow. She should have told him she was staying at the Metropole – *The* place to stay this season, darling.

Why did I say no?

Because I was scared. And have no damn confidence. And, well, wasn't it just a little too much of a coincidence that he should stop to help me out, or am I just being paranoid? I'll have bread and soup alone in my room tonight because I hate sitting in restaurants alone. *Stupid, stupid, stupid.* I could be dining at some snooty restaurant being pampered by the waiters while the Who's Who of Moscow's New Rich ask who is the beautiful mystery woman with the country's most eligible bachelor . . .

In a taxi, heading back to her hotel, she stared out the back window at Alexei Bova's tower, black on black with dark tinted windows, windows you'd usually see in a sunny place like California rather than gray, overcast Moscow. It had a tall spire with a large round cap that overlapped the sides of the building. The 'cap' was intended to be a revolving restaurant in the plans approved by the city. After Alexei constructed the restaurant, he added a glass structure to the roof and all hell broke loose because the Black Tower ended up taller than the Bell Tower.

She remembered other controversies about the building. In fact, Alexei Bova was the darling of the story-hungry news media. Everything he did seemed to explode into controversy. He claimed he was trying to build a new Russia; his critics claimed he was trying to steal the new Russia.

In the mad scramble to convert to a market economy, Bova had entered the real estate market with a vengeance, privatizing overnight major buildings and land by making deals that a lot of people claimed were illegal. But who knew exactly what was legal? She recalled reading that a French fashion house had bought a Moscow building and spent millions refurbishing it, only to have the people who used to work at the location claim the building for themselves and enforce their claim by squatter's rights, setting themselves up in the building until the French company bought them out.

She was halfway back to her hotel when a thought struck her. He called me Lara. Did I tell him my name? *I must have*. Don't be paranoid, she told herself. It was a chance meeting.

She shook her head. I must have told him my name. My memory's shot. My brain cells are dying from the cold . . .

The taxi pulled up in front of her hotel and she sat inside a moment thinking. Returning to her room was not going to get the job done.

She had to go and see the truck driver.

Alone.

Why wasn't I nicer to Yuri? I don't burn bridges, I dynamite them.

The address for Joseph Guk, the truck driver with the perfect driving record, was west of the city, off a major

113

highway. She told the taxi driver where she wanted him to take her and got an argument.

'It's a long way.'

'How much is the fare for a long way?'

'The roads in that area are bad.'

'How much for bad roads?'

'It's probably going to snow.'

'How much?' she asked.

As soon as the official restraints had come off, taxi drivers were the first group in the city to throw both feet into the market economy. Almost every ride had been a memorable financial experience for her. At the airport on the day she arrived, a taxi driver had locked her luggage into the trunk of his cab and then blatantly told her a ride into Moscow was a hundred American dollars. Her willingness to yell for the airport police while she stood in front of the taxi so it couldn't move had quickly negotiated a reasonable fee.

Years of dealing with crooks, perverts, attorneys and cops had made her tough, she thought. But that was before she had tangled with a Moscow taxi driver.

After agreeing to pay double the reasonable fare, she leaned back in the seat and tried to think of a story to feed Mr Guk. Walking up to him and demanding to know why he had been part of a plot to create a phoney accident involving the death of her mother probably would not win any points with Mr Guk.

Chapter 13

Half an hour later, the taxi left the main highway and groaned in and out of big potholes down a narrow road.

Lara saw no pride of ownership, none of the small, personal touches she had expected in the countryside. The area was without warmth or rustic charm. Scattered houses, shacks more than anything else, were flanked by crippled old outhouses and sheds caving in from the weight of snow; fence posts ravaged by winterkill formed the bleached rib bones of the skeleton land. Gray and gloomy Moscow streets appeared bright and cheerful in comparison.

This is a place where people were imprisoned by the land, not fed by it, she thought. She realized there must be places like this in America, land where only snow and rocks and misery grew, but she was a city girl and those places were the stuff of news broadcasts, no more real than a flood in China or a terrorist bomb in Israel.

She shivered at the thought of living in one of the houses without indoor plumbing and having to go out and sit on an outhouse toilet during a sub-zero Russian night.

Several miles down the road, a row of wooden mail boxes next to a snow-covered one-lane bridge told her that she had arrived. The numerical address she had for Guk was on one of the boxes. The bridge spanned a small, frozen creek.

On the other side of the stream were half a dozen homes on large lots, six blighted houses that not even snow and icicle trim could transpose into quaint cottages. Soiled from chimney soot, the dirty snow and icicles added to the derelict appearance of the houses.

The taxi passed the weathered corpse of an old factory before reaching the bridge. A sign, wounded and scarred by time and the elements, said the factory had made chemicals for fertilizer that made the Soviet Union grow.

Lara opened the taxi window and stuck her head out to get a better look at the houses. A smell of snow was in the air, a crisp dry bite to her nostrils slightly polluted by a stench that made her wonder if the chemical factory was still alive – or rotting in death.

'A swamp from factory waste,' the taxi driver said about the smell, pointing to an area near the ruins of the factory. 'It's almost frozen over.'

An icy fog was dropping the sky around them and she could barely make out the swamp about fifty yards from the road. The abandoned factory grounds were dotted with overgrown bushes and weeds, but nothing grew near the slushy swamp, making her wonder what kind of chemicals they had used in their fertilizers.

The risk that they might have to drive out of the isolated area in a winter white-out was making the city driver unhappy.

'You know what area this is, don't you?'

'What do you mean?'

'Citizen R lived somewhere around here.'

Russian criminals were referred to in the newspapers by a code name, Citizen A, B, and so forth, and it took a second for the label to register.

'Is he the one who killed children?'

116

'Killed children and ate their hearts. Twenty-two children they know of, probably more. Runaways they'll never trace.'

Citizen R had been captured before she had arrived in Moscow but the stories about him still circulated. Because of the old regime's refusal to publish horror stories for fear it would cast their 'perfect' society in a bad light, Citizen R and others like him had been even harder to track down in the Soviet Union than they were in the West. A newspaper had recently estimated that most of the serial killers in Russia were still walking around free because the public was unaware of their existence; the paper suggested doing news stories like those in America where descriptions were broadcast to the public.

She wondered if the driver was trying to scare her to turn back – or increase the price again. He had tried to jack up the price on the way and her refusal had turned into a shouting match. She was tired of being ripped off, she told him. It seemed as if the whole country had been storing up greed for seven decades just waiting for the fall of communism when they would stop being exploited and could start exploiting everyone else.

The driver's bitching had started on the outskirts of the city and had increased as they left the main highway for the bumpy road: something was going to break on his cab and he wouldn't be able to get parts to replace it; they were going to get stuck in one of the huge potholes; it was going to snow and the roads would be impassable; the overcast was dropping like a dark blanket from the sky. His final complaint was the bridge.

'I can't drive over that bridge,' he told her. 'It's too dangerous.'

The bridge looked as if it had been sculpted from ice.

'It has a lot of ice on it, but the people over there must drive back and forth.'

He twisted in the seat and glared at her. 'Maybe they don't have bald tires on their cars. Do you want to end up drowned in the river?'

'I'll walk. But you have to wait. I'll need you to take me back to town.'

'Pay me now. For the return trip too.'

She hesitated. 'How do I know you'll wait?'

His glare went red. 'How do you know the sun will rise tomorrow?'

'In Moscow, I wouldn't always bet on it.' She gave him the money. 'I shouldn't be long.'

She got out of the taxi and swung the door closed behind her. She had wanted the taxi to park right outside Guk's house in case she ran into any problems, but the driver would have left tire marks across her back before he left them on the bridge.

The courage and resolve she had felt that morning in her room and in the warm, safe taxi on the way out was rapidly shrinking as the reality of actually facing Joseph Guk neared.

She knew only two things about the mysterious Mr Guk: he was former KGB and he was somehow connected to the death of her mother.

Nervous and wary, she did what she always did: put one foot in front of the other and kept pushing forward. Halfway across the bridge, a frigid wind lashed her, nearly sweeping her off her feet as her leather-soled city shoes slipped on the ice.

The wind gave her another sharp whiff of that stench from the swamp. How do people put up with it? she wondered, realizing at once the naïveté of her question. A little stink was mild in comparison to what many Russians

118

had to put up with. Before Chernobyl, thousands of people, a couple of generations, had lived on radioactive ground at several places in the country because the government had refused to admit accidents had occurred with nuclear reactors.

As she crossed the bridge she studied the houses on the other side. The scene looked like a black and white print of Russia before the Great Patriotic War, the Soviet country-side of the 1920s and 1930s when Stalin had forced socialism down the throats of peasants who had never read a book let alone the Communist Manifesto.

She prayed that the Guk house was one of the two closest to the bridge. The last couple of houses were already dark shadows in the gray mist that had almost turned the already short winter day into night. It reminded her of the tule fog generated in California's great central valley.

A dog barked from the porch of the house closest to her and a second dog, on the porch of the house across the lane, joined the chorus. She ignored them, at least to the extent of not looking at them, following advice she'd heard about not making eye contact with vicious dogs. They were big dogs, junk-yard mean, not the type it would be wise to challenge.

A stout woman was getting wood from a pile next to the third house along the lane and Lara quickened her step to hail her before she went back inside.

'Hello . . . hello.'

The woman ignored her and went into the house without even glancing back.

Friendly neighborhood, Lara thought.

No street numbers were on the houses and she kept walking, looking for a clue to Guk's house. The dogs kept up their barking and snarling as she walked and she tried to muster the courage to barge up to one of the houses and ask where the Guks lived. Being tough in a courtroom or a public place was different from taking on vicious dogs and the people who made them that way.

A couple of times she spotted curtains twitch and someone peek at her from inside a house.

The icy fog was falling faster. She knew she'd have to get her meeting with Joseph Guk over fast or the taxi driver wouldn't wait.

Another curtain fluttered. *Go for it*. At least someone in the house would know she was approaching. She started for the house when she spotted a flat-bed truck parked in the rear yard of the house she had just passed.

The name Guk was painted on the side of the truck. The woman picking up wood had probably been Mrs Guk.

Gathering courage, she resolutely walked to the gate of the Guk yard, opened it, and stepped onto the frozen pathway to the house, forcing herself to move toward it, overcoming weak knees and a faint heart.

The house was as ugly as its neighbors, unkempt and lacking any aesthetic charm – dark wooden walls and a slanted tin roof packed with dirty snow. But it was the largest house along the lane, half again as big as the others. And she had spotted something else that set the place apart from its neighbors. In the back yard, near the parked truck, was a satellite dish. That sort of luxurious black-market item was as out of place next to the shanty as a new Mercedes would have been.

To the left of the front door was a small structure, a four by four square box, and she wondered what it was for as she approached. She was a few feet from the box when a flap on the side of it flew open and a big dog leaped out.

She stumbled back and fell as the animal charged, snarling hoarsely and exposing lethal white fangs. It ran to the end of its chain and reared onto its hind legs a couple feet from her, snapping its jaws, bloodshot yellow eyes glaring wildly at her. She scooted backwards on her rump, putting more space between her and the crazy-eyed dog with snapping jaws and a rabid brain.

The door to the house opened and the sour-faced wood carrier stepped out. 'What do you want?'

Lara stared up at her open-mouthed.

'He's chained. What do you want?'

She took a deep breath and swallowed. 'Mrs Guk?'

'I'm Mrs Guk. What do you want?'

'I'm looking for your husband. I'm from the government,' she said.

'The government?'

'We,' she swallowed again, the lie sticking in her throat, 'the Ministry of Transportation, are compiling a history of the safest truck drivers in the Moscow area to be used as a, uh, an example for others. Bad drivers today, Mrs Guk.'

'Who cares about his driving record? He's retired.'

'There may be some honors given in the, uh, form of financial reward . . .'

Mrs Guk's vinegar expression got a little oil added to it at the mention of money. 'I'll put away the dog.' She grabbed a club leaning next to the house and gave the dog a whack on it's hindquarters. 'Get back in there.'

The dog tried to duck round the woman and fly at Lara again and Mrs Guk hit him on the nose with the club. A couple more blows and the dog disappeared through the flap of the hut.

Lara waited until the woman had dropped the latch on the flap before she started breathing normally again.

'Come in.'

The dog pawed at the flap as Lara hurried by the hut. 'Why doesn't he bark like the other dogs?' she asked.

121

'No larynx.' Mrs Guk made a cutting motion with her hand across her throat.

The dog's voice box had probably been cut out so the dog could attack without warning.

Charming people.

The house was furnished Soviet Utilitarian – big stuffed chairs and couches, bulky tables, big lamps, no elegance, no taste.

Except for an entertainment system that took up an entire wall. Lara's eyes went wide at the sight of the big screen television, dual VCRs, sound system with multiple players. There were floor to ceiling shelves of video cassettes, CDs, and tapes.

Boris Yeltsin's wife probably had a black and white TV and a hand-cranked record player. The retired truck driver and his wife living in shanty town had electronic equipment only available on the black market, and at a price few could afford.

'Which division of the ministry do you work for?' Mrs Guk asked.

Lara smiled and started to answer when her eye caught a picture hanging on the wall behind the woman, a photo of an older man standing beside the truck parked in the yard, with Mrs Guk standing next to him. She was wearing a nurse's uniform.

Fear crawled down Lara's back.

'I asked you where you worked. What division?'

Lara tore her eyes away from the picture and met the woman's stare. Her face had gone sour again. She knew something was wrong.

She fought the urge to run. 'My mother was Angela Patrick,' she said, speaking rapidly. 'She was supposedly killed twenty years ago in a head-on collision with a truck your husband was driving. I know the accident never

122

happened. I want to find out what really happened to my mother. I'm willing to pay.'

The woman's jaw slowly dropped and her eyes grew wide.

'I'm willing to pay,' Lara repeated. Her right knee was shaking and she started edging back from the woman.

A look akin to the mindless rage of the dog lit the woman's eyes.

Lara spun round and headed for the front door. She sensed Mrs Guk behind her and the woman's hand grabbed at her coat as she flew out of the door. Lara didn't look back until she was through the gate.

Mrs Guk was on the path, standing next to the dog hut. She looked mean enough and mad enough to get down on her hands and knees and bark herself.

Lara quickened her pace for the bridge. Halfway there she suddenly stopped dead in her tracks.

The taxi had gone.

Chapter 14

Lara crossed the bridge and started down the bumpy road back to the main highway. It was a good three or four miles to the highway and a gas station. A couple of hours' walk on an icy road in street shoes. She hadn't been bright enough to wear a pair of boots on a trip to the country. She hadn't been bright enough to remember Moscow taxi drivers had the ethics of Mafia hit men.

The white-out had not only obliterated everything more than fifty feet away, it had brought the temperature down to below zero, colder than anything she had experienced in the city. Her feet were already aching and she had only been walking a few minutes. She realized her feet would be frostbitten by the time she reached the main road. Her heart started beating faster and she quickened her pace into a trot.

Her feet slipped out from under her and she fell hard onto her rear. She couldn't run on the damn ice. Her senses told her to go back to the houses, but she kept hurrying away, down the country road. No way would she go back to Guk's shanty town. She was too damn scared of his wife. *The nurse*.

And the rest of them back there, the neighbors with their vicious dogs, the whole mess of them had probably inter-bred for so long she'd find a Joseph Guk and a replica of his beefy wife behind every door she knocked on.

125

But maybe she was the one with the genetic defects. What else could explain her paying a Moscow taxi driver in advance? What else could explain her coming here on her own?

'Cold, scared, and stupid,' she said out loud. She imagined her words going nowhere, just freezing and falling to the ground as soon as they left her mouth.

Her feet began to feel hot and that caused more panic. There was no way in hell her feet were doing anything but freezing. The burning sensation must be what frostbite felt like as it froze nerves and tissue, she thought. They cut off a person's toes, even their feet, from frostbite.

Knowing she'd never make it to the road without permanently damaging her feet, she decided to try for the shacks she had spotted coming in. She would tackle the first one that came in sight – if she could see it in the bloody white-out.

Every inch of her face not covered by her scarf and hat was burning from the cold. She stopped and wrapped the scarf round her head, stamping her feet. Only her eyes were left exposed and they were irritated by the dry frigid air.

But it was her feet that worried her. Losing her toes or feet to frostbite. Being crippled for life because she had paid a damn taxi driver in advance.

She was focusing so much on her frozen feet she almost didn't hear the barking of dogs, the dogs back at the houses of Guk's neighbors.

Someone was leaving the settlement.

She tried to keep calm and concentrate on what she had to do but her breathing was out of control from over-ventilating. She reached into herself to pace her breathing with her stride as if she was jogging along the beach at home. She kept glancing over her shoulder, expecting to see Guk's truck lights coming at her out of the fog, expecting to hear the sound of the engine.

And then she did see something in the fog and her blood ran cold. It was a shadowy figure. A person? A small tree? No, it wasn't her imagination, it was a person, a dark figure with a long coat and . . . the person was wearing a nurse's hat. She was sure of it, the distinctive boxed shape.

Lara ran with her heart pounding in her chest, her nerves electrified, on fire with panic.

A large building was off to the left and she diverted off the road toward it. As she stumbled across the snow the acidic odor she had noticed earlier grew stronger and she realized the building was the abandoned chemical factory and that she was running beside the polluted pond.

The frozen turf was slippery near the pond and she worked away from it, her breathing coming in gasps as her eyes searched the fog behind her. Wind was whipping the mist and visibility had dropped to less than a hundred feet. She couldn't tell if anyone was approaching.

Turning back, she ran toward the building, anger and determination to live and fight rising in her. There might be a telephone, a caretaker, even something she could use as a weapon.

As she approached the building, the dilapidation became more obvious, chipped paint, broken windows, snow-coated debris scattered in the yard. It was not a living factory but the withered ghost of one, rotting in its own putrid stench.

The only entrance in sight was a doorway large enough to drive a truck through. Double doors, enormous slabs of rusted steel, protected the entrance but one of the doors was leaning over, its top hinge broken, leaving a space large enough for her to slip through.

A loading area with a dock for trucks was before her. Just

enough light came from the broken windows to cast the interior in dark shadow. She started to yell for help but stopped. She knew there was no one in the building and a yell would only draw the person stalking her closer.

She went up the steps of the loading dock. Hide, she thought. I have to find a place to hide. Hurrying across the dock, she spotted an open doorway that led deeper into the factory. She went through and pressed herself up against the wall on the other side, forcing herself to stop and get her breathing under control so she could listen. Closing her eyes, she slowly calmed her breathing and focused on sounds. Little noises came to her but she couldn't separate them from the creaks and groans of the old factory turning in its grave.

The room she was in was darker than the loading area and the stench of chemicals worse. She moved slowly round huge metal tanks, some of them several times taller than she was, and what seemed like an endless and mindless array of pipes and valves.

She took each step cautiously, straining to hear behind her, looking around for something to use as a weapon. A piece of steel pipe would have been perfect but all the pipe she saw was attached.

A noise came from somewhere in the factory and she stopped and listened, her heart beating faster. She was scared, terribly scared, but the terror was mixed with anger and she knew this time she would fight back, would not stand petrified as someone attacked her. But she needed a weapon, something to bash that bitch's face with if it was Mrs Guk.

She moved among the maze of piping and tanks looking for a place of concealment. There had to be offices, someplace where paperwork was done, a room with a heavy door and a lock.

Another doorway led into an area of open vats, some of them large enough to swim in. With each step the stench grew more noxious. This was probably some sort of mixing room where chemicals were combined before being fed to the processing tanks in the other room. More fear erupted in her, fear that she might fall into one of the open vats. Some of the containers were set below ground level and had protective railings no more than a couple of feet high. With night closing in outside as each moment ticked by, the factory was getting darker and darker. She couldn't wander around the vat room trying to feel her way out – some vats still contained solutions that she was sure would melt her bones. The odor in the room was fiery, a noxious stench of long-decayed acids that made her lungs burn. With usual Soviet efficiency, the factory had simply been closed one day and left to rot the surrounding environment.

It occurred to her that there was no place safe in the old factory. She had to get back out in the open, back to the little settlement, and make enough noise to let the people there know she was in danger.

The last of the daylight outside glowed dimly through a doorway at the other end of the room and she worked her way round vats and piping toward the exit. She had to hurry, she needed some light to get back to the settlement.

A couple of dozen feet from the doorway she moved cautiously round a large vat that was at ground level. Something hanging over the big vat caused her to stop and stare.

The arm of an interior crane extended over the vat, and as she stared at the object, a scream started, one she couldn't stop. It was a man, hanging upside down with his feet tied to the top of the crane. At first she thought the man was wearing a dark shirt but then she realized that the chest covering was blood.

Lara ran out of the building and fled from the factory mindlessly, not thinking about the direction she took. Stumbling down an embankment, she fell and slid on hard snow to the bottom. She was on the road but visibility was down to less than fifty feet and she was totally disoriented with no idea of where the settlement was. Her mind racing with panic, she started moving down the road, going to her right for no other reason than that was the direction her feet were pointing.

She could still taste the rotted acid from the factory in her throat and her lungs burned now from the freezing cold. Her breath came in great gulps. When she felt ready to drop, she staggered to a stop to get control of her breathing. She looked back down the road and saw something coming toward her, a small dark thing coming at her in the fog like a speeding bullet. She realized what it was and started running again. The Guks' dog was loose.

She slipped, falling to her knees, pain shooting up from ice rocks that cut in. No sound, no warning was coming from the dog but she knew it would be on her at any moment. She ignored the pain in her knees and forced her feet to move again.

Plows had thrown snow against trees lining the side of the road and the embankment ran seven or eight feet high. She went up the embankment on her hands and knees, slipping back because of an icy crust of surface snow, frantically breaking through the crust with her elbows, fists and knees to gain purchase. Almost at the top, she heard a hoarse snarl behind her. She grabbed the lower branch of a tree for support and twisted round as the dog flew at her.

Lara screamed and kicked blindly with her feet. His teeth clenched her shoe and she kicked at his face with her other foot, causing his grip to slacken. He slipped down, jaws snapping. She was able to pull herself up a few inches but he was back again. Kicking blindly, she felt his teeth graze her ankle as she smashed down on his nose with her free foot.

A shrill horn blared and a pair of headlights came at them from the direction of the shanty town. She kept kicking and the dog slid back down the embankment, confused by the oncoming car.

The car skidded into the embankment only feet from her and someone jumped out of the driver's side. A gun fired, the sound of it shattering the eerie quiet of the white-out. Patches of snow from the tree branches overhead splattered down on her.

Seconds later strong hands were helping her gently down the embankment.

'Are you all right?' Yuri asked.

Chapter 15

'I was waiting up the road from the bridge when you left the Guk house,' Yuri told her. He helped her into the passenger side of the car. 'Take off your coat.'

'I'm fre-freezing.'

'The coat will keep out the warmth from the car heater.' He pulled off her coat and draped it over her. 'Watch yourself, I'm closing the door.' He ran round to the driver's side and got in.

'There's a man, a dead man,' she said.

'What are you talking about?'

'Back at the old factory. There's a dead man.'

Yuri drove the car to the rear of the factory. He took a flashlight from the glove compartment.

'Wait here,' he told her.

'No.' She opened the car door. 'I'm not waiting alone.'

When he came round to her side of the car, he had the flashlight in one hand and his gun in the other.

'Show me where you saw the body.'

'It's right inside the rear door.'

He led the way with the flashlight, their feet crunching on snow the only sound in the night. Near the door he whispered, 'Stay back.'

He turned off the flashlight and moved up to the side of the door and listened for a moment. Then, ducking low, he slipped into the factory. When she saw the torch go on she went in and stood beside him as his flashlight swept the vat room.

'Over there,' she said. 'The body's over the vat on the left.'

The beam of the flashlight found the vat and the arm of the crane hanging over it. She gasped at the sight of the object hanging from the crane – a piece of dirty canvas.

'It was there, the body, it was there!'

Without responding to her, he stepped up to the vat and shone the light down into it. The fluid was dark, almost chocolate brown. He put his gun in his shoulder holster and reached down and picked up a metal rod off the floor. Standing beside the vat, he stuck the tip of the rod into the liquid. The fluid foamed and boiled. A moment later he pulled out the rod and shone the light on the end. The tip was missing.

'If a man had been dropped in here, not even the metal fillings of his teeth would be left.'

'If? What do you mean if? I saw a man—'

'It was dark—'

'I'm sure I saw a man hanging there, naked and bloody. I can't believe this is happening.' She was close to tears.

He dropped the rod and put his arm round her shoulder. 'Calm down. Look, I believe you.' He swept the room again with the flashlight. 'Let's get out of here.'

They returned to the car and drove down the bumpy road toward the main highway.

She leaned up against the passenger door, her head pounding. 'You don't really believe me. You think I imagined it. But I didn't. There *was* a man hanging.' She shook her head. 'I don't know what I saw. I . . . I don't know anything anymore.'

'I'll check it out in daylight.'

'Get a crime team out there—'

'I'm going to check it out personally, with my partner Stenka.'

'But—'

'You don't understand. We have limited resources. We don't have enough police to handle street crime and drugs – or the money to pay them. My supervisor would slap me into a night job answering emergency calls if he caught me investigating anything about you.'

'What do you mean?'

'Look, you showed up in Moscow a couple of weeks ago and started stirring up the past. You're listed in the system as a problem foreigner. My supervisor will call it a wild goose chase and pull me into another assignment.'

Her jaws tightened and anger swelled. 'Everyone believes I'm running around imaging things. Fine, let's test my imagination. I'm sure that the dead man is Joseph Guk, the truck driver I came to see. He's supposed to have driven the tanker my mother crashed into.'

'You recognized him?'

'No, not really, it's just logical. He's not at home, he's the man I came to see, he knows about the past. Look, if you don't believe me, let's turn this car round and go back to his house. You can ask Mrs Guk where her husband is.'

'And if she doesn't know? The police have been called several times because of battles between the Guks. He has a habit of disappearing for days at a time on a drunk. When he gets back there's a row.'

'We're just going to leave it like this? Ignore the fact I saw a dead body?'

'Stenka and I will make inquiries on our own.'

'But—'

He reached over and touched her shoulder. 'Trust me.'

'I don't know what to think. I've probably got frostbite on my feet,' she added inconsequentially.

135

He pulled the car over to the side of the road and put it in neutral. 'Give me your feet.' He bent over and lifted her feet onto his lap, took off her shoes and vigorously rubbed her toes. 'They're like ice.'

'I'll put them by the heater.'

'No, I have a better idea.' He pulled up the sweater he wore under his suit jacket and pulled his shirt out of his pants. He tucked her icy feet against his bare flesh under his shirt and sweater. As soon as her icicle toes hit his warm skin he yelped. 'It's okay, just fine,' he said.

She leaned back against the passenger door as he got the car moving again toward the main highway. His strong face and dark eyes were as welcome a sight to her as an angel from heaven. She felt the fear and anxiety leaving her. Maybe she did imagine the body, she thought. And if she didn't, she had a tough cop to check it out.

'Thank you. Not just for saving my feet.'

'It's all right. My job, as a matter of fact. Saving beautiful women from mad dogs.'

'Thank you for calling me beautiful. No one has ever called me that.'

'What? Impossible.'

'And I've never had flowers from a man.'

'Never?'

'Not ever.'

He shrugged. 'I've never had flowers from a woman.'

She felt giddy, light-headed, now that the fear had passed. 'You saved my life. That makes you responsible for me for the rest of your life. It's an old Chinese custom. Chinese-American.'

He swerved round potholes in the road. 'There's a similar old Russian custom that says when a man warms a woman's cold feet on his chest, they will become lovers.'

'I like old customs,' she said. 'How did you know where to find my cold feet?'

'I saw the taxi leave, saw you cross the bridge and head for the main road. I waited to see if anyone followed. When the dog went by I suspected it was trouble but this classic automobile built by heroic Soviet workers decided to give me trouble starting.'

'You were following me?'

'Of course. How else would I have the opportunity to save you? It's another old Russian custom, Russian-American custom.'

'Did you shoot it?'

'The dog? No, it was on the other side of the car. I fired in the air to scare it off.'

'Good.'

'Good?'

'It wasn't the dog's fault. It's a poor animal those people turned vicious. A little like the children in some of my cases, ten-year-olds who stab other children. They weren't born crazy and mean, someone worked to make them that way.'

She played with the knob on his glove box, thinking. She really liked Yuri Kirov. But no one in Moscow seemed to be exactly who or what they said they were. Saving her life had raised a couple of interesting issues. 'How did you know the Guk name? And the fact that they fought?'

She felt his belly tense against her feet.

'How did I know his name? The taxi driver called in the address to his dispatcher. I had Stenka get it from the dispatcher, run it for a name, and check it out. We do have police computers, you know.'

She sighed. 'You've been following me. Do you also have the hotel staff spying on me?'

He shot her a look. 'Of course. This is Russia. Everyone has always spied on everyone else.'

'Why are you following me?'

'We still have one body for sure to account for.'

She didn't like the implication that there was only one body, but she let it pass. 'Have you found out anything more about Belkin?'

'No. And there's been no decision as to whether the cause was accidental or not.'

She rubbed her head. 'Please, give me a break. You know it wasn't accidental.'

He shrugged. 'Anyway, that's how I stumbled onto you.'

'Did you see anyone. Back there, in the fog?' she asked.

'No, just the dog. Why, did you?'

'I'm not sure. It was pretty foggy. What do you know about Guk? And his wife? I think she's a nurse.' Speaking the word 'nurse' made her cringe.

'Only what Stenka told me. He goes off for days drinking and when he comes home he fights with his wife.'

Her feet were beginning to melt and she started to remove them from under his sweater. 'I bet I've given your belly button frostbite.'

He pushed them back against him. 'Leave them. I want them hot so they can dance tonight.'

'Dance?'

'I'm taking you to dinner. To a real Russian restaurant, a rouble restaurant, not one of those hard currency places with food for tourists. You'll see, it's not town food.'

'I . . . I can't go dancing.'

'Why?'

'I don't dance.' Confessing it embarrassed her.

138

'You don't dance? A beautiful woman, no flowers, no dancing.' He nodded his head. 'Yes, now I understand your secret.'

'What secret?'

'You are a nun. Or you have been in prison since you were three years old.'

'Seven. I've been in prison ever since I was seven.' She wanted to explain why, to bare her soul to him, but she wasn't ready. 'Could we . . . could we go to dinner and not dance?'

'An excellent idea. Do you know why?'

'Why?'

'I don't dance either. Honestly.'

'Amazing. You must have been raised in prison too.'

'Something like that,' he murmured.

She sighed and closed her eyes. Going to dinner with a handsome Russian cop who told her she was beautiful was the least she could do after he had saved her life.

She wiggled her toes against his stomach. Her toes were purring. She was warm, safe and happy for the first time since she had been in Moscow.

She woke up and discovered they had been in a traffic jam on the outskirts of the city for over an hour. She went back to sleep again and woke up when they were near the restaurant. She could smell cigarette smoke. He had the driver's side window down and a cigarette hanging out of it. He tossed the cigarette and closed the window as she sat up and struggled into her coat.

'Sorry,' he said, 'bad habit.'

'Cigarette smokers are addicts and cigarette manufacturers are drug pushers.' She smiled to take the edge off her words. 'I read that on a sign put out by the health authorities back home.'

'Is cigarette smoke any worse than the air in the city?'

'Probably not. Actually, smoking is a private matter and is no one else's business.' What a hypocrite I am. Now I'm lying about my opinions because he called me beautiful.

It was toasty warm in the car; just looking at the cold, dark night gave her a chill. He left the driver's side window down a little for air.

She was embarrassed about her confessions about never having been called beautiful, no flowers, not even able to dance. What an idiot. She had violated the first rule of dating: never tell your date your life story. Especially if it makes you sound like a nerd.

'I had this dream while you were driving,' she told him. 'I dreamt that I had told you I had never received flowers from a man. Actually, I receive flowers all the time from men. Big men, small, tall, short, young, old, you know, lots of men.'

'I knew that. I'm a good detective. I realized a woman as beautiful and sensuous as you would be showered with flowers and jewels and furs.'

There was something about Yuri she liked. A lot of somethings . . .

The restaurant, called Moscow Nights, had a line of two dozen people waiting in the dark, chilly night air to get in. The lead couple appeared to be in a heated argument with the doorman. Lara couldn't hear the words as they drove by, but the body language spelled trouble. The people were trying to open the door and the doorman was leaning on it to keep it closed.

'We'll freeze waiting for a table,' she said.

'There are plenty of tables. You just don't understand the system at Russian restaurants.'

He parked the unmarked militia car behind the restaurant and she followed him through a back door that led

into the kitchen. A wave of warm and wonderful food aromas hit her as they entered.

A big man, bigger than Yuri's partner Stenka, looked up from chopping a side of beef with a meat cleaver. He wore the hat and white uniform of a head chef.

'Ah, the police. Give him the drugs and counterfeit money,' he yelled to the kitchen help, 'so he can go back to his dacha and leave us poor people alone.'

'Offering to bribe a police officer. You are all witnesses.' Yuri waved at the other workers. 'Actually, I am not here about drugs and funny money. There are stories about the food. I have been sent to investigate.'

The chef raised the big cleaver. 'I filleted and made shish kebabs out of the last customer who criticized my food.'

'The stories I am to investigate are that the food is wonderful. Which means you must be doing something illegal.' That one got a laugh from everyone. 'Constantin, this is Lara Patrick, a rich American. She has promised to take me back to Texas with her and support me in a life of moral depravation.'

'Ah, a woman whose heart beats with mine. Go on, take her into our fine restaurant. When she is finished with our delicious food and your boring company, send her back here and I will excite her with tales of my prowess as a lover.'

'His prowess has landed him four wives and nine children,' Yuri told her as he led her through swinging doors and into the restaurant, 'not to mention a jail term when he neglected to divorce one wife before marrying the next.'

The restaurant was huge, a wide open area with seating for a couple of hundred people and an elevated stage for a band and entertainment. The color red dominated the place – red flocked wallpaper, long red velvet drapes, red

141

carpeting; grotesque chandeliers hung like big teats from a rosy milk cow. Lara thought it was wonderfully tacky.

'It's only half occupied,' she said as they selected their own table. 'Does Constantin know he's losing money because the doorman is turning people away?'

'This isn't Constantin's restaurant. Like almost everything else, it is owned by all Russians, one hundred and sixty million of them. The restaurant workers get the same pay if they serve one customer or if they serve a hundred.'

'So they turn away business. No profit motive. But surely that's all changing now that you're going to a market economy.'

He shrugged. 'Unless the Communist Party comes back into power.'

'I don't think your people would permit that after communism failed so badly.'

'People will not decide that, guns will. And communism did not fail, people failed. People driven for three decades by the whip of Stalin, under the most brutal and terrifying methods imaginable, built Russia into an industrial and military superpower. In the fifties, while the country still trembled from the shadow cast from his grave, our scientists stunned the world by launching the first space probes. Our doctors showed off their surgical skills by sewing a second head on a living dog. Now, after nearly forty years of peace and tranquillity, our atomic reactors explode in our laps and we have managed even to forget how to grow wheat on fertile soil.'

'You're not saying you need another madman like Stalin to get the country moving, are you?'

'We need vodka and good food to get the country moving,' he said. 'And no more political discussions.'

'Politics? No politics allowed in Moscow Nights,' a waiter said. He set a bottle of frozen vodka on the table and

two glasses. 'By some miracle of the market economy, this bottle of fine vodka broke on the floor of a general's kitchen and yet has turned up here as if it were whole. It is of course an economic illusion and the bottle does not actually exist. Because it does not exist, it will not appear on your bill.'

'Victor, I congratulate you. Your communist mentality and heart of an *apparatchik* has survived the fall of the Party.'

Victor bowed modestly. 'I was a member of the Party until the purge of seventy-three. What can I say? I learned from the best.'

'How's your son?'

'My boy is doing well. He has a job as a plumber. Thanks to you he is not in jail.'

'You have a good boy. I did only what was right.'

'You did only what was human.' Victor glanced around. 'There is some caviar that also escaped from that general's kitchen.' He slipped away to get the fugitive caviar.

'What did you do for Victor's son?' she asked.

'Gave him good advice.'

'Just advice?'

'Maybe a little gentle persuasion. You know, before Victor became a waiter, he was a Russian count with a great estate and two thousand serfs.'

'Really? That's amaz— Wait a minute, there haven't been any Russian counts or serfs for nearly eighty years.'

Yuri grinned. 'A story waiters are using on tourists.' He poured them each a healthy slug of the premium vodka and saluted her with his. '*Na zdorovie*. To your health.'

'Not for me, I don't—'

'This is not liquor, it is liquid platinum.'

'I don't like liquor. Even good liquor.'

'You don't like cigarettes, you don't like liquor, you

don't dance and you wear bulky clothes that cover a lovely figure.'

'How do you know about my figure if it's covered with bulky clothes?'

'How do I know? Did you think I would let you dress yesterday without observing whether you hid something or had a gun?'

'You pervert, you watched through the door. You and Stenka—'

'No, I never permitted Stenka to look. Rank has certain privileges. Besides, I wanted you all for myself.'

'I think I need a drink.' She took the shot of vodka and gulped it.

Her throat was hit with molten lava. Her face turned red and her eyes went wide and watery. She teetered on the brink of choking and spitting it out on the table.

Finally she leaned back and took a deep breath, wiping her wet eyes with her linen napkin.

'Good stuff,' she croaked.

Black Beluga caviar made its way to their table, followed by a delicious eggplant relish, hot and tasty red cabbage borscht, chicken Kiev with a sea of garlic and butter flowing into a bed of rice. Dinner was the best she'd had since being in Moscow.

'I love the way they do the chicken. Usually you get a thin watered-down butter concoction that soaks into potatoes and makes them taste greasy. What did you mean when you said it wasn't town food?'

'There are, or were until a couple months ago, restaurants and stores for the Kremlin elite and only those with special passes could enter. If you were a Chosen One, you could buy a fine pastry sculptured by a French chef. The rest of the people bought lumpy cakes at the local bakery. Kremlin food. Town food.'

She took another slug of vodka and gasped, her eyes nearly crossing as the liquid burned down her throat. When she got her breath back she leaned toward him and confided, 'I've never been drunk.'

'I guessed that.'

'Why? Do you think you can get me drunk and take advantage of me? Listen,' she poked him in the chest with her forefinger, 'I may not be experienced with liquor, but I have an intellectual understanding of it. I know it can take hold of my body, but I would never surrender my mind. Do you understand? It can take my body but I will never permit it to take control of my mind.'

'I understand perfectly.'

The lights went down and sparkles above their heads, ignited by the glow of the chandeliers, turned the ceiling into a star-clustered night sky. The band began to play the folk song after which the restaurant was named, 'Moscow Nights'.

'It's also called "Midnight in Moscow", isn't it?'

'Yes,' he told her. 'Midnight in Moscow on a starry white winter night.' He leaned closer to her and his hand rested on her thigh. 'Lovers in a horse-drawn sled, warm under the blankets, the stars smiling down at them, the man leans over and kisses her . . .'

His face was so close to hers, she thought he was going to kiss her but he stopped and searched her eyes.

She felt goose bumps on her skin. Mesmerized by his dark, soulful eyes, she suddenly wanted to be kissed by this man, wanted to be in his arms. She leaned forward to meet his lips—

And knocked over the bottle of vodka.

'Oh, noooo!' She grabbed at the bottle and knocked a glass of water into his lap.

'Oh God, I'm so sorry—'

'It's okay. Don't move! You almost knocked your plate off the table. Just stay where you are. Have another drink. It'll relax you. I need to dry off in the kitchen. And check in with Stenka.'

When Yuri left the table, she sat back and stared up at the midnight ceiling. Why me, Lord, why was I chosen to be bimbo of the year? She was just starting to feel good from the liquor and she had to make an ass of herself.

On stage a troupe of wild Russian dancers gave way to a man and woman dancing a scene from *Swan Lake*. The restaurant reminded her of a 1940s American nightclub, at least the kind portrayed in movies that played on the classics channel.

Yuri came back with a long face.

Guilt-stricken and embarrassed, she said, 'I'm sorry if I've caused—'

'No, it's not that.'

'What's the matter?'

'We have a new case, Stenka and I. A woman. A possible suicide. I have to meet him at the scene of the death.'

'Oh, I'm sorry. But I'm relieved that you're not mad about the vodka and the wet pants.' She smiled and reached over to touch his knee. His leg felt cold and stiff under her hand and she pulled it away.

He took a sip of vodka and watched the ballet dancers as he spoke. 'The dead woman is a school teacher. Apparently she became upset yesterday after a visit from one of her former students, a young American.'

The warm glow of vodka turned to ice in the pit of her stomach. 'Malinovsky?'

'She fell seven stories from her apartment window.'

'Are they sure it's . . . suicide?'

146

'After a seven-story fall, the only thing they're sure of is that she's dead. She had a history of emotional imbalance. She was apparently very upset after you left yesterday.'

Lara controlled the tremors gripping her and spoke very softly, but firmly. 'I'm not responsible for that woman's death.'

'I didn't say you were.'

'That look on your face implies it. I'm not a nut or a troublemaker and I don't go around causing problems for people. I simply asked that woman about the day I was picked up at school, the day my mother died and I was taken to the airport.'

'Why?'

'I told you, I don't believe the official version of my mother's death.' She told him about the attack on her as a child and when she returned to St Basil's. She suspected that he already knew the story from police records. 'I know someone other than my mother picked me up from school, a woman dressed in my mother's clothes. The same person attacked me the other night in St Basil's.'

'You went to see Malinovsky because you suspected that a woman dressed as your mother picked you up at school when you were attacked as a child?'

'Yes. Look, I don't seem to get across to you what sort of runaround I've been given since I arrived in Moscow. And not just from the bureaucracy. The first person I went to was my mother's best friend, a woman my mother constantly mentioned in her letters home. She also taught at the university. The woman welcomed me with open arms but the moment I brought up questions about my mother's death she literally threw me out. She said I was on a witch hunt.'

'She was a KGB informer against your mother.'

'What? How do you know that?'

'You keep forgetting where you are. You are staying at a hotel where just a few months ago every room was bugged. Every room in every hotel in Moscow was bugged. Every tourist who came to the country had an Intourist Agency guide. When I joke and say everyone in Russia was an informer it is only a little joke because there's much truth to it. Your mother was a foreigner living in Moscow. Everyone who came into contact with her would have been contacted by the KGB and questioned. Those people were not paid agents. They were average citizens. They would answer out of fear for their jobs, their families and their very lives.'

'But that's all gone, the KGB's been disbanded,' she said.

'But the memories and the records are still here. That professor was your mother's friend. No doubt a true friend. But from time to time she would have had to report your mother's activities to the KGB. You brought up a bad subject, a forbidden subject. Few people want to talk about that part of the past because of shame. It is embarrassing for individuals, and to bring up the past would be dangerous to the government. If such revelations were suddenly made public, and people were put on trial for acts that were legal at the time, the country would be torn apart by the turmoil. The past is dead. We are committed to forgetting it.'

'I don't believe there was anything political about my mother's death. I don't believe she was killed by the KGB.'

'Whatever your instincts are, you are causing a great deal of misery to people for what happened long ago.'

'Misery? I'm not causing problems to anyone. Do you really think that my old teacher killed herself? That Belkin was given an accidental overdose? That I just happened to imagine Guk's dead body? That I threw myself out of a window ten stories up?'

'Those matters are still under investigation. And there was scaffolding outside the window.'

'You ... you think I planned it? Jumped out of the window because I'm crazy? One minute you show common sense and the next you sound like a tape recording of an official apologist for the Soviet regime. Just because all you people have something to hide doesn't mean you have a right to hide it. I don't care about your politics and your frightened informers. I'm frightened for my life. *I'm talking about murder.*' Her voice had risen and people at adjoining tables turned to stare.

'The fact that you have come to Moscow hysterical and angry over a motherless childhood does not turn your suspicion into fact. You should go back to America before more innocent people are hurt.'

She jumped out of her chair so fast it went over backwards. 'You ... you ...' Speech was beyond her. So was reason. She reached across and flipped the plate of caviar into his lap. '*Bastard!*'

She rushed out, going back through the kitchen the way they had entered. Flying through the swinging doors to the kitchen, she snapped at Constantin, 'I need a taxi. Now. If that man comes back here I'm going to use your meat cleaver on him.'

The swinging doors behind them slowly opened and Victor, the waiter, stuck his head through first and then his hand holding a pair of shoes. 'Were you leaving without your shoes?'

'Give me those. Keep Yuri out of here.'

'Detective Kirov is busy scraping several thousand roubles worth of caviar off his pants.'

'It'll take an hour to get a taxi,' Constantin said.

'How far is it to the Gorky Hotel?' she asked.

'Too far.'

'I can drop you off.'

The speaker was a woman Lara noticed for the first time, a young woman of about twenty. She dropped a cardboard box on a pile of other boxes. Each of the boxes contained the markings of the army quartermaster corps, the supply division. She wore a Russian army work uniform.

'I'm going in that direction on the way back to my unit.'

'Then get her out of here,' Constantin said, 'quickly. Before Yuri comes back here and I have a dead policeman in the restaurant.' Constantin grabbed Lara and gave her a bear hug and a kiss. 'Call me. I am between wives.'

Behind the restaurant, next to Yuri's little militia car, was a Russian army truck. Lara climbed into the passenger side less adroitly than her benefactor.

The young woman got the truck moving.

'I'm Tatyana. Constantin's my father.'

'I'm Lara.' She didn't ask why Tatyana was delivering army supplies in the middle of the night to the restaurant her father ran. No doubt it was more damaged goods from the general's kitchen.

'Yuri and Lara,' Tatyana said. 'The tragic lovers from *Dr Zhivago*. Just like Romeo and Juliet. I love romantic tragedies, don't you?'

Arriving back at the Gorky Hotel in a Russian army truck did nothing to lessen Lara's already suspect reputation with the hotel staff.

She lifted her chin high and walked across the lobby like Princess Di at a ball.

The porter and night clerk stared at her with the wide-eyed diffidence reserved for presidents and axe murderers.

She passed the unreliable elevators on the grounds that she had used up that day's luck by surviving frostbite and a crazy dog and went directly to the stairway, without giving the staff any indication that she was aware of their existence.

She stamped up the steps, imagining Yuri's face underfoot every time her shoe came down. She had made a complete fool of herself, from her silly confessions in the car while she toasted her feet on his belly to her bimbo act in the restaurant. The only thing that redeemed her from total humiliation was the fact that he was a worm.

I'll never see that bastard again, she thought as she stamped up the stairs.

The floor maid was outside the linen room, busily folding towels on a cart as Lara reached the top of the steps.

'Good evening, Madam.' The woman bowed and smiled, then bowed and smiled again.

Lara noted that she had to unfold towels before she folded them. She stalked by the woman, barely giving her a glance.

Pausing to insert the key into her door, she suddenly looked back and caught the maid staring at her. The woman quickly turned back to unfolding towels.

Lara shoved open the door, flipped on the light and stepped into her room. A couple feet into the room, she stopped and stood still.

On her chest of drawers was a doll. It was dressed as a nurse. Between the doll's legs was a fat candle shaped like a penis.

Lara recoiled, letting out a scream. She started back toward the maid, who dropped her towels and ran.

Lara caught her at the end of the hallway. 'Who's been in my room?'

'No one,' the woman wailed, cowering against the wall.

'Someone's been in my room. Tell me who it was.'

'Nobody, I swear. Just that nurse this morning.'

'What nurse?'

'Right after you left, a nurse told me to let her into your room because you had forgotten your medicine. We all know you are under medical care.'

'Get the bellman up here. I'm leaving this place, now.'

The Moscow Grand was big, expensive and, she hoped, safe. The room doors could be double-locked from the inside. Her fourth-floor room was the cheapest in the hotel, located next to the whining and vibrations from the elevator shaft on one side and the rumble of ice machines on the other. There were no windows. She could barely afford the room. The hotel catered for German and Japanese businessmen. Her windowless room was two hundred dollars a night, five times what she had paid at the Gorky for a two-window room without vibrations.

She stripped down to long underwear and burrowed under the covers.

Chapter 16

In bed the next morning, Lara stared at Alexei Bova's card and fought with her self-respect. She just didn't know how to ask for help. Finally, admitting defeat, she picked up the telephone.

By some miracle of electronics and economics, there was actually a hotel operator who responded at the Moscow Grand when one needed to make a call. She gave the operator the number and was surprised when the woman told her to wait on the line. A moment later the operator came back on and asked her name. Then a man's voice came on.

'This is Ilya, Mr Bova's secretary. How may I help you, Ms Patrick?'

'Mr ... Mr Bova,' she stammered, self-consciously, 'invited me to a party—'

'Yes. That's the Western affair tonight. May I send a limo for you at eight?'

'Uh, yes, that's fine. Eight is perfect.'

'Your hotel?'

'The Moscow Grand.'

'Excellent. The limo will be there at precisely eight. Are you enjoying your stay at the Moscow Grand?'

She looked around her windowless room. 'It's okay. I would have preferred a room with a better view than four walls, but I'm on a budget.'

'I will let Mr Bova know.'

She hung up and banged her fist against the side of her head. What a mouth I have! Let him know what? That Lara Patrick can't afford a room with a window? I'll probably get a call back in an hour. 'Mr Bova regrets to inform you that he doesn't invite people to his parties who can't afford a decent hotel room.' Why can't I just keep my mouth shut?

She jumped out of bed. It was after twelve. She had less than eight hours to get a dress and accessories for tonight. From what Bova's secretary had said, there would be mostly Westerners rather than Russians at the party and that was fine with her. It would be easier raising her mother's case with Bova without Russians listening over her shoulder.

She needed a dress, but she had to be realistic about it. She couldn't afford to spend a lot of money on a dress she was only wearing one night.

Nor could she afford the Moscow Grand. Tomorrow she'd find another hotel on the budget scale of the Gorky, only in another part of the city where there were lots of people and taxis.

What does a dress cost here? she wondered. Could she find something for under a couple of hundred? It was the coat that was going to be the problem. She had no dress coat, period. And the ski jacket she wore with pants and two pairs of long underwear wasn't going to be quite the thing for a party given by Alexei Bova.

If Westerners were the main guests, there would probably be ambassadors, trade ministers, international business executives. They would dress fairly conservatively, she thought. Simple and elegant was likely to be the dress code with some of the younger, better built women wearing less clothes and more cleavage.

Considering the state of the economy, it would be easier to make a deal for a Russian tank than an evening dress.

No time for a luxury soak, she showered, dressed and was out of the hotel in less than an hour. There were no strange looks from the hotel staff as she came down the stairs and crossed the lobby. Apparently her reputation at the Gorky hadn't made it over yet. Last night when she left the Gorky she had the taxi take her to the Rossia Hotel, where she switched cabs; not so much to throw off pursuers as to prevent the Gorky staff from finding out where she went and calling her new hotel and telling the staff she was a nutcase.

Out on the street she walked quickly in the direction of the fashion shops she had seen in the neighborhood of Bova's Black Tower.

Accepting the party invitation had not been part of a sudden urge to become a social butterfly, but the realization that she needed allies. So far she had dealt with clerks and office managers to gain access to government records. At her present rate she would run out of money before she got to the records she needed. Alexei Bova and the stripe of people who surrounded him could open doors. And maybe even get the police to listen and give her protection.

She had stayed in bed that morning, running every move she had made over and over again in her mind. Yuri, and her anger at him, repeatedly sneaked into her thoughts like a puppy craving attention. She could forgive him for tricking her about Belkin, and even his damn cigarettes, but stupidity was unforgivable.

A thought kept popping up in her mind like an itch that would not go away and finally she faced it. Yuri was not stupid. He couldn't really believe that swill he gave her. Was he protecting somebody? And what was he doing at the carnival the night Belkin was hit by the truck?

155

The little doll in her room was the last straw. Now the bitch stalking her was invading her room and leaving calling cards.

She wanted to call up Yuri, to tell him she'd had a visit from the nurse, but her pride and a worse fear – that he might think she was making it up – stopped her.

Yuri is out of the picture, she told herself. And Alexei Bova could open doors for her. How she would approach him, she didn't know. She knew nothing about asking for help, less about networking. And she couldn't just walk up to him at the party and tell him she needed help with several unsolved murders.

The French had invaded Russian fashions and it was a French shop Lara tried first.

She knew from the look of the clothing there wouldn't be anything she could afford. But she had to have something decent. Rich people like Bova probably assumed that all women traveled with six steamer trunks, ready to whip out an outfit for any occasion.

The last evening dress she had bought, the only evening dress she had ever bought, was the one she got for the high school graduation dance no one had invited her to. It was still hanging snug and warm in her Pacific Heights condo with the price tag on it.

'May I help you?' a sales clerk asked.

The saleswoman was wearing a floor-length maroon dress with a slit that came up the side almost to her hip. With a long bead of pearls, a pageboy hairdo, glorious make-up and a haughty attitude, she would have been perfect for Alexei's party, Lara thought. Maybe I ought to tell her to go instead of me.

'I'm just looking,' she said.

She wandered through the store, looking hungrily at the

beautiful clothing, trying to appear as if she wasn't dying to try something on. She needed to find out the price range of the clothes, but was too embarrassed to ask and too self-conscious to rummage for price tags.

Something very European, a black suit with a white shirt, rather elegant even though it was modeled after a man's business suit, caught her eye. A 1920s gangster's hat, a white scarf thrown carelessly over the shoulders, and black patent shoes with white spats set off the outfit.

It wasn't her, much too showy, but what intrigued her about the outfit was that she might get away without a coat. With pants, suit jacket and scarf, she could wear two pairs of long underwear underneath and not look silly without a coat.

She walked round the outfit, trying to get a glimpse of a price tag. She found one sticking out from under the scarf, and it gave the price in hard currency: $500.

A lot of money, more than she had hoped to pay, but did she have the courage to wear it? Was it too flamboyant for her? Too trendy for a conservative party?

She took a closer look. The outfit was really quite clever, very feminine, yet a bit different. It was really an outfit that made a statement. Oh God, the last thing she wanted was to be noticed. But she could get away without an evening coat and a decent coat would cost several times the price of a dress.

'Find something you like?' the saleswoman asked.

'Perhaps. I'm traveling and suddenly need an outfit for tonight. I'm just wondering if this isn't a little too, uh, fashionable, for me. Are the shoes and spats separate or are they included in the five hundred dollar price?'

'Madam, the five hundred dollars is for the scarf . . .'

The Arbat is one of the oldest districts in the city and the one that holds whatever charm Moscow is said to have. The streets once housed the court artisans, the silversmiths and pastry cooks, woodworkers and glass cutters that served the gentry. Later it became a favorite place of the aristocrats, and ultimately evolved into an area of small shops and crafts. Lara decided its present ambience was a chemistry made up of small shops, pickpockets, street musicians, beggars, and beats – the 1950s variety.

After crawling out of the third foreign fashion house, beaten and humiliated, she got on a subway for Arbat Square. One could find almost anything in the area, from souvenir Soviet army flags to handmade lace.

In a shop called Ninocha's she found a classic black dress that came with a short jacket. The top of the dress came all the way to her neck and had full-length sleeves. The skirt extended down to her shoes with a slit on one side that reached to just above her knee.

The outfit was modest and conservative, she told herself, not really old-fashioned. Its charm was that the little jacket would keep her from looking conspicuously coatless.

She already had black shoes and the right color tights. And a silver bracelet watch that looked expensive and wasn't. With the high neckline, the watch was the only jewelry she needed.

Best of all, the whole outfit was $180.

'Am I going to look like I'm wearing my mother's dress to a high fashion party?' she asked the saleswoman.

'A great ballerina wore this dress to her lover's funeral,' the old woman told her.

'It's secondhand?'

'Worn only once. After the cameras captured her suffering, the ballerina gave away all her worldly goods and secluded herself in a convent in France. New, the dress would be $500.'

Lara shifted her weight from foot to foot. 'The outfit seems a little conservative.'

'You are in Moscow. We still preserve the dignity of our women when they attend parties.'

The assistant manager intercepted her at the foot of the stairway when she got back to the hotel.

'Your room has been changed, Ms Patrick. The night clerk was remiss in putting you in that little room by the elevator shaft.'

Oh oh, they've heard from the Gorky. Probably think I'm planning to bomb the place. 'The new room doesn't have padded walls, does it?'

'Padded walls? You want padded walls? I don't believe we have a room with padded walls, but I'm sure you'll enjoy the one we've moved you to. It's the best in the house available at a low level. I mean height, of course. You told the front desk last night you didn't want anything above the fourth floor.'

'I was joking about the padding,' she said, as they went into the elevator. 'You know, padded cell, crazy people.'

'Oh yes, very humorous.' He gave her an artificial laugh.

She looked up at the ceiling of the elevator. Time to change hotels . . .

They went past her old room, down to the end of the hall and round the corner. He paused at double doors, opened one door and stepped aside for her to enter.

She walked in, her eyes growing wide.

It wasn't a room. It was a suite.

Bouquets of flowers lined long tables on both sides of the entry. A table of hors d'oeuvres with a bottle of champagne was in the center of the sitting room. Off to the side was a bowl of fresh fruit, not a piece of which was grown within a thousand miles of Moscow in the winter time.

A maid came out of the bedroom and gave her a small curtsy. 'Welcome to the Tsarina Suite, Madam.'

Lara had to restrain herself from laughing – they must think I'm a rich American. 'I really appreciate all this but I'm afraid there's been a mistake.'

'A mistake?' The man almost jumped out of his pants. 'Have we done something wrong? You don't like the room? The food—'

'No, I'm talking about a mistake in identity. I'm Lara Patrick. I have the room by the elevator and the rattling ice machines.'

'Lara Patrick. Exactly.'

'You don't understand. I can't afford this room.'

'Afford? The suite is compliments of Mr Bova.'

'Alexei Bova?'

'Yes, of course.'

'Mr Bova had all . . . all this done for me?'

'Yes.'

'Oh, well, now I know there's been a misunderstanding. I appreciate Mr Bova's generosity, but I don't permit men to pay for my hotel rooms.'

'Mr Bova owns the hotel.'

'Mr Bova owns the hotel?'

She looked round the room. It was bright and cheerful. Three windows. All closed, the way she liked them. She went over and looked out. A couple of floors below was the terrace to one of the hotel restaurants. If someone threw her out she'd probably only break a leg.

Elegantly carved crown molding decorated the walls and ceiling. Instead of the dull gray-white walls of her elevator shaft room, the suite was decorated in soft pastel colors. The carpeting was so thick and soft she could bury her toes in it. The bedroom was as big as the living room.

She inspected the bathroom. Oh God, a jacuzzi bathtub.

Soaking in a hot tub full of bubbles was one of her favorite luxuries.

She kept a straight face as she held out her hand for the key, the way she thought Katherine Hepburn might handle the situation. 'Since Mr Bova owns the hotel, I suppose we can consider me a house guest,' *and not a kept woman,* she added silently.

'Thank you, Madam.' The assistant manager bowed all the way to the door.

The maid held her ground.

Lara lifted her eyebrows.

'I'm your personal maid,' she told Lara. 'Did you wish me to draw your bath?'

'Yes, yes, that would be nice.'

As soon as the maid disappeared into the bathroom Lara grabbed a cracker and dipped it into caviar, kicked off her shoes and swam her feet in the thick carpeting all the way to the bed. She flopped backwards on the bed and looked up at the ceiling. *Why would a man I had only met briefly do all this for me?*

He's rich. He does wild and crazy things, according to the news media. Maybe he was attracted to her. Hell, maybe he's after *my* body. She looked around the luxurious bedroom. I could learn to like this.

'Just call me a slut,' she informed the ceiling.

Chapter 17

To get rid of the maid for a few minutes, Lara sent her down to buy a can of hair spray. As soon as she left, Lara picked up the telephone and asked to be connected to the United States Embassy, marveling again at the telephone efficiency when the operator told her to stay on the line.

Eric Caldwell, the embassy's Legal Attaché, took her call. Probably thought I'd be on his doorstep if he didn't, she thought. She had been working through him to convince the Ministry of Security to reopen her mother's 'accident' case. He had not been very helpful despite her calls and visits to his office; his excuse was that the infant Russian government was shaky enough without bringing up dirt from the past.

'Mr Caldwell, is there any news from the ministry about reopening the investigation into my mother's death?'

'Nothing further. It is still under study,' he said curtly.

'In other words, they're waiting for my money to run out so I'll go home.'

'You have to understand, Ms Patrick . . .' He gave her the same line he had given her half a dozen times about how long these matters take in Russia, especially in this time of social, political and economic turmoil.

'I had another question, more of a social one, nothing to do with my mother. I've been invited to a party and I thought before I went I should check out my host. His name is Alexei Bova.'

'You've been invited to one of Bova's parties?' Caldwell's voice changed from bored tolerance to envy and amazement.

'Yes. Can you tell me a little about him?'

'Everybody in Russia can tell you something about him. He gets more news coverage here than Princess Di and Donald Trump combined get from the scandal magazines in the West. His parties are something that would make a Roman emperor envious. He once served Chicago pizza at a party. Real Chicago pizza. This madman ordered a Chicago pizza parlor dismantled – ovens, booths, barrels of flour, two Italian pizza makers, the whole nine yards – and had it flown to Moscow for one of his parties.'

'He sounds like one of those Depression day American millionaires who threw ostentatious parties while people starved.'

'Good comparison, and if you've ever read about the Depression, you'll find that the exploits of those wild and crazy rich people got more publicity than the antics of today's rock stars. People loved and hated and envied them. Russians feel the same about Alexei. When they're having a hard time buying milk for their babies, they curse him for his extravagances, but most people are actually proud of his accomplishments.'

'How did he make so much money so fast? The market economy has hardly got going here.'

'Wheeling, dealing, leveraging. Owns his own bank. Uses OPMs – other people's money. That big building, the one they call the Black Tower, is supposed to be an example of free enterprise at work, but Alexei stole the land from the government with a fast paper shuffle. Then millions of dollars in building material came from government factories eager for orders, orders that got filled but never paid. In other words, he built the tallest building in Moscow and it didn't cost him a dime, personally.'

'Isn't that how many self-made American millionaires did it?'

'True, but some of them went to jail along the way. I've also heard that he had to import more millions in materials to finish the building and that money came from depositors. The government has the building tied up in the courts and no one's occupying it except Bova. You must have read about his dacha?'

'I remember something.'

'He grabbed a tsarist country palace that's been a museum,' Caldwell said enthusiastically. 'Bought it from the workers' committee that ran it, with the workers getting more money than any of them would have earned in a lifetime. The government's suing to get it back.'

'How can someone buy something from a committee that doesn't own it?'

'Who knows who owns what in Russia today? Besides, to say he bought it is misleading. What the clever devil did was take out ninety-nine-year leases on the land and the palace. Workers' committees don't have authority to sell the properties they run, but they can enter into contracts. The leasing angle was a loophole in the law that the government's trying to close in the courts. And one other thing of interest,' Caldwell said. 'That Black Tower may have turned into Bova's folly. There are rumors of major structural problems created when he threw it up so fast. Moscow building inspectors won't give it a certificate of occupancy. An empty skyscraper has to be one helluva cash flow problem, especially with the people who put up the money in the first place.'

After she had finished talking to Caldwell, she checked out the bath Anna had drawn for her in the jacuzzi tub.

It looked heavenly. Six inches of bubbles and a temperature you'd boil a lobster in. She hurried into the living room and quickly prepared a tray of hors d'oeuvres, poured a tall glass of champagne, and then, thinking what the hell, brought the bottle of champagne as well as the food into the bathroom.

She stripped off her clothes and slowly submerged into the luxuriously scented water. With bubbles up to her neck, she reached out and took caviar on a cracker. A few crackers later she tried the champagne. It tasted wonderful and tickled her nose. The only champagne she had ever tasted before was the $2.99 a bottle stuff served at weddings. Cold champagne in a hot tub. This was really living. The life of the rich and famous.

She poured another glass. Champagne had none of the kick of vodka. Giggling to herself, she poured the rest of the bottle into the bath water and flipped on the air jets.

She lay back and let the water massage her. Oh, I could get used to being a kept woman . . .

'Does Madam wish me to help her dress for the party?'

Egad, no one had helped her dress since her mother died. Not even her grandmother had helped her dress.

'I'll be fine. But I do need an iron. One sleeve of my jacket is a little wrinkled.'

'I'll iron it for you, Madam.'

'Thank you, Anna.'

Anna had that hardy Eastern European peasant woman build – stout and short. She also had a club foot and walked with a noticeable limp.

I'm going to have to get used to the personal service, Lara thought. At least until she turned down the 'payment' she expected Alexei would want instead of rent and she found herself out of the hotel. No doubt with her growing reputation with the Moscow hotel industry, her next room would be at a homeless shelter.

How can rich people stand to be waited on? She always found herself thanking the bus boys in restaurants every time her water glass was topped up. She'd be hoarse at the end of a day if she had a staff of servants.

Slipping into some red woolly long underwear, she recalled reading somewhere that General Eisenhower's valet used to hold the general's underwear open so the general could step into it after showering. She wondered if anyone held Alexei's underwear for him . . .

Anna brought the ironed jacket into the bedroom. She stared at the long underwear.

'I don't have a warm coat,' Lara explained.

Anna looked puzzled. 'Everyone in Russia has a warm coat.'

Lara smiled. 'What I meant was, I don't have a coat to go with an evening dress. I, uh, left my evening coat at home. This way I'll be able to survive without a coat. I'll roll up the legs and no one will be the wiser.'

'Yes, Madam.'

There was nothing readable in Anna's voice or expression, but Lara could imagine what the woman was thinking. Rich Americans are strange . . .

She felt good. It surprised her that just two glasses of champagne should make her feel a tiny bit tipsy. Not a bad feeling, but a nice, warm, relaxed sensation. No wonder people drink so much in cold climates, she thought. That little glow she got from the alcohol warmed her toes and made her less apprehensive about facing dozens of strangers at the party tonight.

She looked over her outfit in the mirror.

I don't know, she thought. Is it too conservative? She wondered again what ambassadors and business people would wear.

'Is there any more champagne?' she asked Anna.

'I put another on ice after you finished the last one, Madam.'

'Don't tell anyone, but most of the last one went into my bath water. I think I'll have just a glass of the new bottle. Want to join me?'

'No thank you, Madam.'

'Why don't you call me Lara?'

'Yes, Madam.'

Lara sipped champagne as she put on her make-up. The maid stood back, ready to help, but Lara couldn't think of anything for her to do.

'Have you worked for the hotel long?' she asked.

'I work for Mr Bova.'

For Mr Bova personally; that was interesting. She wanted to ask why she hadn't simply been supplied a hotel maid and decided it would be impolite to ask. The woman might even take offense, perhaps think that Lara didn't want her because of the handicap.

Lara rolled up the left leg of her long underwear to above the knee. It created a bulge that showed against the dress so she unrolled it and simply pulled it up above the knee, letting the elastic hold it there. It appeared tight enough to keep from slipping down.

The top of the evening gown looked a bit silly with a shirt of woolly red underwear poking out, but once she slipped on the little jacket that went with the dress, there was no sign of the underwear.

'Well, what do you think, Anna?'

'Very nice, Madam.'

She didn't sound too convincing.

Lara frowned and took another sip of champagne. People who hate liquor have never had good champagne, she thought.

'Well, other than taking a gun down to the fashion district and getting a dress that way, this is what I'm stuck with.'

The phone rang just then and Anna answered it.

'The driver is downstairs, Madam.'

Lara looked at herself in the mirror again. Not glamorous, she thought, but not a spinster school teacher either. About how a poor shop girl would dress wearing her stepmother's evening gown to the prince's ball. She started to giggle at the idea and clamped a hand over her mouth.

'Anna, can a couple glasses of champagne get you drunk? I mean, I'm not drunk, am I?'

The woman shook her head. 'No, Madam.'

'You know what,' she told the blank-faced maid, 'I don't really care what people think. I am what I am and if people don't like it, they can just go to hell.'

She thought about this as she went down the corridor. I don't usually think that way, she told herself, but that's the way I should think. Not worry so much about what the rest of the world thinks about me. I'm a good person. I don't hurt anyone. If this dress is what I can afford and they don't like it, that's their problem, not mine. That's what my mother and father would have said. To hell with what the world thinks.

'Liquid courage,' she said, in English, in the elevator.

'Madam?' the attendant asked in Russian.

'Nothing, just talking to myself.'

She had a new attitude toward things, and it wasn't liquid courage. Champagne doesn't affect me that much anyway. Besides, it's not like real liquor . . .

The uniformed limo driver was waiting in the lobby near

the doors. A garment was folded over his arm. As Lara approached, he unfolded it and she realized it was a full-length black sable cape.

'May I?' he said, holding the cape to drape it round her.

Lara didn't know what to say.

'Your car coat, Madam.'

'Thank you.' She let him put the coat round her shoulders and followed him out to the limo. Inside the back of the limo she took off the cape and examined it. She had seen sable and this was no ordinary piece. It was midnight sable, the finest and most expensive. And there was one helluva lot of it. The coat had to have cost more than the limo she was in and Alexei Bova used it as a 'car coat' for guests?

'Poor sables,' she told them, stroking the coat. She was against wearing exotic animal skins.

The limo was a black Mercedes. She had noticed in the lobby that the driver had only one eye, perhaps a congenital defect because of the way the skin covered the other eye socket area. It struck her that Alexei seemed to go out of his way to hire people with a handicap.

The drive to the Black Tower was short and she was there before she could change her mind and tell the driver to turn round and take her back to the hotel so she could hide her head under the blankets.

A doorman opened the car door for her. Two more doormen were waiting to hold the lobby doors open for her.

'You forgot you coat, Madam,' the doorman told her.

'It's not my coat, it's the car coat.'

There were two more attendants waiting at the elevators. 'Good evening, Ms Patrick,' one of them said.

'Good evening.' She wasn't surprised that they knew her

name. The driver who brought her was supposed to bring a Ms Patrick.

She watched the lights on the elevator buttons as they went up. Forty-nine floors and then the penthouse. Usually her stomach would get a little queasy at such heights, but tonight she felt warm and glowing. She hoped they served champagne at the party. Despite her glow, she worried about what was going to happen when she stepped off the elevator and confronted women in ten thousand dollar dresses laughing at her off-the-rack outfit.

She remembered a story from one of her college teachers, a Polish woman. When the Soviets invaded Poland in 1939, things were a little primitive in the Russian army ranks. It wasn't unusual for the occupying troops to bring women along, some carrying guns, others as camp followers. The Russians were little more than hillbillies, her teacher said, and thieves who broke into Polish homes. The women wore stolen nightgowns on the streets in the mistaken belief that the nightgowns were fancy dresses.

She got a sudden pang of fear and looked at her dress, wondering if she had confused a nightgown for an evening dress and then laughed at her stupidity.

'Sorry,' she told the attendant. 'Private joke.'

'Yes, Madam.'

The elevator stopped at the penthouse level. Lara took a deep breath and launched herself out of the elevator and into the lives of the rich and famous.

She came face to face with the Lone Ranger and Tonto.

Chapter 18

Somewhere in the room a cow mooed and a horse neighed in answer.

With her eyes growing wider and her mouth slowly dropping, she watched General Custer walk by arm in arm with Sitting Bull followed by two older women whose pot bellies were bigger than the rear bustles of the granny dresses they wore.

Across the room on an elevated stage, a pistol-packing mama was belting out the words to 'Elvira' while dozens of Russian cowboys and cowgirls were shuffling, or at least making an attempt at shuffling, to the Texas Slide.

Alexei suddenly appeared in front of her. He wore all black – black hat, shirt, pants and boots. His cowboy hat had a silver band and his silver studded belts held a pair of pearl-handled six-shooters.

'I feel a complete fool,' she said. 'When your secretary said something about Western dress—'

'You didn't realize he meant the Old West. It's our fault entirely for not making that clear. Here's Ilya now.'

A young man dressed as a riverboat gambler came hurrying up. Like most of the men in the room, he wore a pair of six-shooters.

'Ilya, this is Lara Patrick. I'm afraid you didn't make it clear that we were having a cowboy shindig.'

Ilya was grief-stricken. 'I'm so sorry, Ms Patrick.'

'My fault, not yours.' She held out her hand to shake his and then quickly pulled it back. He had a deformed right arm that left the limb and hand much smaller than normal.

He smiled and offered his left hand. 'This one works fine.'

'The mix-up is my fault,' Alexei said. 'It would have been impossible for you to find Western clothes at such short notice in Moscow anyway. I had clothiers come here from Dallas a couple of weeks ago to outfit my guests.'

'Is that where you got your band?'

'Nashville.' Alexei grabbed her arm. 'Come, I'll find you a drink.'

'Alexei, I really think I should go.'

'You can't go. Not unless you plan to leap all the way to the street. I won't let the elevators take you down. Besides, I want you to meet someone, a friend of mine who knew your parents.'

'My parents?' She was stunned.

'Your mother was Angela Patrick, wasn't she?'

'Yes.'

'My assistant, Felix, knew her and your father.'

'Really?'

'You're staying then?'

'Staying? I'm camping out, partner.'

Alexei laughed and took her arm. 'Let me introduce you to Felix. He's something of a snob, literary variety. I keep him around because he adds a little class to my peasant upbringing.'

A waiter came by with a tray of glasses containing a yellowish concoction. Alexei picked up a glass for each of them.

'You'll like this. Apricot-flavored vodka. Not unlike a brandy.'

'I'm not much of a drinker.'

'*Na zdorovie*,' he saluted.

'*Provost*.' She took a sip. 'Hmmmm, it's good, sweet.' It tasted as good as champagne, not at all harsh like the liquid fire she had drunk with Yuri.

In the middle of the room fenced enclosures had been set up, with a cow and bales of hay in one, hay and two horses in another.

The room itself was amazing, an enormous circular cavern with a high ceiling, over thirty feet she estimated, windowed all round. On the side opposite the elevators, a grand stairway led to a second level. The band stage was next to the stairway.

'It was designed to be a revolving restaurant, one of those places you go at night to watch the city lights as you dine,' Alexei told her. 'We're revolving now.'

The movement wasn't noticeable but the scenery outside had changed slightly since she entered.

'I have the system activated during parties. I fell in love with the place after it was built. No one since tsarist times has had an apartment as grand as this one. I look down at the city and the entire city looks up at me.' He laughed. 'You only live once, Lara. If you can do it as a megalomaniac and enjoy pleasures that few have experienced, why not?'

She saluted him with her sweet-tasting vodka. 'Why not?' Another couple of drinks and she'd be ready to stand on the rooftop and yell to the poor people clamoring for bread below to eat cake . . .

'Felix, this is Lara Patrick.'

He was tall, slender, probably in his early sixties, she thought. He had very short, thin sandy hair.

'Felix will tell you how embarrassed he is to work for me while I make sure the kitchen staff don't burn down the place. They're roasting a whole Texas cow over an open pit.' Alexei hurried away.

'Why are you embarrassed to work for Alexei?' she asked.

'Alexei is a charmer – if you like spoiled children with vast amounts of money and no common sense. However, he has one redeeming feature: he has a great deal of money and I have none. It is purely for my own capitalist sense of greed during these times of economic chaos that I tolerate this madman.'

Lara was saved from having to find a response to this by an eruption of screaming and shouting from the far corner of the room. She stood on tiptoe to get a peek at the action.

'A mechanical bull,' she said.

'Straight from Gilley's in Texas. We've had one broken arm so far tonight, a deputy minister of trade.'

'What, uh, is your position with Alexei's organization?'

'Everything but change his diapers, and if he could he would have me do that. Actually, my official position is senior aide. Ilya handles the mundane matters and I have the glory of doing everything from counting Alexei's losses for this Tower of Babel he built to preparing his autobiography. Hopefully his investors will permit him to live long enough to make it an autobiography, but I assure you I'm prepared to be his biographer if he runs foul of a lynch mob.'

Lara laughed hard and then took a sip of the sweet vodka. Felix had the sharp, dry sense of humor of a Mr Chips.

Two urban cowgirls wearing skin-tight, low-cut silky outfits no cattle range ever saw moseyed by and gave longer than polite stares at Lara's dress.

'Don't pay any attention to them,' Felix said. 'Word has gotten around that Alexei sent his personal limo for you tonight and you'll find the young women in the room all have their claws out.'

She took another sip. The more she drank, the less she cared about what other women thought.

'Alexei said you knew my mother and father.'

'In a manner of speaking. I was not a confidant of either. However, they were part of a literary and intellectual scene of which I was also a member. It was back in the sixties, the time in America when many young people were rebelling against the Vietnam War, and here in Russia writers and poets were hiding under their beds writing words that could earn them a trip to the labor camps.'

He raised his glass, extending his little finger as he drank. 'I was the editor of a small literary magazine supported by the university. Obviously, we published only approved items because the switch to the printer was never turned on until the censors had stamped the copy. But I was something of a beacon for writers who sought alternative methods of getting their stories published.'

'You mean underground?'

'Underground and smuggling to the West. I am proud to say that some of the best writings of dissenters against the Soviet regime were passed by me. Anyway, that is history, and you are interested in your parents. I met them both on a number of occasions. They were well liked and popular, although your father's appearance in Moscow was as a shooting star. He flashed through the city and the next thing we heard was that he had been killed in Africa.'

'What was he like?'

'Wild and brilliant. He was British, I seem to remember.'

'Yes, from Wales.'

'A poet and a revolutionary. My feeling about your father is that he was less interested in ideology than in adventure. He just loved a good fight. And romance. He was very handsome. Let's see, he must have died when you were a baby. You've seen pictures of him?'

'I have one picture. He died when I was a few months old. He was already in Africa when I was born.'

'My best recollection of your father says a great deal about his wild and impulsive personality. It was at a party, one of those dull university gatherings where we eggheads try to impress each other with our own brilliance. Your father, after more than adequate drinks, stood the party on its head by climbing up on the railing to the balcony and dancing on it while balancing a bottle of vodka on his head. You have to appreciate that we were on the fifth floor.'

Lara laughed so hard she started choking. She stopped coughing and then hiccupped. 'Oops. I'm sorry.'

'That's all right.'

'I'm not used to drinking.'

'Really? How disappointing. I was hoping you were like your father and that after a few drinks you would stand this party on its head.'

'To tell you the honest truth – *hic* – I am nothing like my father. I am extremely conservative and reserved. I've had more to drink in the last couple days than the last ten years. I discovered I really love champagne. And this flavored vodka tastes soooo good.'

'You'll find out that experienced drinkers avoid sweet-tasting drinks because it's easy to drink too much without realizing it.'

'I'm careful. I also have good – *hic* – sorry, control over it. People seem to surrender themselves to the effects. I believe that while liquor can affect your body movements, it's a matter of – *hic* – mind over matter. It can control my body but it will never take my mind.' She held her breath to try and control the hiccups.

'That's an intellectual approach to drinking I've never

heard before,' Felix murmured. 'But so much of life is mind over matter.'

'What about my mother?' she asked eagerly, returning the stare of two more cowgirls.

'Nasty little things, aren't they?' Felix said. 'Alexei is the most eligible bachelor in Russia. Every woman in this room is anxious to find her way into his bed and into his bank account. No one has yet.'

'The bed or the bank account?'

He shrugged and smiled.

Three cowgirls had grouped together nearby.

'Another one of those looks and I'm going to knock the bitches on their tush.' She put her hand to her mouth. 'Oh my God, I've never spoken like that in my life.' She shook her head. 'Moscow must be giving me brain fever.' She grabbed another drink from a passing waiter. 'Tell me about my mother. People back home say I take after her.'

'As I said,' he looked at her drink, 'you remind me a bit of your father. Your mother was physically like you, an attractive woman, but she was a very serious intellectual. Fiery like your father, but while he might get across his point when language failed by punching his opponent, your mother was more inclined to tear the flesh from the enemy with shearing words.'

'In America,' Lara said, 'my mother had the reputation of a violent revolutionary, but she wasn't violent at all. I've read the reports of the riot that turned violent and through our freedom of information laws I obtained the FBI reports on her. She wasn't militant; things just got out of hand.'

'My recollection is that she was a woman of uncompromising opinion,' he said. 'There was a great deal of pressure placed upon her to write anti-American pieces, but other than the anti-war articles, she refused. She would not back down to anyone, not the devil nor his censors. She was a woman of great moral courage. Had what you Americans call guts. If she saw a man beating a child with a stick, she would not have called the police. She would have grabbed the stick from the man and struck him with it.'

Lara's eyes moistened and she stared down at her drink.

Alexei came up and put his arm round her shoulder. 'Is Felix driving you to tears with boredom?'

'We were just discussing her parents. What do you remember about them, Alexei?'

'You know I never met them, Felix. I told you that earlier. Your memory must be getting as thin as your hair.'

'Aren't you going to introduce me?'

The voice was a commanding one and the three of them turned to a woman in a bright red sequin cowboy outfit, red sequin vest, red sequin chaps, red leather pants and silver-plated boots. The woman was Nashville hot.

'Nadia, this is Lara Patrick,' Alexei said. 'You probably recognize Nadia. She's an anchorwoman on the Moscow Evening News.'

Lara did recognize her. A very attractive woman with classic Slavic cheekbones and dark blonde hair combed back in a wet look, there was an edge of hardness to her that kept her from being beautiful. Whatever it had taken to get her to where she was in life, her body language said she wasn't giving up an inch of the territory without a fight.

She was naked under the loose fitting vest and her breasts flashed every time she moved.

'So nice to meet you,' Nadia said, amused eyes sweeping Lara's dress. Lifting her arm to taste her drink, the vest pulled away, exposing her bare breast to the nipple. 'My mother would love your dress.'

Lara flushed and then paled with anger.

Alexei cleared his throat. 'Felix, why don't you tell

Nadia about that idea we have for her own news program while I give Lara a tour of the penthouse.'

He took Lara's arm to lead her away but she held back and spoke to Nadia in a stage whisper. 'You know, you can hide those breast implant scars with tattooing.'

Nadia's jaw dropped.

Alexei pulled Lara away so fast she stumbled beside him. They were across the room before she realized he was laughing so hard there were tears in his eyes. As he led her up the grand stairway, he asked, 'Do they really do that? Hide implant scars with tattooing?'

'It's an old trick strippers use. Most implants are put in through the areolas. A tattoo artist can turn the scars the same color as the rest of the areolas.' She couldn't believe she was having this conversation with a man she hardly knew. Don't let the liquor take control, she told herself.

'How did you know she had implants?'

'Please. Breasts that firm and perfect only exist in male imagination and the wonderful world of silicone.'

'For a woman who leaves an impression of having led a sheltered life . . .'

'I have led a sheltered life. Personally. Someone recently accused me of having been raised in a convent. But professionally, I'm a big city prosecutor. I've dealt with pimps, perverts, prostitutes, murderers and other scum, not to mention their lawyers and their victims. The Nadias of this world are a piece of cake compared to some slimy bastard who has raped and murdered a child.'

'I'm impressed. You have dimensions I never suspected.'

'I'm sorry, Alexei, I didn't mean to go off like that.'

They stopped at the top of the stairs and looked back down at the party.

'I have the impression,' he said, 'there is more to Lara Patrick than I first imagined. I thought you were some sort of commercial spy and now I find out you are much more complicated.'

'Commercial spy? What do you mean?'

'I thought you had been sent to Moscow by certain business interests in the United States and Western Europe who are trying to get a financial foot in Russia by gaining control of my bank.'

She looked down at her drink. 'I've obviously had too much to drink. I think Scotty has beamed me up.' She handed him her half-empty glass. 'Keep this away from me. I've had several in short order. And champagne earlier. I'm feeling a little numb. Does that mean I'm drunk?'

'It's a start. But liquor takes a while to get into your bloodstream, so the best is yet to come. Haven't you ever been drunk?'

'Drunk? I've never even been buzzed. Now tell me about the commercial thing. Why on earth would you think I was a spy?'

He raised his eyebrows and spread his hands. 'Why do you think I was following you yesterday? And then after we met, you left that terrible little hotel where it appeared you were hiding out in secret and moved into a hotel I own.'

'Following me? You were following me? Why?'

'Isn't it obvious? I thought you were involved with his death.'

'Whose death?'

'Nikolai Belkin's. My chief negotiator.'

Chapter 19

The landing at the top of the staircase spread out left and right.

He guided her left, leading her to the end of the hallway. 'This is a private entrance.' He opened a door to an alcove with an elevator. 'That elevator permits me to come and go without entering the public lobby.'

She was bursting with questions but she kept her mouth shut – she needed time to think.

He opened doors in the hallway on the way back.

'Spare bedroom – there are three. Gym, fully equipped. Personally, I hate exercise. It's only the fact that I have a personal trainer with instructions to flog me if I don't cooperate that I keep in good condition.'

He gave her a brief glance at the master bedroom that was in the corridor to the right. 'Fit for a king,' he told her. 'I will let you see the rest of it some day but right now it would get the guests buzzing with gossip.'

'Let's talk about Belkin,' she said. 'You dropped a bomb and we need to clear the debris.'

'Belkin was a . . . how would an American put it? He was a shit.'

'That's one way of putting it.' The numbness was spreading in her system and her balance felt off just a hair. Take hold of yourself, she thought. She started concentrating on how she walked and talked. She certainly wasn't drunk and didn't want to leave that impression.

'But a very useful shit in certain situations. He talked the same language as the old hard-liners and was very useful in dealing with them. When I heard he was killed, perhaps even murdered, and that an American woman was involved, I was naturally curious. Especially after I found out you were staying at a hotel where it's unlikely an American would register.'

'I'm a poor American. Besides, I speak Russian, so I don't have to stay at a tourist hotel.'

'Well, anyway, I arranged with the hotel staff to spy on you.'

'The hotel staff? I hope they have a photocopy machine.'

'A photocopy machine?'

'With all the spying that goes on, they should mass produce their reports. I can't believe the amount of paranoia in this country. It hangs over everything like winter clouds.'

'In Russia, paranoia is simply heightened awareness. Russians don't have to conjure up fictional enemies, not with everyone in the country ready to put a knife in everyone else's back and the rest of the world surrounding us like vultures as we struggle to get on our feet.'

She shook her head. 'I agree. I've had vultures flying overhead since I arrived in Moscow.' Shaking her head made her mind spin a little and she decided not to do that again.

'However, I no sooner learn that the police are investigating you than the hotel security man disappears, apparently off to the country for his health.'

Lara thought about Yuri. 'Are you also paying the police to spy on me?'

'That would have been my next move, but I wanted a look at you myself. When someone from the hotel called my office to report that you had left on foot, the message was relayed to me in my car. I swung by to get a look at this mystery woman only to find myself in a snowball war.' He grinned. 'The rest is history.'

They went up a stairway and through a door that led to another hallway.

'We are on the roof now. My office is through the door on the left and the outdoor spa is at the end of the hallway.' His office had glass windows all along the corridor. Heavy drapes on the inside kept the room private.

He opened the door at the end of the hallway and showed her the steaming spa. 'I'm sure before the night is over some of my guests will find their way into the spa, with too much to drink and not much to wear.'

He closed the spa door and Lara followed him into the office. If the revolving structure was the crown of the skyscraper, the office was the crowning gem. Floor to ceiling windows gave a panoramic view of the city.

'This is my favorite room,' he said. 'I feel like I own the city when I stand here and look down. The room off to the left is Felix's office.'

She stayed back from the windows. Heights made her head spin and she already felt like a Saturn rocket ready to launch.

'I ... I'm sorry, I don't like heights. Usually it only bothers me when I'm next to an open window, but these floor to ceiling windows are scary.' She swayed, dizzy.

'Are you all right?'

'Yes. Perhaps we should go downstairs. I think I need some food in my stomach.'

He closed the office door and led her back down the corridor. 'You've had a little too much to drink.'

185

'No, it's just vertigo.'

They paused at the top of the stairs.

'You haven't asked me why I came to Moscow,' she said carefully.

'I know why you came to Moscow.' He held her arm as they descended the stairs. 'Mr Caldwell from your embassy called today. A courtesy call to let me know that you might attempt to elicit my help in a case that the Ministry of Security has already decided not to reopen.'

'That bastard.' Her temperature went soaring.

'I wouldn't give him that much credit. I think he was really only trying to get an invitation to the party.'

'Good thing you didn't invite him. I'd kick his butt for snitching on me.'

Alexei gave her a double take.

She had more questions about Belkin but she had a problem getting her mind and tongue to coordinate.

At the bottom of the steps, his assistant Ilya whispered something to him.

Alexei squeezed her hand. 'I'm going to leave you in Ilya's hands for a few minutes while I deal with a crisis in the kitchen. He'll get you some food to, uh, offset the liquor.'

Ilya led her to tall stools at the back of the room as a small person came on stage dressed in a cowpoke outfit and announced a Western show to be followed by a contest for best dressed cowgirl. The announcer reminded her enough of the hustler at the carnival freak show to be his twin.

'I'll get you a plate of food,' Ilya told her after he got her settled on a stool. 'Will you be all right alone for a moment?'

She gave him a cock-eyed grin. 'All right alone? I've been alone most of my life.'

'Yes, I see . . .' He backed up and then rushed for the food tables.

A waiter came by with a tray of drinks and Lara grabbed one. She was dying of thirst. She sipped the drink and kicked her legs as a cowboy performing rope tricks entertained the audience.

Her glass was empty by the time Ilya got back.

'You shouldn't have done that. You need food in your stomach before you get totally bombed.'

She leaned toward him and tapped his chest with her forefinger. 'I'm not as inexperienced at these things as one might suspect. I've handled murderers and rapists. I can certainly handle a little liquor.' She leaned closer to say something else and nearly fell off her stool.

'I think you'd better have some food. That flavored vodka is deceptive. It's as potent as the clear variety.'

'Don't worry, I'm in full control.'

The rope artist was followed by a buckskinned Indian throwing knives at a buxom blonde. Lara clapped for each act, a bit harder than the rest of the audience, but she was feeling really good.

Ilya kept watching her out of the corner of his eye. She thought of asking him if he was the one who held General Bova's underwear in the morning and started giggling at the idea.

Then she saw Nadia and two other girls lining up at the side of the stage and her mood blackened. That bitch. She looks like a cheap slut in that red outfit.

'The judges have cast their votes,' the dwarf in cowboy duds announced, 'and we have the results for the best dressed cowgirl and the two runner-ups. The winner is Nadia Kolchak, with Marina Dolchin and Natasha Florinsky as runner-ups.'

The three women came on stage to thunderous applause. Lara was having a little trouble keeping them in focus but it didn't take much imagination to realize that the judges must have been all men and that the less dressed were the best dressed. One of the women had on a clear plastic cowboy suit – and nothing on underneath.

Nadia took the flowers offered as her prize and stepped up to the microphone a bit unsteadily. 'Thank you, thank you.'

'She's – *hic* – had too much to drink,' Lara slurred. 'Can't hold her liquor.'

'Appears so,' Ilya replied.

On stage, Nadia looked around the room until she spotted Lara. 'Now that we've had the best dressed cowgirls awarded, it's time to give the award to the funniest dressed.' She pointed down to Lara. 'And that award should go to our American guest in the dress that looks like something Stalin's mother wore. To her grave.'

The girls on stage giggled and there were a few laughs in the audience, but not everyone was laughing. They were staring at Lara wondering what, if anything, would happen next.

Lara went black with rage and a devil crawled under her skin. 'And those aren't Western outfits,' she yelled to the girls on stage. 'Those are what call girls wear, not cowgirls.'

Lara unbuttoned her jacket and threw it to the side. Murmurs went through the audience as she reached down and pulled her dress off. She turned to Ilya and grabbed his white cowboy hat and put it on her own head. 'Give me your guns,' she told him.

He started to protest so she unbuckled the gun belts for him and put them round her own waist.

Dressed in woolly red long johns, white cowboy hat and a pair of six-shooters, she announced, 'This is how real cowgirls dress.'

The audience went wild clapping and cheering. Alexei came out of the kitchen and stared.

Lara grinned, and strutted a little, drawing her six-shooters. 'Yahoo!' she yelled, pointing the guns overhead and pulling the triggers.

The guns fired, knocking her backwards. Bullets struck the huge crystal chandelier and glass rained down. It sent the audience stampeding in panic. Nadia, terrified by the shooting and the flying glass, fell off the stage trying to get under cover.

Lara sat on the floor with the two smoking six-shooters in her hands and stared up at the world open-mouthed.

'I didn't know they were loaded.'

Chapter 20

Alexei hustled her out the back corridor and down his private elevator. The limo was waiting. They climbed into the limo and Alexei told the driver to wait, he wanted a word with Ilya before they left. He couldn't stop laughing.

'I don't know why you think it's so funny. Who would be crazy enough to have loaded guns at a party?'

'They're all loaded,' he said, still laughing. 'Live bullets were easier to find at the last minute so that's what I gave them.'

'You are a sick puppy.'

'Me?' He gawked at her red woolly underwear, white cowboy hat and crossed gun belts and began to laugh so hard he started choking.

She shook her head. 'I just don't believe those guns could have been loaded.'

He patted her knee. 'You made a believer out of the rest of us.' He grabbed her and gave her a big hug. 'You made my party. Tomorrow this will be in every newspaper in Russia.'

Oh great, just what she needed.

Ilya appeared at the side of the limo and Alexei got out to speak to him.

She was still buzzed, she could feel it, but the shock of shooting up the most luxurious penthouse in Russia had sobered her.

Horribly embarrassed, dying of shame, devastated were words that occurred to her to describe how she should feel – but didn't. She realized she did have some of her father in her and that the liquor had brought out the crazy and wild side. She didn't feel one damn bit ashamed. There was just one thing that bothered her and the moment Alexei got in the car she hit him with the question.

'Are you going to sue me?'

'Am I going to what?'

'Sue me. For the damages.'

'No, my dear, I'm not going to sue you.'

'But that chandelier must have cost a fortune.'

He patted her knee again. 'Don't worry. In a manner of speaking, it was stolen.'

'You forget, I'm a prosecutor in my country. A champion of law and order—'

'Enforced at gunpoint, no doubt.'

'*Touché.*'

'Ilya tells me that a couple of my drunker guests decided to see who had the fastest draw and straightest shot before everyone was disarmed.' He gave a shout of laughter. 'You'll be happy to know,' he chuckled, 'Nadia's injuries aren't serious. One of the guests is a doctor and he's examined her. She'll be black and blue for a couple days. Here, put these on.' He handed her a pair of silver cowboy boots.

'Where did you get these?'

'I had Ilya borrow them from Nadia. She's lying down and won't miss them. They go nicely with your red underwear.'

'In a manner of speaking, you might say you stole her boots.'

'Exactly.'

Lara struggled into the boots as the limo entered traffic.

'They're a little big, but I'll survive. Why am I wearing Nadia's boots?'

'You need them where we're going.'

'And that is?'

'Dancing.'

'Dancing!' She collapsed back against the seat. 'What is it about this country? Everybody wants to go dancing. Do you know how well I dance?'

'It doesn't matter. Where we're going dancing is merely a polite word for letting out the savage within.'

'Alexei, I've had a few drinks but I'm not drunk enough to go out in public dressed in long underwear. That wasn't me back at your party. That was the ghost of my father.'

'Don't worry, at Planet X you'll be overdressed. The sable cape is yours, by the way. To keep.'

'This cape cost a fortune. I'm not taking it.' She pushed it at him.

His face fell like a little kid told he couldn't have candy. 'But I want you to have the cape. It's unique, irreplaceable. It belonged to Tsar Nicholas' oldest daughter. It's been in cold storage in a musty old museum for three-quarters of a century. You will give it life.'

'How did you get it?'

'I bought the museum.'

'Wait a minute. Are we talking about the museum that people say you stole?'

Alexei shrugged and gave her a naughty little boy smile. 'All right, I stole the museum.'

She sighed. He had an amazing amount of boyish humor and charm, but she knew that was partly an act. From everything she had heard and read, he was a hard, tough businessman. The best in Russia, where business wasn't just war as it was in Japan but all-out thermonuclear conflict.

'I appreciate your generosity, but I don't wear coats made from animals slaughtered so people will look good.'

'You wear cow's leather.'

'People eat cows.'

'Russians eat sables. Hell, we eat people when we get hungry enough.' He shoved the cape back. 'You have to at least wear it tonight.'

'Considering my other alternatives, okay.' She grabbed his hand and squeezed it. 'Alexei, you are generous. You are handsome. Fun. Best of all, rich. But I have to tell you something.'

'Yes?'

'I'm a terrible prude. I'm not going to sleep with you for that fancy suite. And I'm not keeping the coat, stolen or not.'

He leaned over and kissed her cheek. 'Lara, there are fifty women back at my penthouse who would sleep with me for a ride in this limo. And gladly murder someone for that coat. I don't expect anything from you in return because I know you really don't want anything from me. That's part of your charm.' He put his fingers to her lips. 'Now be quiet. We're almost there.'

'There' was a semi-industrial area, small grubby-looking factories and warehouses, some of which appeared deserted. As she stared out of the window she considered his comment about not wanting anything in return. One thing she had learned about people who had possessions was that short of winning the lottery, people usually didn't amass great material wealth if they were generous to a fault. Alexei either didn't fit the pattern or he hid his greed nicely.

The limo went round a corner; a block down the street she could see a long line of people in front of an old warehouse.

When the limo pulled up at the curb, a uniformed attendant opened the door for them. Lara stepped out first, the crowd getting a flash of her long underwear and holstered six-guns under the fabulous cape. The people in line whistled and applauded when she put on her cowboy hat.

As soon as Alexei stepped out, people up and down the line whispered his name. Someone shouted, 'Alexei, throw the poor some money!' The crowd broke out in laughter.

The disco doors were pulled open by a doorman who ceremoniously said, 'Welcome, Mr Bova.'

'The next twenty people are on the house,' he yelled to the bouncer, which brought immediate cheers from the eager crowd.

'Do you own this place?' Lara asked, when they finally made it inside.

'Of course.'

She wondered who he had stolen it from.

They went down a dark stairway illuminated by red lights to another door. She suddenly thought about the reception she had got from the crowd and a big grin spread across her face. That was me they were ooohing about!

Stepping through the door at the bottom of the stairs, they were assaulted by lights, music, people, all from another planet.

On the other side of the door the stairway continued down to a rectangular stage packed with dancers. On three sides of the dance area were tiers of small tables and chairs. A dozen feet above the other side of the stage was a long narrow platform where professional disco performers danced.

Music blasted from a dozen speakers hanging from the ceiling. It penetrated into every pore of her body, a tidal wave of noise – no particular beat or rhythm, just violent sound waves pierced by stormy lightning created by pulsating lights.

The people were everything she expected and nothing she imagined. Roman gods danced with girls in jeans and tank tops, women in sequin evening dresses were partnered with guys wearing G-strings. Girls in G-strings and breast tassels hugged and kissed and danced with ... girls in G-strings and breast tassels.

As an attendant with a flashlight led them down the steps, they passed a glass booth were a man and a woman were taking a shower. They were scrubbing each other and the only covering Lara could see was soap suds.

They were shown to a table chained off from the rest. Alexei's name was on the reserved sign.

'Let's dance,' he said.

There was no use telling him she didn't dance. No one else in the place seemed to know how to dance, at least not in any particular style. People on the dance floor appeared to be swaying and moving arms and legs to whatever private message they received from sound effects that were probably destroying billions of brain cells every second.

As she followed Alexei down to the packed dance floor, she looked up and saw a nun dancing on the small stage above. As the nun's habit swayed, the slits in her habit revealed nudity underneath and a very un-nunish penis and testicles.

A group of beautiful young men, all wearing G-strings and nothing else, separated her from Alexei as they pranced by holding onto each other's hips in a daisy chain.

Alexei was instantly swallowed by the crowd on the dance floor and she stood by herself feeling awkward until someone grabbed her arm and spun her round.

It was Hercules, or at least a kissing cousin to Arnold Schwarzenegger – big bronze arms and chest muscles, raw, naked and pumped, muscles and veins bulging from a neck the size of her upper legs, a sack between his legs overloaded and on the verge of bursting with the heavy equipment packed inside, golden thighs rippling with muscles.

He reached round her with long powerful arms and grabbed her buttocks, one huge paw per bun, and jerked her to him until her chin was almost on his chest and she was staring open-mouthed up at his rock jaw.

'We dance.'

Two hours later, Lara burst out of the doors of Planet X and spun in a circle, the sable cape flying. She whipped out a six-shooter and tried shooting the night sky.

'Oh damn it, Alexei, give me some bullets. I wanna shoot out the stars.'

'Get in the car, you're drunk.'

She started to argue and he pushed her into the back of the limo. As the car started moving down the street, she rolled down the window and stuck her head out and pulled the trigger of the gun. 'Bang-bang-bang,' she yelled.

He pulled her back inside and rolled up the window.

'You're crazy,' he told her.

She grabbed him and gave him a big hug. 'Oh, Alexei, I feel like a little kid. I never had so much fun in my life. God, it feels good, as if I've . . . I've added pieces to my life, as if life's a bunch of little pieces and I've been missing most of them.'

He had been laughing when he shoved her into the limo and now his face turned sad.

'What's the matter? Have I said something to offend you?'

He shook his head. 'No, you said something to make me like you even more. People say I'm a kid that never grew up. What they don't understand is that I'm a grown-up who was never a kid. You know what the mark of a great man or woman is? An unhappy childhood. You name somebody great, a Lenin or a Napoleon, a Pushkin or a Tolstoy, and I'll show you an unhappy childhood.'

She leaned back in the seat with a big sigh. 'I'm too drunk to show you anything.' She closed her eyes and fell asleep.

'Wake up, cowgirl, we're back at your ranch.'

She sat up in the seat of the limo and stretched. 'I feel like I just fell asleep.'

'You did.'

She grabbed his arm. 'Did I snore? Tell me the truth, did I snore? I always wanted to know.'

'A gentleman never tells. Besides haven't your boy friends ever told you?'

'My boy friends were all gentlemen.'

The hotel doorman opened the limo door and she got out slowly, still a little dizzy, followed by Alexei.

He embraced her and gave her a kiss on the lips. 'I have to get back and throw out the guests left over from my party. And check to see how much has been stolen. I will call you tomorrow.'

When she reached the front doors, she remembered she was still wearing the sable cape and she spun round, but it was too late, the limo was already on its way down the street.

'I'll have to return it tomorrow,' she told the doorman, who gaped at her outfit. She realized she was wearing only one gun. She must have left the other in the limo.

As she entered the almost deserted lobby, the two clerks at the front desk and the two bellmen followed her progress with wide eyes. Apparently they were not accustomed to seeing a woman wearing red woolly underwear, six-gun, silver cowboy boots, white cowboy hat, and a sable cape that was one of the national treasures of Russia, walk across their lobby to the elevator.

The elevator attendant kept his face pointed straight at the doors as the elevator rose, but she knew he was watching her out of the corner of his eye.

On the way down the corridor to her room, she checked her watch. It was after two. The sable cape slipped off as she dug into her purse for the room key. Too tired to put the cape back over her shoulders, she opened the door to her room, dragging it beside her.

Her nose was immediately assaulted by the reek of cigarette smoke and she froze in the doorway.

Yuri Kirov was sitting across the room next to an open window, a cigarette dangling from his mouth, his feet up on a coffee table, an open bottle of vodka and a glass on the table next to an overflowing ashtray.

Chapter 21

He glared at her with as much arrogance and contempt his handsome face could muster, starting with the cowboy hat then slowly down to open buttons at the top of her long underwear that exposed her breasts, pausing at the six-shooter, and then down to the boots. He grimaced at the sable cape being dragged on the floor.

Moving from her, his eyes took in the luxury suite as if he was seeing it for the first time, the many bouquets of flowers, imported from Holland and the Far East at prices equaling their weight in gold dust; the food from hours past replaced with fresh delicacies and a bottle of imported champagne on ice.

His features remained rigid and stiff as he locked eyes with her again. 'Sable,' he said. 'I have never even felt sable. And you get sable and all this,' he waved his hand around, 'in one night.'

'It's okay. It was stolen.'

'You are a tramp.'

He smoked too much. Drank too much. His suits were cheap, his shirts wrinkled. His necktie was always loose and cock-eyed. He treated her rotten. And acted suspicious as hell. But as far as she was concerned, Yuri Kirov was the sexiest man in the universe.

And best of all he was *jealous*.

She went to him, dragging the cape of the Tsar's

daughter with her, letting it go when she reached the coffee table. Using her knee, she pushed the coffee table aside until his feet dropped off to the floor.

He didn't move, didn't smile.

She sank her knee into the soft cushion of the chair between his legs, pressing against his groin as she leaned down and took his face in the palms of her hands. She forced his face up so she could look into his eyes, those dark, dark, Gypsy eyes. Very slowly, tenderly, she kissed one eye closed, then the other. Kissing the tip of his nose, her lips moved round his, brushing his lips against hers until they melted together.

She kissed him hard and passionately. An expansion of his groin pressed her leg and the surge fired her blood. She broke the kiss and leaned back, feeling his erection against her leg, pressing harder against it. Her desire was uncontrollable. She grabbed each side of the open top of her long johns and jerked them apart, buttons flying off, exposing her breasts, nipples straining against her bra.

He pulled her down to him, burying his face against her breasts. 'No!' he yelled. He pushed her back and she recoiled away from him, shocked, as he struggled to his feet, banging his leg against the coffee table, almost knocking over the bottle of vodka. He walked round the room like a madman trapped in a prison cell.

'It won't work, it can't happen.'

Hurt and embarrassed, she grabbed the sable cape and covered her chest with it. 'What's the matter?' she asked.

'It won't work between us. I can't give you these things,' he waved at the room.

'I haven't asked you for anything.'

He stopped pacing and stood straight, adjusting his coat. 'I am here on official business.'

'Are you crazy? What do you mean official business?'

'I have to warn you against Alexei Bova. He is not what you think he is. The man is . . . a thief, he is robbing the whole country. He's dangerous.'

'He's the only person in Moscow who's been halfway decent to me.'

'He's deceiving you.'

'Why? What does he need from me? I have nothing.'

'Did he tell you Belkin worked for him?'

'Yes.'

'Did he tell you he used to be KGB?'

'Everybody in this damn country used to be KGB.'

'Everything he tells you is a lie and a fraud. He is the most dangerous man in Russia. Even the government can't stop him.'

'You're jealous of him.'

'My feelings aren't important. Your actions are the problem. You have managed to get yourself entangled with a snake.'

'I'll associate with anyone I like.'

'Then you had better give him an invitation to visit you in America because you are leaving Moscow tomorrow.'

'Like hell I am. I came—'

'You came to uncover a crime. But you have also committed a crime.'

Her jaw dropped. 'What are you talking about?'

His features were stern and unyielding as he made the accusation. 'You have violated Russian law by bribing a guard to gain access to government records. If you are not on a plane back to America by tomorrow night, I will arrest you.'

'Get out of here, get out of my room!'

He turned to the door. She jerked the gun from her holster and threw it at him. It crashed into the wall to the right of the door and disappeared behind a chair. She grabbed the vodka bottle off the coffee table but he was out of the room before she had a target.

It was her turn to pace like a wild animal. Her blood was boiling. She had thrown herself at him and he was running her out of town under threat of arrest. She hated him. Why had he suddenly changed on her?

The door across the room opened and Anna poked her head cautiously out.

'Is everything all right, Madam?'

'What are you doing here?'

'I sleep in this room, Madam. Is that policeman still here?'

'He's gone. For good.' Lara put down the vodka bottle, threw her cowboy hat on top of the sable cape and unbuckled the gun belts. 'Return this stuff to Mr Bova first thing in the morning. And tell him I've left.'

'You've left?'

'I'm returning to America tomorrow on the first available plane.' She sat down to take off the boots and add them to the pile.

'Does Mr Bova know you're leaving?'

'Mr Bova knows nothing,' she snapped. 'Look, I'm sorry, Anna, I just got some bad news. Go to bed, please. I need to be alone.'

She dumped the boots on top of the gun belts and started to walk away when she noticed Yuri had left his pack of cigarettes on the coffee table. Not to mention an overflowing ashtray and the half-empty bottle of vodka. She grabbed the cigarettes and vodka bottle and rushed to the open window.

He was standing at the curb below, getting ready to cross the street.

'Hey!' she yelled down. 'You forgot something!' She threw the pack of cigarettes. It dropped toward the street and disappeared in the dark night. 'Here's your booze.' She sent the vodka bottle flying and watched it explode on the street thirty feet from where he was standing.

She grabbed the ashtray full of butts and threw it out too. Sticking her head out of the window, she yelled, 'Kissing you was like kissing an ashtray!'

He looked up at her, his hands in his overcoat pockets, and shook his head. As she leaned further out to yell something nasty, the pavement came up and smacked her between the eyes; she threw herself back, landing heavily on the floor, her head spinning.

She was so angry at him she had forgotten about her vertigo. Crawling across the floor toward her bedroom, her hand hit something lying on the floor.

A bouquet of roses.

Not the incredibly expensive long stemmed ones that Alexei had delivered by the dozens, but a few scrawny roses. All Yuri could afford, she thought. The roses probably cost him a week's wages.

Oh God. She clutched the roses to her bosom and tried to tell herself she hated the bastard, but the words wouldn't come.

At four o'clock in the morning the incessant jar of the telephone ringing forced her to emerge from under the blankets and fumble for the phone. The receiver fell to the floor and she snaked off the bed and onto the floor after it. Belly down on the carpet, she groaned into the phone, 'Hello.'

'This is Minsky,' a nervous voice told her. 'You must come at once. I found your mother's file.'

Chapter 22

She staggered into the bathroom and threw up. The champagne and vodka that had been so sweet in her mouth had curdled in her stomach. She sat down on the toilet and leaned her head against the wall.

She wanted to die.

She was dying.

If this was the life of the rich and famous, she was ready for a farm in Kansas.

She thought about Minsky's call. She was used to his nervousness, but this time there had been a new ingredient in his voice. Fear. Terror, even.

She had spent a whole day away from her fears. A day of being somebody. Andy Warhol's fifteen minutes of fame.

As she sat on the toilet after puking out her guts, she wondered what lay in wait for her at an underground station at an hour when no one was out on Moscow's dark streets except murderers and rapists.

She stuck her head into the sink and threw up again.

The advantage of staying at a first-class hotel was that there were taxis outside twenty-four hours a day. Dressed in jeans and ski jacket with a scarf over her head and tied under her chin, she got in a taxi and gave the cabbie the name of the metro station. The driver had been asleep at the wheel and he yawned and stretched before he got the cab moving.

Her paranoia was riding high and she watched out the back window to see if they were being followed. They had gone a block when the lights of a car that had been parked on the other side of the street about half a block from the hotel went on.

'Make a right turn,' she told the driver.

'The station is—'

'I know. You'll be paid well. Just make the turn.'

The car to the rear made the same turn. Certain it was Yuri's militia car, she leaned forward to talk to the taxi driver. 'Look, I've been with a friend and I think my husband is following me. Lose him and I'll pay you twenty American dollars.'

She caught a flash of the driver's teeth as he grinned. He hit the gas and spun the wheel into a sudden turn, sending her flying back against the seat and the back door.

Twenty minutes later the driver pulled up at the metro station. She had three tens ready to give him. He turned to her with a big grin and she knew she was in trouble.

'One hundred dollars,' he said.

'The deal was twenty. I'm giving you another ten for the fare, which is a lot more than I owe.'

'One hundred dollars. I know the difference between an unmarked militia car and a husband's car. A hundred dollars or I call the militia and tell them where I dropped you.'

She leaned in closer and dropped a ten dollar bill in his lap. 'Call them. When they get here I'll tell them you raped me.'

She got out of the car and slammed the door. As she walked away, he stuck his head out the window and yelled, 'What about my twenty dollars?'

'If you're still here to take me back to my hotel when I come out, you'll get the twenty. If you're not, I'll give it to the next driver.'

She went down the steps as fast as she could. A trip to

Wales to find out more about her father when this was all over was definitely in order. She had apparently inherited some form of madness from him.

The tea shop was closed and Minsky was nowhere in sight. Five or six derelicts, one of them a woman, had bedded down for the night on benches.

Her stomach muscles knotted. This was not a nice place for a woman alone. For anyone alone.

One of the derelicts got off a bench and walked toward her. She started to turn to go back up the steps when he spoke to her.

'You looking for Minsky?' he asked. He was pale and thin, with an ulcer on his cheek and a grubby beard; his frame was wasted by booze or drugs or whatever his brand of devil was. He held up a folded piece of paper. 'Minsky said to give this to you. He said you'd give me money.'

'Where's Minsky?'

'Sick, I think. He looked real sick when he gave me the paper.'

'Give it to me.'

He docilely handed her the folded paper and she gave him one of the ten dollar bills from her pocket and quickly walked away.

The taxi was waiting outside. The driver didn't even turn to look at her when she got in, he just got the cab moving toward her hotel.

It was six o'clock in the morning, still pitch dark in Moscow. She held the paper up to try and read it in the bluish light of street lamps they passed but couldn't make it out.

'Put on the dome light, please.'

He turned on the dome light without saying a word.

The paper was a one-page KGB document titled 'Report of Death of Foreign Subject'. The top half contained statistical information typed into blocks: her mother's name, date of birth, address, occupation, employer, political status.

The word 'Remarks' appeared on the bottom half and a statement was typed below:

Subject 35-year-old female US citizen died at Charsky Institute. Subject had been taken into protective psychiatric custody for treatment and possible re-education after suffering dangerous delusions concerning death of a friend.

Subject mentally unstable at time of admission. Commited suicide before institute staff were able to implement treatment program.

Subject had history of mental instability and had attempted suicide in the past.

To avoid adverse foreign press coverage, subject's death will be attributed to vehicular accident.

Back in her hotel suite, Lara sat in the stuffed chair next to the window and read the document over and over.

Words from the report spun in her head: *delusions . . . death of a friend . . . mental instability . . . attempted suicide in the past . . .*

The report was designed to say just enough to defame but not to explain. It was dated the same day Lara was put on the flight back to the United States. She couldn't remember the time the flight left Moscow but she was sure it was at night. Her mother's death was listed for that same evening at 7:35 p.m.

Not one word about an attack on Lara earlier that day.

Not one word about her mother picking her up at school and taking her to St Basil's.

Delusions . . . death of a friend . . .

What friend?

She took the picture out of her purse and unfolded it, repulsed at having to look at it. The pounding started at her temples. *Outside their apartment, looking up at the landing above* ... The pounding became a searing pain and she shoved the photo back into her purse.

The one irrefutable fact the document established was that the Soviets had lied about how her mother had died: she had not died in a crash with a petrol tanker.

A lie upon a lie.

Lara's hands shook as she read the report for the twentieth time. Kill her and smear her. The dead can't defend themselves and their living champions can be crippled by clever phraseology: *history of mental instability, attempted suicide in the past* ...

Someone took her mother's life. *Murdered her*. Then they covered their tracks by smearing her memory.

A perfect cover-up, she thought. Some bastard maniac kills a woman and has the power both to feed the press a story about a road accident to satisfy foreign observers, and to have a psychiatric report compiled stating that her mother was a suicide to satisfy the Soviet authorities. Confuse and conquer, that's how insiders manipulated bureaucracies.

Minsky hadn't got the document to her out of love or money. He had been motivated by fear. Someone had put a fire under him to see to it that the paper reached her. By now Minsky was probably on his way 'out of town' for his health. If he wasn't floating in the Moscow River.

Puppet on a string. That's what I am, she thought.

Something was terribly wrong. She had been manipulated into coming to Moscow, that was certain. Someone wanted to open up an old murder case. Or wanted her back for more sinister reasons. She was still no closer to discovering who or why. She had paid a lot of money to get into the archives and came out with nothing more than an address for the truck driver. And the suspicion that the address had been spoon-fed to her.

But the report in her hands changed things. It was much more important, a document Minsky had kept from her. On orders from someone. Suddenly the rules changed and Minsky was ordered to give her another clue about her mother's death.

Why? What had changed?

Someone had the power to draw the document from the KGB archives and scare the wits out of the guardian of it. It scared her, too.

Someone had tried to kill her, had killed Belkin, frightened Malinovsky to death – or killed her – and sent Minsky and the hotel security man running for cover. Could the man hanging at the old factory have been Gropski or Minsky? She was convinced it hadn't been her imagination, that it was a body she saw and not a piece of canvas.

How many people were using her as a pawn, she wondered, and who was the target for the checkmate?

Her hands were still shaking as she looked at the report from the Charsky Institute again.

'. . . dangerous delusions concerning death of friend.'

Dangerous to whom? Who was the friend?

That afternoon she sat in a rental car and watched the Charsky Institute from a block down the street.

The neighborhood was a quiet avenue of small professional buildings. The institute was at the corner of the block and was the only facility with grounds. It needed a paint job and tender loving care. Wooden railings and window frames appeared chipped and dilapidated. Broken windows, three observable from where she was parked, had been boarded in. The grounds, grass, bushes and a dozen small trees, were overgrown.

Something about the place didn't feel right to her and it took her a moment to realize what it was. The second floor windows had steel shutters. Once those shutters were pulled closed and no doubt secured by a padlock inside, the rooms became as secure as prison cells.

The place was a prison in disguise.

It had an abandoned look to it, but she knew it wasn't deserted. Three people had come and gone in the two hours she had been parked down the street. It probably no longer housed patients, she thought, but still had a small number of outpatients.

Darkness fell early in Moscow's winter and although it was still only dusk, lights were already being turned on in the buildings along the street. The only lights she saw at the institute were on the ground floor, and those shone through windows clustered near the front entrance.

Her guess was that the institute had fallen from favor either with patients or, more likely, with the government that paid its bills. The Soviets had been notorious for their use, and abuse, of pseudo-scientific forensic psychiatry as part of their control apparatus, an expense the new 'free' Russian society couldn't afford and probably abhorred.

In her senior year in college she had attended a lecture given by Valerian Davydov, a Russian writer who had survived the 'treatment'.

Given the Soviet premise that their system was perfect there was a certain logic in the view that anyone who disagreed with the system must be mentally deranged. That being so, it ought to be possible to 'cure' them. Anyone suspected of deviant thoughts was sent to a psychiatric ward for 're-education' and 'treatment' rather than being thrown into prison. Those who didn't respond to the 'treatment' were found to be criminally sane and were given appropriate punishment.

The thought that her mother might have been subjected to the mental torture of Soviet psychiatric treatment appalled Lara. She was not convinced that her mother had died the day she herself was put on a plane for the West. The date of death given on the KGB report wasn't necessarily accurate. Her mother could have lived for weeks or months longer while she was battered mentally and physically.

Lara jerked open the car door and started for the institute.

She tried to think up a cover story as she walked but her mind was too tired to be creative. Too tired and too angry. She hadn't gone back to sleep after returning from the underground station. When Anna had come into the room to straighten up, Lara dressed and left the hotel after arranging for a rental car. Then she drove around for hours, more because of the thoughts storming in her head than to throw off anyone who may have been following her.

Yuri's threat of arrest no longer had any power over her. Her mother had been a living, breathing person full of love and courage and exciting ideas. She had been killed and labeled a nut. Getting on a plane back to America was out of the question. Not until she had cleared her mother's name and saw her mother's killer punished would she even think of going home.

She had ended up driving by the institute in the early afternoon. Going there had been the next logical step. The Soviets never threw away anything. Her mother's file would be in the building. Somebody wanted her to see that file. And she wanted to see it too.

Chapter 23

A short stone wall surrounded the institute. The pedestrian gate was open and bent back from age and abuse. As Lara got closer, the building looked even more rundown than it had from the car.

She took the six steps up to the front porch slowly, gathering her strength. This was the place where her mother had died. She had to get that out of her mind and keep it out or she would not be able to function.

It's just a building, there's nothing left of my mother here.

The front door was unlocked and complained as she pushed it open. Butterflies swarmed in her stomach as she stepped into the entry hall and proceeded to the reception area. A reception desk was directly in front of her, with a corridor to the right. No one was behind the counter.

A stairway to the second floor appeared first in the corridor, next an elevator; beyond that, office doors lined both sides of the hallway. To the left were waiting-room chairs, and behind the heavy curtains would be the French patio doors she had spotted from the street. French doors were not a popular architectural item in winter-bitter Moscow. Already attuned to the logic of the way the country had been run, she decided the windowed doors had been added to give the reception area a light, airy and friendly feel, and the heavy curtains had been kept shut to make sure no one enjoyed it. Or to keep out the cold, she begrudgingly admitted.

What she sensed most in the atmosphere was hopelessness, as if all the hope had packed up and moved out, leaving the building to wither.

A call bell, the type tapped with fingers, was on the reception desk. Lara gave the bell's plunger a couple of taps and moved over to check out a directory on the wall.

The listing that caught her eye was the Medical Records Department. In the basement. She went down the corridor to see if there was a stairway. A door labeled STAIRS was on the other side of the elevator. The elevator had a pointer and three positions set out above it: basement, ground floor and the floor above. The arrow pointed to the basement.

She heard the elevator doors slam below and the old beast began creaking its way up.

Must be the receptionist returning, she thought. She stepped over to the door marked STAIRS and opened it, coming face to face with a woman in a nurse's uniform.

Lara quickly stepped back. 'Excuse me—'

'What do you want?' the nurse demanded. The woman had an armful of patient files and a set of keys in the other hand. She stepped past Lara and went to the reception desk. 'Are you here for an appointment?'

'No, I – my mother was treated here.'

'Your mother is not here. We do not have in-patients and the last patient appointment was an hour ago.'

'She wasn't treated today.'

'Not today? Well, what is it you want to know about your mother?'

'I need to see her file.'

'Her file? Your mother would have to come in and discuss that with the doctor. Why do you want to see her file?'

'To fill out family papers. You know, family medical history.'

'Why don't you ask your mother?'

'My mother's dead. She died some time ago.'

'When was she a patient here?'

'Years ago. Over ten.'

The woman's eyes narrowed. 'You want to see a file that is over ten years old?'

'I was told you kept files that old. And older.'

'We have every file for every patient since the institute opened thirty years ago. But no one is permitted to see those files without official authorization.'

'How do I get the authorization?'

'You must go to the Ministry of Public Health. They have the forms.'

'Isn't there some way I can do it more quickly? The ministry will take months. They will just make me fill out more and more forms.' Lara reached into her purse and pulled out a wad of bills. 'Perhaps if I can make a donation to the institute . . .'

The woman's face went dark. 'This is a medical facility, not a kiosk. We do not sell our patient files. No doubt that is what Mr Yeltsin wants, for us to sell our patients' secrets so he will not have to provide money for the institute. What little he gives us now is barely enough to keep the doors open.'

Diehard communist, Lara thought. Flashing money was the wrong move. 'Perhaps if I talked to your director, explained the circumstances.'

The woman turned stiffly and marched to a door behind

the reception area. She knocked, then stepped in, closing the door behind her.

Nervously Lara pushed aside a section of the heavy curtains blocking the patio doors and stared out at the overgrown bushes and weeds poking out of the snow as she waited. One of the door latches was half undone and on impulse she gave it a little nudge that opened it all the way. The doors had a painted shut look, as if they had not been opened in years.

A moment later the nurse came back into the reception area followed by a skeleton of a man with dried skin stretched across his bones. Like the building, he had a look that said all hope had fled.

'I am the director. No files can be seen without permission of the Ministry of Public Health.'

'That would take months.'

'That is the rule.' He disappeared back through the doorway.

Lara turned her back on the woman's triumphant smirk and left the building. At least she had established that her mother's file should still be in the building. And no one had asked her name.

Now she only had to do two things. Get back in her car and drive away so they would believe she had left. Then find the courage to come back after dark and break into the Charsky Institute.

Two hours later she parked down the street and turned off the headlights of the car.

At the institute a dim light, just enough to make the building look a wee less than abandoned, shone above the front door. She watched the building for over an hour and determined someone was inside. Lights went on and off in the pattern a cleaning person might make. Or a nightwatchman. The way things worked, or didn't work in this country, it could also be members of the medical staff doing night duty at a time when there were no patients.

With the fall of darkness, every building on the street had been closed up, leaving behind only the empty sidewalks and an occasional light.

Dense clouds buried the moon and cast Moscow in a shadowless night. The radio said a storm was coming and would hit the next evening.

Keeping the engine running to heat the car was not possible. It would have made her presence on the street conspicuous. Instead, she had sat in the car and nearly froze to death, swearing that once she left Moscow she would never go anywhere again where the temperature fell below balmy.

Unable to take the cold any longer, her courage slowly worming away, she put a small flashlight and a screwdriver into her coat pockets, opened the car door, got out, slammed it, and walked with all the determination a 120-pound woman, cold and scared and all alone, could muster.

Earlier that morning someone had dropped the Charsky Institute in her lap. Now she was wondering if that someone would be waiting in the dark building for her.

Glancing back nervously as she neared the front gate, for the fourth time she determined there was no one else in sight. She slipped through the gate and moved off onto the snow-covered grass, her heart pounding. She moved quickly across the lawn to the side of the building where the French doors were located. She was relying on the heavy curtains to smother the sound of her pulling open the door.

A small patio jutted out from the French doors. Each of the wooden steps leading up to the patio felt rotten underfoot; two sets of double doors faced the patio. The one she unlatched earlier was on the left. She took hold of the knob and pulled. The door didn't budge. She pulled a little harder. It groaned but still didn't budge. She took out the flashlight and shone it at the inside latch.

The latch was closed.

Her heart rate shot up twenty beats and she nearly ran off the porch before a thought occurred to her. If they were setting a trap, they wouldn't have locked the door. Encouraging thought, but now she had to figure out another way in.

All the other doors looked solid. A set of metal doors at the bottom of some steps led into the basement on the other side of the building, but there was no chance of her getting through those without a blow torch. She couldn't break a window and climb through – all the windows on the ground floor were at head height.

No, the patio doors were her only chance and a pane of glass was between her and the latch. The only tool she had was the screwdriver she had brought to use as a jemmy in case the medical records were in locked cabinets. Tapping the glass to break it with the screwdriver would make too much noise.

On impulse she hit the pane of glass with her elbow. She never even thought about it, just gave it a blow with her elbow well protected by her ski jacket.

The glass broke with a sharp shattering sound. She listened breathless for a moment. Not a creature stirred.

Swallowing hard, she looked over her handiwork. The glass couldn't have made much noise inside; fragments had fallen to the carpet and the heavy curtains would have smothered the sound. She hoped.

With her gloved hand, she picked and pulled at pieces of glass until she could get her hand in and open the latch.

She pulled lightly on the door. It made more noise than the glass breaking. Taking the frame with both hands, she slowly worked the door open, every creak and rusty groan adding years to her life. She stepped inside and closed the door behind her.

The reception area was dark but the adjoining hallway was lit by a dim night light.

She moved quickly across the reception area and to the doorway labeled STAIRS.

The stairway was a black well.

A light switch was on the wall next to the door but she didn't dare put on any lights. Not knowing if there was an open doorway below, she was afraid to use her flashlight. She slipped in, letting the door close behind her. The door shut with a click and she belatedly wondered whether it was self-locking. She tried the handle. Locked. That's why the receptionist had the keys in her hand when Lara bumped into her. It must be a patient security system from the old days.

The question was whether she was now trapped in the stairwell. Logic told her they wouldn't lock the whole stairwell, that would be too dangerous in case of fire. The top and bottom would have to be left open. If it wasn't, she'd be trapped till they opened the institute in the morning. Those heavy metal doors leading into the basement from the outside were typical fire doors.

Feeling her way cautiously, she got a handhold on the railing and took the steps one at a time. She checked out the door at the bottom of the stairwell.

Locked.

So much for her damn theories. So much for Soviet planning in case of fire.

The door was a thick, wooden one. She examined it with the flashlight. A quarter-inch gap separated the door from the frame and the lock was nothing more than a normal door handle lock, not a dead bolt. She wiggled the

221

screwdriver into the space, pushing back and forth and pulling on the door until it opened.

Night lighting at both ends of the room gave just enough illumination for her to see the layout. The Medical Records Department was before her, a long, long wooden counter and behind it thousands of mud-brown files on wooden shelves.

She tested the handle to the bottom stairwell door from inside the room. It turned freely. The lock only worked from the stairwell side. She closed the door and was making her way toward an opening in the counter when she heard a noise that made her freeze.

The whine of the elevator.

She spun round and stared up at the floor indicator above the elevator door. It was at the second floor. She watched, frozen in place, as the indicator slipped down to the ground floor mark. The whine stopped.

Breathless, she got her feet moving and went round the other side of the counter. She looked back at the floor indicator. It was still at the ground floor mark. Either a nightwatchman or the cleaning people were in the building. The basement might be the next stop. She had to hurry.

She turned back to the files and shone her light on the rows. These had to be either current files or from the past few years, she thought. They certainly couldn't represent over thirty years of patient care. The old records would be archived. But where?

She found a steel door marked KEEP OUT to the rear of the shelves at the far left side of the room. It was secured with an old-fashioned lock that took a key as thick as her finger.

A key as thick as her finger was hanging on a ring to the left of the door. She tried the key in the lock. It fitted.

It didn't surprise her. There was no one to keep out

anymore. Besides, most people were so obedient during the Soviet regime, the key probably hung by the door and only authorized persons used it; when a Soviet sign said keep out, people kept out.

She pointed her flashlight into the darkness before her.

The light picked up rows and rows of shelves containing file folders. More dinosaur guts. Three light switches were by the door and she tested them and found that they turned on lights in three separate areas of the room. The place was only a small fraction of the size of the KGB archives. That was encouraging.

She turned off all but the light in the far corner of the room. She was too scared to go into the place with no lights on at all, even with her torch. She stepped into the room, closing the door behind her but leaving it unlocked. The door swung open half an inch. She closed it again and it slipped open slightly again. She could have solved the problem by locking the door from the inside, but no way would she lock herself in even if she had the key in her pocket. Very slowly she pushed the door shut; it stayed and she backed away.

Moving quickly down the rows of files, she tried to decipher the filing system. No labels were on the shelves. She started pulling files and found they were alphabetical by patient name and date.

It's a piece of cake, she told herself, just keep moving down the aisles, checking files, going down year after year.

Her mother's file was in the last quarter of the room, opposite where she had kept the light on. It was thin, only a few pages; she knelt down and balanced the file on her knee. With the flashlight in one hand and turning pages with the other, she quickly read the file.

Her mother had been brought to the institute the day Lara had been picked up at school.

The diagnosis was: 'Class 3 mental derangement: delusions. The patient made anti-Soviet statements and claimed that her next door neighbor had been murdered and the crime concealed.' She had been tranquilized and taken to a room. A few hours later she was found dead with a hypodermic needle in her right hand and a needle mark on her left arm. There were traces of potassium in the hypodermic.

There was 'evidence' that the patient had suicidal tendencies and had gained access to a medical cabinet located outside her room.

The cause of death was suicide. The time was the same as that listed in the KGB report, about seven thirty in the evening.

Lara stared at the page and willed her mind to remember.

Standing on the landing outside their apartment, her mother giving her a kiss on the cheek when a woman in white, a nurse, stepped out of the apartment above. Her mother asking if anything had happened to Vera . . .

Chills crawled over her and she started shaking.

Vera Swen. The pretty woman in the apartment above theirs. She used to give Lara cookies and candy.

The woman in the picture, the mutilated woman, was not her mother. It was their neighbor, Vera. And her mother knew something about the killing. Lara had seen something too.

The nurse turned round and looked down at them. The eyes—

The elevator started whining. It was coming down to the basement.

Trying to unzip her jacket with shaky fingers, Lara dropped the flashlight and it hit the floor with a bang.

She grabbed it and turned it off. She fumbled with the zipper until she got the front of her coat open. She stuck her mother's file inside and re-zipped the jacket.

She started to make her way back toward the door and the light switches. She was almost at the door when she heard it creak open. She froze behind a set of shelves, her breathing suspended.

The lights went on throughout the archives.

Maybe they don't know I'm in here, maybe it's a guard who thinks the day staff left the light on.

Footsteps sounded from near the door and she strained to listen. The person stopped, hesitating. Then she heard the footsteps start down the center aisle.

The person was checking each aisle.

Lara crept round the end of the shelves and tiptoed toward the door. She heard the other footsteps stop; with a burst of speed she raced for the door. It was open. She hit the light switches, throwing the archives into darkness, and then slammed the door shut. She groped for the key to lock it and it flew out of her hand. In panic she ran, making a mad dash for the stairs.

The elevator doors were open but she flew by them, fearful the elevator took a key to operate at night.

She went through the door to the stairway and paused for a moment when she remembered. The ground floor door was locked.

She raced up the steps, clicking her flashlight on as she went, praying that the upper floor would be unlocked. There'd be no reason for a lock on that level, she told herself. They had to keep people from getting off the second floor, not onto it.

Breaking onto the upper landing, she flew at the door. It was locked.

She heard the elevator doors slam in the basement and frantically shoved the screwdriver between the door and the jam, using both hands to force the blade against the bolt.

The elevator whined upward.

Driven with strength born from panic, she jammed the screwdriver at the lock and the door sprang open. She bolted through it and ran down a corridor lit with the same dim lighting the lower corridor had. She stopped and stared at the elevator floor indicator.

It was almost at the upper level.

She spun round in panic. Break a window and jump and she'd probably break her neck. It was only the second floor but it was probably equivalent to three stories of a building with average ceiling heights. She ran down the hall in mindless panic and dashed into a room to her left as she heard the elevator doors opening.

In the dim light from the hallway she saw that the room was a recreation area with chairs and card tables. A door on the other side of the room had to lead to the upper patio she had seen from the street. It was locked from the inside with a bolt. She slid it aside and opened the door. It opened quietly. She stepped out onto the patio, her feet crunching on the snow. She started to shut the door and her feet slipped out from under her. The door flew back with a bang.

As she struggled to her feet she got a glimpse of someone entering the recreation room.

Someone wearing a white uniform. A nurse's uniform.

She grabbed a folded wooden chair leaning against the wall and raised the chair overhead.

A cyclone of images swirled through her mind.

The apartment building landing. A stranger in white coming out of Vera's apartment. Her mother asking if something was wrong with Vera. The person turning, looking down at them. The eyes ... The eyes of the woman taking her up the steps in St Basil's.

The door opened to her right and someone stepped onto the patio. Lara got a flash of the nurse's uniform and then the face.

The truck driver's wife, the big woman who drove her out of their house.

She screamed and struck out with the chair.

The woman stepped back to avoid the blow and hit the wooden railing behind her. It gave way with a crash.

Chapter 24

'This woman is a danger to Soviet— I mean Russian society.' Orlov, the Ministry of Security liaison to foreign embassies, paused to pour water into a glass from a plastic bottle on his desk. 'The violations of Russian law and the harm to the citizens of Russia have been nothing less than staggering.'

Lara sat quietly with her hands folded together. Next to her, on her right, was Eric Caldwell of the American Embassy. Yuri was sitting to the left.

'It is only by the most fortunate circumstances that her latest victim escaped with significant but non-fatal injuries.'

Orlov turned his attention from Lara to a woman sitting behind and slightly to the left of Yuri. Lara could feel hate glowing where the woman sat with her neck in a brace, her head bandaged, her right leg in a cast, a pair of crutches propped against the chair. Mrs Guk had not weathered her fall well.

'I resent the statement that I'm the aggressor and this woman is a victim,' Lara said. Caldwell touched her arm with his hand but she ignored it. 'The woman would have killed me if I hadn't fought back. She had chased me up two floors.'

Orlov took a drink of water to wash down what appeared to be a bad taste in his mouth. 'The woman, the unfortunate Mrs Guk,' he nodded at the unfortunate Mrs Guk, 'was performing her duty as the sole night staff at the institute when she discovered someone, you, had broken into the institute.'

'She turned a vicious dog on me.'

Yuri cleared his throat. 'That dog may have got loose by itself. I should remind the deputy minister that Lara Patrick had previously forced her way into the Guk residence and made accusations to Mrs Guk about Mr Guk being involved in a cover-up about her mother's death over twenty years ago.'

'Yes.' The deputy minister washed down more bad taste.

'And that besides breaking into the institute to steal a file, Lara Patrick was found to be in possession of documents from the archives of the former KGB that are still considered state secrets. It appears she bribed an employee of the Russian government to give her these documents in violation of Russian law.'

Lara scooted to the edge of her chair. Caldwell put his hand on her arm as a warning to stay quiet but she jerked her arm away. 'The files confirm that there was a cover-up about my mother's death and my own investigations show there is a second death related to my mother's, a young woman who lived above us.'

'This ministry is not involved in a cover-up of your mother's death or any other death. The files you refer to were not given to you because they are the property of the state,' the deputy minister said. 'The only cover-up, as you put it, was an attempt to save your mother's reputation by keeping her suicide out of the newspapers.'

'My mother didn't commit suicide.'

'That is what the records state, Ms Patrick.'

'Which records? The ones that say she died in an auto

accident? Or the ones that say she died of an overdose of potassium? Isn't it a bit coincidental that Mr Belkin died of an overdose of potassium, administered by a nurse, and that my mother died of the same thing at a facility with nurses.' Lara turned and met Mrs Guk's glare. 'Maybe we should find out how long Mrs Guk has worked at the institute.' Mrs Guk began growling. It was the only sound she could make. Her jaw was wired. 'Over twenty years, I would say. And was she—'

'Mr Minister,' Yuri interrupted, 'I checked Mrs Guk's whereabouts on the night Mr Belkin died. She was attending a Communist Party conference. She's still a member of that organization. There are several hundred witnesses because Mrs Guk was receiving an award for loyalty.'

'That's very convenient,' Lara snapped, 'and what about you, Detective Kirov. You always seem to show up at the right places at the right time. Where were you the night Mr Belkin died?'

Yuri turned to the deputy minister and threw his hands up in exasperation. 'So far she has accused everyone in the room of plotting against her, including the ministry and the American Embassy. May I remind the deputy minister that it has been reported that this young woman recently took off her clothes and fired a gun at a party.'

'You—' Lara started out of her chair toward Yuri but Caldwell got a firm hold on her arm and pulled her back down.

Yuri refused to turn to meet her eye. He kept his face straight ahead, directed at the Ministry of Security official. 'As a police officer, I abhor this woman's actions and yet,' he shrugged, 'I am not without sympathy. In my opinion, she has become so psychologically wound up in her mother's death she has begun to see plots and conspiracies round every corner. My recommendation is that the government cancel her visa so she can return to the United States immediately and obtain psychiatric help.'

'I'm not the one who needs their head examined—'

'Miss Patrick, please,' the deputy minister said.

'I'm tired of being pushed around by this whole damn crazy system you people have. You're all afraid of bringing up the past because the whole country has a guilty conscience. I'm not afraid of bringing up the past. If I can't get satisfaction from the government, I'll make my story public.'

The deputy minister smiled but his eyes were cold. 'We are trying to resolve this situation with as little inconvenience to you as possible. However, if you wish us to proceed officially . . .'

'Shut up or they'll charge you,' Caldwell whispered in her ear.

She pressed her lips together and clenched her hands.

The deputy minister sighed and took a deep swallow of water. 'Miss Patrick has one major factor in her favor. One of our most influential citizens has taken an interest in her, uh, welfare, and has vouched for her. I have agreed to release Miss Patrick in Mr Bova's custody—'

'I'm not a child,' Lara protested.

'As opposed to putting her on the next plane out of the country.'

'I'll be glad to have Mr Bova's guidance.'

'Mr Minister, as a police officer it is my duty—'

'The matter has already been decided, Detective Kirov. There will be no more discussion. Mr Caldwell, I suggest you leave first with your client.'

Lara couldn't drop the matter without making one more attempt. 'Wait,' she said. 'Please, you have to listen, you're my last hope. They say I'm crazy and paranoid, but I have one more question. Mrs Guk is here, but where's Mr Guk? What Detective Kirov hasn't told you is that the last time I saw Mr Guk he was hanging like a piece of meat over a vat of acid.' She locked eyes with the deputy minister. 'Show me Mr Guk and I'll admit that I'm crazy.'

The deputy minister turned to Yuri and raised his eyebrows. 'Detective Kirov?'

Yuri sighed and slowly rose from his chair. As he turned toward the door, Lara's heartbeat doubled. As he reached for the door knob, her pulse started pumping in her throat. He opened the door and stood aside as his partner, Stenka, propelled an older man with disheveled clothes and a hungover face through the door.

'This is Mr Guk,' Yuri said.

'I was set up,' Lara said, moving so fast down the ministry corridor that Caldwell had almost to run to keep up with her. 'And Yuri, Detective Kirov, was part of it. There *was* a body. I didn't imagine it.' She stopped and spun round so quickly that Caldwell almost ran into her. 'And putting me in someone's custody as if I were a child.'

'Better than being in police custody.'

'My own government has not been any help at all since I arrived in Moscow.'

'I've explained on a number of occasions the delicate balance of political and social turmoil in the country.'

'But what about human beings? The Russian government and my country's own embassy are so caught up with the world of politics and the fate of nations that they have forgotten about the fate of people. Horrible injustices were done to two women and God only knows who else. And you have not done one thing to help me.'

'Perhaps, Madam,' the diplomat stiffly tipped his hat to her, 'some of us are less human than you. And less imaginative.' He marched away, a soldier wounded in pride.

She followed Caldwell out of the front door and into a chilly Moscow afternoon, the wind catching her coming out of the door and nearly blowing her back inside. She wrapped her scarf round her face and put on gloves as she came down the steps. A horn honked off to her left as a black Mercedes limo pulled up to the curb.

Alexei stuck his head out of the window. 'Need a ride, cowgirl?'

She hurried down to the limo and got in, giving Alexei a big hug after she shut the door. She took off her scarf and gloves and leaned back as the limo moved in traffic. She was worn out from dealing with idiots.

'Thanks for the help. They were trying to make up their minds as to whether I should be shipped to the airport or to Siberia. Either way it would have been in chains.'

'My assistance was not a major feat. Deputy Minister Orlov has been anxious to invest in a computer opportunity.'

She shook her head. 'It's how it works, isn't it? Money talks in politics.'

'Money talks everywhere. Almost everywhere. There are a surprising number of ethical people in Russia. Mostly people over the age of forty. Raised in an atmosphere of pure communism, many people get guilt complexes just talking about money. On the other side are the hungry tigers. Russia is up for the taking and it's the tigers with the largest appetites who will get the biggest mouthfuls.'

'Are you a hungry tiger?'

He smiled. 'There is an old Russian proverb, one that long outdates communism. It's said that if you distribute all the geese in Russia evenly, giving the same number to each person, the geese will soon return to their original masters.'

'I'm sorry, Alexei.' She laughed softly and took his hand in hers. 'I'm so wrapped up in murder I can't make head or tail of geese at the moment.'

He leaned closer and kissed her. 'What I love about you is your honesty. Women around me usually pretend to be fascinated by my every word.'

'Including Nadia?'

'Nadia is a bitch. She's fascinated by my money and how she can get it. I give her a little and dangle more and she in turn ensures that my public image on the country's most watched news programs is not muddied.'

'And what am I?'

'You are ... you are a lovely gem that's been locked away in a jewelry box in a dusty old attic.'

Embarrassed, she changed the subject. 'Tell me about the geese, why do they return to their owners?'

'Some people gather material wealth, others don't. Those who don't think in terms of gathering geese will soon find their birds have flown to those who do.'

'You gather lots of geese, don't you?'

'I gather toys. Making the money to get the toys is just a means to an end. And it's not difficult to do. You see, it's easy to win when you don't play by the rules.'

'You don't play by the rules?'

'Of course not. There are no rules in Russia. Even if there were, I wouldn't play by them and neither do most of the new rich emerging from this chaos. Look at your own country. The great fortunes were founded by men who violated all the rules. The railroads that opened and united the country were built on land swindled from the government and the bones of thousands of Chinese coolies who died hammering the spikes.'

He squeezed her arm. 'Imagine it, Lara, there's a whole country up for grabs, a country over twice the size of your own. Out of all this chaos some of the greatest fortunes the world has ever seen will be made over the next few years. Now, I can sit around and watch my geese being stolen or I can steal everyone else's.'

She turned away from him and stared out of the window.

'What's the matter?' he asked. 'You don't like my bluntness.'

A question nagged at her. 'Alexei, why are you helping me? If you're lusting for my body, I have two surprises for you. I'm not going to sleep with you and I probably wouldn't be worth the price, anyway.'

'You're wonderful. It's a rarity to find a beautiful woman who doesn't know she's beautiful. And you're right, my motives are base. You're a wonderful centerpiece for my parties. The whole country is talking about your last performance.' He grinned and shrugged. 'I love the attention.'

'At the party you told me Belkin—'

'Stop. No more questions. Relax your mind and your suspicions. This weekend you will step back in time and share with me the glories of a past age.'

She suddenly noticed that they were heading out of town. 'Where are we going?'

'To my dacha.'

'Your dacha? Why are we going there?'

'I am having a party there tonight. Besides, I want to show it off to you. It is the biggest dacha in all of Russia.'

'Is it the palace?'

'Yes, the palace I stole. Seventy years ago the Bolsheviks stole the palace by murdering the prince who owned it. Now, with the stroke of a pen, I have stolen it back. An example of capitalism at its best.'

'Alexei, you have done some nice things for me, a stranger, and you haven't asked for anything in return. You are good-looking and dynamic and rich and generous and crazy. I think I could learn to love you. But I don't think I could ever really like you as a fellow human being. Even with all your charm, you're just too much of a bastard. And I do mean bastard.'

Chapter 25

An hour out of the city, the limo pulled up to a sleigh with two horses waiting by a stone wall.

'It's a troika,' Lara said. 'We're going to take a sleigh ride!'

'You can't arrive at a palace built in the days of Catherine the Great in a car. What's the use of owning a palace if you can't live like a king?'

She jumped out of the limo and went directly for the horses, giving them equal attention. 'Are they cold?' she asked the troika driver. The driver wore a tall hat and old-fashioned greatcoat from a past age. The only thing that separated him from the pictures in history books of an eighteenth-century nobleman's troika driver were dark blotches on his face from a skin disease. Leopard's skin is what the kids at school cruelly called a young boy with the ailment when she was a teenager.

'They're Russian horses, Madam, born with icicles between their teeth.'

'I just remembered I'm not a Russian horse.' She started back for the limo when Alexei stepped out holding the cape. 'Forget something?'

'I'm just going to borrow it,' she said, letting him slip it over her shoulders.

They climbed aboard the troika and let the driver cover

their laps with a huge bear blanket. Lara pulled it all the way up to her chin and snuggled close to Alexei.

She kissed him on the cheek. 'You make me feel like a little kid.'

'I'll tell you a secret,' he said. 'Everyone around me, Felix, Nadia, my business associates, all of them try to make me act my age. They want me to throw away my toys. You're the only one I've found who wants to play with me.'

The troika went through a wide gate in the stone wall and down a snow-covered road crowded by trees heavy with snow and glistening with icicles. Sleigh bells jingled as the horses stomped and blew vapor from their nostrils.

'I can understand your friends. They've already had their childhood. What happened in your life, Alexei? What caused you to skip being a kid?'

She felt his body tense next to hers.

'I don't mean to pry.'

'No, that's all right. You're the first person I've met that I would like to share it with. I don't know who my parents were. And I was a sickly child, the type no one wants. Ugly, too.'

Another orphan, she thought. Yuri had said he was an orphan too. Not so strange in a country where millions were killed by war and politics. The starvation and deprivation during and after the Second World War were almost unimaginable.

'You can't sell me on the ugliness,' she said.

He looked away from her as he spoke. 'Plastic surgery can do amazing things. And I was a teenager during the renaissance of Soviet science and medicine.'

As the sleigh passed a small cottage on the right, a family of four, two children and their parents, stepped onto the porch and waved. The entire family was dressed in peasant costumes, and the man wore a great black beard.

Alexei waved back.

'Don't tell me,' Lara said. 'Those are peasants, serfs, and they belong to the lord of the manor.'

He chuckled and snuggled down in the blanket like a naughty little boy. 'Of course. He used to be a gunnery officer on a battleship and she was employed in a factory that made washing machines that ripped clothes. Now they're both unemployed, but they have a nice little country dacha to live in and all they have to do is wave to the prince a couple of times a month. We should be so lucky.'

'Alexei, you are not just an arrogant bastard, you are a spoiled bastard.'

'Yes, isn't it wonderful?'

They broke out of the forest and the palace was before them, a wide, gray-stone structure with carved frieze along the roof and tall, narrow windows. Four pillars in front flanked a short set of stairs up to the huge doors. The palace extended two tall stories, perhaps as high as fifty feet, and was about a hundred feet left and right from the front entrance before it dropped down to one story at each end. The end wings had ground-floor balconies enclosed by a bronze balustrade.

'It's beautiful. I expected a huge ugly thing like a castle. This is more like a French chateau.'

'There's a private lake in the rear,' he told her. 'I would have it polished for ice skating for the party tonight, but there's a storm coming in and we don't expect the party to go on late.'

'Why don't you delay the party if there's a storm coming?'

'Because everything has been set – costumes, musicians, servants. Besides, I don't care if my guests have to drive home on icy roads in a blizzard. It's a small sacrifice to make to be near me.'

As the troika pulled up at the palace, two servants in livery came down the stairway with a set of wooden steps which they placed beside the carriage. Then they assisted Lara and Alexei as they stepped down from the sleigh.

She had a hard time keeping a straight face as Alexei assumed royal airs. The great hall of the palace was as grand as the exterior. Huge crystal chandeliers hung like pregnant diamonds from the ceiling; gold leaf trimmed the railing to dual stairways that rose to the second floor and also covered much of the elaborately carved ceiling. Between the stairways was a fireplace large enough to burn small trees in. It looked like a forest was on fire inside it.

The great hall was warm and it couldn't have been from just the fireplace across the room. 'There's modern heating, isn't there?'

'No expense was spared by the previous owners, the Union of Soviet Socialist Republics. Modern heating, modern plumbing. It was on the books as a museum, but the most powerful men in the Presidium often used the place to entertain. I didn't really steal this place from the people. I took it from what you call the fat cats.'

Ilya, the assistant she had met at the Western party, came down the stairway to greet them. Lara shook his left hand.

'Miss Patrick's room is ready. I'm afraid Nadia is a bit perturbed. She's accustomed to having the room Miss Patrick is occupying.'

'Alexei, I don't care which room I'm in.'

'I do. I deliberately had Nadia moved down the hall and placed you closer to my suite.' He grinned. 'Royal prerogative. Nadia has been exceptionally bitchy lately. And the price of her friendship has gone up. This is my way of telling her to get back in line.'

'All right, but if the woman scratches my eyes out, I'll sue you.'

'The great American pastime. In this country you'd get an award of six roubles for two eyes. Ilya, show Lara her quarters. Then I want to go over the arrangements for tonight. Is Felix here?'

'He's in his office in the west wing.'

'Do you mind if I take a walk after I check into my room?' Lara asked.

He gave her a kiss on the cheek. 'I can have you carried on a sedan chair by slaves if you wish.'

'How sweet.' The two words came from the top of the stairway where Nadia glared down at them. 'I hope I'm not in the way.'

'Show Lara to her room,' Alexei told Ilya. He beat a hasty retreat toward some inner domain of the palace while Ilya led Lara up the stairs.

Nadia had disappeared by the time they reached the landing at the top.

Grounds covered by winter's mantle extended from the back of the palace to the lake. The lake was frozen. It's too bad there's a storm coming, she thought, it would be fun to skate. The idea brought a vague recollection of being with her mother and skating on a frozen pond in a park near their Moscow apartment.

Storm clouds were brewing, but there was hardly a breeze, and despite her abhorrence of even the threat of getting cold, walking alone in the forest provided needed peace and quiet to do some thinking. Start playing things smart, she told herself. She had to stop being led by the nose. Getting an ally would be the first smart move. Alexei was rich and powerful. A man who could steal a palace and thumb his nose at the government from his perch above Moscow should be able to open doors for her. Yuri obviously wasn't an ally. He had lined up with the keep-the-past-buried mentality she had encountered since she arrived in Moscow. He seemed to have an almost pathologi cal obsession with getting her on a plane out of Moscow.

The thought stuck with her as she walked alongside the lake. Why would a policeman investigating a chain of deaths want a key witness to get out of Moscow? That morning after viewing Belkin's body, he should have taken possession of her passport so she couldn't leave Moscow, not argued with her because she didn't want to leave. And she wondered again about the way he popped up every-where. When the Gypsy woman was warning her about being followed, he was behind the tent. When Belkin was pushed in front of a truck, he would still have been around. When she was being chased by the Guks' dog, he was in the area. What was he doing near the Guks' house anyway? He said he had followed her taxi, but she never noticed a car to the rear.

She really liked him. Liked him better than any man she had ever met. Why was he turning out to be a louse? Damn him. She started walking faster, heading back for the palace. She had thought of the first bit of help she wanted from Alexei: a background check on Detective Yuri Kirov. Most importantly, what case had he been working on the night she saw him behind the carnival tents?

The business about Belkin working for Alexei also bothered her. She needed to know more about Belkin and his activities, but she'd have to tread carefully because Alexei didn't want his fantasy weekend disrupted with reality.

As she approached the west wing of the palace she saw

Felix coming in her direction. He waved and said hello. 'I was also taking a walk,' he said as he fell into step beside her. 'Only my route took me in the other direction. What do you think of Alexei's little toy?'

'The palace? Everyone should have one. Unfortunately, if it was mine, I'd be bankrupt just paying the heating bill for a month. How long is the government going to let him keep it?'

'That is the subject of a meeting we're having tomorrow with the ministry that considers the palace within its domain.'

'They're coming out here?'

'No, we will go to them. Alexei won't allow them on the property. By the way, did I tell you that I might have published one of your father's poems?'

'Really? Do you still have it?'

'I'm not sure. The thought occurred to me a moment ago as I saw you walking. It is a possibility.'

'I'd love to have a copy. I have nothing of my father's, just a few comments about him in letters written by my mother.'

'I will look. I don't have the actual magazines with me, but I do happen to have an index of literature that I've published over the years. It's one of the reference works in the office I've set up here at the dacha. Why don't we take a minute and check it? If a poem's listed, I could get you a copy in a few days.'

They went up a short stairway to the balcony of the west wing and through double doors to a small, cozy library.

'Oh, I love this room,' she said.

It was a stately room but intimate, with thick carpets, a roaring fire, old but comfortable furniture, and book-shelves soaring to impossible heights. Behind a desk hand-carved from Siberian rosewood were tall windows giving a view of the front of the estate. The fireplace was in the wall opposite the desk, with a large mirror above, a clever arrangement that permitted a person to sit at the desk with window light behind while the lovely grounds reflected in the mirror above the fireplace.

'It's different from the other parts of the palace I've seen. It's more . . .'

'Me, more me,' Felix said. 'This room was the one real luxury I've demanded from Alexei for a decade of faithful service. I fell in love with the room the moment I walked in. It was almost bare then, just a few pieces of antique furniture and some volumes about the life of Lenin. The shelves probably hadn't had their fill of books since they belonged to a prince.'

He walked round the room, running his fingers along bookshelves.

'You did a wonderful job.' She almost asked who Alexei stole the books and furniture from, but caught herself. Felix was so proud and pleased with the room he would have taken offense at her joke.

'Let's see,' he said, 'my index is over here. While I'm searching for your father's poetry, why don't you take a look at that stack of pictures on my desk and give me your opinion about which ones should go into Alexei's book.'

'I shall look forward to reading it when it's published.'

'It's sort of a horror story in a way. There are similarities between Alexei and Tsar Peter that are startling.'

'That's quite a compliment.' She picked up the stack of photos and started looking at them.

Felix grinned at her. 'I wasn't talking about Peter the Great, my dear, but Peter III, the eccentric madman who used the palace guards for toy soldiers until his wife and lover had him murdered.' He chuckled at his own humor and she couldn't help but join him. She enjoyed his dry, cutting wit. Alexei must have a thick skin to keep Felix around, she thought.

The first picture was of Alexei receiving some sort of medal. He was in a military looking uniform and an older man with general's stars was pinning a medal on his chest. Alexei looked quite a bit younger in the picture and she mentally dated it about ten or twelve years back. The next picture was a banquet scene. Her eyes scanned dozens of other men at the table in the room, but none was familiar to her except the man who had been in the general's uniform earlier. He was in civilian clothes and so was Alexei and all the rest of the men in the room. She noticed words inscribed on curtains behind the tables: COMMITTEE OF STATE SECURITY.

A chill ran through her. 'Committee of State Security' was the official name of the KGB.

She held the picture in one hand and picked up the next one. Her hand began to tremble as she stared at the picture. It was a party scene, people standing around talking and laughing, drinks in hand. Three people in the foreground leaped out at her – two women holding drinks and laughing and a man bent double with laughter, his drink spilling from the glass he held. The woman on the right was her mother. The woman on the left was Vera, their neighbor. The man between them was Alexei.

'Lara?'

She turned slowly. Alexei had entered the room and was standing near the door.

'I see Felix has put you to work.'

Felix looked up from a book and adjusted his glasses, smiling at Alexei as he said, 'I thought she might give me a hand with the photos for your autobiography. You know how concerned I've been about selecting just the right ones.'

'Excellent. Did you find anything?' he asked Lara.

She put the pictures back on the stack and gave him a weak smile. 'No, I didn't.'

'I'm sorry, Lara,' Felix said, 'but I was wrong about having published your father. I don't see anything by him listed.'

'That's okay,' she managed, forcing a smile.

'Your costume has arrived,' Alexei said. 'You have to go upstairs for a fitting in case any alterations are needed.'

'Of course.' She walked by him, keeping her face neutral.

As she stepped outside the room, Nadia was coming down the hall. She gave Lara a dark look and as the two passed each other, the door to Felix's office slammed so hard it startled both women.

Lara kept walking, not acknowledging Nadia's presence.

Upstairs in her room she went to the window and stared out at the frozen lake and the snow-draped forest.

Miles from town and I'm a damn prisoner, she thought.

Her door opened and she turned as a maid with a club foot entered with a costume draped over her arm.

Anna smiled.

Chapter 26

She had a plan. It wasn't perfect and it would probably get her deeper into trouble, but at least it was a plan.

First, she was determined not to get drunk. Not that she was afraid of making a fool of herself – there was no way she could top her Annie Oakley act. Wearing a white wig, black cheek mole, powdery facial make-up and bold blue eye shadow, wrapped in a billowing pearl-colored gown that gave her the figure and look of a wedding cake (how did women wear these tents two hundred years ago? she wondered), she passed through the crowded ballroom, not recognizable as the woman who shot up Alexei's last party.

She felt slightly less ridiculous in her costume than most of the other guests looked in theirs; eighteenth-century Russian clothing did no more to enhance twentieth-century pot bellies than cowboy outfits did.

Making her way toward the front entrance, a glass of champagne that had barely touched her lips in one hand, a fan in the other, it struck her that everyone always seemed to talk about how Alexei spent money. No one ever mentioned feats of financial wizardry in making money.

The second part of the plan was to get through the crowd and out the front entrance without being seen by Alexei, Felix, or the hoard of spies that she imagined must monitor her every move.

Outside, she'd make a dash for Felix's office. Then, picture in hand, or at least tucked somewhere beneath the billowing dress, she'd return to the party. As Alexei had said, the party wasn't destined to last long, the storm was already blowing arctic air and snow was expected shortly. When that happened, she'd flow out of the front doors with the guests and hitch a ride into town, hopefully with a charitable looking couple in a warm limo.

Simple and neat, she told herself. All she needed to carry it off was a miracle. What she would do when she was back in Moscow she hadn't worked out yet.

Near the vestibule leading to the front doors, she paused to check out the enemy. She hadn't spoken to Alexei or Felix since the incident in the library. At the moment Felix was engaged in a discussion with several people near the center of the room. Alexei had disappeared down the west wing hallway a moment earlier with a harried Ilya on his heels, not on his way to Felix's office, she was sure, but to do battle in the kitchen. That was her interpretation after watching Alexei lashing out at servants and Ilya scurrying behind him patching wounds. Alexei is in a foul mood, she thought, his manner toward the servants not at all like the Old West party where he had simply harangued them to move faster.

She slipped into the vestibule. Only one attendant stood near the great palace doors. She could hear voices in the cloakroom off to the left.

Smiling at the doorman, she said, 'I left something in the car. Be back in a moment.'

'It's very cold outside, Madam. I'll get it for you.'

'That's all right. I love a little fresh air.' Liar. She was going to freeze.

She set her fan and champagne glass on a table next to the door and smiled bravely as he held the door for her. She stepped out into the night air casually, as if she was taking a walk along the beach.

Jesus. It was colder than a witch's tit.

As soon as the big door closed behind her she lifted her dress and ran for the west wing. It was almost impossible to keep the wedding cake dress from dragging on the ground and there was no way to see where she was putting her feet.

Her plan was based on the premise that the palace doors didn't get locked. Lara had heard Alexei tell Ilya that doors on the ground floor should be left open so the guests could wander around and admire the palace. She assumed that meant all the doors. If the doors leading to Felix's office from the balcony were locked, her arms would be frozen brittle and ready to break off by the time she made it back to the front entrance.

The night wind swept inside her tent dress and nearly lifted her off her feet as she went up the half-dozen balcony steps. Her teeth were chattering as she made it to the balcony doors.

The door handle slid down easily and she slipped inside and shut the door, leaning back against it, so damn cold her exposed skin felt bruised. The fireplace was brightly lit and she rushed over to it, glancing up at herself in the mirror above it. Her face looked pale even under the heavy white powder.

She forced herself away from the warmth to examine Felix's desk. The manuscript was still stacked on the desk, but the pictures were not in sight. She started leafing quickly through the thick manuscript to see if the pictures had been tucked inside. A movement caught her eye and she looked up at the mirror above the fireplace. A face in the frosted window behind her was peering in.

Lara spun round but the face had already disappeared.

She ran for the door leading into the west wing corridor, opened it and flew through. At the other end of the corridor servants were busy with food tables lined up against the wall. A group of people with Felix at the head, engrossed in conversation, had started down the hallway. She opened a door to her right and darted through – almost screaming as she came face to face with a woman.

Nadia.

The Moscow Evening News anchorwoman grabbed her arm and jerked her out into the cold night. She slammed the door behind them and the two women stood facing each other, the bitter night air brushing their clothes and clawing at their skin.

'You're spying on me,' Lara said.

'And you're spying on Felix.'

'What do you want?'

'The same thing you do. Felix has something on Alexei. I heard them arguing about you and a picture after you came out of Felix's office today. What's so important about the picture?'

'Why do you want to know?'

'Don't be a fool. Alexei has money, more money than you can imagine. And it belongs to all of us.'

'And you want a share.'

'Just as you do.' Nadia glared at her.

Lights went on in Felix's office, and through a window to her right Lara saw Felix and the people from the corridor enter the room.

'I've got to get inside,' she told Nadia. Her teeth had started chattering again. If she stood outside any longer, she'd be frozen in place.

Nadia spoke in an urgent tone as they hurried back toward the front door. 'Alexei has plenty of wealth for all of us.'

'I don't want his money,' Lara said.

Nadia scoffed. 'You and Felix, Felix the old-time communist, but you've seen how he decorated his office and library. The bastard pretends he doesn't care about money, but I know he has some sort of control over Alexei. Alexei hates him, but he keeps him around. And sometimes Felix acts like he's in charge. I've seen Alexei back down to him. Oh, they do it very subtly, but I can tell when Alexei eats shit.'

Lara wanted to tell her she didn't give a damn about her greed and her plots, but it struck her that she might be able to use Nadia. The woman obviously had an inside track to whatever was going on.

Unable to stand the cold any longer, fifty feet from the front doors Lara broke into a run but stopped as Nadia grabbed her arm.

'Listen to me. We have to get our hands on that book. They're all going back into town tomorrow and returning tomorrow night. They have some big meeting at one of the ministries. I know the routine. Felix will take the book with him in that black attaché case he carries. He never goes anywhere without it. He'll lock it in his office. It's at the top of the penthouse, next to Alexei's office and the spa. I'll meet you at the back street level entrance tomorrow at noon.'

'At the tower?'

'Yes, but you have to get the key to the elevator and the back doors.'

'Me? Why me?' Lara's teeth were chattering so badly the words came out in chips. A light snow was falling.

Nadia grinned with malice. 'Alexei keeps a complete set of keys for everything he owns in a cabinet in his dressing room closet. I've never been allowed in his room. You can get it tonight after he fucks you.'

'After he what?'

'Don't act innocent with me. I'm not the one with the sable cape.'

Lara turned and ran to the front doors. Blood rushed to her head and she felt faint as she hurried into the warm interior. She moved quickly past people to cross the room and get to the roaring fireplace. Standing close to the fire, she roasted each side of her body. It felt heavenly.

People were already starting to leave. She realized she was going to have to make her move to get a ride into town, but she held her ground, staring into the fire. Nadia's proposition was tempting. All except the part about sleeping with Alexei.

Nadia was suddenly at her side holding two cups. 'This will warm you inside,' she told her, holding out a cup.

'I don't want anything to drink.'

'There's no booze in it. I promise.'

Lara took a sip of the drink and eyed the crowd moving toward the front doors. Alexei was there, saying goodbye to guests. If she was going to leave, she'd have to exit by one of the other doors and approach people outside where the cars were.

'I think I misjudged you,' Nadia said.

The drink tasted good, hot and sweet. 'What do you mean?'

'I saw the expression on your face when I mentioned fucking Alexei.' Nadia had stepped closer and her voice was lower, huskier. 'You don't understand what I've had to go through. I'm being pressured.'

Lara didn't have the faintest idea what the woman was driving at. The room had started glowing brighter and then dimmer, brighter and dimmer. People and furniture got bigger, then smaller. Everything was cock-eyed.

She wanted to ask Nadia what was in the drink but her lips felt much too thick to open and close properly and the words came out as baby talk.

Nadia laughed hysterically.

Nadia held on to Lara's arm tightly and helped her down the stairs to the sub-level of the palace. 'You need to clear your head and sweat out some of the cold you've been exposed to,' Nadia told her. 'A sauna will do both.'

Lara nearly fell when her foot struck the floor at the bottom of the steps and Nadia struggled to hold her up. 'You sure don't have much tolerance,' she said. 'I just wanted to make you feel good.'

A maid who had fallen asleep on a bench near the sauna woke up at the sound of the two women approaching and came forward to help.

'Is the sauna ready?' Nadia asked.

'Yes, Madam.'

'Help me get her clothes off,' she told the maid, 'in the sauna where it won't be cold.'

Between the two of them they started stripping Lara of her costume. Lara tried to tell them to stop and to push them away, but her mind was swimming around her head and her hands and feet felt twice their normal size.

When Lara was naked on a sauna bench, Nadia told the maid she could go and then undressed herself. Then she pulled Lara into a sitting position, slipped behind her and pulled her back against her own nakedness. She put her hand round Lara's waist and pressed her against her bare breasts. She whispered in Lara's ear as her hands travelled up Lara's abdomen and cupped her breasts. 'Ever do it with a woman? I like it both ways.' She kissed Lara's neck and tickled her ear with her tongue. 'Sometimes at the same time. I like to fuck a woman's cunt with my mouth while a man's pumping me doggy style,' she whispered. 'You ever had it at the same time?'

The door to the sauna opened and Nadia turned to tell the maid to go away.

It was Alexei, not the maid.

Chapter 27

Lara lay awake staring up at an ornate ceiling and tried to place herself in the universe. She moved her toes and they operated. She tried her hands and arms next. It slowly came to her who she was and that her head had been stepped on by a tyrannosaurus.

She shot up in the bed, her head spinning from the sudden movement.

Where the hell am I?

It was a big room, grand, more than twice the size of the room assigned to her in the palace.

Alexei's room.

She was naked. Not a stitch of clothing on.

'Oh no.'

She crawled out of the blankets and sat on the edge of the bed, her mind taking a swim in a whirlpool for a moment before she rescued it. Think, she told herself. What happened last night? She remembered going to Felix's office. Freezing outside while Nadia talked of blackmail. Something in her drink. The sauna. She felt her bare breasts and blushed. That bitch. She drugged me. And then there was . . . Alexei.

She jumped off the bed and looked at it. Were the three of us romping on it last night? No, she remembered Nadia had said she had never been allowed in his room.

A white terry cloth robe was draped across a chair near

the bed. The robe had a note attached to it: 'Darling, last night was the most incredible experience I've ever had with a woman. Making love to you was a journey to nirvana.'

She collapsed back down on the bed and put her head in her hands. Please God, stop the world and let me off.

Everything was wrong. Alexei. The note. The situation. *Think*, she hit her forehead with her palm, *think*. The consequences of the note were too horrendous for her to analyse at that moment.

They were probably all gone, back to the city. Nadia said they would be leaving. Some big meeting at a ministry. Nadia wanted to meet her at the penthouse at twelve o'clock. The ornate clock on the fireplace mantel said it was a little past ten. The palace was an hour from the city. She could get dressed and be at the tower by twelve. If she wanted to.

She didn't have much choice. It was either the tower or the airport. And she wasn't running away. She was going to get the picture and storm the American Embassy. If Caldwell looked at her cross-eyed, she would go to every foreign news bureau in Moscow and tell them about her mother, the neighbor woman, Alexei and Felix, Yuri and his penchant for hanging around places where people died, Belkin, the man at the acid bath and, hell, being drugged and molested.

She would either make headlines or they'd commit her, but she wasn't leaving and she knew she had absolutely no one to turn to.

She put on the robe and started for the hallway to sneak down to her own room when she remembered Nadia's comment about keys. The bathroom to the suite was bigger than her room at the Gorky; leading off from it was an even larger dressing room. She found a square metal box on the wall in the dressing room. It didn't surprise her it wasn't locked. Hanging inside the box were a couple of dozen keys, each with a little white tag that identified their purpose. She chose a set of three marked 'Tower' and slipped them into her robe. Another tag said 'Tower offices' and she slipped them into her pocket too.

She understood why Nadia would have had a hard time getting to the keys if she hadn't been invited to Alexei's bed – the only way in or out of the grand suite was back through the bedroom.

She opened the bedroom door and checked the corridor. It was clear. She went out and headed for her bedroom, slipping quickly inside, checking the hallway again to see if she had been seen. She quietly closed the door and turned as her bathroom door opened and Anna limped out. Lara heard running water coming from the bathroom.

'I'm running your bath, Madam.'

Lara forced a smile. 'Still here, I see.'

'Yes, Madam. Everyone has gone but the servants. After the clean-up, some will return to the tower, others will stay here. I will go wherever you go.'

No, you won't. 'Order me a car, Anna. Now.'

The storm had passed and left several inches of snow. Gray clouds and a sharp north wind put a dull edge on the day and kept the new snow from looking fresh and white.

As she sat in the back of a Mercedes limo and whizzed past lesser mortals and their lesser cars, she rather regretted that Alexei had turned out to be a louse. It would have been nice to have a rich and famous friend – even though she had discovered that friendship in Moscow had about the same enduring quality as a game of Russian roulette.

People had died around her but she was still alive.

Somebody had gone to a lot of trouble to kill Belkin

when they didn't get it right the first time. But maybe they didn't get it right because pushing Belkin in front of the truck wasn't planned but was done on impulse. Yuri had been there that night. Said he was on an investigation. He saw Belkin and he saw her. Not Yuri, she thought, please don't let it be Yuri.

The school teacher had died, scared to death or killed, murdered either way. Along with John Doe at the fertilizer plant.

Yet she was still alive. There had been plenty of opportunities for someone to kill her after the attempt failed at the cathedral. If nothing else, she had wandered around the city in the dead of night. She certainly wasn't being protected.

If she wasn't being protected, she was being used. The thought struck her and it rang true. It was as simple as that, she thought. She felt the keys in her side pocket. Why have a metal safe for keys and not lock it? No, no, don't get paranoid, she told herself. People aren't used to locking up everything in this country.

Alexei was ex-KGB. No surprise there, so was half the rest of the country. But he hid it while others, like Belkin, rather flaunted it. Why did Alexei hide his past? And what did he have to do with her mother? Could he had been the one that gave orders to . . .

To what?

She would keep the appointment to raid Alexei's office at the penthouse. The rendezvous had been set up by Nadia. The woman was a world-class bitch but stupidity wasn't one of her faults. Like Alexei, she knew how to steal geese. It's time I stole a few of my own, Lara thought. Whatever was in Alexei's autobiography, it was probably her last hope of getting information about her mother's death.

* * *

The limo let her off in front of her hotel. She went inside, walked through the lobby to the restaurant, smiled at the maitre d' and said she had forgotten something, turned round and exited the lobby. The limo was gone. She climbed into a taxi and gave the driver directions that she thought would get her within a couple of blocks of the tower.

The taxi dropped her two blocks from the rear of the tower and she walked slowly toward it, trying not to think about the fact that she was once again in the business of breaking and entering. Actually, she was Alexei's live-in guest. There was nothing wrong with grabbing the keys to the penthouse so she could be waiting for him when he returned from his meeting. Yeah, sure. How many times did I hear a story like that when I was prosecuting a thief?

She had a view of the back of the building for more than a block. Nadia was not in sight. It was almost exactly twelve when she got to the back door. Trying to look inconspicuous, she moseyed down the street a little, then turned and walked back.

Why should I wait for Nadia? The woman's a blackmailer. I'm not trying to hurt anyone, I just want that picture. And a peek at the rest of Alexei's autobiography.

Besides, what were they going to do with the manuscript once she and Nadia got their hands on it? Wrestle for it?

On impulse, she turned and stepped into the little alcove leading to a tall set of steel doors. She fumbled nervously with the keys before finding one that made the lock turn. In seconds, the door was closed behind her and she was in the corridor leading to Alexei's private elevator. Quiet as a crypt, was the thought that came to mind.

She made her way down to the elevator. She pressed the button to the right of the doors. Nothing happened. She fumbled with the keys again and found a small, round cylindrical one that looked as if it should fit an elevator or alarm system. She put the key in, turned it, and the elevator doors slid open.

Scared but determined, she stepped into the elevator and faced the control panel. There were only two choices: UP and DOWN. She hit the UP and the door slid shut. The elevator gave a little lurch before it started ascending smoothly. She examined her key collection, feeling very claustrophobic in an elevator that had about fifty unoccupied floors between the two levels it served.

The night she had shot up the place, Alexei had taken her from the ballroom to a corridor where the kitchen facilities were located and out a back door to the elevator. The third key on the tower ring had to be to the rear door of the penthouse.

God, was that really me that night? Felix was right about one thing, she thought. She had inherited more from her father than she realized. Her mother would not have stormed this building alone; she would have distributed inflammatory pamphlets and led a march on the place.

The elevator slowed and came to a stop along with her breathing. The doors swung open. The alcove was deserted. She breathed again and stepped out.

She went quickly to the door across from the elevators. Her nerves were going to hell and her hand was shaking as she got the key into the lock, twisted it and opened the door. Stepping in, she quietly closed the door behind her.

The interior corridor was unlit. To her left, open doors let in light from windows in the adjoining rooms. No lights on was a good sign. If people were here they'd have the lights on. She went down the corridor unconvinced that there weren't killers hidden in every nook and cranny. Opening a door cautiously, she peered into the grand ballroom. Other than a little light coming from partially opened drapes, the place was cast in darkness and shadow.

She crept in and slowly closed the door, carefully releasing the handle so that it didn't make a sound. Moving quickly across the ballroom, she went up the stairs leading to the second-floor landing. A couple of steps from the top she heard a noise and froze in place. She listened, trying to place it. A door shutting? She wasn't sure.

Probably nothing more than the central heating blowers kicking on, she told herself. *Nothing to fear but fear itself*. At the moment she couldn't remember who had said that. Fighting her instincts to turn and run, she crossed the landing to the gloomy corridor beyond.

The door at the end of the corridor was closed and didn't have a lock. She opened it and looked up at the stairway. A noise was coming from somewhere on top, the faint hum of a machine. The central air machinery, she hoped. She was at the bottom of a dark well, but there was faint light at the top of the stairs. She carefully closed the door behind her and looked up at the gray light. Her mouth was dry and her nerves on fire.

One step at a time, she told herself.

At the top of the steps she paused and looked down the dark hallway. The door to the spa was partially open and she realized the humming noise was the spa pump. Was it on its auto filtering cycle? she wondered. If someone was in the spa, they hadn't bothered to turn on any of the lights along the way. The corridor was dark and narrow. There had to be a light switch at both ends. The short stairway to the offices was immediately to the left of the spa door. Interior windows to the offices were above and no lights shone through them.

She had come too far to let what might be nothing more than machinery running cause her to turn back.

Why me, Lord? Why couldn't I have stayed home, safe with my cat and my condo?

The hum got louder as she went down the dark corridor, her eyes glued on daylight coming through the narrow opening of the door to the spa. Just the spa going through its filtering cycle, she told herself; no one would be in the spa this early.

A few feet from the door her foot kicked something. A metallic object on the floor. She bent down to get a closer look.

It was a gun. A big six-shooter, like the ones from Alexei's party. She heard a noise behind her, from the stairwell area. She picked up the gun and held it in both hands, her heart bouncing in her throat. She listened but the noise didn't come again.

She swallowed and pushed open the door to the spa, her eyes adjusting to the daylight. She stared at the spa, her mind rejecting what her eyes saw. The spa was running. Blood-red water bubbled and foamed. Floating face down was a naked woman, her blonde hair spread out. She knew it was Nadia without having to turn over the body. She turned and ran back down the corridor, holding the gun with both hands.

She stumbled down the dark stairwell and jerked open the bottom door with one hand, the heavy gun in the other. When she was sure no one was waiting to jump her, she started running again, holding the gun with both hands.

Racing across the balcony, she was near the stairway down to the grand ballroom when the double doors of the ballroom burst open. She caught a flash of Yuri at the head of a group of men and guns being raised in her direction; she threw herself down, the gun flying out of her hand as the gunfire exploded in the room.

A few seconds later Yuri was beside her as the other men streamed by. Stenka picked up the gun she had dropped.

'Are you all right?'

'I think so.' She got to her knees and then her feet, ears ringing.

'What are you doing here?' he asked.

'There's a body in the spa, on the roof. I think it's Nadia.' She couldn't remember the woman's last name and she stammered, 'The newswoman.'

'This gun's been fired,' Stenka said, holding the six-shooter with a pen stuck in the barrel.

'It's not my gun,' Lara said. 'I found it upstairs.'

Yuri's features were stone. She suddenly realized she was surrounded by men, all staring at her.

'I didn't kill anybody. Look, I just got here. I went upstairs, saw the body and ran.'

A man shouldered one of the other officers aside. He had gray hair, an air of authority and was dressed in a more expensive suit than the others. 'We saw you running with a gun in your hand,' he said.

'I know Miss Patrick,' Yuri started.

'I'm handling this, Detective Kirov. You and Stenka go upstairs and make a search of the roof. Give me the gun.'

Stenka grabbed Yuri's arm and pulled him away as Lara faced the man, not flinching under his hard look.

Her pulse was beating in her throat; she was hot and sick with fear.

'How did you get in here?' he asked.

'With keys.'

'The elevator people say no one came up.'

'I . . . I came in the back way.'

'We received an anonymous call a short time ago. The caller said a woman with a gun had entered the building and a shot had been heard.'

'I didn't shoot her.'

'How did you know who was in the spa?'

'It was just a guess. I saw her and I thought—'

'You saw her and you shot her.'

'I never shot her!'

'You came in the back way, you say.'

'Yes.'

'Did anyone pass you as you came in?'

'Pass me? No, no, I didn't see anyone.'

'We saw no one either and we came in the front way. No one except you running with a gun in your hand.' He smelled the barrel and checked the chamber. 'A recently fired gun. Two bullets missing. It would be my guess that we're going to find the two bullets from this gun in the dead woman.'

'You have to believe me, I never did anything. My foot kicked the gun. I picked it up, saw her in the spa, panicked and ran. I didn't kill her.'

The man held the gun up in front of her. 'Have you ever seen this gun prior to today?'

'I don't know.'

'You don't know?'

'There was a party. The gun looks like the six-shooters people had at the party.'

'You had such a gun?'

'Yes.' Oh God. She stared at the gun in his hand as if it was a poisonous snake. She'd had two of the guns. One she had left in the limo. The other she had thrown at Yuri when he was leaving her hotel room.

Her mind was in such a fog she didn't catch the man's next words. 'What did you say?'

'I said you are under arrest for the murder of Nadia Kolchak.'

Chapter 28

Survive, survive, survive.

The word kept spinning in her mind.

At the Moscow City Jail, a man took each of her hands and roughly forced them onto an ink pad and then rolled her prints on paper, each finger, palm, side of the hand. She stared down at the prints. How many times had she seen prints of criminals? Exemplars, the prints were called, to be compared with the latent prints lifted from the scene of the crime. She had seen so many; fingerprint cards and criminals went together in her mind like meat and potatoes. Now they were her prints, her marks on the justice system.

Booking photos came next, front and back and each side. She stared at the camera, as she had at the fingerprint cards, a perplexed expression on her face. She couldn't believe this was happening.

After booking, she sat in a chair for nearly four hours before a husky matron, spiritual sister of the truck driver's wife, came into the room.

'Prisoner, stand up.'

Lara stood up.

'Prisoner, turn to your left and walk to the second door on your right.'

The room on the right was a bare concrete box without windows. A long wooden table sat in the middle. A gray smock had been tossed on the table. A pair of rubber slip-on shoes were on the floor.

'Take off your clothes,' the matron told her.

'Shut the door, please.' The voice didn't sound like her own; the words seemed to come to her from some far and distant place where her mind had retreated.

The woman shut the door and Lara took off her shoes and slowly stripped until she was in panties and bra. She picked up the gray smock to put it on. 'Not yet,' the matron said. 'Take off the rest of your clothes.'

Lara turned and looked at her. The matron was holding a gynaecological instrument.

'Prisoners are searched for weapons and contraband.'

Lara lay back on the table and stared up at the cracked concrete ceiling.

Survive, survive, survive.

Holding onto a single blanket, clutching it tightly against her, Lara followed the matron down a cell block corridor. She had lost track of time and knew only that it was late evening. A line of naked bulbs down the center of the cell block cast little enough light to leave the cells on each side deep in shadow.

Her feet were flopping in the ill-fitting rubber shoes, her legs were cold, but her heart was no longer pounding, her nerves were no longer on fire; icy calm gripped her. She felt like a seven-year-old girl being led to an airplane after having been assaulted.

Women in cells on both sides stirred as she was marched through. She heard a snickering voice say that here was a newcomer, someone to take advantage of; in another cell two women, prostitutes, smoked cigarettes and watched her with hard eyes as she went by. From another direction she heard a woman crying for her baby and someone else yell, 'Shut up, you crazy bitch, you killed your baby.'

The matron stopped at a cell door at the end of the block and opened it. She gestured for Lara to go inside. It was a small cubbyhole, the size of a walk-in closet. Cement walls on all three sides, no window, steel bars facing the cell block.

Lara stepped inside and stood, clutching the blanket, her back to the matron as the woman closed and locked the door.

'Murderers get private cells. We don't want to expose our whores and thieves to them.'

Lara went to the rear of the cell and sat down with her back against the cold concrete wall. She wrapped the blanket round her and buried her head in her arms. She thought the matron had left and the woman's voice came to her as a sound from the grave.

'We execute murderers. One shot in the head. And if they're still alive, we tape their nose and mouth shut so we don't have to waste another bullet.'

Down the cell block a woman laughed hysterically, while another shouted, 'Shut up, you crazy bitch.'

It took Eric Caldwell from the American Embassy two days to make a visit to the jail. He was sitting in the attorney visiting room when she was brought in.

'Miss Patrick, how are you?'

They would send the dumbest bastard in the diplomatic corps in her time in need. Through tight jaws she told him, 'I'm cold, unbathed, charged with a crime I didn't commit and suicidal.'

'Yes, well, I'm here to help.'

'Yes, well, I need help,' she mimicked. 'I didn't murder that woman. I need my government to—'

Caldwell's head was shaking 'no' so hard it threatened to swivel off its base.

'The United States government cannot get involved in your case in any manner. Criminal matters are entirely in the sovereign jurisdiction of the Russian government.'

'I can understand that, but I need money. Everything I have is tied up in a condo in San Francisco.'

'The United States government cannot assist you financially.'

'I need an attorney, Mr Caldwell, a good one.'

'The United States government cannot—'

'What can you do? You said you were here to help.'

'We can pass a message to your friends or relatives Stateside and let them know you are in need of assistance.'

'That's all? I'm an American citizen. That's all you can do for me? Stamp some envelopes?'

'You have got yourself into trouble in a foreign country, Miss Patrick. We have no authority here.'

'This country is asking for billions in aid from us and my representative can't pick up the phone and ask for a review of my case? That's all I'm asking. For my government to ensure that I am not being held on trumped-up charges.'

'If you had been arrested for a political crime we might be able to give assistance, but this is a murder case. The Russian government will appoint you a defense lawyer.'

'A Russian defense lawyer is a contradiction in terms. This country has been under totalitarian dictatorship for over seventy years. A few months under a new regime isn't going to change the legal system. Attorneys here have been trained to help the government convict their clients.'

'There is one thing wrong with your reasoning, Miss Patrick.'

'What?'

He smacked his lips with satisfaction. 'There is only one

kind of attorney in Russia – Russian attorneys. You weren't expecting Perry Mason, were you?'

She bent closer to him, causing him to lean back a little. 'No, Mr Caldwell, I'm not expecting Perry Mason. I'm a little more practical than that. I am an attorney, I know my way around a courtroom in a system I can trust. The Russians are still operating under the old Soviet criminal justice system which has almost no safeguards for due process. The police work is primitive and the judicial system is barbaric. I need to find one attorney out there with the same sense of being an advocate that I have.'

'I am also an attorney, Miss Patrick. The justice system here is different from our own, certainly, but I'm sure you will be appointed adequate counsel to guide you through the system.'

'I don't want *adequate* counsel. I'm facing a murder charge in a country which uses capital punishment. Hell, they used to shoot drunk drivers here. I need money and help. We send the whole damn army and navy to Kuwait to help some fat little sheik who lives like a king while his people starve and—'

'You have a very unrealistic view of world events. And of your own situation. I speak both as an attorney and a diplomat. Frankly, your situation is somewhat of a diplomatic embarrassment to your government at a time when we are trying to restructure the world community after the end of the Cold War.'

'Restructure the world community? A diplomatic embarrassment?' She got to her feet and came the closest she had ever come in her life to punching someone. 'You jerk. Don't you ever call yourself an attorney. A law degree doesn't make you an attorney any more than boxing gloves make a fighter. You're not a lawyer until you've been in a courtroom and fought for truth and justice on both sides of the counsel table. And you'll never see a courtroom because trial lawyers have hearts as well as guts and you obviously have neither!'

She rested her head on her folded arms on the table as she waited for the matron to take her back to the cell. Caldwell had fled, angry and speechless after her outburst. She had focused her anger on him and felt no real remorse for doing so. The world seemed to be full of Caldwells, people who appeared to go effortlessly through life without ever once getting punished by God or whoever for never reaching out and giving a helping hand to their fellows.

The door to the interview room opened and she looked up without much interest, thinking it was the matron.

Yuri stood in the doorway. His features were grave. He slowly stepped in, closing the door behind him. Taking the seat across from her that Caldwell had left vacant, he looked around the room for a moment before he met her eye.

'I just spoke to Mr Caldwell of your embassy. He was a bit upset.'

'I clawed him for being stupid,' she said. 'I was the stupid one. I should have sat on his lap instead. I don't seem to have a talent for tact.' She studied his face, trying to read his secrets. 'Did you come to finish the job of killing me?'

'What?'

'You people came through that door shooting to kill. If I hadn't thrown myself to the floor—'

'I never fired at you. I'm in trouble because I spoiled my supervisor's aim when he fired. He believes I'm too emotionally involved in your case.'

'Very convenient, having the police rushing into the room as I was running through the place in a panic.'

'There was a call.'

'Yes, I know, an *anonymous* call. That's convenient, too.'

'I told you to stay away from Alexei. You were seduced by his money and glamour.'

'That's a lie. I was put into his custody, for God's sake. You weren't willing to help me. Your best suggestion was to tell me to get out of the country.'

For a moment she was sure she saw a flash of pain in his face and he looked away. When he met her eye again, his features were neutral. 'It may be better for you to be in jail. It's safer. You would have been dead soon if you'd kept wandering around Moscow sticking your nose in the past.'

'Better in jail? Facing a murder charge? Are we on the same planet?'

'Tell me what happened.'

She ran her hands through her hair. 'I look like hell, don't I? You need money for everything in here, even for soap and a comb.'

'I'll leave money for you.'

'No, thank you. I just have to get to my purse.'

'You have a hard time taking help, don't you?'

'I . . . yes, all right, but Yuri, don't . . .'

'Don't what?'

She almost sobbed but held it back. 'Don't betray me.'

He looked away again as she started talking. She told him about the message from Minsky, about breaking into the institute, and about being take to the palace by Alexei after leaving the meeting at the ministry.

'When I returned from my walk, Felix invited . . . I guess lured me in is more accurate.' She told him about seeing the picture of her mother and the neighbor with Alexei, the party that night, being intercepted by Nadia.

'She asked you to meet her the next day at the tower so she could gather evidence to blackmail Alexei?'

'Yes.'

'But she never told you what she suspected?'

'No, only that Felix must have a hold on Alexei.'

'What happened after you spoke to Nadia?'

Too embarrassed to tell him about the sauna scene with Nadia and waking up in Alexei's bed, she said, 'I had something to drink and passed out. I . . . I'm sure I was drugged.'

'What happened next?'

'Everyone had already returned to town by the time I woke up. I got dressed, took the key . . .' She described the key safe, returning to the city, going to the tower, finding the gun.

'You had returned the guns you wore at the party?'

'Yes – no. I left one gun in the limo the night of the Western party. I threw the other gun at you as you were leaving my hotel room. It hit the wall by the door and that's the last I saw of it. I . . . I don't know if it was the same gun as the one I found near the spa. Most of the guns at the party looked the same.'

'So you had access to the gun that killed Nadia?'

'It might have been—' A terrible, ugly feeling suddenly overwhelmed her, choking off her words. 'Yuri, you asked that question as if you were doing it for the record. Are you . . .'

He turned away, refusing to meet her eye.

She leaned across the table and jerked open his suit coat. A transmitter was clipped to his shirt pocket with a line of wire going to his coat.

'*You're recording me!*' She hit him with her fists. 'How could you! How could you!'

The door flew open and a man rushed into the room, followed by Stenka.

The man grabbed her, spun her round and jerked her arm into a hammer lock so hard she cried out.

'Don't hurt her!' Yuri grabbed the man's arm and the man shook him off.

'Back off,' he told Yuri. He slammed Lara into her chair and then turned to Yuri and Stenka.

'Detective Kirov, Detective Stenka, you may leave. This case is now in the exclusive jurisdiction of the Moscow City Procurator's office.'

Yuri stepped closer to him. The man was not much taller than Lara but almost as broad, a shaved head on an eight-ply body, giving him the appearance of a blunt-nosed artillery shell.

Yuri tapped his chest. 'Don't ... touch ... her, Vulko. Question her, do your job, but touch her and I'll be back.'

'You are dismissed, Detective Kirov.'

As he left the room with Stenka, Yuri gave her a shamefaced glance.

Vulko sat on the edge of the table and stared down at her, his look a mixture of amusement and contempt. The dim light in the room cast shadows in the pockets of his rough face. He lit a cigarette, a brown thing almost like a cigar, and blew out foul-smelling smoke.

'You have got to Detective Kirov's heart, I see. Inside his pants, no doubt, too. I'll report the matter to his supervisor and he will be reassigned walking a patrol.'

'Who are you?' she demanded.

'Nikolai Vulko, Chief Investigator, Moscow City Procurator's office.'

'What do you want?'

'I am here to question you about the crime you have committed.'

'I haven't committed a crime. I want an attorney present. And an official from the American Embassy.'

He chuckled, a hoarse rasp. His pinstriped suit was baggy and wrinkled, his white shirt open at the collar with salt and pepper chest hair poking out like a bunny's tail. She noticed he had no eyebrows, not even the residue of having shaved them.

'You have no right to have an attorney present, you have no right to have a representative from your embassy present. Your only right is to answer the questions I ask. Do you understand?'

'No, I don't understand a legal system where I have no rights.'

'Don't try to play games about legal theory. We are not in a debate. You are in jail, not the marble halls of a law university. In your country you are a prosecutor, correct?'

'Yes.'

'And you understand that what you call a prosecutor, we call the procurator.'

'Yes.'

'Good. We are getting somewhere. I am a chief investigator for the prosecutor's office. The police arrest the criminal and gather evidence at the scene of the crime. At that point an investigator for the prosecutor's office takes over the investigation. We prepare the case for trial, uncovering all the facts and evidence and put it in an orderly fashion for the court.'

'Are you here to twist round everything I say or to look at the facts objectively and help me out of this terrible mess?'

'I know the facts. I am here to listen to your confession and to see if there are any mitigating factors to what appears to be a crime of intentional murder with aggravating circumstances.'

She tried to word her response carefully. She knew what a prosecutor's investigator was, at least in the context of an American courtroom. They took a second look at the evidence gathered by the police and in the right case they could make a recommendation that would result in charges being dropped.

'I did not kill Nadia. I went to Bova's penthouse and found her dead. I found the gun on the floor, panicked and ran.'

He chuckled hoarsely again, a cancerous throat rasp, and shook his head. 'No, you misunderstand. This is not America, we do not play legal games. There is one path, the path of justice, and in this case there is a fork in the road: if you explain your actions, accept responsibility for them, show repentance for the terrible deed you have done and offer explanations, you take the path to being sentenced for murder with mitigating circumstances. If you fail to repent and do not offer satisfactory explanations, you take the path to murder with aggravating circumstances. It is as simple as that.'

'You're not listening to me,' Lara said. '*I didn't kill anyone*. I can't confess to a crime I didn't commit.'

He reached out and roughly took her chin in the cup of his hand. 'You are the one not listening. You must tell me the truth. Admit that you fired two shots and took the life of Nadia Kolchak.'

Lara struggled out of his grip and fell backwards off her chair. She scrambled to her feet, nearly in tears. 'Don't you touch me. Touch me and I will report you to my embassy.'

He blew out laughter and smoke and raised his shoulders and hairless eyebrows. 'Do you think we Russians care about a report to your embassy?'

'Maybe you'll care if it's reported in newspapers around the world that an American woman has been manhandled in a Russian jail by a Russian investigator. Maybe my congressional representative back home might want some questions answered before they vote on aid for Russia. Maybe your own career—'

'Prisoner, your threats do not bother me. You have totally

misunderstood the situation because you are ignorant of Russian legal procedures. We have more than sufficient evidence of your crime. I am here to accept your offer of repentance and mitigation to place before the procurator.' He blew more foul smoke from the brown cigarette. 'So, I ask you the question again. Why did you kill Nadia Kolchak?'

'I . . . did . . . not . . . kill Nadia Kolchak.'

He dropped his cigarette on the floor, then got off the table and stamped the cigarette out.

'You have made, shall we say, a fatal mistake.' He paused at the door to the room. 'Perhaps no one has told you. Murder with mitigating circumstances is punished by up to ten years in prison.' He grinned. 'Murder with aggravating circumstances is punished with death.'

He opened the door but paused and turned back to her again. 'Russian death sentences do not stay around the courts for years with appeals. Justice is sure and swift. You've chosen the bullet.'

Back in her cell she curled up in a corner and covered herself with the blanket. Anger helped steady her nerves. She had been betrayed again. There wouldn't be another opportunity for betrayal because she would never allow herself to be tricked again. Or allow herself to get emotionally attached. She had trusted Yuri. And cared for him. She understood the emotions that turn love to hate and hate to murder.

She wished she had a gun to kill him. Not for being a smart cop, but for the hurt he gave her heart.

And she'd put another bullet in that bastard with a polished head and no eyebrows.

Chapter 29

The next morning she stood in line with other women waiting to go into a courtroom. The women were being called in one by one, some for pleas and sentencing, others for the appointment of an attorney. She was weak and queasy. She had not had the courage to go to breakfast with the other prisoners. Two days in jail and she had not eaten. It wasn't a hunger strike; she just did not have the fortitude to march in line to the mess hall and eat. Other than the one trip to the visitors' room, she had not left her cell day or night. Not even for a shower. She didn't know how much weight she had lost; the smock she wore was designed for an elephant.

A hole in the corner of her cell was her toilet; a trickle of water could be directed into the hole from a rusty tap a couple of feet above. The water was bitter with an iodine taste but so far it hadn't killed her. The cell had a dirty mattress with a sheet stained from God knows what. She used a corner of the sheet to wash herself under the tap.

Eventually she would have to break down and join the other prisoners for food and showers. Being forced into line with them for the court appearance had broken some of the ice for her. She knew from hearing the other prisoners talk and some taunts directed at her that she was a celebrity prisoner – the news was full of the 'love triangle murder'.

Her hair was in knots, her face a wreck, the smock she wore would have embarrassed a pregnant cow, but her mind was still functioning and she tried to think as a lawyer, running the facts over and over in her mind. The case was based on circumstantial evidence, no one actually saw the killing, but when you're caught red-handed by police officers with a smoking gun in your hand, it was almost as strong as a case with eye witnesses. In her courtroom in San Francisco it would have been a no-plea-bargain case – the evidence was too strong to offer a lesser offense. Premeditated murder without special circumstances meant a life sentence without possibility of parole back home, a bullet in the brain in Moscow. She would rather have the bullet than spend the rest of her life in prison.

A matron grabbed her arm and pulled her out of line.

'Prisoner, your lawyer is here.'

She followed the woman, wondering what was going on. Lawyers were being appointed in the courtroom.

The man waiting for her in the attorney interview room was about forty years old with dark, slicked-back hair tied in a pony tail, a narrow face and patrician nose. He wore an expensive pinstriped, double-vested Italian suit, hand-painted silk tie, and Balley loafers with tassels.

He introduced himself. 'Viktor Rykoff. I'm the best lawyer in Moscow.'

She recognized his type – smart, successful, high-priced big city lawyer. Some of them really were the best but a lot more were better at promoting themselves outside the courtroom than performing their dance steps in it. If Russian lawyers were developing along the lines of their American counterparts, 'best' probably meant the most financially successful. Many a household legal name in America got famous handling high profile cases that they lost.

'Who sent you?' she asked.

'The gods, American and Russian, are smiling on you. Even the dead communist ones. Your case is getting great media attention. For over seventy years there have been no crimes of passion in Russia – at least none that were allowed to be so well reported. Because you are making history, I am here to help.'

He was telling her he wanted to share the limelight. She had no problem with that – if he was good and if he could be trusted. But she took an instant dislike to him. He reminded her of the lawyers whom prosecutors and prisoners call 'dump trucks' – they drive the case all the way to the day of trial with their bullshit and then dump the client when it's time to perform.

'You're the best lawyer in Moscow. I'm the most frightened defendant in the city. And I don't have any money.'

He winced. 'A rich American . . .'

She shook her head. 'Poor American. I have a condo in San Francisco with equity in it. That's all.'

'San Francisco. That's halfway round the world.'

'I thought you wanted to share these historical moments with me.'

He spread his hands and smiled. 'True, but sharing is so much more palatable when there is money on the table.'

Except for poets and crazies, she hated pony tails on middle-aged men. She got up. 'Well, I'll be—'

'No, no, please sit down. I won't let something like money get in our way. This is Russia and we have not converted our legal system to the market economy yet.'

'Can you get paid by the court?' she asked.

'Not enough to feed my BMW.'

'BMW? I see. You have converted to the market

economy even if the country hasn't. What do you know about my case?'

He shrugged. 'You killed one of Russia's most popular women in a heat of passion over one of the country's most famous men.'

'I see. And how does heat of passion line up as a defense in Russia?'

'It's not a defense. The crime of murder is punishable by death. If a judge believes there are mitigating circumstances for your actions, you can be spared the bullet. In this case, there will be great pressure on the judge from all sides. Your case is the first of its kind to get this type of attention in the country. The whole nation will be waiting to see how it is judged.'

'So the judge will be on the hot spot.'

'Exactly.'

She thought for a moment. 'Something bothers me. You indicated you'd take my case, but you haven't asked me anything about it. You haven't even asked if I'm guilty.'

He shrugged again. 'This is Russia. Your case will be won or lost in the judge's chambers by the pressures that are applied, not by the actual facts. We may even have to create facts.' He leaned toward her. 'Do you have jewelry? Perhaps something Bova gave you?'

'You mean for your fee? No, nothing of any value.'

'A pity. The more money, the more justice. Just like America,' he laughed.

What a pig, she thought.

He got serious again. 'Don't worry, I will still take your case. Our strategy will be to stall the case for a long time, long enough for the news people and the public to get bored with it. That will take pressure off the judge.'

Panic welled up in her. 'I . . . I don't want the case stalled. I need to have it forced to trial as soon as possible. I can't

stand jail. Besides, my instincts tell me that the criminal
justice system here is a slow-moving bureaucracy, a fat
cow. If we push hard it's likely neither the police nor the
prosecutor will be ready for trial.'

He frowned. 'Your instincts. We have to get one matter
settled immediately. I am the lawyer, you are the prisoner.
It is *my* instincts that we will be following. And my instincts
are to delay the trial until the right moment and when that
moment comes, we move in for a kill.' He made a chopping
gesture with his hand.

'But—'

'We do it my way or you can go inside and take your
chances with a court-appointed lawyer. Has anyone told
you about court-appointed lawyers? They are still practicing Soviet justice. They sit on your legs while the
prosecutor beats a confession out of you.'

She stared down at the table. Her instincts were screaming against it but he was the only game in town.

'Today the judge will order your case to the city courts.'

'I don't understand.'

'This court is the people's court. It does not handle death
penalty cases. You are being sent to the next higher court.'

'I'm not entitled to any sort of hearing before being sent
to a higher court?' she asked. 'A hearing to establish that
there is enough evidence to bind me to a higher court? No
hearing on being let out on bail?'

'You had the hearing. Chief Investigator Vulko came
and spoke with you. You refused a statement. He made a
decision to move your case to the city court for trial as a
death penalty matter.'

'He made the decision? He's just an investigator for the
prosecution!'

'You misunderstand. You are thinking like an American.
The case is prepared by the prosecutor's office. It is the

prosecutor's decision to make it a death penalty case, but a chief investigator's opinion would rarely be ignored.'

'How about the court's opinion? Doesn't the people's court judge look into the case to see if it has any merit?'

He became a little exasperated. 'Theories, theories, those are theories. I am telling you what happens in the real world.'

'I'm sorry. Where I come from we call those rights, not theories.'

'Next time kill someone at home.' He held up his hand. 'A joke. Listen to me, the important thing is that I am taking care of your case. You made a very serious error when you refused to speak to Vulko last night and offer mitigation. He made it a death penalty case, so it is being transferred today. There will be no more mistakes.'

'He said I didn't have a right to have an attorney present.'

'He was speaking the truth. But there are ways of handling this matter without antagonizing the chief investigator on the case. Leave it to me. I will take care of everything.'

When she returned to the line of prisoners, the woman in front of her asked, 'Is Rykoff your attorney?'

'Yes. Is he good?'

'He's wonderful. He was my sister's attorney when she was charged with stabbing her boy friend.'

'Did he get your sister off?'

'Get her off? Of course not. She stabbed her boy friend.'

'Then why do you think he's such a good attorney?'

'He said nice things about my sister to the judge.'

'Did the things he said get her a lighter sentence?'

The woman shook her head in wonderment at Lara's ignorance. 'Of course not. Everyone gets equal justice. But not all lawyers say nice things about their clients.'

Wonderful, Lara thought. I've got a lawyer who can give a nice eulogy when they put a bullet in my head.

'What are you charged with?' Lara asked.

'Stolen boots.'

'Boots?'

The woman shrugged. 'I worked in a boot factory. Each day I wore to work a pair of rubber shoes I could fold and put in my purse and wore a pair of boots out. I did it to feed my baby. That is my mitigating circumstance. I did it to feed my baby because my boy friend stole my money.' She gestured as she talked and Lara saw track marks on her arm. Her 'baby' came in a hypodermic needle.

The door to the courtroom opened and the woman with the sister who stabbed her boy friend stepped inside. As the door was swinging shut, Lara got a flash of two men huddled together in the courtroom.

Yuri and Rykoff.

'What's the matter with you?' the door guard asked.

'What?'

'Are you ill?'

'I'm all right.'

'You're next,' he said.

Betrayal upon betrayal. Yuri wasn't going to be satisfied until she was dead. Or insane.

The guard was talking to her again.

'Move, prisoner. Into the courtroom.'

She forced her shoulders back and held her head high as she stepped into the courtroom. The lighting was much brighter than the holding area and she cringed at how awful she must look, but she was determined not to let her chin drop.

The courtroom was packed and a stir went through the gallery as she entered. A metal railing ran a dozen feet into the room and she walked along it into the prisoner's dock, a wooden box with a step to elevate her, making her visible to the whole courtroom. It was hot and stuffy in the room; the heat was gagging.

She ignored a hundred pairs of eyes and found Yuri's. He was standing at the back of the room. She locked eyes with him for a moment and then deliberately looked at Rykoff. The attorney smiled and nodded. Without changing her expression she looked back at Yuri. She wanted to let him know she wasn't falling for his trick.

As she listened to the judge stating her name, the case number, and the charges, thoughts of herself in court, at the prosecutor's table, shuffling files as the cases were called flashed through her mind. The courtroom was designed like those in America, the judge's bench at one end of the room, the exit doors on the other side of the room, the spectator gallery taking up about half of the portion closest to the exit door, a railing called the 'bar' cutting off the spectators from the counsel tables, clerk's desk, witness box, and the dock.

The most obvious difference was the lack of a jury box and the presence of three people on the judicial bench. The judge was dressed in a suit; he wore a white shirt and a tie. On each side of him were the assessors, two citizens chosen to sit in on cases with him for a couple weeks before other citizens took their place. Lara was not certain what their exact role was, whether they had as much power as the judge or were just courtroom decoration.

The judge was smoking a cigarette and the ashtray in front of him was nearly overflowing and smoldering from butts not quite extinguished. Just beyond the ashtray were bottles of soda pop and mineral water. The assessor to the right of the judge was a thin, sickly-looking woman whose eyes were half-closed. She was leaning away from the judge as if she was being blown away by the smoke. The other assessor, sitting on the judge's left, was an older man dressed in heavy woollen workman's clothes. He, too looked barely awake, and Lara could see sweat on his face.

Opposite her, on the wall, was a poster of Lenin, as mandatory in Russian public buildings as images of Christ in Christian churches. Cracked and faded, the picture gave a sinister cast to the revolutionary's otherwise distinguished face; the dark, stern features and goatee reminded her of a faded old movie poster of the count from Transylvania.

The judicial atmosphere was not as dignified as she was accustomed to, but she reminded herself that the communists had deliberately tried to make the justice system available to the common man. Too bad so much of the 'justice' ended up practiced under the table, she thought.

Viktor Rykoff stood up at the counsel table. 'I will be representing the prisoner.'

'No, he will not, your honor.' She said 'your honor' out of habit; she had no idea what the proper way to address a Russian judge was. 'I have discovered that Mr Rykoff has a conflict of interest. He will not be representing me in this matter.'

A buzz went through the audience. Rykoff's jaw dropped. He swung round and looked at Yuri who shrugged his shoulders and shook his head.

The judge stared at her as if she was a candidate for a mental competency hearing. Even the two assessors perked up. 'You don't want Mr Rykoff for your attorney.' It was more an echo than a question.

'We have a conflict of interest.'

'Mr Rykoff is one of the best attorneys in Moscow,' the judge said.

A conflict of interest apparently didn't mean much in a Russian courtroom. A surge of strength went through her –

she was in a courtroom, thinking on her feet. 'I believe, your honor, that Mr Rykoff is associated with one of the police officers in this matter. I would like to inquire as to his relationship with that officer and why he would offer to represent me free.'

'This is ridiculous!' Rykoff exploded. 'The woman is a mental case. She needs a doctor.' He turned and stamped out of the courtroom, jerking open one of the double doors with such force it banged against the wall.

The judge peered down at her above the rim of glasses riding his nose. 'I will give you time to hire an attorney.'

'I don't have the money for an attorney. I need to have one appointed by the court.'

He gaped at her. 'You do not want Rykoff and you want me to appoint you an attorney?'

'Yes.'

The judge shook his head. 'This is a free country,' he told the audience. She didn't know if he was joking but a titter went through the audience. 'She doesn't want Rykoff and wants me to appoint her an attorney.' The titter turned into a buzz.

He adjusted his glasses and consulted papers in front of him for a long moment, finally looking up and calling a name.

'Marya Gan.'

There was complete silence in the courtroom for a moment and then a young woman stood up and came forward.

Several things instantly struck Lara about her. She was young, a few years younger than Lara, in her mid-twenties. She was also Afro-Russian, a very uncommon racial mixture; one of the few people of African heritage Lara had seen in Moscow other than tourists in Red Square. And she was very scared.

'I am Marya Gan,' she told the judge in a nervous voice.

The judge pulled his glasses down his nose and grinned at Lara as he spoke. 'Marya Gan, member of the Collegium of Law, I appoint you as attorney for the prisoner.'

Marya Gan looked frightened enough to crawl under the counsel table.

Ten minutes later Lara and Marya stared at each other across the table in the attorney interview room like two doves coming face to face in a burning forest. The Russian attorney had black hair, almost to shoulder length, dark cinnamon eyes, and smooth skin shades lighter than ebony.

'I've never handled a criminal case before,' she told Lara.

'Never? Not one?' Lara tried to control her voice but the words squeaked.

'A few cases of prostitution. A man who beat his wife. A case of theft. A watch.'

'A watch.' Lara nodded.

'A cheap watch,' Marya said. 'Plastic. He gave it to me as a fee.'

Rykoff had a BMW and Marya had a plastic watch.

'Have you won any trials?'

'I've never had a trial.'

'Great.' Lara dropped her head into her hands. She felt like taking off her head and bouncing it on the table.

'The judge was mad at you. I was here today to be appointed to a prostitution case. He appointed me to your case to punish you.'

'Jesus Christ.' It was the most complex thought she could muster.

'Mr Rykoff is one of the best attorneys in Moscow,' Marya said. 'I can beg the judge to—'

Lara looked up at her. 'Has he ever got anyone off?'

'Anyone off?'

'Has Rykoff won any cases? Walked his client out of a courtroom. Got a not guilty verdict.'

'Not guilty? Criminals are almost always found guilty. They wouldn't be on trial if they weren't guilty.'

'God help me.'

Marya stood up. 'I'm going to talk to the judge.' She turned to leave.

'Wait, please,' Lara said.

Marya shook her head. 'I can't represent you. You need a more experienced lawyer. The judge expects you to apologize for refusing Mr Rykoff.'

It was Lara's turn to shake her head.

'I'm black,' Marya said.

Lara understood. Blacks and Mafia were favorite Russian scapegoats for everything and anything that went wrong. 'A black woman in a white male-dominated system,' she said. It was a thought, but she expressed it aloud.

Marya's chin went up a notch. 'I have had to fight.'

'It must be tough for you.'

'It's been hell. I have to work twice as hard as anyone else and do three times better.'

Fight and win, Lara thought, every step of the way. One thing about Marya had struck her from the moment the young woman had turned to her wide-eyed in the courtroom: she was without guile. She had clear, honest eyes. No plots, no intrigue, no hidden agendas.

'When the August coup was attempted and people manned the barricades to face off the KGB and tanks, where were you?'

Her chin went up another inch. 'At the barricades.'

'That's what I thought.'

'I will go and talk to the judge now.'

'Wait. You're embarrassed, aren't you? Because you lack experience.'

'Embarrassed? I am terrified.'

Good, Lara thought, I fight best with my back to the wall.

'Before you go back to the judge,' Lara said, 'may I ask you a question?'

'Yes.'

'A moment ago you said all people charged with crimes are guilty. Do you really believe that?'

'Most people charged with crimes are guilty,' Marya said. 'All the people I have represented have been guilty of what they were charged with. But the police make mistakes. They make many mistakes, not just from stupidity, but from malice. You have been a prosecutor. Have you ever prosecuted an innocent person?'

'No. But I chose not to prosecute a number of people because I believed after reviewing all the evidence that they were not guilty.'

'From what I have heard about your case, the facts all appear to point to your guilt. But I have not heard all the facts. I have not heard your side.'

'What if I am guilty? If you were my attorney, how would you handle my case?'

Marya thought for a moment. 'In America, attorneys are taught under the British system – they are gladiators who go into a courtroom to advocate their client's position. That's not how attorneys in Russia have practiced.'

'The question is how you practice,' Lara said.

'I'm going to be a gladiator, not a sheep. I did not become an attorney to handle traffic tickets,' Marya said.

'Going to be?

'Why are we having this conversation? I can't handle your case. I'm not experienced. In Russia—'

'They have the death penalty. That's what frightens you, isn't it?'

Marya looked away and then met Lara's eye. 'If I handled your case, even if you were found guilty and executed, I would be famous. If I represented you and you were found not guilty, I would probably be made President of Russia. After I changed my color and sex, of course.'

Lara smiled.

'No, don't smile. This is not a matter to joke about. Yes, I am frightened, terrified, that I could make a mistake and have your blood on my hands. But I am not as frightened as you must be because with me it is only feelings. For you it must be a living hell.'

Neither woman spoke for a moment. Marya kept her position by the door and Lara rubbed her face with her hands. Finally, she asked Marya, 'Tell me the truth. Is Rykoff a good lawyer?'

'He is smart and rich. He has a fancy German car. And he says nice things about his clients.'

'And?'

'He has no heart, no feelings. If he gets paid enough, he makes deals in the judge's office. Sometimes the judge gets paid too.'

In other words, he can be bought. And I would be the lowest bidder, she thought. 'Assume I'm innocent, that I didn't kill Nadia Kolchak. What would it take to win my case? You've heard the facts, I'm supposed to have killed this woman in jealousy.'

'The news reports say that the police caught you with the murder weapon in your hand.'

'What would it take to win if I'm innocent?'

'Nadia Kolchak was very well known. Because of her exposure on television, she was one of the most popular women in Russia. The public is interested in the case.'

'What would it take to win?'

'The truth,' Marya said.

Lara smiled. She was weary and weak, but she had got the response she was after. 'Marya, it may just be delirium from lack of food or insanity from being in this mess, but if you are willing to stay on the case, I want you to be my attorney.'

Marya stared at her. 'Do you understand that criminal trials in Russia begin with a confession by the accused? If you don't confess, the judge will give you the maximum penalty. That's death in this case.'

'You're telling me that I have to stand up in court and tell the judge I'm guilty or he will give me the death penalty?'

'Yes. That's how the system works. If you do not confess, then you are not repentant and will be punished severely.'

'I have no intention of confessing to something I didn't do. This trial isn't going to start or finish with me being repentant for a crime I didn't commit. I'm going in to fight for my life with everything I have.'

Marya shook her head. 'You don't understand Russian trials. The chief investigator prepares the case for the court and the rest is mostly just procedural.'

'You aren't describing a justice system, but a court system that would—' Lara stopped and took a deep breath. 'I have to stop thinking like an American lawyer. But in any court system the truth must win out.'

Marya came back to the table and slowly sat down across from her. 'You will need more than truth to win this case,' she told Lara. 'If you do not confess to the crime, before the court will show you mercy you will have to enter the courtroom walking on water.' She suddenly grinned. 'You're a smart lawyer,' she said, 'but you forgot to ask me one thing.'

'What?'

'Which side of the barricades I was on.'

Chapter 30

They returned to the courtroom and the court called the case of Lara Patrick.

'I have had a discussion with the accused,' Marya said, 'and I will be representing her.'

The judge didn't look happy and the two assessors both turned to him, three heads with one mouth. 'I believe I made a mistake, Attorney Gan. This is a very serious case and your name was not on the list for the appointment.'

'I am satisfied with Marya Gan as my attorney,' Lara said.

'So be it. This case is transferred to city court.'

Classic example of a judge throwing a hot potato into someone else's lap, Lara thought.

'The defendant objects to a transfer to city court,' Marya said assertively to the surprise of everyone, including Lara. They had discussed making an objection and Marya had told her it would be useless. 'The defendant denies guilt in this case. Even if one is to believe the rumors circulated by the news media that this was an affair of passion, the crime would be that of an intentional killing in a state of great emotional excitement. Thus this matter can stay in the people's court.'

An expression of deep distaste spread across the judge's face. 'Case transferred to city court,' he barked.

Braced by the fact that she had an attorney she trusted and

liked, Lara got up the courage to go to lunch with the other women. No one bothered her, but the sour cabbage and soup and piece of black bread that the meal consisted of attacked her stomach with a vengeance and she ended up heaving her guts into her toilet hole.

Dinner wasn't any better. Knowing she needed food for survival, she had joined the dinner line and was served the same soup, warmed over, and a piece of the same bread. She gave the soup to another woman and ate the piece of bread.

When she returned to the attorney conference room early that evening, Marya was sitting at the small table. Police reports were stacked in the center of the table. A writing pad with a freshly sharpened pencil was placed on each side.

'How is jail food?' Marya asked.

'Rotten cabbage in sewer water.'

A paper bag hit her leg. Marya was bending down, her arm under the table. Lara took the bag and opened it on her lap. A wonderful aroma hit her nostrils, sending a sensation of pure joy shivering down her spine.

A Big Mac from McDonald's.

Lara started to say something and Marya said, 'Whisper.'

'It must have cost you a week's wages.'

Marya giggled. 'My friend works there at night. He smuggled it to me. I don't have a week's wages to spend.'

A stolen Big Mac. Somehow that made it even more delicious.

Another bag hit her knee.

'Chocolate for energy,' Marya whispered.

'Oh, I love you. But next time bring me a cake with a saw in it.'

'A cake with a saw? Why would you want that?'

'It's an old American joke.'

Marya said in a normal voice, 'I've arranged to have some

of the money in your purse released and deposited to your jail account. You will be able to buy necessities with it. I've given the guard a bag with comb, brush, toothpaste, a toothbrush and some other things.'

'Marya, I don't know what to say.'

'The things I have brought, they are not of good quality.'

'I understand. You must take half the money in my purse.'

'No, no, I won't do that. Now we must get to work.'

Lara dropped the subject rather than embarrass her.

'Now,' Marya said, dropping her voice back to a whisper, 'before we go through the police reports, let's talk about the past. When we met yesterday after the court session you told me about your suspicions concerning what the man Belkin had said to you about a young boy being charged with a mutilation killing.'

'Yes, after I realized that the woman in the photograph I was sent wasn't my mother, it occurred to me that Belkin wasn't just making conversation, that there might be a connection with the death of our neighbor.'

'You were correct. I reviewed court records for that time. A young man, actually a boy of seventeen named Alexander Zurin whose address was the same as the one you gave me for the apartment you shared with—'

'Pasha,' Lara interrupted her. 'Pasha is the familiar name for Alexander.'

'Yes.'

'I remember a boy in our building who used to tease me, a nice boy, his name was Pasha. Was he the one charged with Vera Swen's murder?'

'Charged, convicted, and sentenced to life imprisonment.'

'He's still in prison?'

'No. He volunteered to do road work in Afghanistan during the fighting there and was killed.'

'He was innocent.'

'Innocent? Just like that without knowing any of the facts? I compliment you, you have become an expert on Russian jurisprudence.'

'I remember him. He called me little cat.' Little Kosca. 'He was a nice boy, not the type to murder and mutilate a woman.'

'The court records say that the woman lured the boy to her room to seduce him. The police theory is that he failed to perform sexually, she said something about his manhood and he killed her in a rage.'

'He confessed, didn't he?'

'How do you know?'

'Because he didn't get the bullet.'

Marya grinned. 'You're right. He foolishly denied the crime at first but then confessed. He received a life sentence because of the heinous nature of the crime. He probably would have been sentenced to death even with the confession, but his age kept him from the executioner's bullet.' She shuffled papers in front of her. 'But enough of the past, we must go through the police reports. Because of the importance of the case, the coverage in the news media, the police have been more active than usual. They have found witnesses against you.'

'Marya, the secret to my case is in the past. Tell me what else you learned about Pasha's case.'

'That's all. Court summaries of the records.'

'Can you get to the actual police reports?'

She hesitated. 'I'm not sure.'

Lara stared at her. 'You're avoiding telling me something.'

'I . . . I already tried to look at the police reports. The police file on the case is missing.'

'You mean stolen.'

'I don't know.'

'I do. Whoever took that file sent me one of the crime scene photos from it.'

'Lara, I know how . . . how important it is to you to piece together the past, but there is so much we need to deal with now. You are charged with a murder *now*, not twenty years ago. We must focus on that.'

'All right, but . . .' She clenched her teeth. 'All right, you mentioned witnesses the police found in Nadia's case. Witnesses to what?'

'Your violent and irrational nature.'

'My . . . oh, yes, the party. Marya, I have to explain that to you.'

'I don't think you will be able to come up with a rational explanation for shooting up a party in your underwear with half the new gentry of Russia watching.' There was awe in Marya's voice.

'I was drunk. For the first time in my life I was drunk. I didn't know what I was doing.'

'There are more witnesses, people interviewed when this man Belkin was hit by the truck.'

'I had nothing to do with that. He was injured at the park and later given an overdose in the hospital.'

'In the police reports, an elderly couple state that a young woman, a foreigner who spoke Russian with little accent, was acting strange. You are the person Detective Kirov identified as the irrational woman.'

'That's nonsense.'

'Lara, I don't understand. It is not just the Nadia Kolchak death that these reports mention. There is a school teacher who died after she talked to you. School officials believe you are responsible for her death because the woman was screaming and distraught after you spoke to her. There are interviews with the staff at the Gorky Hotel who say you appeared to be irrational much of the time. A hospital report of fainting and falling from a window at—'

'Fainting and falling hell. I was pushed.'

'And an ambulance record of fainting in Red Square.'

Lara turned pink. 'That one's true. But you have to understand, everything is being bent out of shape. None of it has anything to do with the charges against me, none of it is evidence related to the case against me. It's all speculation, hearsay and innuendo.'

'It's all proper evidence in our courtrooms.'

'That's ridiculous.'

Marya shuffled the papers in front of her again. Lara could tell she was disturbed.

'You're wondering what you've gotten yourself into, aren't you?' she said.

'For myself, I don't wonder. When I left today I was interviewed by the press. My face is being beamed by satellite around the world. Already, I am famous. My telephone has not stopped ringing. But I wonder how things will go for you. I believe you are a good person, but some of these things . . .'

Lara laid her hands on the table, spreading her fingers. 'I understand. So let's start from the beginning. I was born in Moscow. My mother was . . .'

For an hour she related every move she had made since arriving in Moscow and everything she remembered from those days as a child in the city.

Marya started to make notes and then, as the story grabbed her attention more and more, she put down her pencil, leaned forward in her chair, propped her chin in her hands, and listened.

After Lara had finished her tale, both women remained silent for a moment before Marya picked up her pencil and started writing and talking.

'Point one: two women died twenty years ago. One by alleged suicide; the other by an act of insane violence. Point two: you have been lured to Moscow by someone connected to these deaths.'

'Connected, or has knowledge of,' Lara interjected.

'Either way, it certainly wasn't by the teenage boy, he's dead.'

'Get me anything you can on his death. So far about everything I've read in official documents has been a lie. So who knows?'

Marya made a note. 'Next point: something is going on today that is connected to the people from the past.'

Lara started to say something and Marya motioned her to whisper.

'Nadia believed that Felix was blackmailing Alexei. I'm not sure I accept that, but I know something is going on between them beside the normal work relationship. I told you about the picture. Alexei lied when he said he didn't know my mother. He knew her and the neighbor woman.'

Marya shrugged. 'Knew or attended the same party once. You believe Alexei was ex-KGB. Both women, as foreigners, would have had a KGB agent assigned to them. Alexei may have been that agent, or the supervising agent.'

'All right. But that's a little too simple. Bova is not just a person from the past. In this cast of characters, he has to be a star performer,' Lara said.

'I accept that. Point four, Alexei Bova is hiding something. Five, Detective Yuri Kirov is hiding something.'

'Felix is hiding something too. Nadia was trying to dig it all out – for profit.'

'So, what occurred in the past is important today. When it all erupted, you ended up taking a fall for Nadia's death. Intentional or accidental?' Marya wrote.

'Good question. How would anyone know that I would be sure to take the keys and go to the penthouse?'

'Well, that hardly requires second sight. Since you arrived in Moscow you've bribed your way into the most secret KGB archive, and broken into a renowned psychiatric institute, never mind falling out of a window at St Basil's and shooting up the Black Tower. What's breaking and entering into the penthouse of the richest man in Russia after all that?'

'Oh, God.' Lara hid her face in her hands.

'Let's discuss the crime in hand. Nadia was killed by two wounds made by a .38 caliber weapon. The bullets are being compared to ones taken from the ceiling that you fired during the party. I haven't seen the reports yet.'

'They will match up. Whoever set this up would be that thorough. Alexei, Felix, Ilya, any one of that group could have got hold of the gun I left in the limo. But the one I threw at the wall in my hotel room, I never saw it again. It could have ended up in anyone's hands. What about the maid, Anna? Have the police interviewed her?'

'No, she's not available.'

'What does that mean?'

Marya shrugged. 'A quote from the police report. It could mean anything from deceased to vacationing at a Black Sea resort.'

The two women were quiet for a moment before Lara asked, 'Were any other marks found on Nadia's body? I'd like to see the autopsy reports.'

'I'm having everything copied for you. The report mentions only the two bullet wounds.'

'But did the pathologist examine the body for other marks?'

'The autopsy was limited to an examination of the two wounds.'

'That's not a full autopsy!'

'That's a Russian autopsy. Things you take for granted in your country such as disinfecting chemicals and rubber gloves are not in good supply in Russia.'

'Marya, that body has to be examined. We need to have an independent pathologist appointed to do our own autopsy. We're also going to need an investigator who can track down—'

Marya reached across and put her hands over Lara's. 'The court isn't going to appoint a pathologist or any other expert for you. You have to share the prosecutor's experts. And its investigator, Vulko.'

'That's insane. Experts are loyal to the side that pays them. And it's not just a question of loyalty. Opinions differ, especially expert ones.'

'You don't have to convince me. But it is the Russian way. Experts are neutral because we are . . . were . . . a communist society.'

'But it didn't work under your communist society. Why would it work now?'

'I didn't say it worked. I said it was the Russian way. And the economy makes it worse. With the bad economic conditions, the court will not pay for experts for a person charged with a crime.'

'Great,' Lara said through a mouthful of hamburger. 'Okay then, tell me about courtroom procedure. Start at the beginning and take me step by step through a trial.'

Marya was about to answer when a thought struck Lara and she asked, 'Are we being recorded?'

'I believe so.' Marya shrugged. 'That was often the custom under the Soviet regime. It's hard to break old habits. Now, you understand there are no jury trials.'

Marya didn't seem intimidated by the possible eavesdropping and Lara mentally shrugged it off as par for the course.

She was trying to get herself in tune to the Russian criminal justice system. Thinking like an American could be fatal.

'Right. A judge and two lay persons decide the case.'

'Yes. Two citizens will be appointed by the court. But don't let the presence of three people fool you, the decision will be made by the judge.'

'The citizens don't have equal voting rights with the judge?'

'Possessing a right,' Marya said, 'and using it are two different things. The idea of having citizens share a judge's authority, reducing the power of the judge, is good Marxist-Leninist theory. But except on rare occasions the citizens merely rubber stamp the judge's decision. They would not be chosen to serve as lay judges if they were not the type to follow the judge's lead.'

'Your rules of evidence, the rules governing oral testimony and other written and physical evidence, what are they?'

'The rules are what the judge says the rules are.'

'Do you understand the English legal term hearsay?' Lara asked.

'Yes. Unsworn testimony, things people heard and said out of court. That is all admissible in a Russian trial.'

'That would mean matters of speculation, what people believe or imagine can be admitted.'

'The judge can exclude evidence, but the favored policy is for everyone to have their day in court.'

'Everyone? I thought this was the defendant's day in court.'

'Not in Russia. In law school they told us that in America you have two sides in a criminal case, the prosecutor representing the state, and the defendant. The prosecutor speaks for the state and the defendant speaks, through an attorney, for his or her side. True?'

'True.'

'In Russia there are usually more than two sides to a criminal case,' Marya said. 'The first thing that happens after the judge calls the case is that the defendant is told to step forward and explain why he or she committed the crime. You are expected to confess. You have no right to remain silent, no right to refuse to testify.'

'No right against self-incrimination. Confession is good for the soul.'

'Exactly. After the criminal steps forward and explains the reason for committing the crime or, less often, denies the crime, the judge asks the criminal questions about how the crime was committed and the person's motives.'

'We call that cross-examination,' Lara said, 'conducted by attorneys, not judges, in America and Britain.'

'Yes, cross-examination. After the judge examines the accused, the prosecutor asks more questions. If the judge has been very thorough, the prosecutor may not ask any questions.'

'The purpose must be to fill in things the judge missed.'

'That's right. Now, after the judge and the prosecutor ask questions—'

'The defense attorney—'

'No, I told you, there are more than two sides to a Russian criminal case. At this point questions might be asked by another interested party, let's say a psychiatrist if the accused's sanity is questioned. This psychiatrist or psychologist may simply be used as an expert by the prosecution or he may take a full part in the proceedings as a party. Next, a lawyer representing the victim's interests can question—'

'Wait. Are you telling me that the victim or the victim's family are a party in the courtroom? They can have an attorney who asks questions and participates in the trial?'

'Yes, they can employ an attorney or ask questions themselves.'

'I don't believe this. So first the defendant is called forward and is asked to confess. Then the judge cross-examines, followed by the prosecutor, experts and any other interested party, including the victim in person?'

Marya nodded.

'Is Nadia's family getting a lawyer?'

'They already have one. In fact he almost shoved me down the courthouse steps this afternoon so he could get in front of the news cameras. He told the nation that he would work to ensure that Nadia's killer is punished, that she deserves the bullet.'

'Wonderful. Is this guy any good?'

'He's one of the best lawyers in Moscow.'

'Sounds familiar.' Lara stared at Marya. 'You're not telling me it's Viktor Rykoff, are you?'

'The very one. I caught the afternoon news just before coming here. I got three seconds on screen before they cut to Rykoff. He said very nice things about Nadia. And cried.'

Lara wanted to scream. 'How can the man talk to me about my case and then represent an adverse party? That's a conflict of interest.'

'The goal of the Russian judicial system is to seek the truth. What you tell an attorney can also be used against you.'

'That destroys the attorney-client relationship.'

'That relationship has not been important in our society. It is important to me and to attorneys like me who are thinking in the new ways. But, Lara, you have to accept that good or bad, right or wrong, the Russian system is the one we are dealing with.'

'I'm sorry, Marya. I just . . . Tell me, is there a time when the defense attorney gets to ask questions?'

'Yes, of course. After the judge, the prosecutor, the victim and any other interested party, the defense attorney may ask questions. And after the defense attorney has finished, the defendant is allowed to speak again and to question witnesses.'

'You mean the defendant and the defendant's attorney can both question witnesses?'

'Yes. It's very democratic.'

'More like a circus,' Lara said. 'It's just for show, especially if the case starts off with a confession. To me, a trial is like a chess game – it's about making the right moves, taking apart your opponent piece by piece, marching in experts to defeat your opponent's experts, putting on critical evidence at well-timed moments to capture just the right effect with the jury. In America and Britain, trials are battlefields. Russian trials sound more like bureaucratic hearings.'

'You are probably right. They are not battlefields, certainly. I have not told you the worst part. When you begin a trial with a confession—'

'Which would stop an American trial.'

'Exactly my point. In your country, once the accused admits guilt, there is no trial. In Russia, we usually start the trial with an admission of guilt. If you start with the concept that the accused is guilty, the rest is just a formality.'

'So you have been telling me.'

'But you have to understand how the Russian system actually operates. The judge has before him a person accused, a person who usually has confessed. The judge will thereafter go through the facts of the case. In America, these facts would be presented to him by the prosecution through witnesses and evidence in open court. In Russia, the judge has been given a statement of the case prepared by the prosecution's investigator and the judge will use that as a road map. From that road map he will call witnesses he wants to hear from and ask to see evidence that interests him.'

'But that's all from the prosecution's side. By the time the case is called, the judge will be totally prejudiced against the defendant.'

'Now you understand the role of prosecutors and people like Chief Investigator Vulko. They provide the judge with a direction and the judge follows it. But there is one fundamental right that no judge would deny a defendant.'

'What? To be found guilty?'

Marya smiled. 'They have that right, too. No, the right I speak of is the last word.'

'The last word?'

'Yes. After everyone else has spoken, after all the evidence has been put forward, after everyone – the prosecution, the defendant, the victim or the victim's family – have had the opportunity to ask questions and testify, there comes the grand finale,' Marya waved her hands dramatically, 'and the judge turns to the defendant and says, "Give us your final word."'

'Help, that's the word I'd choose. I'm sorry, what's the purpose of the last word?'

'To throw yourself at the mercy of the court. To explain why the crime was committed.'

'The first word is a confession, the last word is a plea for mercy. I'm not sure there's much justice in between. How did you ever become an attorney in this crazy system? No, that's a stupid question. You were born in this system.'

'I'm very proud to be an attorney.'

'Of course you are. And so am I. I worked hard to get a law degree and pass the bar exam. And I know that there must be tremendous prejudices and obstacles put in your way. Were your parents like mine? Foreigners living in Russia?'

'My mother was Russian. My father was a diplomat from

the Sudan. When he returned to Africa, she chose to remain here. As a white Russian woman in Africa, she would probably have felt as I do about being a black woman in Moscow.'

'But, you're half Russian.'

'No, I'm *black*. If my father had been a Georgian or even a Turk, I might be called half Russian. Or maybe even simply Russian. When your skin is black, no one cares about your bloodlines. Do you know how I got my name, Marya?'

Lara shook her head. 'Tell me.'

'It was one of Pushkin's favorite names for heroines. You know who Pushkin is?'

Lara told her she knew who the great Russian writer was.

'Did you know that Pushkin was part African? His grandfather was a black slave Peter the Great elevated to nobility because of his services in war.'

'I didn't know that.'

'Neither do any of the other white people in Moscow. A number of black people came here from Africa and America attracted by the great egalitarian society. The Soviets used them as propaganda pieces for foreign consumption, but the Russians themselves never accepted them as equals. Now, because so many of these people have been relegated to menial jobs and live under the scorn of their neighbors, there is much crime and prostitution among them.'

Lara nodded and tried to keep her next thought to herself but Marya had already anticipated it.

'You're wondering if the criminal cases I've been appointed to all involved people with black skin.'

'Yes.'

'I told you the judge wanted to punish you,' she said. She stared down at the papers in front of her.

Lara leaned forward and put her hands on Marya's and whispered, 'Then he made a mistake, my friend. Because you and I are going into that courtroom ready for combat while the rest of them are only prepared to put on a show trial.'

'You don't understand,' Marya whispered. 'The prosecutor and Rykoff will get together with the judge and limit what we can do.'

'They're not going to limit us. You said that the case was getting incredible news attention. Russia's anxious to show its newfound democratic face to the world. We're going to go in there and open our mouths, Marya. We're going to say things that are going to be repeated around the world.'

'The judge will shut you up.'

'American lawyers are shut up all the time. All we do is turn round and say the same thing in another way. You're not a good lawyer until you've been held in contempt at least a couple of times.'

Marya shook her fists. 'I'm so excited,' she whispered. 'New ideas, new approaches. We'll turn the Moscow court system on its ear. You just tell me what to do, how to win.' Another thought occurred to her. 'How many cases have you defended?' she asked.

'Defended?' Lara had been a prosecutor. 'This will be the first.'

Chapter 31

The police reports told them little of any value in terms of constructing a defense: while sitting naked in the spa, Nadia had been shot twice, once through the chest and what appeared to be a *coup de grâce* in the back of the head. The hot, circulating water made it difficult to pin down an exact time of death. The police theory was that Lara was captured within minutes of shooting Nadia. Despite the autopsy report acknowledging the fact that the hot water made it difficult to gauge an exact time of death, the pathologist who did the report set the time of death at precisely one minute before Lara was captured.

The tail was clearly wagging the dog. Time of death was a required entry on the death form. The time of death could not be determined precisely by the physical evidence, so the pathologist provided a time based upon the officer's statement as to when Lara was captured. If Lara had done the killing, it was a reasonable conclusion.

'My arrest in the building, murder weapon in hand, obviously saved the pathologist a great deal of thinking time,' Lara commented. 'There's something else that doesn't add up,' she went on. 'The police say that they received an anonymous tip that a woman carrying a gun had entered the tower and a shot was heard. I want the tape of that anonymous call.'

'What tape? Stop thinking like an American. If they have

a tape, they won't give it to us. And if they don't have a tape, they won't tell us they don't have it. I'll find out what I can about the call, but don't expect a tape recording.'

Lara tapped the report. 'It also says that no one in the area reported hearing shots, which is in my favor.'

Marya shook her head. 'There was heavy construction work going on down the block. The police claim a bomb exploding would not have been heard.'

'But the anonymous caller claims to have heard a shot. And don't you find it interesting that Yuri Kirov and his group of officers were the ones who responded to the anonymous call? There are thousands of police officers in Moscow and the one who responds is the same guy I've been tripping over every time I turn round. According to the police report, Yuri met up with the other officers in the lobby.'

'The tower is not far from the main police headquarters,' Marya pointed out.

'Whose side are you on? Just joking, but I still want to know everything about that call. If the call wasn't taped, I want to know the exact time it was received, who received it, who that person reported to, when the officers left the police station, how long it took them to get to the building, up the elevators and through the penthouse doors.'

'Do you also want to know their brand of cigarettes? An officer will testify about the call at the trial. Perhaps not the officer who received it, but—'

'No, we don't wait for the trial to find out about the call. You should never ask a question during a trial that you don't already know the answer to because the answer might sink your case. We need to know everything that will help us and everything that will damage us before we enter the courtroom. Keep reminding yourself that you're not an administrator of justice in the old system, you're a gladiator fighting to the death in the new.'

'I keep reminding myself that I am a gladiator,' Marya said, 'and a voice keeps whispering in my ear that I'm really a mouse.'

'Then be Mighty Mouse. Listen to me, Marya. I am being framed. To frame a person for a crime like this, everything has to run like clockwork. What we need to do is uncover the inconsistencies; remember that word, glue it to your brain, *inconsistencies*. What's an inconsistency? I arrived in the penthouse only a minute or two before the police came crashing in. That means that the call to the police was probably made before I entered.'

'If the call was made before you even entered,' Marya interjected, 'and it had to have been because of the time it would take the officers to get there, and someone, perhaps a shopkeeper, spotted you entering *after* the call was made . . .'

'You're getting it. We need an investigator to go door to door and find people who saw or heard something. I might be able to establish I was still at the dacha or on my way into town when the shots were fired. Someone might have heard the shots, whatever the police say about the sound being muffled by the construction, might have seen me enter the building without a gun. The investigator can track down the maid Anna and talk to her. She would know what happened to the gun I left at the hotel.'

'It is the same bullet,' Marya said. 'I was told the report was not finished but here it is. One of the two bullets removed from the ceiling matches one of the bullets that killed Nadia. The other bullet found in the ceiling matches a gun the police found packed and ready to be returned to where the guns were rented.'

'Wait. You say the bullet matches one of the bullets that killed Nadia. Was she shot by two different guns?'

'No. Both slugs were fired from a .38, but one of them was too damaged to be compared with the .38 slug from the ceiling.'

'We need a ballistics expert to go over the results and personally examine each bullet. If Moscow police ballistics are as scientific as their autopsies, we'll probably find one bullet came from a cannon and the other from a pea shooter.'

'But the ballistics expert says—'

'Marya, remember, that's *their* ballistics expert you're talking about. Our expert might find it was fired from an entirely different gun. Ballistics experts render opinions based upon evidence and many times the evidence is subject to more than one interpretation. Remember, question, question—'

'Question everything. My boy friend has a friend in the army who is a ballistics expert. He'll probably help.'

'Good.' Lara continued talking as Marya took notes. 'Let's assume it's the same gun, the gun I carried back to the hotel from the party. Yuri, Detective Kirov, knew I had it – hell, I threw it at him. He could have come back later and got it. Alexei, or perhaps his staff, people like Ilya and Felix, would have known about it if Anna returned the gun to one of them. If Anna didn't pick up the gun, another maid could have found it and turned it over to anyone in the world, especially in a country where everyone is still spying on everyone else.' She ran her hands through her hair and pulled. 'God, I don't know what to think. It's all too complicated.'

Marya looked up from her writing. 'You were the last one seen with the gun and the one caught with it. How do you explain that under Anglo-American jurisprudence?'

'You punt.'

'Punt?'

'It's a joke. An American football term. When the other team's got your back to the wall, you kick the ball to get out of it. Meaning you take a gamble or do something brilliant – or you just close your eyes and jump.'

'What is our brilliant explanation?'

'I was framed. We'll know more after we get an investigator. You said the court won't help with that.'

'Don't worry, I have friends already working on it.'

'Marya, I'm so glad you're my attorney.'

The young Russian grinned. 'I woke up this morning and pinched myself, wondering if this was really happening.'

'I did a reality check myself and found out the nightmare was real,' Lara said. 'Did they test the gun for fingerprints?'

Marya took a minute to skim through the reports. 'Fingerprint tests were unnecessary because the police had observed you holding the gun.'

'But what about other people who held the gun before me?'

'Your prints would have wiped out—'

'No, absolutely not. I only grabbed the gun by the handle. I don't even remember touching the barrel. That's sloppy police work. Even if I smudged some prints, there might be others.' Lara got to her feet, her voice rising. 'We have to have the gun tested for prints.'

'Not so loud.'

Lara sat wearily back down and whispered, 'Sorry. I keep forgetting we're being bugged. We need a fingerprint expert appointed by the court immediately and an order to the Moscow police to turn over the gun for examination forthwith. And crime scene pictures, not photocopies of pictures; I want duplicate prints. Make sure they turn over all prints, not just selected ones. And besides checking for witnesses and searching for Anna, the investigator should interview the people on the prosecutor's witness list. And we'll need background checks on all the key players – Alexei, Felix, Ilya, Belkin, Nadia, and don't forget Detective Yuri Kirov. And that security man at the Gorky who turned me onto Belkin, we need to locate him. He conveniently dropped out of sight after Belkin was killed.'

Marya wrote frantically. 'You will need to enlist the Russian army to act as investigators.'

'Try to find us a pathologist. We have to conduct our own autopsy.'

When she was through writing, Marya looked up and asked, 'Is this how criminal cases are fought in America? With an army of experts?'

'The toughest case I ever prosecuted involved a teenage girl who had been strangled. The defense attorney not only got the court to appoint a defense pathologist to do another autopsy on the body, he watched the autopsy.'

'The defense attorney won the case?'

'No. I was there too, handing his pathologist forceps and scalpels. The second autopsy came up with a critical piece of evidence – the young woman had been strangled from behind by a left-handed person. That was deduced from the fact that the damage to tissue was more severe on the right side of the victim's neck than the left side. If I hadn't been standing by, that information would never have been revealed.'

'The defendant was left-handed?'

'Yes.'

'I really admire you. I have never heard of an attorney attending an autopsy.'

'Don't admire me. I was sick for a week afterwards. Once, in a moment of temporary insanity, I had a pathologist lead me through an autopsy on a Jane Doe, an unidentified body, with a knife wound. Our theory was that the defendant stabbed her in the stomach. The defense position was that the wound was self-inflicted, hari-kari style. By participating in the autopsy, by observing the position her body had to be in for the incisions in the layers of flesh and organs to line up, I was able to explain how the murder occurred.'

Marya's mouth dropped.

Lara took a deep breath. 'I hated every moment of it but I told myself I was doing it for a woman who had lost so much she didn't even have a name for a grave marker. She had been pretty, too, but . . .' Lara choked up.

'Now I know what you mean about being a good lawyer, Lara. You have to be a doctor, a detective and a scientist.'

'Don't forget actor, psychologist and occasionally avenging angel.'

Marya's face twisted with a surge of emotion and she burst into tears. It was Lara's turn to gape as the young lawyer hid her face in her hands and wept.

'Marya, what's wrong?'

'There will be no experts, no tests,' she sobbed. 'They will convict you and you will die because I can never be the lawyer you need.'

Lara got out of her chair and went round to the other side of the table. She put her hands on Marya's shoulders and squeezed. 'I feel like a fool,' she told Marya, 'telling you what a great attorney I was back in the States. The truth is I always had a team of investigators and experts at my beck and call because I had the power of the government behind me. This is the first time I've had to wing it.'

'You do have to wing it. We both do. The court will never appoint experts. No fingerprint expert, no pathologist, no investigators. I told you, I can get friends to help to knock on doors, someone to look at the bullets—'

'Just do what you can. If we can't get our own pathologist, get as much information as you can from theirs. The
only thing I ask is that you try, and that you shake off the
mentality that a defense lawyer is an arm of the government. You're young and tough and part of the new Russia,
Marya. Don't let the old ways,' she almost said 'kill me',
'don't let the old ways make us lose.' She pointed a finger
down at the young attorney. 'Stop crying. We're tough
lawyers. We can do it.'

Marya wiped away her tears. 'We're tough lawyers. We
don't cry. But, Lara, I don't know what to do, I can't get
you the things you need. If you had money ... I thought
all—'

'Don't say it, don't call me a rich American. If I hear that
phrase one more time I'm going to run screaming into the
night. Or at least back to my cell.' Lara suddenly thought
about Marya's other clients. 'What about the rest of your
law practice? How busy does it keep you?'

Marya laughed. 'The rest of my law practice takes a few
hours a week.'

'Take half the money in my purse. It'll help with taxi
fares and snacks while you run around.'

Marya waved away the offer. 'I take the metro and pack
my lunch. I don't know a pathologist, but I have my own
doctor who can answer medical questions.'

'It won't help.' Lara shook her head.

Marya looked as if she was going to cry again. 'Lara, I
can't get a pathologist to let me conduct an autopsy. That
just isn't done in Russia.'

'Don't worry about autopsies. I'll go through the pathologist's report and see what we need to have filled in. When
you don't have your own experts, you try to get enough out
of the opposing experts to add to your case or impeach the
expert at trial.'

'I can't do anything about background checks. That would violate the privacy of our citizens,' Marya said out loud, then leaned closer to Lara and whispered, 'My boy friend works in the military records division of the army. Most of the men we're investigating should have military records. Even if they didn't serve, there will be background checks.'

'Great.'

Lara stood up and gave Marya a big hug. Marya put her own arms round Lara and squeezed.

'We're going to make it happen,' Lara told her.

Marya gave her a high five. 'Right on, sister.' She giggled. 'I saw that in an American movie.'

It was after ten o'clock before they decided to call it quits. They hugged again before Marya left. Lara sat wearily at the counsel table, waiting for the matron to return from letting Marya out.

The woman unlocked the conference door and gestured for Lara to come out. Lara waited while the woman relocked the door. The woman spoke to her as they walked back toward the cell block.

'You are making a mistake,' she told Lara.

'A mistake?'

'The black girl, she's no good.'

'Why do you say that?'

The matron glared at her. 'Are you stupid? She's black. If she was good, she'd be white.'

Jesus.

'No one will listen to her in court.'

'I hope that's not true,' Lara murmured.

'What did she tell you about herself? Did she tell you her father was an African diplomat?' The matron laughed. 'Everyone in the courts knows about her. Her father was a driver for one of the African embassies. And her mother was a whore, a prostitute and a drug addict. That's why they give her the prostitution cases. They say it's in her blood.'

Lara didn't speak and the look on her face annoyed the guard. 'Didn't you hear what I told you, prisoner?'

'I heard you. All I can say is that I must have one hell of a lawyer. A woman who could crawl out of the gutter and make it all the way to the Moscow courts by the time she's twenty-five must be one tough lady. I'm glad she's on my side.'

The matron grabbed Lara by the arm and pushed her down the corridor. 'Move, prisoner.'

Lara kept her mouth shut the rest of the way back to the cell. The woman opened the cell door and as Lara started to step into the black hole, she realized someone was there.

'Shhh. Don't make a sound.' It was Alexei.

In the next cell a woman started whining about the noise and the matron told her to shut up or she'd take away her food privileges.

Alexei pulled her into the cell.

'I can only stay a minute. I paid my way in.' He laughed, an almost girlish giggle. 'Imagine paying your way *into* jail.'

She didn't say a word.

'I know this is hell for you. But it's just for a short time. I can't get you out yet, but I will. There's too much publicity about the case right now. When the publicity stops, I'll buy your way out.'

'I'm charged with murder, Alexei, not shoplifting.'

'Everything is for sale, if you have enough geese. But it's too soon. I even had to leave the penthouse in disguise tonight just to come over here. Camera crews and reporters have the tower staked out twenty-four hours a day. Darling, at the right time I'll grease the right palms.'

She hated the way he called her darling. A melodramatic

ring came with it. There was melodrama to everything about him right now, as if being the prisoner's savior was another role to play, riding up to the gallows at the last moment and cutting away the hangman's noose with his sword.

'You've made me famous all over the world,' he told her. 'Our love affair and you killing Nadia is getting more news coverage than the war in Yugoslavia.'

Anger blew the roof off her emotions. She grabbed him by the lapels. 'How dare you say I killed Nadia. I never touched Nadia.'

'Shhh, calm down. I didn't mean that.'

'Understand that. I never touched her.'

'Then who killed her?'

'Why don't you tell me?'

'Me? I never killed her. I was getting tired of the bitch, and she was a bitch even if I shouldn't speak harshly of the dead. I was tired of her constant demands for money and frankly bored with her as a lover, but that's hardly a reason to kill her. I was already letting her know her days were numbered when I brought you into my life.'

'Nadia was trying to blackmail you. She knows Felix has something on you.'

'What did she tell you?'

'Exactly that. What does Felix have on you? And what does it have to do with that picture of you with my mother and our neighbor?'

'Felix isn't blackmailing me.'

Something about his voice told her he was telling the truth. It wasn't so much a ring of truth to what he said, more the way he tossed aside the idea, as if blackmail was insignificant compared to what was really going on between him and Felix.

'You're right about the picture. I didn't even realize the

picture existed. I don't remember your mother or the other woman. Apparently there was a party at Felix's apartment, I was there, pictures were taken. When you showed up at my cowboy party, it struck a cord. He found the picture and used it.'

'Used it for what? You said he isn't blackmailing you.'

'I can't explain.'

'I'm facing a murder charge. You damn well better start explaining.'

'It has nothing to do with Nadia or the charges against you. The past, Felix is part of my past.'

'What part of the past?'

'Not your mother. I . . . I used to be KGB.'

'You and half the other people in this country. What does that have to do with anything that's happening now?'

'I can't explain. You'll just have to trust me.'

'Trust you? I'm in jail accused of murdering your girl friend who was hot to blackmail you and told me she knew secrets you were hiding, and you want me to trust you?'

'What did Nadia tell you?'

'Nothing. Unfortunately, by the time I arrived for our appointment someone had put two bullets in her. If you want me to trust you, answer a question honestly. Anna returned my cowboy outfit to you, the hat and boots. Did she return a gun too?'

'Who's Anna?'

'The damn maid you had spying on me.'

'Oh yes, the one with the club foot. I don't know what she returned. She would have given the stuff to Ilya. If he wasn't there, Felix probably would have taken it. Is one of the guns supposed to be the gun that killed Nadia?'

'That's what they say.'

'The police were digging holes in the ceiling. They must have been looking for a bullet to match.'

'They were and they did. The murder weapon was one of the guns I fired that night.'

'That's bad.'

'Bad?' She laughed, a harsh grate in her throat. 'It's worse than bad. I feel like my life's been thrown in front of a runaway train. I need to talk to Anna. Or at least have my lawyer talk to her.'

'I don't know where she is. I'll ask Ilya to locate her.'

'If you want to help me, find her. If she can testify she returned the gun—'

He was shaking her head. 'I remember now. Ilya mentioned that the maid had returned your outfit but not the gun. You left one gun in the limo.'

She shivered listening to him.

'Ilya asked me to speak to you about the missing gun and I forgot.'

'I don't believe this.'

'Is it important she returned the gun?'

'Of course it's important. That would get the murder weapon out of my hands and into someone else's. It's the difference between being convicted of murder and having a fighting chance.'

'Don't worry. I'll have Anna found and she'll testify that you returned both guns. It's as simple as that.'

'That's perjury.'

'It's only perjury when you get caught.'

She shook her head. 'No, no, you can't do that. Find Anna so my attorney can talk to her.'

He suddenly looked as if he had eaten something that left a bad taste. 'I've heard about your attorney. You have to get rid of her. I'll get you the best attorney in Moscow.'

'I've already fired the best attorney in Moscow. I'm keeping the one I've got.'

'That's insane. Do you know her background?'

The matron came back to the cell. 'You have to leave. Its time to change shifts. Hurry.'

Alexei took hold of Lara. She held her arms against her chest so she wouldn't touch him intimately.

'I love you, darling,' he said. 'I'll get you out of this. You must have faith and trust me.'

He was back to his role-playing.

'That night when we made love . . .'

She tensed against him.

'It was . . . it was the first time any woman has satisfied me. Nadia was nothing.'

'Hurry,' the matron hissed.

Alexei tried to kiss her on the lips but she turned her head to give her cheek.

'Find Anna,' she told him.

He left and she sank in a dark corner of her cell and wrapped her blanket round her.

She was exhausted. She tried to put some of the things Alexei had said into a sensible order, but the thoughts kept melting away, all except one: Felix wasn't blackmailing Alexei. She told herself she shouldn't believe that statement but she intuitively knew it was true. And it raised an interesting question.

Why would two men who obviously had nothing but contempt for each other, two men who were drastically different in temperament and ambitions, two men who had nothing in common, stay together as . . . as what? And for over two decades?

Just before she fell into a deep sleep another thought slipped into her mind like a snake slithering under the threshold of a door.

Alexei wasn't rich and eccentric. He was rich and crazy. Rich. Crazy. KGB. Felix. Blackmail. No blackmail.

None of it made sense.

Chapter 32

Marya was waiting for her in the attorney conference room the next morning.

'A city court judge has been appointed to handle the trial. He is going to take me off the case.'

'What? Why?'

'Because of the publicity. I don't photograph well. Sorry, I don't mean that. The real reason is a good one – I'm not experienced.'

'We've already been through this. The attorneys experienced enough to have handled murder cases are all products of the Soviet era. Rykoff was probably a lawyer at least a decade before Gorbachev took power. I don't want that type of lawyer. Marya, I don't want you as my lawyer because I like you, I want you because you're young and fresh and your mind isn't totally polluted with outdated ideas.'

'Telling the judge that the best lawyers in Moscow are dinosaurs practicing outdated Marxist-Leninist theories is not going to win you any favors.'

'Then I'll have to use my thermonuclear bomb. This is the actual trial judge?'

'Yes.'

'How was he selected?'

'Selected? You mean by chance or deliberately?' She leaned close to Lara and whispered, 'Judge Rurik was probably selected because he looks good on television. As you pointed out, this case is a chance for the new Russian justice system to show the world its face and he looks distinguished.'

'Does he have any brains?'

Marya thought for a moment. 'He is probably not the worst judge for your case. I've heard that he is honest.'

'Has a prosecutor been assigned?'

'We will know this morning. We're going into court in a few minutes. They say the Chief Prosecutor himself might handle the case. You talked about a thermonuclear bomb. What did you mean?'

'I don't know. I guess I'll have to punt.'

For the first time since she had been in jail she got to see the corridor of the courthouse. She was taken down the public corridor to a meeting in the judge's temporary office.

'Judge Rurik's courtroom and chambers are being painted,' Marya told her. Two jail matrons accompanied them.

'A color that will look pretty on camera?' Lara murmured.

A sideways look from Marya was her answer.

High-profile cases are the worst, Lara thought. Everyone involved, from the judge and lawyers to witnesses, started performing for the camera. She hated it when the press invaded the cases she was handling back in San Francisco. It wasn't the fact that the press covered the story. What bugged her was the news-hungry, sensation-hungry media trying the case on television and in the newspapers rather than letting justice take its natural course in the courtroom.

They paused in front of a door and one of the matrons knocked. The door was opened a moment later by a woman who told them to wait for the prosecutor to arrive.

'Have you seen the Chief Prosecutor in trial?' Lara asked. 'Is he any good?'

'I've never seen him. I'm not sure if—' She stopped as the elevator doors down the corridor opened to reveal three people. They stepped forward with almost military precision, a woman at the leading edge in a navy-blue uniform, a step behind her two middle-aged men, both carrying briefcases.

Lara recognized one of the men: Vulko, the chief investigator who had almost snapped off her chin. He was shorter than the woman and the other man but he made up for it with his bulk.

She turned to say something to Marya about Vulko and did a double take: Marya was staring wide-eyed at the three people coming the hallway.

'Stalin's Breath,' she whispered.

'What?'

'That's what they call her, Stalin's Breath. Her name is Svetlana Petroff. She's a senior prosecutor, the toughest in Moscow. She once attended an execution of a murderer to see what it was like.' Marya stared at Lara with a mixture of horror and dismay. 'She didn't get hands-on experience with a corpse in an autopsy room like you did. She pulled the trigger at the execution herself.'

Stalin's Breath marched down the center of the corridor with people veering out of her way like waters parting for Moses. The snap of the steel caps on her heels echoed off the walls like small arms fire. Her bearing was pure military, her dark blue uniform with gold stripe crisp as a general's; her hair was blonde, short and combed straight back, her jaw rock, her eyes stone. She was all woman, but Lara had the impression of a pumped body under the uniform, a female Schwarzenegger.

The woman stopped abruptly, dismissing Marya with a

cursory glance that said Marya didn't even qualify for her contempt, and then took a long, drawn-out look at Lara, a fighter sizing up an opponent.

Marya suddenly shot forward and stuck out her hand. 'Good morning, Prosecutor Petroff. I am Marya Gan, attorney for the accused. It gives me great pleasure that a prosecutor of your stature is on the case.'

Svetlana Petroff flinched, hesitated and then shook hands. 'Good morning, Attorney Gan.'

She quickly disengaged her hand from Marya's and opened the door to the judge's chambers without knocking. As Marya and Lara waited for the prosecutor and her two shadows to pass through the doorway, Marya shot Lara a grin. At least they had discovered one chink in Svetlana's armor: the most feared prosecutor in Moscow might not be able to handle a curve ball. She had been caught off guard by Marya's warm handshake. She's a machine, Lara thought, she'll mow down everything in her path; to beat her I'll have to sneak up behind and hit her over the head.

Vulko gave them what he no doubt considered to be a pleasant smile as he passed by. Following the procession, Lara and Marya, with the two guards to the rear, entered an outer office and walked past a secretarial desk into another office.

Judge Rurik sat behind his desk and waited for them to trail in. He looked a little like Boris Yeltsin, thick, prematurely white hair capping a large head and broad face. Marya was right, Lara thought, he would look both Russian and judicial for a camera.

With the two matrons behind Lara, the room was crowded and Lara had to edge back to keep from rubbing shoulders with Vulko.

'I am relieving you as attorney,' the judge told Marya. 'I have no doubt that you are a fine attorney with a strong commitment to justice, but it is premature for you to handle this type of case. It was an error of the people's court judge to appoint you to a complex case involving the death penalty.'

'My client does not want to relieve me,' Marya said.

'Your client does not have a choice in selection of counsel. The government is paying, the government decides who shall be the defendant's attorney.' He gave Lara a look that invited her to challenge his remark.

He was right, Lara thought, defendants weren't given the right to choose appointed counsel in the States either. She was about to argue that she wanted Marya to remain, her only leverage being that she would take her case to the news media, when Marya punted.

'I am remaining as counsel for Lara Patrick. She is paying me. I am no longer appointed, but privately retained.'

The judge's eyes shot to the prosecutor.

One could almost see the wheels turning in Svetlana's mind as she analyzed the situation: was the defendant setting her up by having an inexperienced attorney so she could later claim her attorney had not been competent?

Lara remembered what Marya had told her about Soviet prosecutors – under the old system they had had some power to overrule even judges.

'There is an easy solution,' Svetlana told the judge. 'She can keep Marya Gan as her attorney. But in view of the complexity of the case and the potential penalty, we will appoint an attorney to assist her retained attorney.'

Lara and Marya exchanged looks, both with the same thought: two attorneys might be better than one. That's usually how it's done in the States with death penalty cases, Lara thought.

'Who would the court appoint?' Marya asked.

Stalin's Breath answered. 'Mr Venrenko.' She nodded at

the man to her right. 'He came today prepared to take over the entire case.'

Venrenko was a short, skinny man with a receding hairline and large black mustache. His clothing was neat, his shirt starched stiff, his shoes and his briefcase polished.

'Mr Venrenko is a prosecutor!' Marya said.

'No, as of last week he went into the private practice of law.' Svetlana gave him a small smile. He did not return it. 'His liking for foreign cars is stronger than his loyalty to me after many years as my assistant.'

'Your assistant?' Lara exploded. 'You're going to have your assistant appointed as my attorney?'

Marya grabbed her arm.

'This is Russia,' Svetlana told her, speaking as to a child. 'We seek justice. Our courtrooms are not theatres in which attorneys compete for top billing. Mr Venrenko has been a prosecutor for nearly thirty years. He will bring his fine sense of justice and honor to your case.'

Lara looked at him. He did not return her gaze. 'If he's been around that long administering justice, I suppose he was a prosecutor back during the days when writers and poets were tried for thinking and sent off to mental wards and forced labor camps.'

Marya audibly groaned beside her and Lara suffered instant regret, realizing the judge was probably around then too.

Svetlana started to say something but Lara cut her short by addressing the judge. 'Your honor, I'm not taking Mr Venrenko as my attorney. There are already two attorneys on my case – Miss Gan and myself. I'm an experienced attorney.'

'You are not experienced in Russian law.'

'I have chosen Miss Gan as my attorney. I am satisfied with her.'

'Fine,' Svetlana snapped. 'Let's get a transcriber in here. The defendant's wishes will be placed on the record and she will sign it. I will have the statement distributed to the news media. We will also add that this course of action is against the advice of the court and the Moscow City Procurator's office.'

Mr Venrenko remained silent.

'Why do they call her Stalin's Breath?' Lara asked. They were back in the conference room.

'It's the scent she uses. It smells like the after-burn of an artillery shell. Goes with her personality.'

'Is that story about her firing the executioner's gun true?'

Marya avoided her eyes. 'It's not a rumor. I heard Svetlana tell the story to one of my law school professors when she was at the university to give a speech.' Marya looked up. 'In many districts volunteer executioners are used.'

'Volunteers? You mean ordinary citizens?'

'Yes.'

'But they must ... they must botch some of the jobs.'

'Some of the volunteers have had a lot of practice. During a recent hunt for a serial killer the chief investigator did background checks on the citizens who volunteered to perform executions. He discovered his killer among them.'

'All right, let's drop it. I don't want to talk about it.' Lara spread the police reports on the table.

Marya reached down and picked up a paper bag. Lara had seen one of the matrons give her the bag on the way in.

'Your purse,' Marya said, handing it to her. 'I had it brought in from the property room. I can't leave it with you, but you said the picture that caused you to come to Moscow is in it.'

Lara opened the purse. 'My money's gone.'

'I have a receipt for it.'

'I insist you take it all,' Lara told her. 'Just leave me twenty American dollars for soap and toilet paper. You can't refuse this time. You're going to need it now that you're not getting paid.'

'I'm okay right now. If I get desperate, I'll take a little. I may be only twenty-five years old but I've spent almost my entire life as a communist. I get embarrassed even talking about money.'

Lara found the picture of the mutilated woman. 'This is it. I'm not surprised it's still there considering the police work on my case. I'm certain that the woman is the neighbor upstairs at the apartment building where my mother and I lived. You can only see about half of her hair, but it's the same cut and color as the woman in the party picture Felix dropped on me.'

Marya's face twisted in repulsion. 'Poor woman. Some really crazy bastard did this. It's the work of a madman.'

'I had our forensic people back in San Francisco examine it before I came to Moscow. We have a large data bank on killers in the States. The nature of the wounds, the high number of them, the fact that they cover so much of the body, that both breasts and the sex organs have been mutilated, the appearance of depth to the wounds, it all points to a killer in an insane but methodical rage rather than, say, a lover who grabbed a kitchen knife during an argument and attacked in the heat of the moment. Forensics counted forty-six wounds.

'In our experience, the type of killer who would inflict this sort of mutilation is a sexual psychopath who is liable to kill again. And again. There's a seventy-eight per cent probability that some other time, before or after this attack, there was at least one other attack.'

'You're saying this is the work of a serial killer.'

'A high probability is the best that forensics would come up with. This type of person tends to kill more than once, so yes, it probably is the work of a serial killer. But there is a small possibility that it only happened once.'

Marya shook her head. 'No, this person has killed more than once. No one could be that crazy only once in a lifetime.'

'That's how I feel too. But I've not been able to trace another killing. Sick crimes like this were never reported publicly under the Soviet regime. So it's not a matter of going down to the library and looking through old editions of *Pravda* for news reports. Another problem is the lack of a signature.'

'A signature?'

'Serial killers, either intentionally or unintentionally, often leave a clue linking them to the crime. It can get pretty bizarre – we've had men who kill only strawberry blondes or people born on Fridays, or tall people or short people. Some eat their victim's heart, some cut in a certain way or in a particular pattern. In this case, our forensic people could find no distinguishing features other than the high number of wounds itself, but that's not a reliable criterion. Forensics said the killer was right-handed, but so are most people.'

'What about the cross?'

'What cross?'

Marya pointed to a mark on the woman's right hand. Lara leaned down closer to get a better look. A vertical line intersected by a horizontal line was in the area between the woman's right thumb and index finger. 'The cross bar is a bit high up,' Lara said.

'That's a common design here.'

Lara still wasn't convinced. 'There's another, smaller cross bar nearer the top of the vertical line.'

'Russian crosses usually have that. Haven't you ever looked at the crosses at St Basil's?'

Lara took her hand off the picture. She met Marya's eye and held it for a long moment. 'It's possible,' she said quietly. 'The marks do look like a cross. But they might also be wounds inflicted when she raised her hand to protect herself. It's a natural spot for such wounds. Other than the cross-like shape, there's nothing about the marks to give them any other significance.'

'Not to someone in San Francisco, perhaps, but there is to me,' Marya said.

'What do you mean?'

'You've heard of Ivan the Terrible?'

'Of course. Fifteenth century—'

'Sixteenth century,' Marya said.

'Russian ruler. Mad as a hatter—'

'Also very cunning. Made Stalin look like a monk when it came to insane violence. Stalin drove his wife and son to kill themselves, the son by alcohol. Ivan killed his own son. He also founded the *Oprichnina*, a secret police force that made the KGB look like circus clowns in comparison. Ivan had them slaughter whole cities when he felt like it. Anyway, he was also a religious maniac with a rather Dark Ages view of the world.'

'He had St Basil's built,' Lara said. Speaking of the church made her throat constrict.

'True. And he had an obsession about freaks.'

'What do you mean?'

'People with deformities. He believed that deformities – a hunchback, a twisted limb, things of that sort – were marks of the devil, a sure sign that the devil had played a role in the person's creation. Someone told him that devils could be driven away with the sign of the cross, so he sent his black-robed *Oprichnina* riding through the country looking for freaks. Whenever they found any, Ivan's men scarred one of their hands.'

'With the sign of the cross,' Lara said.

'Between the thumb and the index finger,' Marya told her. 'What's the matter? You look ill.'

'It just occurred to me that the room where I was taken to be attacked as a child was filled with crosses.'

The two women stared at each other for a moment and then Lara examined the picture again. She did not see a deformity on the woman.

'She doesn't look like a freak.'

'Maybe she wasn't a freak,' Marya said. 'Maybe it's the killer who is.'

Chapter 33

A week passed with growing madness for Lara as she fought trapped animal sickness, imagining fires in which the flames and smoke attacked her while she was locked in her cell, going through out-of-body experiences that took her onto a plane bound for home. Marya visited frequently, at least once every day, and it helped but the worst times were at night after lock-down when sounds of anger and fear, women loving women, women beating women, or just plain insanity and viciousness, robbed her of sleep. She lost a lot of weight from her already slim frame.

Lara had never experienced life in jail before although she had been inside a number of them because of her job. Now she questioned whether she could ever go back to being a prosecutor – assuming she survived Russian justice. It was not that she believed the women trapped behind the bars didn't deserve the punishment – most of them spoke freely of their crimes and their only regrets were that they had been caught. But now that she had experienced the hell she didn't think she could live with its knowledge. Her feelings were something akin to a person supporting the death penalty for heinous crimes but not wanting to be the executioner.

Much of her time was spent going through the police reports and outlining tactical moves for the case, tactics she went over with Marya. The two often locked horns.

Marya's points were usually well taken. Lara was approaching the trial in the Anglo-American fashion, strategic combat between two opposing sides. 'Advocacy' was what the British called the system of justice they gave to America. It was based upon the concept that the state was a powerful force and unless opposed would rob people of their liberty.

'Your system gives more rights to criminals than victims,' Marya snapped during one of their arguments.

'Wrong, we give equal rights to everyone. Everyone is presumed innocent and the state must prove the charges against them beyond a reasonable doubt, not to protect the guilty, but to protect the innocent. When criminals have fewer rights than other citizens, a government can take away the rights of good citizens simply by labeling them criminals. That's what happened here in Russia.'

'But look at what happened to the crime rate when controls were taken off,' Marya said. 'Before the fall of the Soviet regime, we could walk the streets day or night safely. Now criminals are taking over the streets.'

'You're forgetting something. The people have also taken over the streets from an oppressive government. There's always a certain percentage of criminals in any society,' Lara argued, 'just as there is a percentage of people with mental disorders and ones with red hair. Liberty doesn't encourage crime, poverty and poor police protection does. And even if it did, I'd rather be free and have to worry about an occasional mugger than live in a totalitarian regime with a soldier on every corner and my neighbors spying on me.'

The arguments were therapeutic for both of them, allowing them to let off steam. And they served another purpose: Lara gained more insight into the Russian legal system and Marya learned more about the Anglo-American

one. Somewhere in between was the right strategy to carry
the day in a Russian courtroom where no one knew exactly
what the law and procedure was because the old establish-
ment had fallen and rules were being implemented and
discarded almost daily.

Lara pointed out over and over again, to drive home
the point and to stir Marya's gray matter, that the police
and the coroner had done inadequate jobs investigating
Nadia's death. The autopsy report was a prime example:
the pathologist tracked the bullet into Nadia's chest and
the one in the back of her head, establishing the cause of
death from gunfire wounds. But because the pathologist
had not approached the autopsy objectively and had
merely set out to confirm the police assumption that
Lara had shot the woman, he had not thoroughly examined
Nadia's body.

'I tried to see the pathologist twice. He's avoiding me,
but what does it matter about the rest of her body if it's
certain the gunshot wounds killed her?' Marya asked.

Lara felt like banging her head on the table out of
pure frustration. 'We already went over this three times.
What if she had been drugged and taken to the spa? No
blood tests were done. What if she had been grabbed
and physically forced into the spa? There was no examination for bruises or marks besides the entry wounds on
her body. She was naked in the spa. What clothes did
the police find? Where did they find them? Did she have
sex before being killed? Was she killed somewhere else
and her body taken there? She might have been killed,
or at least overpowered, somewhere else, and put in the
spa to entrap me.

'And what about keys? There's no mention of the police
having found keys among Nadia's personal effects. How
did she get into the penthouse? Did she come in the public

entrance? What time? Was anyone with her? Can the elevator attendants set a time? If she undressed and got into the spa, she had to have been there for a while before I arrived. Not to mention the time it takes for the spa to heat up.'

'I spoke to the elevator attendants,' Marya told her. 'They had already given statements to the police. They claim Nadia didn't enter by the front.

'Then find out how she entered.'

The next evening when Marya returned, the young Russian attorney was dragging at the heels. 'I was at the morgue standing in front of the pathologist's office when he arrived for work this morning. He said he was too busy to see me right then. After three hours of waiting I realized he would be too busy until one of us died from old age. I went away and returned after five o'clock when I was sure he had left the office. I talked an assistant pathologist into letting me view Nadia's body.'

'Terrific. I'm proud of you.'

'Don't pin the Order of Lenin on me yet. When he slid the body out of the cooler, the smell and appearance were . . . not pleasant.'

'Not just the smell, but to think that the person on the slab was a living, feeling human being a short while ago,' Lara said.

'It was awful. But at least the assistant was kind enough to examine the body for me. There were marks on both of Nadia's upper arms that could be bruises and an open cut in the scalp under the hairline. It is possible that someone held her arms prior to death, that she was hit on the head. But . . .'

'All right, but what?'

'But the wound on the head could have been caused by

340

hitting her head in the spa after the first shot. Because of the hot water, it's not possible to tell when she got the wound.'

'And the arm bruises?'

'He didn't find them particularly important. He said if Nadia bruised easily, she could have got them while making love.'

'But from what you've told me, it is possible that she was treated roughly before she was killed.'

'Yes, but a dozen other inferences are also possible.'

'Were you able to learn anything about the key?'

'No key was found in Nadia's effects.'

'People on the street, the neighborhood . . .'

'Myself and a friend combed the neighborhood for witnesses. None jumped out and bit us.' She sounded very tired.

'Thank you.'

'For what? I have done nothing to help the case.'

'You have done a great deal. We're narrowing down the evidence. You've discovered that there were signs of violence on Nadia's body. I'm really grateful for what you're doing.'

Marya's tired frame swelled with pride. 'Tomorrow I will talk to the judge and demand that he provide funds for experts of our own. The old ways are gone and the new ways must increase the rights of the individual. We can no longer be at the mercy of the government.' She slammed her fist on the table.

After Marya had left, the matron told Lara to stay in the room, she had another visitor.

A moment later Yuri entered the room.

Lara stood up and turned her back on him. She knocked on the door for the matron.

'I'm ready to go back,' she said.

The matron looked from Lara to Yuri. 'No, not yet,' he said.

The woman shut the door in Lara's face. Lara swung round to Yuri. 'What do you want?'

He lit a cigarette and took a long drag. He appeared worn and haggard. His eyes were tired, puffy. 'I've been trying to help you.'

'Trying to help me? You came in here with a body-wire and taped me—'

'Vulko ordered me to do it. If I had refused, I would have been jerked off the case immediately. Luckily my supervisor's given me some leeway to continue to investigate despite the fact Vulko's taken over.'

'Why should I believe you? We're probably being taped right now.'

'You have to believe me. I'm the one who lined up Rykoff for you. I had a little thing on him.' Yuri shrugged. 'He wanted your case anyway. He's supposed to be a good lawyer.'

'I've got a good lawyer.'

'You have to get rid of her. You don't understand the system. She won't get respect in court. She's too young, inexperienced ... and the wrong color. It's an old boy's network and she's not a member.'

'I'm sticking with her. She has one quality that I haven't seen in anyone else in this whole damn city – she's honest.'

'Lara, I'm sorry, I'm ... really sorry. But in some ways it's not as bad as it seems. You're—'

'Are you crazy? I'm in jail, charged with murder. I'm facing execution. The only consolation is that I might be lucky enough to die of food poisoning or freeze to death in my cell before trial.'

'You're alive. I kept trying to get you out of the city, back to America. And you kept fighting it, going back out onto the streets at night. You should be dead. You're safer in jail, protected, until I can get to the bottom of things.'

She sat down and crossed her arms and legs and stared up at him. He was a wreck. 'You look worse than I do.'

'I haven't been sleeping.'

'What are you worried about?'

'Worried about? You think I want you in jail?'

She stood and moved around the room, her adrenaline pumping, her arms still folded across her chest, drilling holes in him with her eyes. 'You don't make sense to me, Detective Kirov. You wear a different face every time we meet. You showed up at my hotel room claiming to be investigating Belkin's death, but I saw you the night before at the carnival. What were you doing at the carnival?'

'I was conducting an investigation.'

'What kind of investigation were you conducting behind a fortune teller's tent and a freak show?'

'I can't reveal that. It's police business.'

'Funny thing, that freak show you were hanging around. Marya thinks freaks have some sort of connection to the killings. She's checking it out. Anything you want to tell me?'

'I don't know what you're talking about.'

'And you knew nothing about me, no name, no nationality, that night at the carnival. I was just a woman walking with Belkin?'

'Yes.'

'Yet within hours of Belkin's death you were at my hotel room. How did you know I was staying at a hotel? How did you find the hotel so fast? Moscow has seven or eight million people and dozens of hotels. Yet by early the same morning you were banging on my door.'

He followed her with tired eyes as she walked round the room. 'I told you we found your name on Belkin.'

'There's something else that happened that morning that makes me wonder about you. We had coffee together and got into an argument because you wanted me to leave Moscow. Why would a police officer investigating a murder want a material witness to take the first flight out of the country?' She stopped and moved closer to him, keeping her eyes locked with his. 'Every time I made a move, you were right on my heels. Every time something bad was happening, you always seemed to pop up. And every time we spoke, you tried to get me to leave the country.'

She started pacing again, rolling ideas off her tongue. 'A policeman trying to get rid of a witness? That doesn't compute. Unless the policeman has something to hide himself. Now that's an interesting premise, isn't it, Detective Kirov?'

If Yuri found the premise interesting, he did nothing to reveal it in his expression. He continued to meet her fierce gaze with tired, half-closed eyes.

'That led me to some conclusions. You said you spotted Belkin and started following him. What if instead of Belkin you were following me? You see me with Belkin and Belkin gets hit by a truck. I leave you to go and see my old school teacher and she dies. I tell you about the archives and the next thing I know Minsky has disappeared. I pay a visit to the truck driver and you're there, too. I was really grateful to you for saving me from that dog, but I find it hard to believe that you followed my taxi down that long, straight, almost deserted road without me spotting your car. You know what? I wonder if you didn't arrive there *before* me.'

'Your imagination has been infected by the mental diseases that float in the air around this place,' he said.

'Being in jail has one benefit, Yuri. It gives you time to think. Hours and days and nights of sitting in a damn cell all alone with your whole life passing before your eyes.'

'You're in this jail because you refused to follow my warnings. I told you Bova was trouble.'

She changed tack, realizing she would get nothing out of him with a frontal attack. 'Tell me about Bova.'

'What did you find out about him?'

'I asked you the question. I know he's rich and he's crazy. That Nadia was killed in his spa. It strikes me as unlikely that he killed her. It doesn't make much sense to kill her in his own penthouse when he had the largest country in the world to do it in.'

'Don't assume a criminal will act logically,' he said. 'Especially if he's crazy to begin with. And I don't know how rich he will remain. The government is locked in battle with him because he's stolen everything from oil fields to fishing boats. Most of his gains went into that tower, a monument to himself. The government's keeping it empty by refusing to issue the occupancy permits. There are rumors that he will collapse financially at any moment. When that happens, there'll be trouble.'

'What kind of trouble?'

'The kind that gets people killed. It's not his money that went into the tower, the dacha, his fancy cars, or anything else. The money belonged to others.'

'The news media claims he is some sort of financial wizard.'

He shrugged. 'One hundred and sixty million of us Russians don't understand money-making. Market economy is a phrase we hear but don't know the workings of. I've done a great deal of checking on Bova. He seems to lose money on everything. The things he stole, like the oil wells, bring in no income – the government has seen to that. It's more like a game he plays for fun rather than for profit. He owns a bank and the bank makes investments. But even before he ran into trouble with the tower he seemed to lose two dollars for every dollar he invested and yet he still made a profit. Being an economically ignorant ex-communist, I don't understand how he does it.'

'Money laundering,' she said. 'It's the only business in the world where you can lose money and still make a profit. The very nature of the game is that for every dirty dollar you handle you'll lose half of it, but the remaining half is clean, and it's straight profit.'

Yuri nodded. His eyes were veiled and she couldn't read his face. 'I've suspected money laundering, but we don't have the resources to track such activities. Banks and other businesses conduct themselves as they want because the government agencies are incapable of monitoring them.'

'Is Bova involved in drugs? Money laundering for drugs?'

'He's not involved in drugs, I'm certain of that.'

'Then what is it?'

'The matter is still under investigation.'

'When's the investigation going to be concluded? About the time I'm being executed? Don't give me that investigation nonsense. I'm in jail and facing charges now. I need answers. Nadia knew something about Alexei. She suspected that Felix was blackmailing him. What does Felix have on Alexei? Is it money laundering?'

'Felix and Alexei go back a long way.'

'What does that mean?'

'I'm investigating their affairs.'

She stepped close to him, her eyes searching his face. 'Why are you doing this to me? What are you hiding? Something tells me that I've been caught up in something more than a fight over dirty money. My instincts are screaming that if I knew who was behind my mother's death and that of our neighbor, I would know who put me in this jail.'

He grabbed her arms and squeezed tightly. 'You fool,' he whispered. 'You stumble around with your eyes closed, stepping on poisonous snakes, trying to find out who slashed Vera Swen without any idea what you're sticking your nose in. The only reason you're alive is because you're in jail.'

She slowly drew back from him until he dropped the hold on her arms. She rubbed her arms where he had grabbed her.

'Nadia had bruises on her arms where someone grabbed her before she was killed. Did you give her a lecture too? Right before she died?'

Chapter 34

Marya brought someone with her when she returned the next evening.

'This is Vladimir Andreevich Dzhunkovsky.' She smiled. 'We call him Vlad.'

Vlad was a tall, gangling young man, at least six foot three, Lara estimated, with a thick bushel of wheat hair; thin, bony and awkward were the thoughts that came to mind when she looked at him. The glasses he wore were thick, the type kids at school used to call Coke bottles.

'Vlad is an expert on guns and bullets.'

'Ballistics,' Vlad corrected. 'More precisely, I am knowledgeable about projectiles ranging from small arms ammo to artillery shells. My rank in the army is lieutenant.'

This was the ballistics expert Marya had mentioned. With two bullets as the obvious cause of Nadia's death and little doubt in her mind that the bullets came from the six-shooter she had handled, a ballistics expert didn't offer much hope but at least it was another straw to clutch.

'What exactly do you do with, uh, projectiles?'

'My unit tests the efficiency and accuracy of ammunition. We fire thousands of rounds from dozens of different types of weapons. We change the amount of charge in the shell, the size and shape of bullets, and sometimes even the length or rifling of barrels. We have the most advanced technology in the world for tracking small arms fire with lasers,' he said with pride.

'Sounds impressive.' But how the hell will it help me? Lara wondered. 'Are you also qualified to compare the rifling marks on bullets to determine whether they were fired by the same gun?'

He grimaced and waved away the question as if it was beneath his dignity. 'Child's play. I have used the comparison microscopes and periphery cameras required for such examinations many times, usually after a training accident when we are sent the bullets to determine which weapon fired the shot. But my special expertise is tracking the path of bullets. Except at very short range, a bullet fired from a gun does not follow a straight line. I employ lasers to trace the paths. From those studies, we improve the effectiveness of ammunition.'

'In this case, we have a very short range,' she said. 'Have you looked at the photos of the bullet that struck Nadia in the chest and the bullet they dug out of the ceiling? The prosecution's ballistics expert says that they come from the same gun.'

'He hasn't seen them because I left my copy with you,' Marya said. She was sifting through the stack of reports as she spoke.

'You'll see from the reports that there were two shots,' Lara said. 'Nadia was sitting in the spa, facing the door to the interior, her back to the spa rim, when she was shot. The bullet went through her chest and out of her back, embedding in the rubber liner of the spa. She was then shot again, probably while floating face down in the spa. That bullet went into the back of her head. It was also recovered. A third bullet recovered from the ceiling of the penthouse matches one of the bullets that killed Nadia. I, uh, allegedly fired that one into the ceiling a few days earlier.'

Vlad smiled a little shyly. 'I heard about it. It was on television.'

'Here.' Marya handed the ballistics report to Vlad.

'I could make a more accurate comparison by doing my own examination of the bullets, but we can start with the police laboratory report.'

While he read the report, Lara asked, 'Any success on getting the judge to appoint a pathologist?'

Marya's lips pressed. 'No pathologist, no investigators, no fingerprint analyst, no experts at all. Vlad is my friend and the best friend of my boy friend, who is also in the army. He will assist us for nothing.'

'That's kind of him. I appreciate it.'

Marya shook her head. 'I know that he may not be able to help. But . . .'

Lara smiled. 'In this case a ballistics expert is a shot in the dark.'

Marya laughed. Lara liked the sound. The young attorney's laughter was spontaneous and honest, a reflection of her personality.

Marya's pretty face became serious again. 'I spoke to the judge and the prosecutor. Svetlana telephoned me this morning and instructed me to appear within the hour for a conference with the judge.'

'A conference with the judge? Without me?'

'I think Svetlana planned it that way. She told the judge that you intend to make your mother's death an issue at the trial.'

'Of course I'll make it an issue. It is *the* issue in this case. I was lured to Moscow because of my mother's death and I'm sure her death has something to do with Nadia's.'

'The judge will not permit you to raise the subject during the trial.'

'Why not?'

Marya spoke fast, mimicking Svetlana's military tones. 'We are a struggling nation trying to build a new Russia from the ashes of the old. To keep our people united we must bury the past and look to the future. The defendant will attempt to make this case into a political trial to divert attention away from her heinous crime.'

Lara's face went crimson with anger and frustration. 'She's trying to kick the only defense I have out from under me. If we can't mention my investigation into my mother's death, other events won't make sense. How can I explain what I was doing with Belkin when he was hit by a truck? The school teacher? The institute? Breaking into Bova's penthouse? It all goes back to my mother's death.'

'I know how you feel,' Marya said. 'But the judge did ask me one good question, and I had no answer for it. He asked me to list the evidence that linked your mother's death to Nadia's death.'

'Belkin was murdered, the school teacher is dead, the murder of Vera Swen—'

'Those are events. What physical evidence links them to Nadia's death? The prosecution theory is that you and Nadia were conspiring to blackmail Alexei and that you killed Nadia because you wanted Alexei and his money for yourself.'

'The picture,' Lara said. 'Both pictures. The one sent to me in San Francisco, the one of Alexei with my mother and Vera. The picture with Alexei Bova in it was my motive for going to the penthouse, for dealing with Nadia. It proves he lied to me about knowing my mother and it shows a connection between the past and someone alive and involved today. Marya, we need that picture.'

'I have requested the picture through the police, but what chance is there that Felix will admit to having it and turn it over to the police?'

Lara shook her head in frustration. 'No chance.'

'My boy friend did some of those background checks you asked for,' Marya said. 'The army's central records department came up with some interesting and puzzling things about your friends Felix and Alexei.'

'What do you mean?'

'Felix's file was coded for special handling.'

'Which means?'

'There are different reasons a file might be marked special. The person may have risen to political or military prominence or might be the son of someone prominent. Or they could be KGB. The higher the rank, the more special and inaccessible the file.'

Marya shot a sideways glance at Vlad. He was engrossed in the pictures of the bullets and the crime scene report. She indicated with a movement of her head that she wanted to speak to Lara off to the side. The two women got up and moved away from the table and spoke in low whispers.

'Vlad is very trustworthy,' Marya said, 'but I don't want him to overhear things that might get him or my boy friend into trouble.'

'I understand.'

'My boy friend is a computer genius. He loves to play with the computer programs and has managed to gain access to secret files. The regular file on Felix contained what you would learn by being his next-door neighbor. But my boy friend peeked into the secret file the army maintains on Felix.' Marya grinned. 'The army and KGB were very competitive. Each maintained secret files on anyone of importance in the other's service.'

'I wasn't sure Felix had been KGB,' Lara said. 'But that didn't seem very important. So many people in this country are either ex-KGB or were KGB informers.'

'He was KGB,' Marya says, 'but not just KGB. He reported directly to the head of the Finance Directorate.'

'What's the Finance Directorate?'

'The department that handled the money to pay not only a million or so internal agents but KGB agents all over the world. It was answerable directly to the Chairman of the KGB himself.'

Lara nodded. 'Alexei is rolling in money. Felix handled finances. Probably trillions of roubles, worth a lot more then, before hyper-inflation started. Money was probably funneled out of the KGB during the Gorbachev years when the upper echelon knew the system was heading for collapse.'

'Exactly,' Marya said. 'But Felix's government position was not the most important thing my boy friend discovered about him. The army's file on Felix has been edited. It's hard to explain. My boy friend says it's not a true confidential file, that everything in it was accessible to any ministry. He suspects Felix's job at the KGB was a cover for something else. Whatever it was, it had to have been big. To have a dummy army file is one thing, to have a dummy secret file means you are very important.'

'Important to whom?'

Marya shrugged. 'To the KGB. There are not many other choices. You understand what I am saying, a great effort was made to make Felix appear innocuous.'

'Alexei has a lot of money.'

'Not that kind of money, nobody has in the Soviet Union. This sort of thing is not arranged with money anyway, but with power.'

'Why do you think it was done?'

'Why, I can't tell you.' A big grin spread across her face. 'But I can tell you what his file originally contained.'

'How?'

'Erased files can be resurrected if there are no special programs blocking it. The top secret file storage system has a retrieval program for erased files.' She grinned again. 'It's the old Soviet mentality showing itself again.'

'Marya, what did the damn file say?'

'Back in the sixties and seventies, your mother's era in Moscow, Felix was the editor of a literary magazine. He rubbed shoulders with all kinds of writers, ones who wrote pieces the government approved and ones who wrote pieces that had to get smuggled out of the country to be published under anonymous names.'

'And he turned them over to the KGB,' Lara said, taking a guess. 'He told me he was a beacon for people with literary aspirations and bragged about how he assisted dissenters. No doubt he helped them, right off to the forced labor camps.'

'Exactly what the secret report says. But there were dirty rumors about him on the street and in the mid-seventies he became employed directly by the KGB's finance department.'

'Why finance if he came out of a literary background?'

'At a guess, knowing how the KGB operated, he knew someone at a high level, probably the Finance Director himself. When I speak of the KGB Finance Director, I am speaking of one of the great power players in the Soviet Union. The KGB was not just a spy organization, it was an army with a gigantic bureaucracy which employed over a million people. The Finance Director had direct access to the Chairman of the KGB. Felix had a staff job at the Finance Directorate as an assistant to the Director until March 1985.'

'What happened in March 1985?'

'Gorbachev came to power in March 1985.'

'The beginning of the end,' Lara said. 'They had to have

seen it coming, all the old boys at the KGB. The economy was going to pieces, there had already been serious food shortages and the man selected to lead the country was crying out for new thinking. A fortune in roubles was flowing through the KGB coffers. Probably even more significant was the hoard of gold, gems, and art the KGB had unofficially confiscated over the years. I bet a bunch of fat old boys got together to make sure their feet would stay warm during the long Russian winters to come.'

Vlad interrupted their conversation. 'May I see the crime scene pictures mentioned in the reports?'

'What did you think of the prosecution's ballistics report?' Lara asked as Marya dug out the pictures for him.

'Very accurate. Obviously the same gun.'

'Wonderful,' Lara said.

'How tall are you?' Vlad asked.

'How tall? About five feet five inches. In meters, centimeters—'

'I'll work it out,' he told her.

Marya gave him the pictures and came back to the corner to continue the whispering huddle with Lara.

'You're going to tell me that your boy friend ran Alexei, found a regular file and a secret file that had been edited.'

'Bova's record is stranger than fiction. There was no file, period.' Marya's voice rose with excitement. 'Do you understand the significance of that? Bova is male, Russian, and a resident of Moscow. If you weren't born in Moscow, you needed a special permit even to visit the city, let alone live here. The Soviet government apparatus kept track not just of every baby born, but every paperclip manufactured. It's impossible not to have a military record, even if it was just for being rejected for service. Not to have an army file, not even a secret one, is to sit on the knee of Lenin.'

'Something like the right hand of God,' Lara murmured.

'Whatever. Lenin's knee is an old Russian expression I just made up.' Marya chuckled. 'My boy friend was so fascinated, he used a military program to access other government files and found no reference to Bova prior to six or seven years ago. If Alexei Bova doesn't exist on paper in this country, Alexei Bova doesn't exist, period.'

Lara was stunned. 'That doesn't make any sense. You're talking about one of the most famous men in the country. He has to have been put under a microscope and examined by everyone.'

'You're thinking like an American again. We've only had a free market economy a short time. No one had heard of Bova until he suddenly appeared as an entrepreneur who founded one of the new banks. There was nothing unusual about that, most of the new capitalists popped out of nowhere. One day a friend of mine worked behind a computer in a city office. The next day she became an importer of computers.'

'But there has to be background material on Bova. The news media must have investigated his whole life.'

'No, there's no way they could. We don't have a data base on social matters. We don't even have telephone books. I know someone who works for one of Moscow's new scandal magazines, the kind that are always showing pictures of three-headed babies born to farm girls who were raped by Martians. She took a look at Alexei's background material in her magazine's file. It's the most mundane file imaginable. He's supposed to have worked in the accounting office of a very small company that imported raw material for government factories.'

'A private company?'

'I don't know. The company went out of business in 1985 and all the files were lost in a fire. The eerie part is that all the employees died in the fire.'

357

'But I saw a picture of Alexei Bova at a party, a party that took place over twenty years ago.'

'You saw a picture of a man. Who says his name was Alexei Bova back then?'

'You're right,' Lara said. 'And we're back in 1985 again. Let's imagine for a moment that there was a scheme to put together a nest egg for KGB inner circle members and that Felix was part of that scheme. Alexei was another part.'

'The most important part,' Marya said. 'The man who would handle the money.'

'Money that needed to be laundered.'

'I apologize for my ignorance, but as a reformed communist I'm still not absolutely certain what money laundering is.'

'Dirty money, that is money earned illegally, comes in the form of cash. People don't usually buy drugs, fence stolen goods, take bribes, or conduct any other criminal activity except with anonymous cash. Major drug traffickers end up with millions of dollars in cash. But our society doesn't operate on a cash basis and they can't just deposit it in a bank because questions would be asked about where it had come from. So it's laundered, it's carefully fed to the bank through businesses which both legitimize the money and disguise its source. If you happen to own a bank, laundering naturally gets much easier.'

'May I see the pathologist's report, please?' Vlad asked.

When Marya returned to the corner, Lara asked her if her boy friend had come up with anything on Yuri.

'One thing of interest but I don't know how to tie it up. He has an extensive army file because he was a military policeman before entering the Moscow police department. His military service was honorable.'

'That's what I was afraid of. Having a solid background is worse than no background. At least with Alexei we have grounds for suspicion. What's the one thing of interest in Yuri's background? Has his file been edited?'

Marya pursed her lips. 'He was seriously wounded in Afghanistan and cited for extraordinary performance of duty. He had followed an escaped prisoner into the desert, a murderer, my boy friend said, who had been brought in from a prison camp in the gulag to do road work.'

'Why would they bring a prisoner from Siberia to Afghanistan?'

'Afghanistan was the Soviet Vietnam. You couldn't get ordinary citizens to build roads across the desert, so the government brought in forced labor crews.'

'Even murderers?'

'If the man had been in prison a long time. I don't know his background. Yuri Kirov was wounded in 1984.'

Lara looked at her. 'Pasha, Alexander Zurin, the neighbor boy convicted of the murder of Vera Swen, died in prison in 1984. Did your boy friend give you the name of the prisoner?'

'No, but I can ask him. It's sure to be in the file.'

'Find out for me.'

'You think that there's a connection between Detective Kirov and the neighbor boy?'

'I don't know what to think. My head is spinning.'

'I'll ask my boy friend tomorrow. Keep your fingers crossed. The one thing we haven't been able to tie in with the case against you is the death of your mother and this Vera person years ago.'

'Except for the picture with Alexei in it.'

'Except for the picture, and I don't think a judge would give much weight to such a picture. There must be evidence with a link to the crime,' Marya said. 'I've thought about the cross on the hand that might be the mark of a serial killer. I don't know how to research it. I've talked to a couple of lawyer friends and one of them knows someone who works with court records, but it all turned out negative. The court doesn't keep records of such things. If the police do, they're not saying anything.'

'In America you'd go to the news morgue,' Lara said.

'What is a news morgue?'

'It's what we call the records room of a newspaper. The place where past editions are stored. The sort of gruesome killings generated by serial killers would make front-page news. You just go back to year one and start forward, skimming the headlines for stories.'

'That doesn't work in a country where the stories never made the news because the government kept them from the public,' Marya said.

'Yes it does.' The statement came from Vlad and caught them both by surprise. They hadn't realized they had been talking loud enough to be heard by him.

'The stories *were* obtained by the press,' Vlad said, 'but were never printed because the censors cut them. All the rejected news stories for the past several decades are available to researchers. I read about the archive in the newspaper. The censored stories have been gathered at Moscow University's School of Journalism. The archive is open to scholars.'

'I'll go there tomorrow,' Marya said, 'after my day in court. I'm still taking classes at the university and have a student card. I can say I am doing legal research into old cases.'

'Good. Thank you,' Lara said. Then to Vlad, 'Were you able to come up with anything that will help?'

He shook his head. 'I will have to conduct an actual experiment using models, but I'm not hopeful.' The tall youth stood up, grimacing in frustration. 'I can't see any way to prove that you didn't fire the second shot.'

It took a moment for both women to digest this remark and then it was Marya who asked the obvious question.

'What about the *first* shot?'

He raised his eyebrows. 'But of course Lara couldn't have fired the first shot.'

Lara and Marya slowly looked at each other and then at Vlad.

Lara's voice trembled as she asked, 'Why couldn't I have fired the first shot?'

'You're too short.'

Chapter 35

Marya stopped by the university to check out the archive of censored news stories after she finished at court early in the afternoon. She discovered the archive was not at the university, but in an annexe a few blocks away, a three-story building that once housed a student affairs department. At the annexe she got into a line for admission. A notice pinned to the wall announced the cost of a ticket to spend two hours in the archive.

Marya's turn came and she stepped forward to the counter where a clerk asked for identification. Marya passed over her university permit and her identification as a member of the Moscow Collegium of Lawyers.

The clerk examined the law membership and looked up at Marya with contempt. Marya knew what she was thinking – what was this black girl doing with a law degree when good 'Russian' women were sweeping the streets?

'We have sold the quota of tickets for today. You will have to come back another day.'

'Tomorrow?' Marya asked.

'You can return tomorrow if you like.'

'May I buy the tickets for tomorrow now?'

'All the tickets for tomorrow are sold.'

Lara would scream at this mentality, she thought, but she understood what was really being said.

She dug into her purse and pulled out a British pound

coin, less than two dollars but worth nearly two thousand roubles at the current exchange rate. The coin had been a gift from an exchange student from Glasgow and she had been saving the money for her boyfriend's upcoming birthday.

She let the woman see her slip the coin between the rouble notes necessary for admission for the rest of the day and evening.

'It is a matter of great urgency for me to obtain access to the reports immediately. An important legal case depends upon it. You appear to be a person of some importance in this facility,' she told the dull-eyed, stupid-looking bitch she would have preferred punching on the nose, 'and I appeal to you for an act of mercy.'

The money was whisked off the counter and a stamped ticket pushed across to her.

'Next!' the woman said to the person in line behind Marya.

Marya took her ticket and headed for the elevators, mentally grumbling about the system. The market economy has come to the university, she thought. Pay for services, bribe the employees, what next? she wondered. Will they start charging for attending college?

Another notice said that reports of crime were on the second floor. Someone had penciled in the words 'that never happened' after the word 'crime'.

Students hung around the lobby, willing to assist with research for a small fee, but the cost of the ticket had used up her money for dinner that night and lunch the next day; she decided she wouldn't need help.

When she got off the elevator on the second floor she experienced instant regret that the Soviets never threw anything away. Gray bins, hundreds of them, were on tables spread over the entire second floor. Another paper notice on the wall told her that the censored press releases went back to the end of the Second World War, nearly fifty years ago. Rows were by year and each bin contained approximately one week of reports, the signs said.

She examined the contents of the closest bin. The news stories that were never released were printed on standard government-issue typing paper. Each release was a summary of a crime, usually a page or two in length.

There were probably thousands of reports for the three decades she wanted to cover. She needed information only on women brutally killed but the reports were not categorized other than by date.

She spent a few minutes leafing through the bins for the year prior to Lara's mother's death and then went down to the first floor and hired two students to help. It cost her food money for a week, but her boy friend would understand and help out.

'I'm looking for crimes of insane violence, mutilations particularly,' she told the young man and woman, 'especially anything in which a mark resembling a religious cross was found on the victim.'

She sent the male researcher to start at reports that began ten years ago, instructing him to move forward, the young woman to start ten years back from him. She began another ten years back, so in total they would cover the past thirty years. They spread out and went to work.

Marya had expected to find only serious crimes in the bins. To her surprise, most of the crimes reported on the sheets in the bins were commonplace – simple muggings, thefts, indecent exposure, prostitution, and the like. In order to arrive at the correct statistical results for the crime rate in general, the censors had barred the publication of tens of thousands of common crimes. Buried among reports of the theft of a coat on a metro and pilfered widgets from a factory was an occasional violent crime.

The reports were quite detailed, even a simple theft took a couple of typed, single-spaced sheets. After reading for a while, Marya decided the reports on lesser crimes were probably word for word duplicates of the actual police reports, while major crimes, a rape or murder, were summaries.

Her fingers flew through the reports, eyes scanning the short summary paragraph at the top of each one. Unless it involved the murder of a woman, she quickly skipped the rest, resisting the temptation to read on because she had limited time. There was no way she could pay her way back into the news morgue without asking for money from Lara and she was determined that Lara's little nest-egg stay untouched. She had a dreadful feeling Lara was going to spend a long time in a Russian prison, and the money would help her survive.

Skimming through the bins, she decided that Russians had no criminal finesse. Thieves seemed to be stupid, stealing whatever was to hand rather than what was most valuable; killings tended to be impulsive and particularly bloody because, once again, the typical Russian murderer grabbed whatever weapon was handy, like the husband who beat his wife to death with an *empty* vodka bottle after an argument about his drinking. Police work was just as primitive; if the culprit wasn't caught red-handed and confessed, a little beating was amazingly soul cleansing.

A nagging worry ate at her: what if she came across an arrest report of her mother? She didn't remember how old she was when she found out her mother had been a prostitute; the knowledge had just always been there, perhaps first coming as a taunt from other children at school, or a yelling match her mother had had with a neighbor woman, or kitchen talk between her mother and other whores.

She knew her mother had been arrested more than once and that she had been a drug addict; she also knew that in her helpless way her mother had loved her and tried to provide for her. Her mother's sister had taken her in at the age of ten. She rarely saw her mother after that, just a couple of visits as she deteriorated more and more from the drugs that destroyed her life. Marya's aunt had been a woman of great courage and resolve to take in the black child of a whore in a society where even divorce could ruin a career.

Marya had worked harder than anyone else she knew, unconsciously feeling that getting high marks and the certificates of accomplishment that came with them made up for her mother's shabby background. She had gone into law because of a comment a friend had made. Lawyers were not a highly paid and influential class of professionals under the communist system, despite the fact that Lenin himself had been a lawyer. But, a friend told her one night while drinking beer in a cafe near the university, lawyers know the law. They know what their rights are.

Having spent her short lifetime feeling that others considered her somewhat less than a Russian, somewhat less than a citizen, sometimes even somewhat less than human if the taunts of children and stares of adults were any clue, knowing her rights was a concept that appealed to her.

Getting a law degree with outstanding grades had not placed her on a path to success in the great utopian society. While whites, mostly males, went immediately into good jobs in the vast Soviet bureaucracy, she had been relegated to travelling by metro from courthouse to courthouse, getting appointed to minor cases. It had not just been the courts that were a problem, but the defendants too – not even blacks wanted a black attorney.

Only the prostitutes didn't seem to mind. Not that she told them her mother was a prostitute, although she knew it was common knowledge around the court system. Once in a while a whore would mention her mother. Early on she understood that the prostitutes didn't object to her representing them not because they were liberal minded but because they usually had no belief in their own worth; they were the dregs of society, and they probably thought they were only getting what they deserved.

Lara's case had catapulted her from an attorney for whores to the front pages and the evening news. She was surprised that the clerk downstairs hadn't recognized her as the attorney on the most notorious murder case to hit Moscow in anyone's lifetime.

With the case came a chance at fame and fortune in the new Russian legal system – or an opportunity to be a laughing stock, she thought. But more important than her own fate was that of her client. After speaking to her for only a few minutes, Lara Patrick had placed her life in her hands. Marya was not one to take the obligation lightly.

Ninety minutes before closing time Marya reached the end of her ten-year search with hands that were empty but soiled from the dusty records. Her hired help was still buried in the bins. She took a break to wash her hands before rounding up the two researchers. Both had papers in their hands.

'I found nothing,' she told them. 'Did either of you come up with anything?'

'I found one,' the woman told her, holding up a sheet of paper. 'About twelve years ago. A man was killed, a derelict.'

'Same here,' the young male student said. 'About five years ago, a man killed, a pervert, with a history of hanging around men's rooms.'

'I told you I wanted reports of *women* mutilated,' Marya said.

The two researchers exchanged looks. 'No, you didn't,' the woman told her. 'You said you wanted violent crimes involving mutilation, especially if they mentioned crosses. The one I found was a man whose penis and testicles were cut off. Slashes on the man's right hand resembled a cross.'

'Same here,' the male student said. 'Penis and testicles cut off, a couple of slash marks on the right hand between the thumb and index finger. The report didn't mention any connection between the death and any others. No serial killer stuff.'

'Mine didn't either,' the woman said.

Marya was stunned. There was a serial killer leaving the mark of Ivan the Terrible's cross – on men, not women.

'You're right,' she told the students, 'I've been stupid. I was only looking for deaths of women, so we'll have to go over my section again as well as finish both of yours.' She checked her watch. 'You two carry on. I have to make a phone call.'

From the lobby pay phone she called her boy friend's apartment to tell him to have dinner without her. 'Lara and I have been focusing on the wrong type of killer,' she told him. 'I don't know what it means or how it all fits into the scheme of things, but the killer has gone after at least two men. Add in a woman victim and you have a killer that does not select his victims based upon sex. Something else sets the killer off. I'll bet we come up with something when we go through my section again. I wasn't even looking for male victims.'

After she hung up she turned to leave and noticed that

another woman had left her purse on the shelf under the telephone next to her.

'Excuse me,' Marya called to the woman walking away. 'You forgot your purse.'

The woman turned round and took the purse from Marya and smiled her thanks.

You would think a nurse would be more careful about things, Marya thought as she headed for the elevator.

Marya and her two researchers raced through the bins, covering almost a thirty-year period by closing time. Marya turned up another male victim in her section. The mark of a cross had been found on his right hand and his sex organs, too, had been mutilated.

Other than mutilation by knife and the mark of Ivan the Terrible, none of the cases had anything in common.

It wasn't difficult to understand why no one had made a connection between the killings. The long time span between them, the fact that each killing took place in a different Moscow police district, the lack of public disclosure would all make linking up the killings difficult, but the most crucial reason was the nature of the Soviet bureaucratic mentality. No official wanted to be the bearer of bad tidings by coming out and saying that there was a maniac loose on the streets of Moscow.

One killing was written off as the work of a foreign visitor of homosexual tendencies, despite the fact that the victim was not identified as a homosexual. Homosexuality was simply a good scapegoat in a country where gays who came out of the closet went straight to prison. The report stated that the KGB had taken over the case. That was standard procedure – crimes involving foreigners were always investigated by the KGB, not the local police. But other than speculation, there was nothing to link a foreigner to the killing. The KGB was just as good at tossing back hot potatoes as the rest of the bureaucratic machinery and could have done so in this instance – unless the case was taken by the KGB in order simply to bury it.

Marya thought about that point. The KGB could monitor any murder case and a phone call to a supervisor at the local police station would get the investigation transferred to the KGB with no questions asked and a big sigh of relief from the police.

If we're able to find three in the censored news morgue, how many more occurred that never made it this far? Marya wondered. Lara came to Moscow to unravel one murder and stumbled onto a series of killings.

At closing time she gave the two researchers an extra bonus and left the annex. Her generosity had robbed her of even the metro fare and she set out with a quick pace for the twenty-minute walk to her boy friend's apartment. She was too excited to go home. She wanted to share her discoveries with her boy friend, perhaps invite over some friends and hold a 'think tank' session.

She pulled up her coat collar and put her head down against the wind. She reached a street corner and waited for a break in the traffic before crossing. A horn honked and a car pulled up beside her. The electric window went down on the passenger side and Marya leaned down to see who was in the car.

It was the nurse, the woman whose purse she had found, returning the favor by offering her a ride. Marya welcomed the thought of not having to make the long walk in the cold.

'You're a life saver,' she told the woman as she slipped into the warm car.

Chapter 36

At four o'clock in the morning Lara was awakened by the sound of her cell door being unlocked. She shot up from the mattress on the floor.

'Who's there?'

In the dim light she could see the outline of a man.

'It's me,' Yuri said.

She stood up, clutching the blanket to her. 'Why are you here?'

'Your lawyer is dead.'

She heard his words but they had no meaning to her. 'What do you mean? What are you talking about?'

'Your lawyer's dead.'

She ran from the words, retreating into a corner of the cell. 'You're trying to scare me. I don't believe you.'

He stepped closer to her. 'Marya Gan is dead. Her body was found along the river bank.'

'No ... dear God, no ...' She swayed dizzily. He reached out with his hand but she recoiled from him, stumbling on the mattress and crashing against the wall. 'Oh God, Marya, no, no ...' She slid down onto the floor clutching the blanket.

Yuri's tired voice came to her from the darkness.

'Her body was found in Gorky Park. Her throat was slashed. Her purse gone. A mugging.' He sounded like an electronic voice in an elevator calling off floor numbers.

'A mugging? There was no mugging!' she screamed. 'It's a lie, more lies.'

Curses came from down the cell block. A matron standing behind Yuri said, 'Keep your voice down, prisoner.'

'Get out of here,' Yuri told the matron. The woman stepped out of the cell and Yuri closed the door. He sat down on the mattress. A match flared in the darkness and for a moment she saw the profile of his face, grim and hard. The match went out and the smell of tobacco filled the air.

'Poor Marya,' Lara said quietly. She trembled from a clammy cold that gripped her body. 'She wanted to help. She wanted to be a good lawyer. She was a good lawyer.'

'There was a ticket in her pocket for admission into the censored press release archive. Was she working on something for you?'

'Working on something for me?' A fog had seeped into her head. She heard his question, repeated the words, but the meaning was lost on her. She leaned back and put her head against the wall of the cell. She wished she was dead. It was her fault, her damn fault, sending her out onto the street. She wished God had taken her life instead of Marya's.

'You were right,' she told Yuri, 'I'm safe in here. And I sent Marya out to be killed.'

He took a long drag on his cigarette and blew out smoke. He smoked for a while, then stubbed out the cigarette and lit another. She watched the outline of his face for a second time.

'I should have returned home. I should have left Moscow. She'd be alive now if I hadn't been a fool.'

'It's too late for should haves,' he told her. 'Tell me what she was working on, why she went to the archive.'

'She was working on my case.' She knew that was a

stupid answer, but it was hard for her to think. 'She went to the archive to find reports of women with crosses on their hand.' She shook her head, trying to shake out some of the fog. 'Marya noticed that Vera Swen had a mark on her hand, a cross that Marya said was the mark of Ivan the Terrible, a scar he used to put on the hands of freaks to ward off the devil.'

'The mark of Ivan the Terrible,' he murmured. 'I remember that from school. Deformed people were infected by the devil and the cross would drive the devil out.'

'Marya thought it might be the signature of a serial killer. She went to the censored news archive to look up stories kept out of the newspapers during the Soviet era.'

'This was her first trip?'

'Yes.'

'So you don't know what she found. Would she have told anyone else? A roommate, a boy friend?'

'She has a boy friend. I don't know his name. He's in the army. Works in the records department.'

'What else was Marya working on?'

'My case.'

'Be specific.'

She was quiet for a moment and then said, 'No, I'm not going to tell you anything else.'

'You don't trust me.'

'Tell me what happened to Marya.'

He took another deep drag of his cigarette and slowly exhaled it. 'I told you. Her throat was cut. No sign of sexual assault. Just a quick slash, and then several deep puncture wounds in the back. As if she had been sitting, maybe in a car, and someone suddenly turned and slashed her across the throat. She probably clawed at the door handle and the killer stabbed her in the back a couple of times before she fell out.'

A horrible taste of bile clogged her throat as she listened. She wanted to scream and run and cry but she sat with her back to the wall, a prisoner to the terror.

'My gut feeling is that she was killed in a car,' Yuri continued, 'but the local militia station commander is calling it a mugging. Someone runs up to her with a knife, slashes and stabs and grabs her purse, is the commander's version. But there's little blood where the body was found. If she'd been killed at that spot there would be more blood.'

'What else ? Tell me what else.'

'I went to the university annexe and spoke to the guard. He had come on duty about closing time and saw Marya leave. There aren't that many black people in Moscow, so he had no problem remembering her.'

'What else?'

'He remembered another woman leaving about the same time. He remembered her because of the uniform.'

'It was a nurse, wasn't it? Tell me, was it a nurse?'

'The guard remembered a woman in a white uniform leaving about the same time.'

'Get out of here. *Get out!*'

Tears welled up inside her and she began to cry. She buried her face in her arms as he got up and left.

A moment later she realized someone had re-entered the cell and she looked up. The matron had returned after letting Yuri out and was glaring down at her. It was the same jail attendant that had let Yuri in the first time he came and who had let Alexei sneak in. 'Foreign bitch. You make noise that can get me into trouble.' The woman kicked her, hard.

Lara launched up from the floor in a rage, screaming, 'You've been spying on me! How many people are paying you?'

The matron fled the cell.

Lara cried for the first time since she was a child. Cried for the loss of her mother. For the loss of her youth. For the loss of hope. And most of all she cried for Marya. 'She's dead,' she sobbed, 'she's dead.'

From down the cell block a woman whined, 'She's dead, my baby's dead.'

Chapter 37

Vlad came to see her two days later. Lara was red-eyed and haggard. She had hardly slept since Yuri had awakened her with the news about Marya. Her eyes were swollen and pain never left her head.

'She called her boy friend's apartment from the news morgue,' Vlad told her. 'We tracked down two students who helped her do the research. They had already talked to a policeman named Kirov.' Vlad told her about Marya's discoveries at the archives – three men killed, their sex organs mutilated, the sign of the cross slashed between thumb and index finger.

'Three men,' Vlad told her, 'a doctor, a derelict and a pervert.'

'What kind of pervert?'

'A guy with an arrest history of hanging around men's toilets in parks and soliciting other men for sex. He was fairly young, twenty-seven years old. He would follow a man into a toilet and try to enter the same stall as if by accident. If the man in the stall wasn't disturbed by the sudden intrusion . . .' Vlad shrugged his shoulders.

'One day he followed the wrong person. How did the other two die?'

'The derelict, a man in his fifties with a history of arrest for being drunk in public, was also found in a public toilet, this time at a metro station. The doctor didn't fit the pattern. He was killed by someone waiting in his car, probably crouched down in the back seat. He had been giving an evening lecture at the university hospital.'

'What kind of doctor was he?'

'A noted, elderly surgeon who taught at the medical university. He was something of a pioneer in Soviet plastic surgery back in the forties and fifties, exciting decades for Soviet medicine—'

'And Soviet witchcraft,' she interjected.

'Yes, things are starting to come out about that era, not just what happened in mental hospitals. Some of the medical practices were as bad as those for industry and agriculture. They say some Soviet doctors did experiments that would have made Hitler blush. Anyway, this doctor had retired from full-time teaching and now only taught an occasional class on surgery.'

Pain swirled in her head. 'It doesn't make any sense, none of it. Only two of the victims have anything in common – killed in a public toilet. The doctor's killing doesn't fit with that, and neither does age, occupation, or social milieu. And there's no common element with the murder of Vera Swen.' She shook her head. 'Or with the person stalking me. That was a nurse, a woman.' The nurse at the top of the landing coming out of Vera's apartment, the woman who took her out of school and tried to kill her at St Basil's, a nurse at the bedside of Belkin as he lay injured on a hospital bed, the nurse who left the news morgue at about the same time as Marya . . .

The nurse, the nurse, the nurse.

'There has to be a nurse mentioned in one of the reports. Or a woman at least.'

'The researchers didn't say anything about a nurse. Or a woman. Of course, when the doctor was killed a nurse's presence might not have been considered significant since the killing took place near a hospital.'

'Were any of the crimes solved?'

'In the doctor's case, a man who had been treated at the hospital for a mental condition and who had previously served a prison term for a knife attack on another doctor was suspected of the crime. He was found dead, a suicide, when the police arrived to arrest him. The police listed him as the assailant and closed the case. The case of the pervert was similarly "solved",' Vlad, said. 'A man who was arrested with him a few years before, someone caught in the act with him, was picked up by the police. He had a heart attack and died under police interrogation. The police report mentions a confession, but the reference to the confession was so vague one can't be sure exactly what the man had confessed to.'

'And the derelict?'

'The derelict's death was attributed to a foreign homosexual. The toilet was in a tourist area.'

'It could only happen in a secret society,' Lara said, not keeping the disgust from her voice. 'A free society with the news media watching the police and lawyers exposing police malfeasance in courtrooms would never permit these crimes to be swept under the rug.'

'Besides the bad system,' Vlad said, 'there was a long lapse between the killings, five or six years, the fact that the killings were not centered in a single Moscow neighborhood—'

'It's no excuse. We're not talking about bad police work, we're dealing with corruption. Someone with power pulled strings that caused each investigation to go astray.' Lara shook her head again, trying to get her brain to process the data into a neat and orderly pattern but it wouldn't cooperate. 'The killings in the public rest rooms appear random, unplanned, a typical serial killer strike – a victim and an opportunity suddenly arises. But the killing of the doctor smacks of premeditation. And the killing of Vera causes the whole pattern to ... to disintegrate. Hell, there is no pattern.'

'Of course there is. The same mark, the killer's trademark, is on each body.'

She thought about the power and ruthlessness it would take to cover the tracks of the killer and a wave of fear for Vlad swept her. She reached across the table and grabbed his hands. 'Vlad, I want you to leave Moscow until my trial is over. Go to Siberia, the Black Sea, anywhere, just get out of Moscow until it's over.'

'Your trial won't start for months. You must get a new attorney. The court will delay the trial.'

'No, I'm not getting another attorney. I'm defending myself. In court this morning I signed away my right to an attorney. The judge was ready to appoint a former prosecutor, a hack who would hold my arms while that bitch Svetlana stepped on my face. I'm pushing the case to trial.'

'You shouldn't do that. You will need a lawyer—'

'Vlad, I am a lawyer. Not a Russian one, but Marya was the only Russian lawyer I could trust. It's my life on the line and I'm the only person I trust with my life.' She squeezed his hands. 'I'm worried about you. And Marya's boy friend.'

Vlad shook his head. 'I'm not leaving. I will be at the trial, in the courtroom, so when you turn round you will see a face that you know and who supports you.'

'I can't let you—'

'Don't worry about me. I've been playing with guns since I was seven years old. I can protect myself. I came here in a car with Marya's boy friend and another friend. They're waiting outside for me – with enough fire power to take on a small army. I'm going to help you at the trial, not just for you, but for Marya.'

'Vlad—'

'It is all arranged. I've made models. We can establish the angle of the shot to the victim's chest by the powder burns on the door frame and the bullet embedded in the spa liner. That angle shows that a person several inches taller than you fired the shot. I can't do anything about the second shot, the one to the back of her head. It was fired at close range while the body floated in the spa and I can't determine the angle. But once we eliminate you as the author of shot number one, the other doesn't matter.'

Lara looked away and said nothing. Vlad was her only hope now but there was something that bothered her about his theory. It sounded logical. Too logical, too easy. There had to be a catch and right now her mind wasn't capable of tracking the progress of a fly on a wall let alone the path of a speeding bullet.

She was also terribly afraid for the young man's safety.

'I trust you, Vlad. I know you'll do what you can. And I hate to admit it, but you're my only hope. But I'm worried—'

'Worry about preparing for your trial. I'll do my part. I'm not running. Marya was my friend.'

'Mine, too,' Lara said. 'Mine, too.'

They were silent for a moment. Lara was drained, emotionally and physically.

'I have that other information you asked for,' Vlad said.

'Other information? I'm sorry, Vlad, I don't even remember what I asked for.'

'You wanted to find out from Marya's boy friend the

name of the prisoner who was killed trying to escape when Detective Yuri Kirov was wounded in Afghanistan. The prisoner's name was Alexander Zurin.'

'Alexander Zurin.' She stared blankly at Vlad, trying to get an incomprehensible piece of information to fit a puzzle that kept changing shape. 'Pasha.'

'This information means something to you,' Vlad said.

'Yes, it means something to me. Pasha Zurin was the boy next door who was convicted of killing our neighbor.'

'I don't understand.'

'I don't understand either. Yuri Kirov is one of the links,' she told the mystified Vlad. 'I thought he was just playing cop or a little more, but there's a chain that extends back over twenty years and Yuri is a link in the chain.'

'A chain?'

'A chain of murder and deceit,' she told him.

Seven days passed, each day filled with growing anxiety and mounting impatience before she was brought into the courtroom for her trial. For the first time she was not put in the prisoner's dock, but taken to a counsel table.

There were two other counsel tables, one for the prosecution, the other for that strange creature of Soviet-Russian law, the *obhchestvenni* – representatives of the victim's interests. At the pre-trial conference she had been told that Rykoff would be there with Nadia's sister, and that a representative of Nadia's employer, Moscow News, would also be at the table.

Svetlana had not made her appearance yet. No doubt she was waiting for exactly the right dramatic moment, Lara thought.

The presence of Lenin on the wall and the heavily armed soldiers created a feeling that she was not just in a foreign country, but an earlier era. And something else, an undercurrent she felt from the audience that she had never felt in an American courtroom where stern-faced bailiffs ensured that spectators sat quietly and did not disrupt the proceedings. In this Russian courtroom she sensed something close to arrogance in the audience, as if they, too, were arbiters of the justice that would be handed down.

She wondered if this was Judge Rurik's regular courtroom or if it had been selected with the foreign and local press in mind. The courtroom was impressive, large, old and venerable, with heavy wood tables, dock, and bench, and wood paneling on the walls.

The gallery was full when she was brought in, with standing room only at the back of the courtroom. The smell of damp wool was in the air and she could see wet footprints down the center aisle. Two rows at the front had been set aside for the press. She had already decided that with every word she said, every move she made, she would keep the press in mind because an informed press was the only thing that could keep her fighting on her feet if the system decided to railroad her to the nearest prison.

Yuri was at the back of the courtroom, leaning against the wall to the left of the big double doors leading out, a raincoat folded over one arm, an umbrella in the other hand. She let her eyes touch his for a moment before she scanned the rest of the gallery.

Alexei stood on the other side of the doors, resplendent in a double-breasted Italian suit and hand painted silk tie; the media people pressed close so they could report having been 'in touch' with the great man.

If this was a trial back home, the people in the gallery would be the jury panel, usually forty or fifty citizens from whom twelve would be selected to decide the case. There were no juries in Russia, but Marya had told her to face the gallery and let the people there see the honesty in her eyes because the spectators could get very loud if they thought the court was being misled.

She suddenly had the sensation of being an observer rather than a participant. Her mind wandered up to a corner of the ceiling and looked down on the mob in the gallery waiting for the guillotine to fall, her head dropping into a basket, looking up from the basket at a fly on the wall, a fly with her face.

The double doors at the rear of the courtroom snapped opened and Stalin's Breath entered leading her troops. She wore her sharp military-style uniform; Vulko was in a business suit and so was a harried looking young man who closely resembled Svetlana's previous assistant, the one she had tried to palm off on Lara as her second attorney.

Before taking a seat at the counsel table, Svetlana paused and gave Lara a formal nod – quite different from the look of contempt Lara got from Vulko. For some reason he disliked her personally. It wasn't just a matter of police versus criminal suspect, her personality did not mix well with his.

Svetlana nodded to another person in the courtroom and Lara twisted in her chair to see who it was – a well-dressed gentlemen in his early sixties with a closely trimmed beard, conservative but well-tailored suit, and stiff white shirt with striped tie. He gave the impression of a professional man, perhaps a doctor. It occurred to her that he might be an observer sent from the Foreign Ministry because of the attention the case was getting from the foreign media.

The audience stirred as the judge and two assessors entered the courtroom and took their seats. This was the first time she had seen the two assessors. The one on the judge's left was a short, heavy woman of about forty-five or fifty, a foreman at a brake lining factory. The other assessor was male, early sixties, thick glasses and chubby. The information sheet said he was an administrator with the street department. As she looked at him, he leaned toward the judge like a faithful dog to hear some whispered comment, and she was reminded of what Marya had told her about the assessors' role in the proceedings – they would follow the judge's lead. The judge was the most important, perhaps the only trier of fact, and he was a professional and had no doubt seen about everything there was to see in a courtroom. He would be almost impossible to sway with courtroom tactics. No, she told herself again, it's the press I have to play on.

Judge Rurik called the case and briefly, for the record and no doubt the press, introduced the participants in the courtroom, starting with Svetlana and her staff, moving to Rykoff and Nadia's sister, then to the representative from Moscow News, a young woman with thick glasses and short blonde hair whom Lara was certain she had seen as an anchorwoman on the news program.

'I have read the investigation reports and they appear to be complete and in good order,' the judge said, nodding at Vulko who rose slightly to give the judge a small bow. Lara imagined him snapping his heels and giving a Nazi salute.

The judge went on briefly to summarize the facts set forth in the report: the call to the police from a 'concerned but anonymous citizen' reporting a woman entering the tower with a gun, the police rushing in; Lara seen with a gun; Nadia, a prominent news media personality, found dead—

'My sister was loved by all in Russia,' Nadia's sister cried out. From the audience came a chorus of muttered sympathy.

'I watched her show every night,' Rykoff said.

'A great loss for our country,' the judge said. 'A wrong that we are here to punish.'

The circus has started, Lara thought. Judges in America and Britain would not have permitted such theatrics. Marya had warned her but she was still taken aback that people could make totally irrelevant and inflammatory remarks in a courtroom.

It was a moment before she realized the judge had spoken to her.

'Lara Patrick, come forward and tell us what you know about this matter.'

You have no right to remain silent, Marya had said, *no right to refuse to testify. The court will call you as the first witness and you will be expected to confess your sins. Confession is good for the soul . . .*

Chapter 38

Lara stood at the counsel table. She cleared her throat and looked up at the judge and the two assessors in a display of more confidence than she felt.

'What do I know about the crime? I know a young woman lost her life. I know I stand accused. And . . . I know I am innocent.' She took a deep breath. 'Nadia Kolchak's life was taken not because of anything I did, but because of a failure of the Soviet regime to protect—'

'Miss Patrick,' the judge interrupted. 'We are not here for a history lesson about the failings of the Soviet justice system. This is the time and place for you to take responsibility for your acts. Tell us about how you came to take the life of Nadia Kolchak. Tell us about the blackmail Nadia Kolchak proposed, about the jealousy between you and Nadia over Alexei Bova, and how you felt driven to take Nadia Kolchak's life in a sudden rage of anger and passion.'

Tell us mitigating circumstances and you won't die from a bullet, was what he was signaling.

She was at the fork in the road.

Her right knee trembled and she leaned against the table to steady herself. Her eyes met the judge's eyes and in a strong, clear voice she said, 'This case didn't begin with the death of Nadia Kolchak. The events that led up to the death of Nadia began—'

'My apologies.' Svetlana rose at the prosecutor's table. 'If the judge will permit, I need a few minutes to investigate a matter of importance.'

The judge frowned. 'It is a bit unusual, Madam Procurator, but if it is a matter that recently arose . . .'

'Yes. I need ten or fifteen minutes.'

'The court will be in recess for fifteen minutes.'

The judge and assessors left the courtroom and Svetlana followed them through the door that led to the judge's chambers and the holding tank further down the corridor.

A few moments later one of the courtroom guards told Lara, 'Follow me.'

She would have preferred to have been left at the counsel table with her papers rather than be put in the holding tank for the fifteen-minute break, but she didn't bother trying to argue. She got up and was escorted by the guard to the rear door of the courtroom.

In the rear corridor, she turned in the direction of the holding cell and the guard caught her arm. 'This way,' he said. He took her in the opposite direction, pausing at the door to the judge's office. He knocked and then opened it, standing aside so Lara could enter.

She stepped into the room and the guard shut the door.

At the other end of the room Svetlana stood at a window, smoke from her cigarette surrounding her. She turned slowly, the dull gray light from the window making the smoke a glowing halo around her, creating not so much a cherubic impression as that of an avenging angel.

'Do you want to live?' she asked Lara.

Lara stared at her, at a loss for words. 'Do I want to live? Is that a question . . . or a threat?'

Svetlana chuckled, an almost manly rasp. She moved away from the window, leaving a trail of smoke in her wake as she stood and looked at the law books lining the wall behind the judge's desk.

'This is a very bad time for Russia,' Svetlana told her. Lara wasn't sure if the woman was talking to her or just thinking aloud. 'Not since the Great Patriotic War has there been such fear. For my entire career it has been a crime to make a profit from the sale of goods or services. Suddenly, people are told that if they do not make a profit, they will no longer have homes and their children will starve.

'As a prosecutor, I have been privy to reports of madness in rural areas where the supply of food and fuel have been the lowest, stories of atrocities that I did not believe it possible for good Russians to commit.'

She turned and challenged Lara with a look. 'We will survive, Mother Russia has always survived, but the struggle will be long and hard. And once we have survived we will cut off the economic heads of the Japanese, the Germans, and you Americans just as we did the Mongols, the French, the Germans, and every other invader.

'You Westerners, you're fat and comfortable. That's why the Japanese beat you in the war of the dollar. Now the Japanese are fat and comfortable. But there is no fat, no comfort in Russia. Russia is a hard place. It has always been a hard place – hard to grow crops, natural resources buried deep, weather that makes most of the country a frozen hell. Hard life,' she said, 'makes hard people. That's why we beat you at the Olympics, why we beat you into space, why we were able to face the Nazis in our city streets and beat their tanks back with our bare hands. You know how we defeated Hitler and Napoleon? We plowed under our food, poisoned our water, killed our horses and tore down our bridges. We burned our own cities.

'Look at America, pushed about by little third world countries, trying to police the world with as much grace as an elephant turning in a bathtub. Your country is fat and lazy and sloppy. You Americans and your British friends believe you have won the Cold War but what we have done in Russia is just shed an old coat that has become tattered. We will rise from the ashes stronger and faster, and when we come for you, we will go for the jugular.'

Lara stood silently, wondering why she was getting the history lesson. Svetlana put out her cigarette in an ashtray and sat on the edge of the desk.

'Did you make deals with criminals when you were a prosecutor?' she asked Lara.

Lara thought about the question and answered it honestly. 'I was tough. But I hope I treated people fairly. If the defendant had evidence that rebutted or mitigated the crime, I wasn't afraid to dismiss charges or be lenient. But I never made deals in the sense that I offered anything less than what the evidence showed the person deserved.'

'I never make deals,' Svetlana said. 'I have been a prosecutor for eight years. In every case I have handled the criminal was found guilty of the charge that I originally filed. There is no compromise with me. Justice is not blind to me as it is in the West.'

'Justice is blindfolded to make her impartial,' Lara said, 'not to make her ignorant.'

'I am offering you a ... what do you call it, a plea bargain?' The words came out in a rush as if Svetlana was spitting out something foul.

Nerves fluttered up Lara's throat from the tight knots in her stomach. 'What exactly are you offering?'

'Your life.'

'I see. And what do I have to do for my life?'

Svetlana slipped off the edge of the table and returned to

the window, her back to Lara, speaking to the gray day outside.

'This is a new day in Russia. New rules. The Procurator General has received calls from the Foreign Ministry and the Economics Ministry. The bureaucrats in those departments know nothing about this case except what they read in the newspapers, nothing about the process of administering justice, but they fear the publicity being generated by putting a woman on trial who has blood ties to both America and Britain at a time when Russia is looking to the West for loans.'

'It's not just me, is it?' Lara said. 'It's the rest of the killings. You don't want that to come into the public eye. My mother's death, our neighbor, all the others.'

'You are barred from mentioning those deaths in court because they are not relevant to this case.'

'You will have to gag me. That would look pretty for the foreign press, wouldn't it? An example of the justice system of the new Russia at work.'

Svetlana waved her hand as if she was shooing away a pesty insect. 'It doesn't matter. There will be no trial. My instructions are to give you back your life.'

'In exchange for what?'

'You will plead guilty to killing Nadia Kolchak with mitigating circumstances. You and Nadia were competitive lovers for Alexei Bova. We can leave out your mutual greed for his money. In the heat of the moment, overwhelmed by your emotions and sexual rage, you murdered Nadia.'

Lara's knees shook but she kept her voice calm as she answered. 'I already told Vulko, I am not going to prison for something I didn't do.'

'There is another part to the deal. You will have to serve only one year. After that, you will be released and immediately shipped out of the country. The excuse will be that some close relative is gravely ill.'

'I have no close relatives.'

'Then you can have one of mine. Don't talk nonsense when you are witnessing a miracle.'

'I'm not accepting the offer.'

'What?'

'I'm not pleading guilty to something I didn't do.'

'You are insane.'

'I am *innocent*. I don't think that means anything to you. You say every case that came before you in eight years was black and white. I was a prosecutor for less time, but I learned that there are some innocent people in this world. That's where your system fails. Justice isn't just blind in Russia – she had her eyes gouged out by people like you.'

Svetlana stepped close to her, close enough for Lara to smell her perfume, the acrid scent of spent gunpowder, close enough for Lara to feel the heat of her anger and contempt.

'Put the past on trial,' Svetlana whispered, 'and you put Russia on trial.'

She suddenly realized Svetlana was holding something in her hand. She looked down. Svetlana had a small caliber automatic only inches from her stomach.

She stared wild-eyed at Svetlana, wondering if the cold bitch had lost her mind, unable to believe her own eyes as Svetlana's grip tightened on the gun, the trigger finger slowly contracting, drawing back the trigger . . .

A flame popped up from the top of the gun.

Svetlana smiled and slowly raised the lighter to her cigarette. She blew smoke in Lara's face.

'Put Russia on trial, and I will pull the trigger myself at your execution.'

Chapter 39

When Lara was returned to the courtroom by the guard, Svetlana was standing at the railing to the gallery talking to a man on the other side. It was the distinguished looking individual Lara had noticed earlier.

Svetlana took her place at the prosecutor's table after Lara was seated.

The judge and the assessors returned to the bench and the judge nodded down at Svetlana.

'The defendant has denied the crime,' he said. 'You may proceed with your evidence.'

Lara flinched and rose at the counsel table.

'Your honor, I'm not through with my statement.'

'You have denied the crime. That is sufficient. If you do not wish to admit your guilt, there is no use wasting the court's time. We will proceed with the evidence.'

'But I want the court to know—'

He waved away her objection. 'A trial in Russia is not a melodrama in which those accused of crimes give speeches. You are entitled to cross-examine witnesses, present your own witnesses, and at the end of the trial, you will be given the last word.' He nodded at Svetlana again. 'Proceed.'

'My first witness is Chief Investigator Vulko of the Moscow City Procurator's office.'

The chief investigator gave a simple, straightforward

395

narration of the results of the police investigation. He began with the anonymous phone call and moved forward chronologically.

'When officers arrived at the Bova penthouse and entered the front door, the first person they saw was the accused. She ran across the landing at the top of the stairway. She had a gun. Fearful for their lives, the officers began to fire their own weapons.'

Vulko went on to describe the scene of the crime, showing the murder weapon 'taken from the defendant's hand', describing Nadia found dead in the spa, two gunshot wounds, two empty cartridges in the gun Lara had been caught with.

He wasn't there, she thought. It's all hearsay, every word of it. Multiple levels of hearsay as he testified to what one officer told another officer who told him . . .

She realized with a start that the prosecutor had no intention of calling the other police witnesses: Vulko was it. What he said would convict her without her being able to poke holes in the story. It would be impossible to cross-examine him effectively when everything he testified was told to him by other people.

He then expanded his testimony into the subsequent police investigation, including the taped conversation between Lara and Yuri in the jail.

'Is it your conclusion, then,' Svetlana asked, 'that the accused was involved in a scheme to blackmail Alexei Bova and that she murdered Nadia Kolchak after Miss Kolchak discovered the scheme?'

'Objection.' Lara jumped to her feet. 'There is no foundation for the question.'

'No foundation?' the judge asked.

'There is not one shred of evidence in this case that I was involved in any manner with blackmailing Mr Bova. On the contrary, the only evidence concerning blackmail are my statements that it was Miss Kolchak who was planning to blackmail Mr Bova.'

'Objection overruled.'

'But, your honor—'

'That is not the correct way to address a Russian judge.'

'Your ... Judge, Mr Vulko has testified to the truthfulness of facts he knows nothing about. Now he has drawn an impermissible conclusion from the evidence. In order for him to draw a conclusion from the evidence, there must be facts supporting that conclusion. There are no facts supporting this conclusion.'

'Madam, you are in a Russian courtroom. I am a Russian judge. You are not a Russian attorney. You were given the opportunity to accept a Russian attorney for this trial—'

'My attorney—'

'Sit down! Do not interrupt me again.' He pointed his finger at her.

She sat down, her jaws tight. It wasn't an argument she was going to win. If she opened her mouth they would probably have her cuffed and gagged.

'Under Russian law,' he told her, his tone more neutral, 'the chief investigator is allowed to draw inferences from his investigation which he believes are warranted. He is only permitted to draw reasonable inferences but we are not bound by the rigid legal rules of the Anglo-American system of justice. The chief investigator is given great latitude under our system,' he said, obviously for the benefit of the gallery and the media people, 'but so is the defendant. Miss Patrick will be given great leeway in presenting her defense. No rigid rules of evidence will hackle her. She will be given every opportunity to present her case without restraint from artificial rules that keep the truth from the courtroom.'

There's one thing wrong with your analysis, Lara thought. The chief investigator wasn't propounding the 'truth' but a conclusion drawn from thin air. Those 'artificial rules' of evidence used in British and American courtrooms were not designed to keep the truth from the courtroom but to keep people like Vulko from making groundless accusations.

She kept her thoughts to herself, careful to keep her features blank. The trial was a farce and she wasn't going to improve her position by mouthing off and giving the judge an excuse to gag her.

Vulko elaborated on the blackmail scheme and then Svetlana announced, 'No more questions.'

Lara started to rise to ask questions as the judge said, 'Mr Rykoff, it is your turn.'

She sat back down. She had forgotten. The representative of the victim's family was next. And then Nadia's employer, the news station, would have a shot.

Rykoff stood up, reintroduced himself to the court and the gallery.

The knowledge that he had discussed the case with her and then had turned around and offered his services to an adverse party infuriated her. So did his body language. He was there to get attention for himself and not justice for the victim's family.

'Chief Investigator Vulko,' he said, 'Nadia Kolchak was a great asset to the new Russia, was she not?'

'Objection. No foundation. No evidence has been admitted that Mr Vulko had any knowledge of Miss Kolchak prior to her death.'

Before the judge ruled, Rykoff held up his hands. 'No, no, it is all right, Judge. I withdraw the question.' Rykoff shot a look at the audience and then, in a pandering tone of voice asked, 'Chief Investigator Vulko, have you ever watched the Moscow News on television?'

The gallery roared with laughter. Lara sat back and folded her arms, her face burning.

She studied the corner of the ceiling where she had earlier been a fly looking down at the courtroom. The fly was gone and a spider had taken its place.

Rykoff stopped the pretense of asking questions and began making a speech to the court and audience, feeding maudlin 'facts' about Nadia's past life, starting with her childhood. As Rykoff talked about the flower of Russian youth, portraying Nadia as something of a cross between Joan of Arc and Mother Teresa, Lara closed him out of her mind and thought about the Nadia she knew.

Whatever Nadia was, and she certainly wasn't a saint, she didn't deserve to be brutally murdered.

As Rykoff droned on about the loss to Nadia's family and to all Russia, Nadia's sister sobbed beside him. Lara didn't know if the woman's tears flowed from her sense of loss or the melodramatic atmosphere that Rykoff had created. In the States she would have asked for a 'side bar' to object to the testimony out of hearing of the jury, but there was no jury and she wasn't in the States.

Half an hour later Rykoff took his seat and the Moscow News representative stood up.

'Mr Rykoff has presented to the court the great loss to the family and to all Russia. What Mr Rykoff has said is true. We at Moscow News . . .'

Her mind wandered and she was startled a few minutes later by the judge addressing her.

'The defendant may question the witness.'

Lara stood up, rustled her papers for a moment, and then met Vulko's eye.

'Let's go back to the scene of the crime, Chief Investigator. My recollection of your testimony is that you were not present when I came into contact with Moscow police officers at the penthouse, is that correct?'

'It is not required under Russian law that I be present in order to testify. I am permitted to conduct an investigation in which I question police officers and the defendant and testify as to the results.' He looked at the prosecutor and then at the judge, both of whom gave nodding confirmation.

'So everything you know about what occurred at the scene of the crime you learned from other officers.'

'I am permitted to do so.'

'I am not asking whether what you did was permissible, Chief Investigator, I am asking about the procedure you followed. What you know about the scene of the crime you learned from other officers. Isn't that true?'

'Yes.'

'And it's true that you did not *personally* observe any of the activities.'

'Under Russian law—'

'And, Chief Investigator, in testifying to those things that others told you, you have not left out any of the important facts that should be before this court, is that correct?'

'Of course. I placed all the facts before the court.'

'But not having been at the scene, you did not pick up all the ... the *little* details, things like,' she shrugged, 'well, whether my hair was in a bun or hanging loose.'

He grinned. 'I don't know whether you combed your hair.' Laughter came from the gallery.

'Or the expression on my face.'

'Or the expression on your face.' His grin widened.

'If you don't know the expression on my face when I first

contacted the officers, you cannot judge if I was running in terror from the real killer, can you?'

'I don't understand what you are getting at. I—'

'You testified for the prosecutor that I came running onto the landing with a gun, but you don't know what my demeanor was, you don't know if I was running in terror.'

'You were running in terror. You were terrified because the police were confronting you.'

'Excuse me, but you just testified that you knew nothing about my demeanor. Going back over your previous testimony, you mentioned the fingerprint tests the criminalist took at the scene of the crime. The criminalist told you about all the results, and you testified about all of them, didn't you?'

Smelling another trap, Vulko's eyes narrowed and he sat upright in the witness chair. 'He told me his results.'

Lara's eyebrows went up. 'Why don't you tell us now which of the results you failed to tell us about?'

Vulko hesitated, knowing he was being set up but not knowing which way to turn. He exchanged looks with Svetlana. 'I testified about all of the results.'

Good, she thought. The idea was to commit him completely to his prior testimony or get him to expand upon it.

'Now, Officer – excuse me, Chief Investigator, no fingerprint tests were done on the gun that has been identified as the murder weapon. Is that correct?'

'No fingerprint tests were done on the murder weapon,' he repeated slowly, seeing if any of the words bit back. 'No, there were no fingerprint tests done on the murder weapon because—'

'Because it was found in my hand, isn't that correct?'

'Yes, that's correct.'

'In my statement to the officers at the scene, I said I had

found the gun on the floor and had picked it up just before they entered, isn't that correct?'

'That was your statement. They—'

'And despite—'

'Judge, she is cutting off the witness,' Svetlana objected.

'I apologize,' Lara said, not meaning it. She was deliberately cutting him off to keep him from justifying every negative response.

'Let the witness finish his answers,' the judge instructed.

Sure.

'Now, Chief Investigator, if someone had handled the gun before I did, I would not necessarily have smeared all their prints, would I?'

'I can't say—'

'Isn't it true that you can't say whether someone else handled the gun before me, someone who might have shot and killed Nadia Kolchak and dropped the gun on the floor? And isn't it true that person would now be on trial instead of me if the police criminalist had simply done a fingerprint test on the murder weapon?'

'Objection,' Svetlana shouted. 'She is asking multiple questions and not giving the witness a chance to answer.'

'She has made her point,' the judge told Svetlana.

'It is also true, is it not, that no paraffin test was conducted to see if I had fired a weapon?'

'No paraffin test was done.' His jaws were noticeably tighter and his eyes narrower. He was not getting the respect a chief investigator expected from a 'defense' attorney in a courtroom.

'Paraffin tests are of no use to the Moscow police in criminal investigations, is that your testimony?'

Vulko hesitated and looked at Svetlana. A gun fired will often leave gunpowder residue on the hand of the person pulling the trigger. The tests involved applying paraffin wax to the hand and then removing it. Chemical treatment of the wax ascertained whether any gunpowder particles were present on the hand. Lara knew paraffin tests were not completely accurate, but police agencies all over the world still used them and offered the results as evidence in court. The arresting officers in this case should have had a paraffin test performed on her.

Vulko's dilemma was that if he damned paraffin tests as being inaccurate or unnecessary, the testimony would be repeated in the news media and would come back to haunt him in cases in which the police relied on the tests.

'A paraffin test was unnecessary because you had the murder weapon in your hand when you were captured.'

Relief flowed through her. He thought he had avoided the trap but that was the answer she wanted. 'No paraffin test was done to see if I fired a weapon because I was seen with the weapon in hand. No fingerprint test was done because I was seen with the murder weapon. Is that your testimony?'

'Yes,' he said stubbornly.

'So, your testimony,' she said slowly, 'is that the police officers in this case failed to perform standard, scientific tests that might have cleared me of this crime because they had already made up their minds about my guilt before they conducted an investigation.' She did not give him a chance to rebut her. 'The police officers failed to do their duty, failed even to conduct a rudimentary investigation, because they thought they had caught the criminal red-handed. Now, Chief Investigator, no one saw me pick up the gun, did they? It's my word alone that I found it on the floor, isn't it?'

'It's your word alone.'

'And no one saw me shoot Nadia Kolchak, did they? It's my word alone that I did not shoot her, isn't it?'

'It's your word alone.'

'It's my word alone,' her voice rose, 'because the Moscow police failed to conduct tests that would have cleared me, isn't that true?'

'Objection! Objection.'

Lara sat down while Svetlana voiced her objections. She had finally managed to wake up the two assessors. She glanced behind her to the audience and noted that the news media people were writing frantically. Her eyes swept Yuri's and Alexei's face. Both men gave her a smile of encouragement, but there was something in the expression of each of them that disturbed her. It was as if they knew something that she didn't know. Their looks made her uneasy and she wondered if she had forgotten some critical issue.

The judge ruled in Svetlana's favor and threw out the question, but as he had noted previously, Lara had made her point.

'Ask your next question,' he told her.

Trials combined the subtlety of chess moves with guerrilla war tactics and it was time for her next move. She could keep on tearing apart the police investigation – the officers had not even bothered to question potential witnesses at business establishments near the back entrance to the penthouse – but she decided that this was a good time to leave Vulko alone. She had made several major points and didn't want to obscure them by going on to make smaller points.

'No further questions,' she said, with a sense of dread that she had forgotten some vital fact.

Chapter 40

The court called a noon recess. Lara sat alone in the holding tank behind the courtroom, unable to eat the sandwich of rancid beef and stale bread provided for prisoners on trial. The feeling she got from the people watching the proceedings bugged her – she didn't understand what they knew that she didn't. Things were pretty bad when the spectators were better informed than the defense attorney.

Returning to the courtroom, she briefly met Svetlana's eye and the woman gave her a small smile and a nod. She's up to something, Lara thought. She's too smug.

Vulko was just the opposite. He gave Lara a look that told her he'd like an opportunity to give her some good old-fashioned police 'attitude adjustment'.

The judge and assessors took the bench and the judge ordered Svetlana to call her next witness.

Svetlana rose from her seat at the prosecutor's table. 'The procurator's office calls Dr Zubov of the Serbsky Institute.'

The announcement sent a shock through Lara as she turned and watched the distinguished looking man Svetlana had spoken to earlier rise from his seat in the gallery and proceed into the arena of the courtroom.

The Serbsky Institute. In her mind the name was identified with KGB psychiatrists who certified intellectuals and dissenters insane while helping turn them that way with 'treatment'. But she realized that to most Russians it was a prestigious name, the most prominent psychiatric organization in the country.

She glanced at Yuri, staked out in his place at the back of the room. His features were dark. Her eyes shot to Svetlana. The woman's usual intense glare had folded into a smirk.

Dr Zubov took the stand, bowed slightly to the judge and assessors, and adjusted his glasses before he turned to face Svetlana.

'Dr Zubov, please tell the court your professional background.'

Zubov adjusted his glasses again and looked up at the judge and assessors as he spoke. 'I am a graduate of Moscow University and have served...' He went on to detail nearly forty years in the service of Russian psychiatry, over twenty-five of it at the Serbsky Institute.

Lara did some quick calculations as he talked. Forty years of service would make him a young psychiatrist back in the early fifties, the last days of Stalin and Beria, the rise of Khrushchev. Zubov, she decided, would have been about thirty-five or forty during the trials of the intellectuals in the late sixties. Just about the right age in his profession to have been a major player in the institute's destruction of some of the finest minds in the country.

'Dr Zubov,' Svetlana said, 'are you familiar with the psychiatric case of a woman named Angela Patrick?'

Lara gave an involuntary start at the mention of her mother's name.

'Very much so,' the psychiatrist said, 'although I was not directly involved in the patient's treatment. I practiced at the Serbsky Institute at the time that the woman was a patient at the Charsky Institute. However, it was my responsibility to review certain patients at other institutions. One of those was Angela Patrick. Dr Komoson, my colleague at the Charsky Institute, was the principal doctor assigned to the case, and we had discussions concerning Angela Patrick's condition. As you may recall, this was over twenty years ago. Dr Komoson passed away ten years ago.'

'Doctor, have you also recently had the opportunity to review the psychiatric file of Angela Patrick that is maintained by the Charsky Institute?'

'Yes. As recently as yesterday.'

'What was the course of treatment for Angela Patrick at the institute during the period she was treated there?'

'I should mention that Miss Patrick was only briefly treated at the institute. Sadly, she was in a very advanced state of mental deterioration at the time of admission.'

'Could you define what you mean by an advanced state of mental deterioration?'

'The woman was suffering from severe paranoia, untreated paranoia. Her mental condition had degenerated to the point where she was having delusions and was suicidal. Unfortunately, because she had not been treated at the institute before her admission, though the paranoia was easy to diagnose, her suicidal tendencies were not immediately recognized. As a result, no suicide watch was placed upon her. In retrospect, this was an error because she took her own life shortly after admission.'

'Doctor, what exactly is paranoia?'

'Paranoia is a psychotic disorder characterized by delusions of persecution or grandeur. In general, it involves an extreme distrust or fear of others.'

Svetlana looked at a report in her hands. 'Can you tell us whether paranoia is a hereditary condition?'

A bolt of shock went through Lara.

Svetlana slowly turned toward her and stared at her, thus focusing the attention of everyone in the courtroom on Lara. The good doctor peered at Lara over his glasses, the judge and assessors stared down from their lofty thrones, every head in the audience turned toward her.

Lara started to rise to object to the question, and sat back down. It was a set-up and she couldn't win with an objection.

'There is certainly some evidence that paranoia, like other mental conditions, has a hereditary factor, but even more important than that is conditioning or what you might call the behavioral factor. Children, for example, commonly adopt the behavior pattern of the parent or parents that raise them. The child's attitude toward other people, work ethic, even politics and the family dog, is very much molded by the behavior patterns consciously and subconsciously taught to them by their parents. A person raised by a parent suffering from psychotic paranoia tends to have paranoid characteristics to one extent or another. Sadly, some succumb completely to the disease.'

Svetlana turned and gave Lara another long look.

Lara's face turned red. She tried to maintain her composure, to keep anger and fear under control, forcing herself to take careful notes of what the man said when she really wanted to leap to her feet and call him a quack.

'Doctor, have you had the opportunity to examine the defendant in this case, Lara Patrick?'

'Yes, I have.'

'That's a lie!' Lara leaped to her feet. 'I've never seen this man before he appeared in court.'

Svetlana smiled tolerantly. 'If Miss Patrick could be persuaded to take her seat, we will explain.'

Lara sat down. The woman had set another trap for her, had caused her to jump on command and make her look foolish.

'Please explain, Doctor, about the examination.'

'I did not examine her in my office. Such examinations are of little clinical value. The most valuable are those in which the patient is examined without knowing she or he is being watched. Those are the type of observations I conducted in this case.'

'Go on, tell us about the examinations.'

'Miss Patrick was observed while she was in jail – in her cell, in the corridors, and in the interview room. There were several hours of observations.

'What did you conclude from these observations?'

'This is ridiculous, your honor,' Lara told the judge. 'There is no foundation for any of this testimony. We haven't been told who made the observations, when they were made, what was observed—'

'Miss Patrick is correct,' Svetlana interjected. 'Doctor, please tell us how these observations were made.'

Lara knew she had stepped into it again.

'I can show you,' the psychiatrist said. He reached into his briefcase and took out a video tape. 'Miss Patrick was video-taped on a number of occasions. I have selected portions that illustrate the reasons for my conclusions.'

On cue, the door to the rear of the courtroom opened and a guard came in pushing a television-VCR combination unit. As the man was plugging in the set, Svetlana asked, 'In regard to your views concerning Miss Patrick's psychiatric state, perhaps you can give us that opinion before we see the tape. That way, we might better understand why you arrived at your conclusions.'

Dr Zubov adjusted his glasses and cleared his throat. 'It is my opinion that Miss Patrick suffers from the same sort of psychotic paranoia that her mother suffered from.'

'Are you saying that Miss Patrick is insane, Doctor?'

'The word insane has a psychiatric and a legal definition.

From a psychiatric point of view, my opinion is that Lara Patrick's mental state caused her to interpret falsely the acts of those around her, to imagine conspiracies, to interpret innocent behavior as threatening behavior. For example, the matter in which she reacted to what she believed was the Guk woman's intention to harm her. That imagined threat generated fear within her and she struck out, nearly killing the woman.

'Thus I find Lara Patrick, from a clinical point of view, to be a very dangerous woman due to mental disturbance. However, in a legal sense, no disorders of the nervous system appear present. She appears to be neurologically intact. I have no doubt that the killing of Nadia Kolchak was in some ways triggered by the defendant's paranoia, but the killing was motivated by profit, not from a mental defect in the defendant.'

'What you are telling us, Doctor, is that the defendant is a disturbed and dangerous woman who could kill out of imagined fears, but in the case of Nadia Kolchak, the defendant killed out of a sense of greed.'

'Yes—'

'This isn't psychiatry!' Lara yelled. 'It's witchcraft!'

'Silence!' the judge snapped. 'If you disturb the proceedings I will have you gagged.'

Svetlana used a remote control to start the VCR playing.

A burst of static was followed by a scene of a jail matron backing away from Lara in a cell. Lara's hair was wild, her face was twisted with rage. 'You've been spying on me! How many people are paying you to watch me?'

The next scene was of her in the interview room, screaming at Yuri, attacking him with her fists as she accused him of plotting against her.

Lara shrank down in her chair at the counsel table.

In the video she looked crazy. And dangerous.

Chapter 41

Her turn to question the psychiatrist came and she approached the task with dread. She wanted to rip the bastard's lying tongue out but she had to keep cool and professional, do and say nothing that would support his allegation that she was paranoid.

She slowly stood up at the counsel table, pushing her chair back to get a little room to be nervous in. She sensed the guards closing in on her from the rear and the judge shook his head, indicating that she could have the freedom to move a little when she asked questions. An encouraging sign from the judge after a psychiatrist had just labeled her a dangerous nut.

'Dr Zubov, you mentioned mental conditions. Isn't it true that a *physical* condition can also affect a person's mental state?'

He thought about the question for a moment. He had been in the courtroom when Vulko testified and he was wary of traps. 'Yes, certainly, being physically ill with a disease, for example, might bring about depression.'

'Did my mother's limp in any way affect her mental condition?'

'Her limp? Well, a limp ... a limp does not cause paranoia—'

'But isn't it true that her limp...' she paused. 'You

411

did say you actually saw my mother in person, didn't you?'

'Yes, many years ago, of course.'

Lying bastard. 'And you recall the limp?'

Hesitation. 'Yes.'

'Which leg was lame, Doctor?'

'Which leg?' He smiled and shook his head, a school teacher gently scolding a naughty child. 'It's so long ago, I don't remember which leg.'

'That's good, Doctor. In fact, that's about the only truthful statement you've made in this court.'

'I object—' Svetlana started.

'There was no limp, your honor, I made that up. I just wanted to see how far he would go to lie for the prosecution.'

A stir went through the audience. The judge started to say something and then shut his mouth.

'I should tell the court—' Zubov began.

'Excuse me, Doctor, but there is no question before you. Now, tell me—'

'Madam,' the judge said sternly, 'this is not an American courtroom. We do not play legal games. If a witness wishes to explain an answer, he has the right to do so and you have no right to restrict that answer. Dr Zubov, what were you about to say?'

'The defendant is correct, I do not recall a limp. However, the reason was not that I was lying but that it was so many years ago. I simply accepted that the suggestion made by the defendant about her own mother must be correct.'

'Thank you, Doctor. The court is well aware of your high qualifications and, certainly, it was a long time ago. You may proceed, Miss Patrick.'

She shifted gears, knowing that to continue to impeach

him about what he didn't remember was not going to work.

'Have you ever been falsely accused of murder?' she asked Zubov.

'Accused of murder? Of course not.'

'Ever been held prisoner in the Moscow jail?'

'No, of course not.'

'Would being falsely accused of murder, stripped naked, enduring an intimate body search and being held prisoner in a cold, brutal jail tend to affect one's mental state, Doctor?'

'Yes, certainly. And if one were suffering from a mental disease such as paranoia, such deprivations would aggravate the condition.'

'Your opinion is based upon my actions in the video, is that correct?'

'You say video as if it was a movie. My opinion is based upon genuine actions recorded on video tape.'

'Thank you, Doctor. You were not present, you did not witness the events, did you?'

'No, of course not.'

'And you personally do not know whether this jail matron had been paid by someone to spy on me in jail, do you?'

He floundered for a moment, trying to avoid the obvious. 'Miss Patrick, my opinion—'

'Dr Zubov, I asked a simple question. You do not know whether this woman was being paid to spy on me. Isn't that true?'

He smiled. 'Of course she's being paid to spy on you. She's a jail matron. That's her job.'

A ripple of laughter went through the audience.

'Exactly. She's paid by the government to spy on prisoners, true?'

'I would imagine that is one of her functions although I don't claim to be an expert on jail procedures.'

'But you do know enough about jail procedures to know it would be a crime for a jail matron to take money from a private party to spy on an inmate. Isn't that correct?'

He hesitated, trying to step round the trap.

'I'll take your silence as an affirmative, Doctor. And since you have no knowledge as to whether this woman was corrupt and had violated her sworn oath of office, you don't know whether my accusations against her were paranoid delusions or frustration at having been mistreated, do you?'

'I have heard no evidence that she was a paid spy, but I have witnessed your behavior and it convinces me that your reaction to her was one of paranoia.'

'Tell me, was the murder of my attorney also a product of paranoid delusions on my part? Did I imagine her death, did I imagine she had been murdered?'

'From what I understand, you have not imagined her death at the hands of another. It is not the situation that is created by paranoia, it is the *interpretation* of the situation. Men and women are being murdered with increasing frequency here in Moscow, crimes that were unheard of in the past. Your interpretation is that your lawyer was murdered as part of the grand conspiracy against you. My interpretation is the one accepted by police – that she was the victim of a random act of violence.'

'Was the death of our next-door neighbor when I was a child also imagined?'

He shrugged. 'People die all the time. Every day, in every part of the world. Some violently.'

'And some murdered,' she said.

'And some only murdered in one's imagination.'

More chuckles came from the audience behind her.

'Tell me, Doctor, when you "examined" my mother, were you wearing your KGB uniform?'

'Objection!' Svetlana snapped. 'KGB affairs are a matter of state secrecy. There is no KGB issue in this matter.'

'The question is stricken,' the judge said. 'Ask your next question.'

'My next questions concern the KGB and this doctor's involvement. Is the court telling me that I cannot ask these questions?'

'Yes. You heard my ruling.'

'Then I have no more questions.' She sat down, satisfied with the ruling. There was probably nothing to be gained from a KGB line of questioning, so being prevented from asking was better than falling on her face. At the end of the trial, when the witness had left the courtroom, she'd accuse him and the prosecution of being involved in a KGB cover-up.

She stood up again. 'Just one last question, Doctor. As I recall, you mentioned you have been with the Serbsky Institute for nearly three decades. How many of Russia's bright minds, how many intellectuals—'

'Object—'

'Were destroyed by your diagnosis of mental illness to keep them from telling the world the truth?'

'That question is stricken!' the judge shouted. 'Miss Patrick, you are out of order. You are attempting to create a political cause out of a simple murder trial. I will not permit it.'

'It goes towards impeachment, your honor,' she snapped back. 'If this man has used his medical degree as a tool to suppress dissent in the past, I should be allowed to inquire whether he is doing it again.'

'You have heard my ruling. And stop addressing me as "your honor". That is a form of address used in a society where the classes are divided. In Soviet – that is, Russian courts, all are equal.' He nodded to Svetlana. 'Does Madam Procurator have any more questions?'

'Yes, just one. Doctor, you have now had a chance to have a face-to-face exchange with Miss Patrick. Has that in any way altered your opinion of her mental state?'

'Yes.' He stared directly at Lara. 'The defendant's line of questioning leads me to conclude that the mental disease she is suffering from has deteriorated. The conspiracies she imagines now include not just those in direct contact with her, such as the victim, Nadia Kolchak, and the jail matron, but persons such as myself, the members of the court, the KGB.'

Lara looked away and said nothing. She had made points, but an accusation of being crazy was like one of child molesting – the accusation didn't have to be proven, it was enough that the charge had been made. Svetlana had beaten her. She had turned down an offer to spend just one year in prison and now she was facing the death penalty, or at the very least the rest of her life in a Russian prison.

Deep in a haze of frightening thoughts, she heard the judge ask if Svetlana had any more witnesses and the prosecutor replied that she would call the pathologist to the stand briefly to elaborate upon the cause of death. 'But I will have to call her later because she is not available at the moment,' Svetlana said, 'so this would be the time for the defendant to put forward her defence. If she has one.'

Lara struggled to her feet. 'I call . . .' She paused and looked to the rear where Vlad was pushing the double doors into the courtroom open with his back. Yuri was standing nearby and he grabbed one door and held it as Vlad backed in, pulling a handtruck loaded with cartons. 'I call Vladimir Andreevich Dzhunkovsky.'

Judge Rurik frowned. 'What is the purpose of this testimony?'

'The purpose? Mr Dzhunkovsky is an army ballistics expert. He will be testifying regarding ballistics.'

'We already had Chief Investigator Vulko testify as to the ballistic expert's findings,' the judge said.

'That was the prosecution's evidence. I am presenting evidence as to the defence's ballistic findings.'

'The procurator's office has no objection to this testimony,' Svetlana said.

The hair on the back of Lara's neck rose. Something in Svetlana's voice . . .

'Proceed,' the judge said.

Vlad was sweating. She could see he was extremely nervous. This was probably the first time he had appeared in a court.

As she watched him set up, she glanced at Svetlana. There was no emotion displayed on the prosecutor's face. If anything, her features were placid and neutral. Vulko was casually leafing through a report, not paying any attention to Vlad setting up his equipment.

Something was wrong. She looked back to the audience and met Yuri's eye. He looked concerned, worried.

She focused back on Vlad and on the equipment he was arranging. He had set up his laser device in the open area of the courtroom, between the elevated position of the judge and assessors and the counsel tables, the area in American courtrooms called the 'well'. The laser had a base about a foot square that appeared to be heavy and Lara imagined it was the source of the beam. A framework of metal tubing came vertically out of the base and extended up four or five

417

feet. At the top of the tubing a pipe stuck out horizontally. At the end of the horizontal pipe a real pistol had been attached. The gun had been modified so that the laser pipe became part of the gun barrel.

Clever, she thought. The beam will go through the pistol. Vlad had some showmanship in him.

The rest of the display appeared to be a cardboard mock-up of a section of the spa. Then Vlad unfolded the upper half of a cardboard female figure and set it on the spa display. The cardboard torso had a bullet wound in the chest.

After Vlad finished setting up the display, the judge looked at it as if he was a theatre owner and the equipment the props to a play that couldn't pay the rent.

Lara began her questioning of Vlad by laying a foundation for his expertise, his training, education, and experience. After getting specifics, she asked him about his laser work. He explained the operation of lasers and how lasers were utilized in his work.

'Projectiles fired from weapons, whether we're talking about small arms such as handguns and rifles, or artillery pieces, will soon divert from a straight line after they leave the barrel. The lasers we use for the distances involved maintain a straight line. By comparing laser paths with the paths of projectiles, we are able to determine the best way to make bullets and artillery projectiles more accurate. That involves adjustments and experimentation with the chemical composition of the charge, the size, shape, and weight of the actual projectile, barrel length, and many other factors.'

'Thank you. Now, please explain to the court the purpose of the equipment you have set up.'

'This is a laser device that emits a beam. I have modified a pistol so the beam passes through the pistol's barrel. For the purposes of this demonstration, you can think of the modified pistol as the murder weapon.'

He pointed at the cardboard contraption at the other side of the room. 'That assembly is the exact size, shape, and height of the spa. The mock-up of a woman is based upon the size of the victim, Nadia Kolchak. That wound in the chest is exactly where the shot struck the victim.' He walked over to the display and lifted up the cardboard torso so the rim of the 'spa' to the rear was visible. 'This hole in the spa rim was made by the bullet after it passed through the victim's chest and exited her back. The criminalist removed the bullet from the hole and stated in his report that he was able to do so without enlarging the original hole. He did that by taking apart the rim rather than digging out the bullet.'

'Have you studied the criminalist's report and the pathology report in this matter?'

'Yes.'

'And did those reports reveal anything else in regard to your study?'

'Two shots struck the victim. The first shot struck her in the chest while she was sitting in the spa facing the door from the interior of the penthouse. The second shot was to the back of the head. The only gunpowder residue was found on the door frame at the entrance to the spa. Because no residue was found farther up the hallway, the criminalist concluded, and I agree, that the shooter fired the first shot standing in the doorway.'

'How would gunpowder residue get on the door frame?'

'When a gun is fired a spray of gunpowder follows the bullet out of the chamber. This fast moving "dust" can stick to nearby objects. In this case the criminalist conducted tests that showed such residue struck the door frame. From the residue, he concluded, and I concur, that only one shot was fired from that position.'

'Does the gunpowder residue tell you anything about the person who fired the shot?'

'Only within narrow limits. The residue provides a clue as to where the killer was standing when the trigger was pulled, but it tells me little else other than the shooter was of adult height. Not a child or a dwarf.'

Vulko guffawed. 'Well, that eliminates a few suspects.'

Loud laughter burst from the audience. Lara ignored it and plunged on. 'And you determined which shot was fired first from—?'

'The pathologist's report. The pathologist said the first bullet entered the chest. And from the general description of the crime scene found in the criminalist's report, it appears the distance from the killer to the victim was about twenty feet. The shot struck the victim in the chest, made a clean path through the body—'

'What do you mean by a clean path?'

'Bullets are often deflected from a straight line by bone or cartilage in the body. This bullet passed straight through soft tissue and exited, burying itself in the rubber rim of the spa at the victim's back.'

'And what about the second shot?'

'It's hard to tell anything about the second shot because it hit the victim in the back of the skull at one of the thickest points of the skull. The bullet shattered the skull and veered. From the other facts, I conclude that the victim's body convulsed in the spa after being hit by the first shot, that the killer approached the spa and, when the body was face down, shot the victim at close range.'

Lara couldn't help herself – she glanced again at Svetlana, but the prosecutor's face revealed nothing. Its very neutrality worried Lara. Svetlana's silence felt like the cross-hairs of a telescopic lens aimed at the back of her neck.

'Did you conduct any examinations of evidence or any experiments in this matter?' Lara asked.

Vlad nodded. 'Yes. I visited the scene of the crime. Mr Bova was kind enough to allow me in,' he nodded at Alexei standing near the back of the courtroom. 'And in my laboratory I fired a pistol of the same caliber and type as the murder weapon to determine a number of factors about it, including how widely the weapon spread gunpowder residue, what distance the projectile pushed forward in a straight line, and the range of recoil. By recoil I'm referring to the "kick" of the gun when fired by people with different grip strength.

'I also conducted a number of tests involving shooting stances, specifically in regard to how people of various height and strength would hold a weapon when firing at an object of the victim's size at a range of twenty feet.'

'Are the tests and experiments you conducted standard procedures in your field?'

'Yes. Obviously, in most cases an expert is not a witness to the actual crime. Like the police, the criminalist and the pathologist, I base my conclusions upon the evidence found at the scene and the reasonable conclusions that can be drawn from that evidence. The tests and experiments supplement the investigative results and enable me to reach opinions concerning the incident. Naturally, an expert's opinion is only as accurate as the data it's based upon.'

'So, from your study of the criminalist's findings and report, from your personal observation of the murder scene and from your own tests, did you arrive at any conclusion about who fired the fatal shot?'

'Well . . . no.'

'No?' Lara froze.

'I don't know who fired the shot. But I know you could not have fired the shot.'

A wave of relief washed through her and her knees went weak. She cleared her throat. 'I'm sorry, that's what I meant to ask. Please tell the court how you arrived at the conclusion that I could not have fired the fatal shot.'

'May I demonstrate?'

'Yes, go right ahead.'

Vlad turned on the laser mechanism. He went to the dummy torso and made adjustments back and forth. When he finished, a laser beam funneled through the pistol barrel struck the chest of the cardboard torso where the 'bullet hole' had entered the chest. Standing next to his equipment, he spoke up to the judge and assessors.

'Besides making adjustments for variables such as recoil and shooting stance, I needed two critical pieces of information about the shot. First, I had to know the exact *angle* that the bullet entered the victim. In this case that angle was possible to determine from the chest wound. From that angle I drew a straight line back, initially on paper and later with the laser. That line was the path the bullet followed from the gun to the victim.

'The second critical factor was where the person was *standing*. If I didn't have this information I wouldn't know where along the bullet's path to place the gun. Where the gun was placed along the path determined the height the gun was held when it was fired.

'Thus by knowing the path the bullet followed, as determined by the angle of entry and where the shooter stood, and making adjustments for other variables, I was able to reach a conclusion about the height of the killer.'

'And that conclusion?'

'That the gun,' he pointed at the pistol, 'was held at this height and angle at the time the shot was fired.'

'The height and angle that you presently have your demonstrative weapon adjusted to?'

'Yes.'

'And how did that tell you that I did not fire the shot?'

'Would you step over here, please.'

Lara came to where Vlad was standing by the machine.

'Stand beside the laser equipment ... that's right. Now put your hand in the grip of the pistol.'

A murmur swept through the audience and the judge and assessors straightened in their chairs as Lara reached up to grasp the pistol butt. It was obvious that she would have to be much taller in order to hold the pistol in a natural firing position.

The judge's eyes went to Svetlana and the Chief Investigator at the prosecution's table. Svetlana simply lifted her eyebrows but revealed no other expression.

'That's all the questions I have,' Lara said and walked back to the counsel table.

'No questions from the procurator,' Svetlana said.

Lara bumped into her chair as she swung round to stare at Svetlana. A 'no questions' response was impossible. To leave the testimony uncontroverted would result in an acquittal.

'No questions?' the judge asked. 'Are you telling me the procurator's office has no questions?'

'That's correct,' Svetlana said.

The judge looked at Vlad. 'You are trained by the army? This demonstration, it is something your commanders would approve of?'

'My commanding officer helped me construct the model,' Vlad said.

'And it is your conclusion that Miss Patrick could not

have fired the shot to the victim's chest, the first shot, because the angle of the shot demonstrates that it was done by a taller person?'

'Yes.'

'Your model shows the exact height of the killer?'

Vlad hesitated. 'Not the exact height but a mid-range representing the height within a few inches either way. I can't calculate the exact height because of variables such as grip strength and weapon handling experience, but I established a range of height and determined that the killer was considerably taller than Miss Patrick, at least five or six inches taller.'

The judge turned to Svetlana. 'You have heard this testimony and you have no questions?'

'No questions,' Svetlana said.

Another stir went through the audience. Lara sat rigidly in her chair, ready to break into pieces from the tension. Something is terribly wrong, she thought, I've missed something, oh God, I've missed something critical.

'However,' Svetlana said, 'as soon as this ... this person,' she gestured at Vlad, 'clears away his toys, we have another witness to call.' She turned and smiled at Lara.

It was the same smile she had given her when she pointed the pistol at her in the judge's chambers.

Chapter 42

'The procurator's office calls Dr Uspensky.'

Another psychiatrist? Lara wondered. Were they going to try and prove Vlad was crazy too? The name sounded familiar to her but she could not place it.

A mousy little woman, wearing a heavy wool jacket and shirt that looked more like a military uniform than street clothes, made her way to the witness stand. The woman could have been thirty or sixty – her ill-fitting clothes and stringy hair looked the latter. She had droopy eyes, fat round cheeks, and white unhealthy looking skin. She reminded Lara of an albino salamander that hadn't seen the light of day for ages.

Svetlana rose to address the witness. 'Dr Uspensky, please state your occupation.'

'Pathologist,' the woman said.

Pathologist? Who the hell is she? She didn't write the pathology report, Lara thought.

'And by whom are you employed?'

'Moscow City Office of Pathology.'

'And did you examine the body of Nadia Kolchak, the victim in this matter?'

'Wait.' Lara got to her feet. 'I'm being sandbagged,' she told the judge.

He scowled at her. 'Sandbagged?'

'Sorry, it's an American legal expression. This witness

has been withheld from me and is now being called to give some sort of surprise testimony that wasn't revealed to me in the reports I was given.'

'Has the defendant received any information about this witness?' the judge asked Svetlana.

'Of course she has. Dr Uspensky is the pathologist who did the autopsy on the victim. I believe the defendant's confusion is that the chief pathologist signed the reports. However, he did so in his function as Dr Uspensky's supervisor. The chief pathologist never actually examined the body.'

'But I assumed that the person preparing the report was the person who performed the autopsy.'

The judge's scowl grew. 'It is for that sort of reason you were asked over and over again to take a lawyer who understood Russian procedures. It is common practice for a chief pathologist to sign a report. Who signed the report makes no difference, anyway. This witness did the autopsy, she can testify about it.'

'This is unfair, I should have been told about this witness so I could be prepared.'

'You don't need to prepare for the truth. The truth is simply there. You keep raising the sort of technical objections that the Anglo-American justice system is based upon. We are not interested in technicalities, but in the truth. If you believe the witness does not speak the truth, you may question her but this is not a game we are playing where the truth is excluded because no one told you about it. Or you did not ask.'

'But I should be able to prepare for this witness. She's a technical witness. I don't know the nature of the testimony—'

'Sit down and we shall both find out,' the judge said.

Lara sat down, anxiety crawling over her like a bad case of hives.

'Dr Uspensky, you performed the autopsy on the victim, Nadia Kolchak, is that correct?'

'Yes.'

'And what were your findings in regard to the cause of her death?'

'She was shot twice, once in the chest, once in the back of the head.'

'From your examination of the deceased, were you able to determine which shot struck her first?'

'Yes,' the pathologist said.

Lara felt the trap opening beneath her feet. They had had her bugged and video taped, Svetlana knew everything she and Vlad had talked about. She had known exactly what Vlad's theory was, what he was going to testify to, and had been ready for it. A sense of horror sent goose bumps creeping up the back of her legs and into the small of her back.

'And which shot struck her first?'

'The shot to the head.'

'How do you know the head wound preceded the chest wound?'

'The occipital artery was severed as a result of the head wound, creating hemorrhaging. In order to have hemorrhaging to the extent I observed in the surrounding tissue, the heart must still have been pumping.'

'How do you know that the chest wound was not inflicted prior to the head wound?'

'A comparison of the hemorrhaging. There was almost no hemorrhaging in the chest area. That means that the fatal shot, the shot that killed the victim, was the first shot, the shot to the head. The victim didn't die immediately, and was shot again, this time in the chest, perhaps only a few seconds later, but in those seconds the victim died. However, before the heart stopped, it pumped out enough blood to create hemorrhaging.'

'Hemorrhaging in the head wound, the *first* wound,' Svetlana emphasized. She shuffled papers in front of her. 'I noticed that in the pathology report, the one signed by the chief pathologist, reference is made to, and I quote the report, "the first gunshot wound, a wound to the chest". You are familiar with the passage I am referring to?'

'Yes, but the reference is not to the first shot that struck the victim, but the first gunshot wound that 1 examined. I started by examining the chest wound and then turned the body over and examined the head wound.' She paused and glared at Lara. 'No one asked me which shot I thought struck the body first,' she said defensively. 'What did it matter anyway? Either shot was fatal. The victim was shot in the back of the head from the doorway. The impact of the bullet would have pushed the body forward, across the spa, even causing it to turn over and convulse violently from death throes. The killer moved in closer and fired the shot that struck the victim's chest, probably to ensure the victim was dead.'

Lara felt hell boiling at her feet. Vlad had testified that he needed to know where the killer stood and the exact angle of entry to make calculations. He couldn't calculate the angle of the wound that shattered the skull because the bullet had veered on entry. Now he wouldn't be able to determine the height of the killer by the angle of the chest wound because he couldn't establish where the person with the gun was standing when the chest shot was fired.

She stared up at the corner of the courtroom ceiling and realized that the fly was gone because the spider had eaten it.

Chapter 43

Lara walked beside the matron in a weary, unsteady daze. News of the court proceedings had spread through the cell block and whores and thieves and women who had stabbed their husbands and lovers stood in their cells and jeered at the fallen prima donna, the foreign celebrity prisoner who starred on the nightly news.

'Got your ass kicked in court today, foreign bitch.'

'Stalin's Breath is coming for you.'

'Hey, give the executioner a blow job and he'll grease the bullet for you.'

The jeers and taunts didn't affect her. She was cold and dead inside.

Locked in her cell, she curled up in a corner with the dirty blanket wrapped round her. She trembled but not from the cold; fear racked her body because she didn't have the strength to fight it.

Svetlana had beaten her, trampled on her and kicked her.

Fatal error, Lara thought, I committed a fatal error. I thought and acted like an American attorney. Marya had warned her, told her the prosecution would eavesdrop on conversations in the visitor's room, but Lara had not heeded the warning. The old adage that an attorney who represents himself has a fool for a client came true. A Russian attorney, any Russian attorney, would have known not to make such an amateurish mistake. She and Vlad had openly planned her 'surprise' defense while Svetlana and Vulko listened at the keyhole and laughed.

Dumb American mentality, raised on a diet of truth, justice, and the American way, she had been clobbered in a courtroom by people who had survived by manipulation and deceit. Even Rykoff, shit that he was, would not have fallen into the trap. He would have known he was being spied upon.

She should have seen it coming. The tip-off had been when Svetlana had not called the pathologist in logical trial order. Stalin's Breath would never have permitted a key witness to testify out of order.

The last word.

That's what it had come down to. She had the right to the last word and tomorrow was the final day of trial, the final moment of trial. Svetlana had spoken her piece, asking the court for the death penalty while Lara had sat numbly at her place at the counsel table and Nadia's sister had cried out for justice, 'a life for a life'.

She had thought of the 'last word' as being analogous to the closing argument by a defence attorney. But that was thinking as an American again. This was Russia – brutal, harsh, cold, tough, lean and mean. The last word was a plea for mercy, a plea for one's life, to an omnipotent system that was accustomed to going to the extreme.

There was nothing to argue in her last word anyway. She hadn't presented an iota of evidence that had any credibility. No clever phrases, no winning legal strategies came to mind. She was expected to go before the court on bended knee and beg for mercy. At the moment she was so tired and beaten she didn't have the energy to do anything but crawl up to the judge's bench and cry.

'Lara?'

He was at the door to her cell. She recognized the voice and the figure.

'Hurry,' Yuri whispered. 'I don't have much time.'

She got up and went to the cell door, taking the blanket with her.

'What do—'

'Shhh. We have to talk quickly. I had to bribe my way in. The guards have orders from Vulko not to admit anyone.'

'What is this, another trick? Haven't there been enough already?'

'Listen to me, the trial has gone badly.'

She started to laugh but her jaws were too tight and it came out as a choke.

'You have to turn things round tomorrow. It's your only chance.'

'Do you think I haven't thought of that? I have no chance. It's finished.'

'You focused on the wrong thing during the trial. You tried to prove your innocence, that you didn't do it.'

'What was I supposed to do? Go for an old-fashioned Russian confession?'

'There's a critical piece missing. Who did it?'

Her mind wasn't working on all fours and she stared at him a little stupidly. 'Who did what?'

'Who killed Nadia? Why was she killed? You tried to prove your innocence. It's easy to prove guilt with circumstantial evidence. Your only hope was to prove someone else did it.'

'I have no proof someone else did it although I've got plenty of candidates.'

'You have to think it out.'

'Are you crazy? The trial's over, I'm finished.'

'*Think it out*. It's your only chance. There's a chain. It

started with your mother and Vera Swen and ended up with Nadia.'

'Nadia was trying to blackmail Alexei.'

'And being blackmailed herself. You have to put together the chain of evidence. You have all the pieces, you just don't have them in the right order.'

The door to the cell block clanged open.

'I've got to go,' Yuri whispered. He reached through the bars and squeezed her arm. 'Good luck, Kosca.'

Yuri disappeared down the dark hallway and Lara faded back into her cell, back to her corner. She had stopped shaking and her mind was humming.

She didn't know if her trial tactic had been a mistake or not. The trial had provided no clues as to who had killed Nadia or why.

But something gnawed at her, something Yuri had said.

She fell into a troubled sleep and awoke with a start in the middle of the night.

What Yuri had said had caused the pieces of the puzzle to fall into a clear pattern. She suddenly realized who had killed Nadia. And how it was linked to the death of her mother's neighbor.

Chapter 44

'What is your final word?'

Lara rose and looked to the rear of the courtroom before turning to face the judge. The courtroom was packed, every seat filled, with people standing at the rear near the double doors leading to the outer corridor. The audience had a mean look; they had come for a lynching, not a hand slap.

Alexei stood to the left of the doors, smiling with false hope; Felix, stoic, stood beside him. Both men were holding raincoats. The courtroom again smelled of wet wool. Yuri was to the right of the doors, wearing the cheap raincoat he had had on the night of the carnival. The shoulders of the raincoat were wet and he held a long black umbrella, tapping it in the palm of his hand as if it was a club he was getting ready to use.

Her eyes held Yuri's for a moment. His face was impassive; no messages were passed in the look they exchanged, but her heart pounded and her throat tightened – with fear, with crushed passion. She turned to the judge and assessors.

'There is a British-American expression that an attorney who represents himself has a fool for a client. I am one of those fools. And because I am a fool, I lost this trial. The prosecutor beat me – not because I am guilty, but because she played the game better than I did.'

The judge shot a glance at Svetlana.

Lara continued, 'In America we have adopted the British system of jurisprudence, which this court dismisses as a bad system because it depends too much upon the skill of the attorney and trial tactics. After the experience I have had in this courtroom, I totally reject that argument because there is one thing that is fundamental to the Anglo-American system which I have seen no sign of in the Russian system: fair play.'

Svetlana started out of her chair but the judge waved her back down. 'This is the defendant's last word. Let her speak her mind.'

'Thank you,' Lara said. 'I am not going into great detail about all the deviations from fair play and reasonable trial procedures. Put simply, I was set up. The prosecutor spied on my strategy meeting, withheld evidence and a witness, all to lead me into compiling a defence she could sweep away with one grand gesture. In other words, the prosecutor played the role of Western advocate, but without the rules that the fair-minded British drew up for the game. It's easy to win when you don't play by the rules. I thought I was the best lawyer for the job because in my country I am a good lawyer. But that doesn't count in a system where the rules can be broken by the state. I was an easy mark for the prosecutor's dirty tricks.

'I am not asking for the court's sympathy or even its mercy. Just its understanding. I did nothing for which I should be on my knees. I did not kill Nadia Kolchak. More significantly, it was never proven in this courtroom that I did kill Nadia. What was proven was that the woman died, violently, at the hand of another, and sometime after her death, police officers observed me in a panic and holding the murder weapon. That scenario, coupled with an alleged blackmail scheme, led to my arrest.

'The evidence was circumstantial because no one saw the crime. The evidence was damning because I was at the murder scene with the murder weapon in hand. But the evidence was incomplete. The court did not permit me to fill in the gaps, and I was led into presenting a non-viable defence by a prosecutor withholding evidence.'

She left her position behind the counsel table and moved in front of it, the judge and assessors to her right, the rest of the courtroom to the left. She was in the well, the area lawyers and defendants in British and American courtrooms were forbidden to enter during trial because it brought them too close to the throat of the magistrate.

'I am accused of trying to blackmail Alexei Bova, one of the richest men in Russia. I, too, thought there was a blackmail motive, not on my part, but an attempt by Nadia to blackmail Alexei. Last night I realized I was wrong. Nadia was not trying to blackmail Alexei – Nadia herself was being blackmailed.'

She stopped and poured a glass of water from the pitcher on the counsel table. Her hand shook and she spilled some. The courtroom was filled with an aching silence, as if it was preparing for a cry of outrage or triumph at any moment.

'In order to understand what brought me to stand over Nadia with the murder weapon in my hand, we have to go back, back before I returned to Moscow a few months ago, back to when I lived here as a child.'

'Miss Patrick—'

'The truth, your honor, is there. You said the court was interested in the truth so let's bring it all out. The first truth is that a woman, a woman who lived next door to my mother and me, died over twenty years ago. Her name was Vera Swen and she was probably Scandinavian, at least that's what Nikolai Belkin told me. She died violently and was mutilated. That is a fact, not a delusion of a paranoid mind.'

Her voice quivered and she took a deep breath to still her nerves.

'The second truth is that my mother believed the woman had been murdered and that there had been a cover-up. That is a fact.' She held up her hand as the judge started to interrupt her. 'Oh yes, I was in the courtroom when a psychiatrist was paraded in to tell the world that my mother and I were both psychotic paranoids. A psychiatrist who never examined either of us and who made his name during the most shameful era of so-called Russian psychiatry. Anybody in this courtroom who believed that man needs their common sense overhauled. Leaving aside questions of his credibility, we still have something very significant that we haven't dealt with: a trail of bodies going back twenty years.

'My mother and Vera Swen both died violently. All the psychiatric mumbo-jumbo in the world isn't going to change that. I spoke to Nikolai Belkin. Belkin ended up dead within hours. I spoke to my old school teacher. She also died. I arranged to meet Nadia Kolchak and she was murdered. And my attorney was killed while I was being held in a jail cell.'

The judge shifted uneasily in his chair. 'Miss Patrick, I have tried to give you great latitude because of the seriousness of the charges and the ultimate punishment you are facing, but you have done nothing but relate events. You have not managed in any way, other than your own relationship with people who died, to link the deaths in the past with the deaths in the present. Tell me,' the judge said, 'tell the assessors, tell all of us how the death of Nadia Kolchak is in any manner connected to the past or to any of the other deaths you have mentioned.'

'First,' Lara said, 'we have to deal with one more truth. The night I spoke to Nadia at Alexei Bova's palace, the night before she was killed, she spoke of blackmail, but I now realize she was speaking about what was happening to her, not about her plans for Alexei. Before that I had met Belkin and had a strange reaction from him: he was "selling" me access to KGB files, a task he obviously hated, and showed little interest in getting money from me. Why? Because he was being forced to do it. Belkin was being blackmailed too.

'I've since discovered,' she turned and found Yuri's eyes at the back of the courtroom, 'that Belkin had a morality problem. I don't know what Nadia's problems were, perhaps they were linked to her past before her success, perhaps even to Belkin's criminal activity—'

'Lies! Lies! The bitch defames the dead!'

The outcry came from Nadia's sister.

'Give her the bullet!' someone shouted and a grumbling of approval swept through the gallery.

Rykoff patted Nadia's sister on the shoulder and told her in a stage whisper loud enough to be heard all over the courtroom, 'Let her speak. By showing no remorse she's pointing the executioner's gun at her own head.'

Lara took another sip of water. Silence returned to the courtroom, but she could see from the sullen faces in the audience that they had already passed judgment on her and their verdict was guilty.

'The obvious questions become, who was blackmailing Nadia and Belkin? And why? The person blackmailing them had an obvious link to the past because he had sent me a picture of a mutilated woman from a twenty-year-old police file. That picture lured me to Moscow to re-examine the facts surrounding my mother's death. The idea was to get me to Moscow and force Belkin and Nadia to lead me to where the blackmailer wanted me. The blackmailer had access to old police files, access to more recent information on Belkin and Nadia, and had probably also checked me out and discovered my occupation in America.'

Lara looked back to Yuri again. He stood stiffly next to the door, his face still expressionless.

'A Moscow police detective has access to the type of information that I've mentioned. Someone like Detective Yuri Kirov.'

Heads in the audience turned from her to Yuri like spectators at a tennis match.

'Detective Kirov was present, hiding in the background, that night I first met Belkin. He knew Belkin was a sex offender. Rather conveniently, he was the investigating officer when Belkin died. He was on hand when I found a dead body and was attacked by the Guks' dog. Guk was the truck driver who was driving the truck that *didn't* kill my mother. The court, I'm sure, is aware that there were various "official" versions of my mother's death, none of them true.

'But, as I was saying, Detective Kirov followed me to the Guks' house. I had the feeling he had arrived there before me. If he had been following me, he was doing it very quickly.'

One of the assessors, the woman, started to laugh but it died in her throat at a glare from the judge.

'My old school teacher died after I left Detective Kirov to visit her. Later Detective Kirov was with me when he called his partner and got news of her death. Was it just a coincidence that he was with me? Or had he planned it that way?'

Lara kept her eyes on Yuri as she slowly walked toward the railing separating the gallery from the arena. Tension was building up in the audience.

'Detective Kirov. Always there. He was even with the other officers when they broke in to Alexei's penthouse and saw me with the gun. But a funny thing about that – the police report states he met the other officers in the lobby.'

'Miss Patrick,' the judge said, 'you will not find favor with this court making a groundless accusation against a Moscow police officer. We have only heard words. No evidence has been put before us.'

'You want a connection to the past killings and the present ones? The link is a teenage boy who was convicted of the murder of Vera Swen. His name was Alexander Zurin. He was our neighbor when I went to school here in Moscow. He used to tease me and call me "little cat". Little Kosca.

'Detective Kirov's military record indicates that he was on duty in Afghanistan in 1984 when Alexander Zurin escaped from a work crew. Another coincidence?' she asked the judge.

'That is speculation, not evidence,' the judge said, but his voice carried a note of uncertainty in it that she had not heard during the entire trial.

She swung round and glared at Yuri, tears blurring her eyes. 'If you want evidence, get a fingerprint expert into this room and take Yuri's fingerprints. I believe it was Alexander Zurin who survived terrible wounds in Afghanistan, not the military policeman sent to capture him. Alexander Zurin came to Moscow using the identity of Yuri Kirov, and ultimately sent for me as part of a blackmail scheme to—'

Yuri shoved a man out of the way and burst through the double doors to the outer corridor.

No one moved in the courtroom for a frozen moment.

'Get him!' the judge screamed at the guards.

'He's jammed the outside handles,' a guard pushing at the doors yelled back to the judge.

'Break down the damn doors,' Svetlana snapped.

Chapter 45

Moscow was cold and gray and drizzling when Lara came out of the jail. Darkness was falling, twisting the already taut city in its icy grip. Within a few hours the rain would turn to snow, covering the city's secrets with a false blanket of purity.

No one was waiting for her. The crowd of gawkers, the news hounds and Alexei's limo were all at the front of the building. She had bribed a jailer to let her out the back. She was sick of crowds, sick of living in a cage where she had to hear other women's body functions, sick of notoriety. Instead of the fifteen minutes of fame Andy Warhol had decreed for everyone, she felt tabloid dirty, victim of the sort of notoriety that goes with Elvis sightings and two-headed babies.

Her brain was muddy. Drained physically and mentally, she didn't want to see anyone, talk to anyone. Yuri had fled the courtroom, leaving her innocence in his wake, but instead of being exhilarated, she was an emotional zombie, the thrill of being free chilled by exhaustion and heartbreak.

A sharp breeze cut through her clothes as she went down the steps to the street, but she didn't care – winds symbolized freedom. In jail you didn't have the right to get warm or cold but had to take whatever was given. Her baggy clothes whipped in the wind. The clothes were the

441

same as she had worn into the prison, but she had lost a piece of her soul.

Hailing a taxi, Lara told the driver to take her to the Grand Hotel. Alexei had sent a message that he would be outside the jail waiting with the limo to take her back to the hotel where her belongings still occupied her old suite. She wondered if Anna would be there, spying for Alexei as she limped around the room.

Her plans were to pick up her luggage and take the first flight out of Moscow, going anywhere, preferably home, but if necessary she'd take a flight to Mongolia to escape the city. Her credit cards and nearly a thousand dollars were in her purse – a surprise to her, she had expected the jailers to rob her but nothing had been taken.

As the taxi pulled up at the hotel, the doorman approached with a professional smile that turned into a gawk as he recognized her.

He flew over to open the front doors for her, whispering, 'Congratulations, you're on all the news.'

Walking across the lobby caused something of a sensation in the large hotel. People stopped and stared. She kept her eyes averted, occupying herself with fumbling in her purse for her room key as she headed for the elevators. She wasn't ready for stardom – or freakdom – and she wasn't sure what role the public would cast her in.

Alone in the elevator, some of the energy created by tension oozed out of her and she was dragging as she went down the corridor to her room. If Anna was there she was going to order the woman out, barricade the door, unplug the phone, soak the stink of jail out of her with a champagne bubble bath, crawl into a real bed with clean sheets . . . No! She'd pack and head for the airport.

She unlocked the door to the suite and stepped in, turning on the light and swinging the door shut. As it closed, a hand flew round her face and clamped over her mouth.

'Don't scream,' Yuri whispered in her ear.

He let her go and she stumbled forward before spinning round to face him. 'You're insane, what are you doing here?'

He grinned without humor at her. 'Hello, little Kosca.'

She wanted to scream, to rush for the door, but her feet were glued to the floor. 'Why, Yuri, why?'

'You're in danger,' he told her. He moved closer and she backed away from him.

'Stay away or I'll scream.'

'Don't be stupid.'

'You're a murderer.'

'I've never murdered anyone.'

'You confessed to killing Vera Swen.'

'I was a terrified seventeen-year-old kid in the hands of a sadistic cop who beat the shit out of me. He took me into Vera's apartment and had me touch things so my finger-prints would be all over the room. Then he said my mother would be arrested as an accomplice if I didn't say I did it. My mother was sick, it would have killed her. Hell, my arrest did kill her. Think about it.' He jabbed his finger at his temple. 'Use your brains. I wasn't the one responsible for killing your mother and covering it up through the KGB. I was only seventeen. That sadistic cop who grabbed me right away for Vera's killing saved my life. If he hadn't coerced a confession out of me I would have been found hanging in my cell with a suicide note confessing the crime.'

'The real Yuri Kirov—'

'I escaped during a fire-fight in Afghanistan and tried to cross the desert. Kirov was a military policeman in charge of the prison detail. A guy about my size and build, not a bad person at all. He caught up with me in a jeep. It was cold and he had me wearing one of his coats on the way back when a mortar round hit. Hell, I didn't even know they thought I was Kirov until I woke up from a coma with half my body reconstructed.'

'I . . . I don't understand.' Weak-kneed, she stumbled to the couch and sat down. He sat down beside her as she hid her face in her hands and sobbed. 'It's too much, it's too damn much. I don't understand.'

'You were right about most of it,' he said. 'I was blackmailing Belkin and Nadia. I knew there was something rotten about Alexei and his crowd and that they knew Vera and your mother. Belkin was a scum who liked to hurt women. I zeroed in on him as the killer and squeezed him with a sex offence charge. He swore he didn't kill Vera but thought he knew who did. He's the one who gave me background on Nadia's past that I used to rope her in. And I had checked you out, found out you were a prosecutor, and lured you to Moscow with the picture of Vera Swen.'

'Why? Why me?'

'To try and shake the killer out of the trees. Belkin had two candidates – Alexei and Felix. Both knew the women, both are a bit weird. My days as Detective Yuri Kirov were numbered. If I didn't bump into someone from the past, I was sure some routine check of fingerprints would someday trip me up. I had to find out who killed Vera. I lured you to Moscow for bait to draw out the killer.'

'Last night you deliberately exposed yourself to me. You knew I would use it against you in court today.'

He grinned again, and this time there was a trace of hard humor in it. 'That's why I stationed myself by the door with the umbrella. I even had a friend's motor scooter parked on the street. The only thing I wasn't sure of was whether you would pick up on me calling you Kosca or if I'd have to reveal my identity in open court and make a dash for the door.'

She bolted off the couch and he followed, the two of them circling the room like a couple of jungle beasts getting ready to fight. 'Do you think you did me a favor?' she asked. 'You lured me to Moscow, nearly got me killed, got me charged for murder and left me in jail to rot.'

'You were safer there.'

'Fine. Let's call the police so they can tuck you in a nice safe cell.'

'Don't be a fool. I wouldn't survive a night in jail. Money would pass hands and I'd be found hanging in my cell the next morning, a "suicide".'

'What about me?'

'I paid jail matrons to watch over you.'

'Did Alexei kill Vera Swen?'

That stopped him and they stood and faced each other. 'Alexei . . .'

'What about Alexei?'

'I don't know. I haven't put it all together. There is something strange about Alexei, something I can't put my finger on. He was KGB. Protected, super-protected. He had a strange relationship with the head of the KGB's Finance Directorate. An old KGB agent I got to know told me that Alexei was the Director's "woman".'

'His woman? Alexei's gay?'

'That's the rub. I've checked him inside out. If he's gay, he hides it incredibly well. And there's another crazy thing about Alexei.'

'He doesn't exist. On paper.'

'You— Oh, Marya's boy friend, the army computer wizard. Yes, Alexei has no past history. I spoke to families of the people killed in the small factory where Alexei was

supposed to have worked. His name was not familiar to any
of them.'

'What about the KGB Finance Director? Where does he
fit in?'

'He died two years ago. He was one of the most powerful
men in the Soviet Union. I'm sure that he was responsible
for diverting KGB-controlled assets for his own use. I think
Alexei inherited control of it when the Director died. I'm
not certain Alexei's much of a money manager.'

'He's not a money manager at all. He told me a proverb
about Russian geese returning to their owners. Alexei
would have roasted all his geese in one big banquet.'

He stared at her bewildered. 'Geese?'

She swept the question away with her hand. 'Never
mind. Yuri . . . Pasha . . . Hell, I don't know what to call
you.'

'Lara, I'm sorry for everything I put you through, for
dragging you into this. That's why I kept trying to get you to
go back to America, because I . . . I cared for you. I don't
want anything to happen to you. Stuff a bag with a change
of clothes and head for the airport.'

'Oh God, Yuri.' She went to him and they hugged each
other in silent desperation. 'What's going to happen to
you?'

'Russia's the largest country in the world. There has to be
a tree somewhere I can hide under.'

Abrupt pounding on the door startled them.

'Alexander Zurin, you were seen entering the hotel, we
know you are in there. Give yourself up.'

The command came from Yuri's police department
supervisor. Yuri jerked away from her and drew a gun from
the back of his waist band.

Lara clutched at the gun. 'No! They'll kill you!'

'Get down!' He grabbed her arm and spun her away from

446

him, but lost his balance and stumbled back as the door to the room crashed open.

Lara heard the sound of gunfire exploding in the room, watched dazed and stunned as Yuri fell against the window, saw his body crashing through.

She stood frozen in the center of the room, staring helplessly at the window as police poured into the room. She couldn't move, couldn't think. An image of Yuri's shattered body on the street below flashed and then a dark cloud soaked into her brain and the image was gone.

Someone took her arm and she turned and stared at Alexei with a brain-dead expression.

'Come, darling, I have to get you out of here.'

With a firm grip on her arm, he led her through the doorway and out into the corridor.

Chapter 46

Alexei propelled her down the corridor to the elevator. A police officer with a walkie-talkie blocked their way in. 'Call your supervisor,' Alexei told him.

At that moment the police supervisor stuck his head out of the door of the room and yelled, 'Get down the stairway, all the way to the basement.'

'These people—'

'Let them go. Get down the stairs.'

Alexei pulled her into the elevator and the doors closed behind them. Lara stared blankly at the two doors. Alexei put his arm round her shoulder and whispered something but her mind didn't let his words in.

She was remembering . . .

A cold winter day, a school day. Her teacher saying her mother had come to pick her up. Walking toward the cathedral with a woman wearing her mother's coat and scarf . . .

She had a sudden flash of Yuri crashing through the window and she cried out in pain.

'What's the matter?' Alexei asked.

'Yuri . . .' The computer in her head was rejecting the data as unbelievable. A chill gripped her body. She knew she should focus on the here and now, that there was something about Yuri, something about Alexei, that she should focus on, but when she tried to concentrate the thoughts retreated into the dark corner of her brain where the terrible secrets of the past had been locked since she was a child.

Alexei led her out of the elevator, his arm still round her shoulder. She was as catatonic as she had been the day policemen walked her across an airport terminal to a plane when she was seven years old.

Stenka, Yuri's big Cossack partner, was standing near the elevators, walkie-talkie in hand, and he quickly moved in front of Alexei, concern narrowing his eyes as he observed Lara's state of shock.

'Nobody's allowed to leave the hotel.'

'I'm not a nobody, you fool. Get out of my way.'

Stenka's broad forehead creased with a heavy frown and his fists clenched. The police supervisor's voice erupted from his walkie-talkie and Stenka answered the call.

'Get out and cover the front of the hotel,' the supervisor said.

'What about Bova and—'

'The hell with them. Cover the front.'

Stenka reluctantly let them pass, following the richest man in Russia as he steered Lara across the lobby.

In front of the hotel Alexei ushered her into the waiting limo.

Stenka stood on the curb and watched the limo move down the street as he radioed his supervisor. He kept his voice neutral, hiding his emotions as he asked, 'Did you find Yuri?'

'No, damn it. He dropped only two stories and hit the restaurant balcony. There's blood up here, he's wounded or bleeding from the fall, but he's nowhere on this damn balcony. He might have already made it outside. I've called in a city-wide alert . . .'

Something caught the big Cossack's eye as he was

listening to the radio call. A white handkerchief was on the street. He hadn't noticed it before because it was near where the limo had been parked.

He stepped into the street and bent down and examined the handkerchief. It was stained with blood.

He straightened and stepped back, leaving the handkerchief where it was. About where it would be if it had dropped out of the limo's driver door, he thought. Why would a limo driver have a bloody handkerchief? And lose it?

He looked up at the hotel. The balcony was at the next level but it was too far to jump without breaking a leg. Of course, someone could have come down the inside stairway, out the side entrance to the hotel, saw the limo waiting nearby . . .

He stared at the limo disappearing in the distance, a thought burrowing its way into his thick skull.

Chapter 47

Night had closed in on the city as the limo pushed its way through heavy traffic along the Moscow River embankment. The drizzle had turned to light snow and Lara stared at the flakes hitting the window beside her. *Focus, focus, focus.* The word kept bouncing around in her mind but it didn't land anywhere. She knew she was in the limo, knew she was with Alexei, but her mind had locked up on her with the horrible knowledge that she had again lost someone she loved and was once more alone.

Alexei rambled on and on beside her, talking mostly to himself because she was only catching a word here and there as he gloated and laughed about how she had been the final blow to his house of cards.

'It's all tumbling down,' he told her. 'That bastard Yeltsin has sent in armed guards to take over the tower and the palace. They've seized my bank and are doing an audit. My, uh, investors, as you might call them, are dangerously annoyed. They have lost everything they worked so hard to steal while they were in the KGB and they will no doubt be arrested.'

He laughed again. 'They made that fool Felix my controller, but he never had any control. The money passed to me and they were never able to get it back. All they could do was sit back and hope that my investments would make them more money. It did for a while, until the overwhelming stupidity of the government caused the whole economy in this country to collapse.

'They never understood that I wasn't really one of them. I used the money for what it would buy me, not what it would make them. Felix thinks I still have millions hidden. He's right. How does Brazil sound, my darling? Hot beaches, hot music and color. Have you noticed how everything in Moscow is gray? In Brazil there are greens and blues and reds...'

Grays, Moscow was winter gray again.

It had been a gray day when it all began. Snow had started falling when she left the school with the person dressed in her mother's gray coat and red scarf.

The woman had kept a tight grip on her little hand. A couple of times she had tried to jerk her hand loose and had told her mother that she was holding her hand too tightly, but the pressure of the grip remained.

They entered the cathedral and started up the stairs, the woman pulling her up the steps as she became frightened and hung back. The woman looked at her and Lara saw eyes that weren't her mother's. In the room at the top of the stairs the woman had gestured to her...

'Come closer.'

'What?' Lara snapped out of the grip of memory. 'What did you say?'

'Say? I asked you about Brazil, whether we should go there.'

'No you didn't. You told me to come closer.'

'No, darling, I'm afraid you're hearing voices in your head. I was talking about Bra—'

'*You're lying!*'

'Lara—'

'Don't tell me I'm hearing things. I know what you said. You're playing a mind game with me.'

'Control yourself, darling.' He reached out for her and she batted away his hand. 'Dr Zubov said you had a bit of—'

'You knew my mother.'

He leaned back in the seat and sighed. 'The picture taken at the party. Yes, I knew your mother. I knew a lot of people. I was at that party because Felix was having an affair with Vera Swen.'

'I'm not interested in Felix.'

He shrugged and grinned with boyish charm and innocence. 'All right, I didn't want to tell you this because I thought it would drive you away. I had an affair with your mother—'

'Liar!' she shouted at him. 'You never had an affair with my mother or Vera Swen, and you never slept with Nadia.'

The Venetian blind on the window that separated the passenger area from the limo driver was down and half closed so that only a vague outline of the driver's head and hat could be seen. Alexei closed the blind even tighter before he turned back to her, his face red and stiff with anger. 'You seem to have become privy to my sex life, even that part of it that occurred when you were a child. Have you suddenly developed psychic powers? Or is paranoia your only mental ability?'

'You made a major mistake, Alexei. You bragged about what great sex we had the night I passed out at the palace. Not a bad boast considering I was dead to the world and woke up naked in your bed.'

His features suddenly turned stricken with grief. 'Don't say it, Lara. I really like you. I love you and that's the truth. You're the first woman I've ever really loved, the only person I've loved in my whole life. It was your innocence, your freshness, your purity . . .'

'It's strange, but I believe you really do care for me. But I can't live a lie. And I can't take any more nightmares. You never made love to me, Alexei. I think you've never made love to any woman.'

'You can't say that—'

'Yes, I can. You made a blunder when you claimed you made love to me. Alexei, listen to me. I'm the oldest virgin left in the world. I know I never made love to you. I passed out a virgin and woke up a virgin.'

He laughed with an edge of hysteria. 'And you think I'm the crazy one.'

'It was important to you, wasn't it? To make me believe you had made love to me. That's why you kept changing girl friends, why women like Nadia were so frustrated. You never made love to any of them, did you?'

'You don't understand. I was used, always used. The Director used me as a . . . a . . .'

'As a woman,' she said. 'When I met Belkin in the park he talked about a freak he knew. That was you he was referring to. Now I realize he was testing me, seeing how I reacted when he dropped the hint.'

'A freak,' he said.

'You were out there that night, too, dressed as a nurse. That's what you do, isn't it? Dress up as a woman? As a nurse. You killed him because you thought he was selling your secret to me. What is it about you? What is it about deformed people?'

'Deformed people?'

One part of her wanted to reach out and touch him and tell him everything would be all right. She really cared for him, but she knew he was sick.

'It's too late for lies. You surround yourself with people with deformities. Even your limo driver is blind in one eye,'

'Hire the handicapped,' he giggled.

'A pervert followed you into a rest room and pushed

open your stall. That's how it happened, isn't it? What did he see that made you kill him?'

Alexei shook his head. 'You shouldn't talk this way.'

'The derelict, did he do the same thing? Maybe it was an accident. Did he push into the wrong stall and die because of what he saw? And the doctor? What did he see? Is that when you started playing nurse? To get to him?'

'The doctor made me what I am.' His voice was very low, a barely audible whisper.

'What are you, Alexei? What are you hiding? What is so damn wrong that you have to leave a trail of murder behind you?'

He suddenly became calm and the panic left his eyes. Cocking his head, he stared at her as if looking at her for the first time. 'I was wrong about you,' he said. 'I thought we were alike. Suppressed childhood, loners who never ran with a pack. But Lara, I'm beginning to wonder if the psychiatrist wasn't right about your mental state.' He leaned over and patted her knee. 'Don't worry, my dear, we'll have plenty of money wherever we end up and I'll get you the best treatment.'

His patronizing voice snapped her own icy calm and broke the wall that had held back emotions buried since she was abused and nearly murdered as a child. *I'm just a goddamned doll, another toy in his fantasy world. If I'd got close to his secret he'd have smashed me too*. Rage swept through her as a violent fever, wiping away all common sense, and before she knew what she was doing she hit him, her fists flying at him, beating at him. 'Bastard! You killed my mother and you hurt me. You hurt me!'

Alexei slapped her face and she was thrown back against the door. She clutched at the door handle and flew out as the door gave way. He made a grab at her clothes but she fell out and hit the moving pavement at twenty miles an hour. The limo was in the second lane from the curb and she tumbled all the way to the gutter. A car moving down the curb lane swerved to avoid her, crashing into the car beside it.

Her stunned body reacted with a charge of adrenaline and she got herself out of the gutter and on her feet on the sidewalk as traffic went crazy with a chain reaction of crashes.

Her feet propelled her into a snow-covered park that ran alongside the road as her mind relived horrors.

Yuri crashing out of the window of the hotel. Her mother strapped to a bed in a psychiatric ward while Alexei dressed as a nurse gave her a lethal overdose. The freak show...

What did Belkin tell her? That he knew a freak?

Black riders in the night storming into villages, pulling the deformed out of houses and putting the sign of the cross on their hand.

He was the Director's woman, Yuri told her.

A woman.

'The doctor made me what I am,' Alexei told her.

Ugly thoughts raced round her mind. Bottled up tears broke loose and she cried, for Marya, for Yuri and for her mother, victims of the devil.

She staggered across the park, her eyes half-blinded by tears and falling snow. The night was freezing but her feverish rage kept her moving. Through the haze of snow cloaking the already midnight shade of the night she saw a blur of colors, a riot of colors set aflame by powerful lights.

St Basil's Cathedral.

The limo had been going along the Moscow River embankment with Red Square off to the side. She was right back where it had all started. An hysterical giggle escaped her almost frozen lips. Life is a circle, she thought. I ran halfway round the world and came back again. She had returned to Moscow and her feet carried her again and again to the place where the nightmares began.

Fear fanned the hair on the back of her neck and she slowly turned. Someone was out there, part of the white-out created by the fury of snow. The person was coming toward her, unhurried. A moment passed before the person became visible enough for her to distinguish the shape and form of a nurse in a white uniform and hospital cap.

Chapter 48

She ran, panic beating in her throat, terror winging her feet. The picture of Vera Swen's mutilated body flashed in her mind, cut and slashed and—

Anger fought with panic but she knew she had no chance against the strength of a madman with a knife.

What little she could see of Red Square was deserted, the great parade area dark and lost under the falling snow. She ran to the closest source of light, the cathedral built with the bones and blood of a madman's enemies, and burst in.

An old man sitting on a wooden chair next to a table with his dinner laid out jumped up as she rushed into St Basil's.

Breathing hard, she said, 'There's a killer outside, he's coming.'

The guard's eyes went wide. 'A killer?'

'We have to call the police. Hurry. Where's the telephone?'

'On the wall.' He pointed at the curtained alcove that led to the stairs to the main tower. 'In there on the wall.'

'Lock the doors,' she told him. 'I'll call the police.'

The old man headed for the front door and she hurried into the alcove. It was a pay phone. She stared at it as if it had come from outer space. It took a damn coin and her purse was back at the hotel. Moscow police had an emergency number that didn't require a deposit but she didn't know the number.

She rushed back through the curtains. The old man was down the hallway leaning with his shoulder against the wall near the door.

'It's a pay phone,' she said. 'What's the—'

He turned with visible effort to face her. His face was twisted with pain and he held his abdomen as if he was keeping his guts from spilling out. Blood soaked through the cracks between his fingers. Pressed against the wall, he slowly slid to the floor.

Horrified, she turned and ran up the stairs, taking the steps two at a time, her heart racing, mindless panic driving her up.

And then it snapped, that terrible surge of panic, and she forced herself to stop running and catch her breath and get back her mind and senses.

She was doing exactly what he wanted. He was driving her back up the stairs to where her nightmares had originated. She was playing right into his hand but there were no other cards on the table.

She continued up, getting angrier with each step. She didn't want to die; she would fight the bastard until her last breath. There were no more buried fears or smothered passions. Fire within had swept it all away and now there was only cold, deadly anger.

The most dangerous of God's creatures was a trapped animal and she had her back to the wall and nothing to lose.

Somehow she would kill the bastard before he took her life.

Nearing the room at the top she heard the sound of footsteps below, feet shuffling, and she froze for a moment wondering if she had heard more than one person. The sounds died and she continued up.

At the top landing she went into the room of crosses, the room she had been to twice before in her life, the womb of her nightmares. The window was latched. She undid the latch and pushed open the wooden shutters. The scaffolding that had saved her life had been removed. Wind blew the shutters closed as she stepped away from them.

She took one of the crosses off the wall, a large wooden one. If she could stun him with the cross and push him out of the window . . . Panic rose, choking her throat, and she beat it back as she crouched in a dark corner and raised the wooden cross over her head.

Footsteps reached the top of the stairway. Her hands tightened on the cross.

The steps came down the corridor. People she loved had been killed because of his madness. Now he was going to kill her.

She saw the shadow first, a dark shape in the dim light outside the door. The shadow was vague but it wore a hat. Her hands on the cross trembled and she nearly dropped it. Her lungs were on fire from holding her breath and her mind screamed *kill him, kill, kill, kill!*

The shadow paused in front of the doorway and she held her breath. As the shadow moved into the room, she was so intently focused on the hat that her eyes started to cross. The fire within blew the roof off her head and she screamed as she swung the cross at the person who had entered.

The cross slid against its target, scraping instead of striking, and she felt herself lose her balance. She fell forward, following her swing. Colliding into the person in the doorway she cried out and drew back, awkwardly raising the cross, her head coming up to face him.

Her heart stopped.

'Yuri!'

She recoiled from him in shock, dropping the cross. Her

heel caught on a ridge of the wooden floor and she stumbled back. The shutters at her back flew open as she hit them and her momentum carried her into the opening, a sheer drop of a hundred feet—

Strong hands grabbed her by her coat and jerked her back inside. As Yuri pulled her back in, the cap he wore fell off.

A chauffeur's cap.

'You bailed out of the car too fast. I was driving.' His face and shirt were streaked with blood. 'Alexei is back there somewhere. And just behind him will be Felix and his men.'

'Yuri.' She reached out and touched him. 'I-I thought I had lost you.'

He hugged her. 'It's a good thing you hate heights. A room on the tenth floor and I would be dead.'

'A temporary respite,' a voice said.

Felix was in the doorway. A man beside him had a gun in hand. Sounds of other people on their way up came from the stairwell.

He stepped into the room and shone a flashlight around. 'So this is the famous chamber where Alexei terrifies little girls and,' he said to Lara, 'young women.'

The man with the gun stepped into the room and to one side as another man entered with Alexei in tow.

Alexei's hair was disheveled, blood ran from the top of his head down the side of his face. He looked ridiculous in a white nurse's uniform with a nurse's cap askew on his head.

Felix shook his head. 'What would all Russia think of their boy wonder if they saw him now? What would they think if they knew he liked to cut out other people's sex organs?' Felix shot Lara a look. 'You realize of course that he was on his way here to finish off what he started over twenty years ago. And you were right about him. Your virginity was quite safe with him.' He smiled with pleasure at the surprise on her face. 'We had the limo bugged and the driver is on our payroll – the driver we found unconscious on the front floor of the limo.'

He gave Alexei a look of utter contempt. 'He's a freak, a man stuck in a woman's body. We called them sex freaks when I was a kid, people born with the sex organs of both a man and a woman. During the age of Russian medical miracles, when they were sewing two heads on a dog and reprogramming brilliant minds with dulling drugs, they experimented with Alexei, cutting off his under-developed penis and testicles and leaving him with a vagina. It was very clever of them and the process works quite nicely for a feminine personality trapped in a male body and needing a sex change, but . . .'

Felix turned back to Yuri and Lara. 'You see the anomaly, don't you? You can turn a man with a feminine personality into a woman by cutting off his sex organs and feeding him female hormones. Alexei was a young teenager when they did the operation. The surgeon thought he was doing Alexei a favor – cutting off the under-developed penis that was too small to be functional, increasing the size of the vagina to make it functional for sex, and giving the youth some female hormones.'

Sobs erupted from Alexei.

'It was the sort of quack medicine that went along with the quack psychiatry that you complained about during the trial,' Felix told Lara. 'The problem of course is that not only is the operation irreversible, but nobody asked Alexei if he wanted to be a woman, or even if he could be a woman. The female hormones merely messed up his mind more than it already was.'

'The first victim, the doctor?' Lara asked.

'Yes, it was the doctor who did the surgery. You more or

less guessed the rest. The two found in the public toilets had barged into the wrong stall. There have been others.'

'Why was Vera Swen killed?' Lara asked.

'A very sexually liberated Scandinavian. She made the mistake of grabbing Alexei between the legs and laughing about not having felt anything.'

'You killed Nadia and the school teacher,' Lara said.

'No, I don't kill people. I have them killed. Your old school teacher was a security risk. So was Nadia. She was getting too close to Alexei's secret. We thought she was just after the money. Had we known our friend the police officer, er, escaped murderer, was controlling her, we would have taken him out instead. You should be grateful, Lara. I let you live and showed you the photograph to keep Alexei in line. Framing you for Nadia's death killed two birds with one stone.' He grinned at his own wit. 'The rest is history and I am afraid you two will soon be history too. According to the official version being prepared right now, Detective Kirov kidnapped Lara from the limo, brought her here and threw her out of the window before shooting himself.'

'What about Alexei?' Lara asked the question.

Alexei lifted his head to meet Lara's eyes, his face filled with pain and shame.

'This piece of dog shit will be taken to a dacha belonging to one of our, er, investors, and will be coached into revealing where he has hidden the remaining assets of our cartel, those the bastard didn't squander playing prince.' His lip curled. 'I've always hated him. But he caught the eye of the head of the Finance Directorate of the KGB many years ago, when Alexei was in his late teens. The Director had what you might call strange tastes in sexual partners. I suppose a sexual freak like Alexei doubled his pleasure by—'

466

'Stop it,' Alexei screamed. The words caught everyone in the room by surprise. Alexei's actions were a blur to Lara as he launched himself at his tormentor, sweeping up the slender-framed Felix in his arms and rocketing him across the little room to the window. Felix went backwards out of the window, a death grip on Alexei, a cry of terror escaping from his mouth as they both flew out the window in a free-fall down to the pavement a hundred feet below.

The man holding the gun followed Alexei's movements across the room, trying unsuccessfully to grab him. Yuri crouched to block him and hit the man on the side, sending him crashing against the crosses on the opposite wall. As he bounced off the wall, Yuri hit him with an elbow to the nose, shattering the bone, sending blood flying. The man went down, still holding the gun. Yuri dived for the gun and Lara threw herself at the second man by the door. Gunfire exploded. The man by the door was knocked sideways before Lara touched him. She froze, staring as he started to recover and level his gun at her. Another shot sounded and he collapsed, his weapon spilling from his hand.

Stenka appeared in the doorway, gun in hand, a big grin on his face.

Lara and Yuri walked out of the front of St Basil's. He took her hand and she leaned her head on his shoulder as they walked.

Twenty years of trouble had been shed in the cathedral. It wasn't a rebirth, there were wounds to heal, but for the first time since she had walked out of a classroom with someone masquerading as her mother over twenty years ago she was free of fear. And she was free of guilt too. She now knew why seeing the person in the nurse's uniform – Alexei – coming out of Vera's apartment had been locked deeper in her mind than even the abuse Alexei had

467

subjected her to in the room of crosses. In the child's mind, her sighting of the nurse on the landing above had somehow led to losing her mother. It made no sense except to a traumatized seven-year-old, but the chains of that guilt were gone now and in her heart she knew her mother was at peace.

She would carry the warm memories of her mother now without having them polluted by fear and horror. And the memories of Marya would be there too, with her wide smile and big heart.

Snow had stopped falling and a gloomy frozen mist shadowed Red Square. As they walked side by side, they heard the powerful voices of a mass rally coming from the other end of Red Square.

'I'm free,' she said, squeezing Yuri's hand. Yuri, Alexander, Pasha, she didn't know what to call him but still thought of him as Yuri. 'We're free. Do you hear that, Yuri? We're free to do anything we want, go anywhere.'

'Are you going back to America?' he asked.

'Are you coming with me?'

The question popped out of her mouth. A few months ago she would have thrown herself on a bed of hot coals before she spoke to a man in that manner. She had not ended up as the world's oldest virgin by being forward with the opposite sex.

The noise of the rally was getting louder and louder, the stamp of thousands of feet, an army of voices, and the glow of torches.

Moments later the rally came streaming by them, thousands of people marching shoulder to shoulder in a long column that extended back somewhere deep in the foggy mist. Hundreds of torches lit up the night sky. Flags were illuminated by the torches, a golden hammer and sickle on a red background.

'Hard-line communists, outlawed by Yeltsin,' Yuri told her. 'They want to overthrow the new government, restore the Communist Party as the ruler of Russia, throw out the free economy movement and bring back the Cold War.'

'I know,' she said. 'I've seen them before.'

They walked for a moment in silence, listening to the slogans of the political dead who wanted to rise from their graves and take their place once again among the living. To poison the world again, Lara thought.

'Maybe I won't go back to America,' she said.

'I'm glad you said that. I don't want you to go back.'

'Russia is the New Frontier. I guess they could use a good lawyer in this town. In fact, they need a whole damn legal system. Two people I loved, my mother and Marya, died needlessly because the system didn't work. I could help make one work. I would kick the ass of Stalin's Breath if I ever had a trial with her.'

He stopped and took her face in his hands. They were warm and heavenly on her cold cheeks. She wanted his whole body next to her. 'Is that how American women talk?' he asked. 'Kick her ass? Is that any way for a lady to talk?'

'Yuri . . . Yuri . . .' She spoke slowly, choosing her words very carefully. 'I am not going to tell you that you are an old-fashioned Russian chauvinistic male and get into a silly argument with you. I'm not going to argue with you about who won the Cold War. I'm not going to lecture you about smoking. I'm just going to be me and—'

'And I'll just be me.'

She thought for a minute. She would never get used to the smoking. 'Well, we'll talk about that.'

He kissed her tenderly and her whole body melted against his naturally, lovers meant for each other.

'Can they do it?' she asked.

'Do what?'

'Those people. The diehards. Can they take back Russia? Turn back the clock?'

'Ask the geese,' he said.

More Compelling Fiction from Headline Feature

THE FOUNDATION

A RIVETING THRILLER OF CORPORATE
INTRIGUE IN THE TRADITION OF *THE FIRM*

F. PAUL WILSON WRITING AS
COLIN ANDREWS

Quinn Cleary has always wanted to be a doctor.
But her family is poor, so the only way to make
her dream come true is to win a place at The
Ingraham, the gold-plated medical school
which accepts only the best students but
where tuition is free – funded by the powerful
Kleederman Foundation.

Within this vast, isolated complex, her life
seems just perfect – particularly as she begins
to fall in love. But, as term progresses, Quinn
starts to notice a subtle change in her fellow
students. Even the freest of thinkers are
becoming strangely rigid in their views. When
she confesses these suspicions to her
boyfriend, Tim, he laughs her off . . . until he
discovers a tiny microphone. Suddenly Tim
disappears, without trace.

As Quinn's panic grows, so does her conviction
that something very strange is happening at
The Ingraham. And that, unless she can rapidly
uncover the truth, she also may soon disappear
from the face of the earth . . .

FICTION / THRILLER 0 7472 4252 6

More Thrilling Fiction from Headline Feature

'Easily the best horror writer working in Britain today' *Time Out*

Ramsay Campbell

THE LONG LOST

David and Joelle Owain are enjoying a weekend break in Wales, when their leisurely drive through the June sunshine leads them to a strange abandoned village and a tiny offshore island. There they become trapped overnight by the fog and tide.

It is also there that they first encounter Gwendolen – an old woman whom David discovers may be his distant cousin. Since she appears to have no friends nearby, the Owains take her back to Chester and find her a place in a retirement home just down the road.

But when Gwen is invited to the Owains' annual barbecue, she insists on preparing a very special treat for her fellow guests. And from that night onwards the lives of several ordinary people will never be quite the same again . . .

FICTION / HORROR 0 7472 3998 3

ABOVE THE EARTH,
BELOW THE EARTH,
THERE'S NO DEATH MORE HORRIFYING

Gary Gottesfeld

ILL WIND

When a massive earthquake uncovers a large
Indian graveyard in Beverly Hills, forensic expert
Wilhelm Van Deer – known as 'the Dutchman' –
is confronted by more bones than he can cope
with. But he soon realises that some of the remains
are not as old as they should be, nor the manner of
death as straightforward as first appears.

Digging deeper, he comes across weird
underground passages and strange paintings of
giant centipedes. Somehow these discoveries are
linked to mysterious deaths that occurred over
twenty years earlier, but there are powerful
anonymous people now determined to keep their
dark secrets buried for ever.

When the chilling murders begin anew, the
Dutchman sets out to catch a maniac – an elusive
psychopath obsessed with a grotesquely unusual
method of killing . . .

FICTION / THRILLER 0 7472 4168 6

A selection of bestsellers from Headline

HARD EVIDENCE	John T Lescroart	£5.99 ☐
TWICE BURNED	Kit Craig	£5.99 ☐
CAULDRON	Larry Bond	£5.99 ☐
BLACK WOLF	Philip Caveney	£5.99 ☐
ILL WIND	Gary Gottesfeld	£5.99 ☐
THE BOMB SHIP	Peter Tonkin	£5.99 ☐
SKINNER'S RULES	Quintin Jardine	£4.99 ☐
COLD CALL	Dianne Pugh	£4.99 ☐
TELL ME NO SECRETS	Joy Fielding	£4.99 ☐
GRIEVOUS SIN	Faye Kellerman	£4.99 ☐
TORSO	John Peyton Cooke	£4.99 ☐
THE WINTER OF THE WOLF	R A MacAvoy	£4.50 ☐

All Headline books are available at your local bookshop or newsagent, or can be ordered direct from the publisher. Just tick the titles you want and fill in the form below. Prices and availability subject to change without notice.

Headline Book Publishing, Cash Sales Department, Bookpoint, 39 Milton Park, Abingdon, OXON, OX14 4TD, UK. If you have a credit card you may order by telephone – 01235 400400.

Please enclose a cheque or postal order made payable to Bookpoint Ltd to the value of the cover price and allow the following for postage and packing:

UK & BFPO: £1.00 for the first book, 50p for the second book and 30p for each additional book ordered up to a maximum charge of £3.00.
OVERSEAS & EIRE: £2.00 for the first book, £1.00 for the second book and 50p for each additional book.

Name ....

Address ....

....

....

If you would prefer to pay by credit card, please complete:
Please debit my Visa/Access/Diner's Card/American Express (delete as applicable) card no:

Signature .... Expiry Date..............